PRAISE FOR

olfer

#1 *New York Times* Bestselling Author
IndieBound Bestselling Author
USA Today Bestselling Author
Wall Street Journal Bestselling Author

"There's **more in Colfer's magic kingdoms
than Disney** has dreamt of."
—*USA Today*

"In the Land of Stories, Colfer showcases his talent for
crafting **fancifully imaginative plots and
multidimensional characters**."
—*Los Angeles Times*

"**Will please fans of the series** while offering
an entry for new readers as well."
—*Booklist*

"A **thoroughly satisfying** adventure."
—*Publishers Weekly*

"A **dynamic, engrossing fantasy** that will have readers
staying up late and dreaming big."
—*School Library Journal*

"It will hit big with its **combination of earnestness
and playful poise**."
—*The New York Times Book Review*

BY CHRIS COLFER

The Land of Stories Series

The Wishing Spell

The Enchantress Returns

A Grimm Warning

Beyond the Kingdoms

An Author's Odyssey

Worlds Collide

The Ultimate Book Hugger's Guide

A Treasury of Classic Fairy Tales

The Mother Goose Diaries

Queen Red Riding Hood's Guide to Royalty

The Curvy Tree

Trollbella Throws a Party

Goldilocks: Wanted Dead or Alive

A Tale of Magic ... Series

A Tale of Magic...

A Tale of Witchcraft...

A Tale of Sorcery...

CHRIS COLFER

Illustrated by Brandon Dorman

LITTLE, BROWN BOOKS FOR YOUNG READERS

LITTLE, BROWN BOOKS FOR YOUNG READERS

First published in the US in 2021 by Little, Brown and Company
First published in Great Britain in 2021 by Hodder and Stoughton

1 3 5 7 9 10 8 6 4 2

Text copyright © Chris Colfer, 2021
Illustrations copyright © Brandon Dorman, 2021
Cover art copyright © Brandon Dorman, 2021. Cover design by Sasha Illingworth.
Hand-lettering by David Coulson. Cover copyright © Hachette Book Group, Inc., 2021

The moral rights of the author and illustrator have been asserted.

*All characters and events in this publication, other than those clearly
in the public domain, are fictitious and any resemblance to real persons,
living or dead, is purely coincidental.*

All rights reserved.
No part of this publication may be reproduced, stored in a retrieval system,
or transmitted, in any form or by any means, without the prior permission in
writing of the publisher, nor be otherwise circulated in any form of binding or
cover other than that in which it is published and without a similar condition
including this condition being imposed on the subsequent purchaser.

A CIP catalogue record for this book
is avilable from the British Library.

ISBN 978 1 510 20247 4

Offset by Avon DataSet Ltd, Arden Court, Alcester, Warwickshire

Printed and bound in Great Britain by Clays Ltd, Elcograf S.p.A.

The paper and board used in this book
are made from wood from responsible sources.

Little, Brown Books for Young Readers
An imprint of Hachette Children's Group
Part of Hodder & Stoughton
Carmelite House
50 Victoria Embankent
London, EC4Y 0DZ

An Hachette UK Company
www.hachette.co.uk

www.hachettechildrens.co.uk

To all the "Caretakers" out there who are fighting for our planet and all its inhabitants. Thank you.

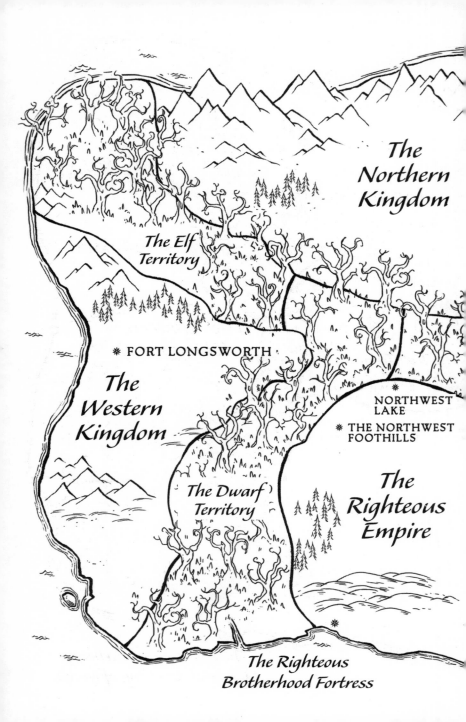

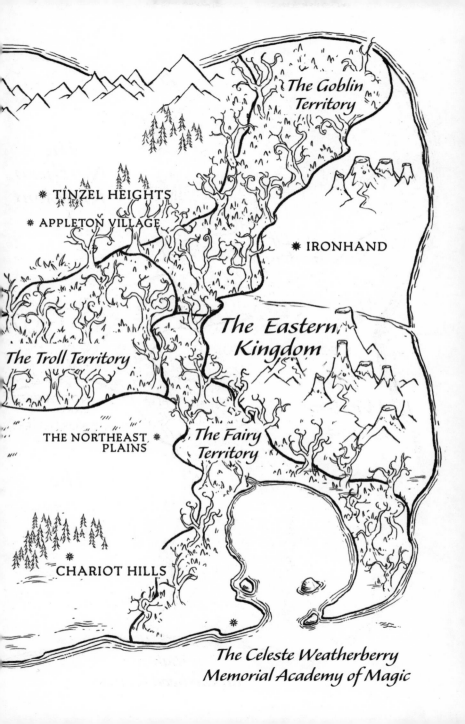

PROLOGUE

CREATURES FROM THE DEEP

The woman was woken by the sound of footsteps. It was still dark when her eyes fluttered open and lazily drifted toward her bedroom door. However, the disturbance wasn't coming from the hall beyond her chambers, but from behind a colorful mural on her wall. She immediately sat up in her large bed, wide awake. Just *one other person* knew about the secret entrance to her bedroom, and their presence could only mean *one thing.*

A frantic knock came from inside the wall.

"Ma'am?" asked a gruff voice. "Are you awake?"

"Yes, come in," the woman said.

The secret door slid open and a man covered in dirt peered inside the room. His sunken eyes were wide with excitement, but his body was stiff with fear.

"Well?" the woman asked impatiently.

The man nodded slowly, still in disbelief of the news he was about to share.

"*We found it,*" he said breathlessly.

The woman flung off her bedsheets and jumped to her feet. She threw a robe over her nightgown, stepped into a pair of slippers, and charged through the secret door. The man escorted the woman down a hidden corridor that snaked between the walls of her spacious residence. The corridor led to a steel staircase that spiraled through the floors below and into the ground beyond the basement.

The duo descended the steps at a feverish pace, causing the stairs to sway and creak. At the bottom, they entered an enormous man-made tunnel that wove through the earth like the hollow root of a gigantic tree. It stretched for miles and miles underground, reaching depths humanity was never meant to reach.

The tunnel was an extraordinary achievement and had taken centuries to construct. If it hadn't been shrouded in complete secrecy, it would have been considered a wonder of the world—but once someone entered the tunnel, very few were permitted to *leave* it. The dirt walls were lined with the graves of all the unfortunate souls who had died while digging it and the people who had threatened to expose the project.

The man and woman spent hours climbing deeper and deeper, never stopping for a moment of rest. The man's lantern barely illuminated the ground below their feet as they trekked through an infinite tube of darkness. The farther they went, the hotter it became, and their clothes were dampened by perspiration. A smoky stench of scorched earth filled the air, making it difficult to breathe. The pressure increased, too, causing their eardrums to throb and their noses to bleed. But still, the pair pressed on, too determined to stop.

Boom-boom... Boom-boom... Boom-boom...

At five miles below the surface, a faint noise echoed from ahead.

Boom-BOOM... Boom-BOOM... Boom-BOOM...

The sound increased with every step they took. It thumped in a consistent rhythm as if they were approaching the earth's beating heart.

BOOM-BOOM . . . BOOM-BOOM . . . BOOM-BOOM . . .

Eventually, they saw a bright light that strobed with the thunderous beat. Against the light, the woman could make out the silhouettes of people standing in a row. Their thin bodies were chained together and they clutched shovels and pickaxes in their trembling hands. These prisoners-turned-slaves were the last generation of diggers the tunnel would ever need, because they had just made one of the greatest discoveries in recorded history.

The diggers were frozen with shock as they stared ahead, but the woman stepped past them and gazed with fearless wonder.

They were facing a pair of double doors that were over two hundred feet tall and one hundred feet wide. The doors were made from iron that glowed bright red from the heat behind it. Something very big—and very hot—was trying to escape through the doors, but the handles were bound shut by a monstrous chain. As the doors were pushed, flames and magma spewed out from between the cracks, offering glimpses into a world of fire and chaos beyond them.

"At last!" the woman gasped. "We've found the *gates of the underworld!*"

"Ma'am?" her exhausted and sweaty companion asked, a nervous quiver in his hoarse voice. "What do we do now?"

The woman's eyes went wide and a devious smile grew across her face. She had been waiting not just *one* but *several* lifetimes for this moment.

"*Open them,*" she ordered.

CHAPTER ONE

THE RIGHTEOUS EMPIRE

I t had been almost a year since the Southern Kingdom's last sunrise. The citizens would never forget the horrifying afternoon when Prince "Seven" Gallivant marched his Righteous Army of the Dead through the countryside and took Chariot Hills by storm. There, the prince sat upon his late grandfather's throne in the Champion Castle and declared himself—not the new king of the Southern Kingdom—but the emperor of a new *Righteous Empire.*

Unfortunately, there was nothing anyone in the Southern Kingdom could do to stop him. It was well within the prince's legal rights to change his newly inherited kingdom however he wanted. But not even his most loyal followers could foresee the horrors he had in mind, and soon they began to resent the monster they had helped create.

The emperor's first act was to dissolve the Southern Kingdom's military and replace it with his Army of the Dead. His second act was to strip the Justices of all power and give their positions to the clansmen of his devoted Righteous Brotherhood. Third, the emperor eradicated the Southern Kingdom's constitution and created a new one based on the principles of the Brotherhood's oppressive *Righteous Philosophy.*

Under the new laws, all schools and churches were shut down—the only thing citizens were allowed to study or worship was the emperor himself. All the markets and shops were boarded up—food and supplies were now distributed at the emperor's will. All the talking creatures—elves, dwarfs, trolls, goblins, and ogres—were exiled to their respective territories and banned from returning. The borders were permanently closed, and any communication with the outside world was strictly forbidden.

The emperor also placed his entire population under harsh curfews and social restrictions. No one was allowed to be outdoors from dusk until dawn, citizens needed permission to travel beyond their homes, and it was illegal for people to gather with anyone outside their immediate family. Additionally, all forms of creative expression, such as art, music, and theater, were outlawed. The only clothes the citizens were allowed to wear in public were the drab black uniforms the emperor provided. Private residences were routinely searched for money, jewelry, weapons, and other valuables, and they were taken as "donations" to the Empire.

The emperor's dead soldiers patrolled the streets day and night to make sure the new laws were being followed, and the walking corpses weren't shy about making grotesque examples out of people who disobeyed. So the citizens stayed in their homes to avoid trouble, all the while praying for something—or *someone*—to liberate them from this new nightmare.

However, the most severe change to the constitution

was the law regarding magic. The Empire sentenced people to death simply for *sympathizing* with the magical community. The broad decree gave the emperor the right to imprison anyone he thought *might* be supporting his magical enemies.

In the months following the emperor's succession, the Army of the Dead rounded up over one hundred "magic sympathizers," and they were quickly sentenced to hang without any evidence or trial. Strangely, although the verdicts were rushed, the actual executions were put on hold. The emperor never gave an indication of what he was waiting for, but secretly he was saving the executions for a very *strategic* occasion.

In his first weeks of power, the emperor demolished the University of Law in the Chariot Hills town square and constructed a massive coliseum in its place. The coliseum towered over the other buildings in the capital—it had enough seating for thousands of people—and was purposely built with only *two* entrances, making it difficult to enter *and* exit. The project was finished just two weeks before the Righteous Empire's one-year anniversary. On the evening of its completion, the emperor ordered all citizens of Chariot Hills to the coliseum to witness the delayed executions of the "magic sympathizers."

The Righteous Brotherhood—dressed head to toe in their ghostly silver uniforms and armed with their glowing bloodstone weapons—herded the tired, hungry, and dejected citizens into the coliseum. The emperor was already there when his people arrived, standing in a private balcony at the very top of the coliseum. He radiated crimson light thanks to his bloodstone suit, cape, and crown that curled around the sides of his face like the horns of a ram.

The emperor never looked down as his citizens filled the seats—he only had eyes for the land *surrounding* the coliseum. He held a pair of binoculars tightly against his eyes, scanning every inch of the horizon and every patch of the evening sky.

"Your Greatness." The emperor's High Commander bowed as he stepped onto the private balcony. "The citizens are seated and the soldiers are in position, sir."

"And the archers?" Seven asked.

"Stationed throughout the coliseum and on every rooftop in the capital."

"And the entrances?"

"Completely surrounded, sir," the High Commander said. "I'm confident we've created the most secure structure in the world."

"Secure enough for *her*, High Commander?" Seven pressed.

"If she finds a way inside, she won't get out alive."

Seven grinned under his binoculars but didn't lower them.

"Good," he said. "Let's begin."

The High Commander hesitated. "Sir, are you certain she'll show? Given the extra security measures, it would be extremely risky for—"

"Trust me, High Commander, *she'll take the bait!*" Seven said. "Now proceed. I've waited long enough for this moment."

With that, the High Commander turned on his heel and faced the center of the coliseum. At his signal, two clansmen began turning a lever, and a heavy caged door opened behind them. More clansmen came through the door, escorting over a hundred prisoners from a dungeon belowground. The hands and feet of the "magic sympathizers" were wrapped in thick chains, and they could barely shuffle forward as the clansmen shoved them into the arena.

Although the citizens wanted to scream at the sight of their friends and family in chains, they remained as quiet as possible. Still, a few cries escaped their lips and echoed through the quiet coliseum.

"Start with the Evergreen family," Seven called over his shoulder.

Five clansmen plucked the five members of the Evergreen family from the long line of prisoners. Justice Evergreen and his wife, their sons Brooks and Barrie, and Barrie's wife, Penny, were all dragged up the steps of a tall wooden gallows and placed in a row behind a single noose. The citizens were impressed by how stoic the Evergreens remained—some of them even seemed *eager* to be there. Mrs. Evergreen eyed the noose with a wide and creepy smile, Penny was so excited she was practically buzzing, and Brooks gave a thumbs-up to the people in the crowd.

"How dare you treat us like criminals!" Justice Evergreen shouted. "For God's sake, I am a *Justice of the Southern Kingdom*! I've devoted my life to preserving the law!"

"No, you *were* a Justice," Seven scoffed. "And soon you'll cease to exist at all."

"Shall we start with the former Justice, my lord?" the High Commander asked.

"No, hang the younger brother first," Seven

instructed. "If that doesn't get the Fairy Godmother's attention, nothing will."

The clansmen pushed Barrie forward and fastened the noose tightly around his neck.

"Oh, w-w-woe is me!" Penny cried. "I can't b-b-believe I am about to witness my husband's d-d-death! What a c-c-cruel world!"

"Don't worry, Jenny—*I mean, Penny*!" Barrie could barely speak with the rope around his throat. "It'll all be over soon."

"P-p-please show him some m-m-mercy!" his wife pleaded.

"I suppose in some ways hanging him *is* rather merciful," Brooks said. "It's much quicker than being burned, drowned, crucified, or boiled. And it isn't nearly as messy as beheading, impaling, drawing and quartering, crushing by stones—"

"*Pssst! Brooks!*" Justice Evergreen whispered. "*Zip it! It's not your turn to speak!*"

"*Oh, sorry!*" Brooks whispered back. "*I didn't realize I said that out loud.*"

"Well, *I* agree with my son!" Mrs. Evergreen announced theatrically, making sure everyone in the coliseum could hear her. "You call this a public execution?

I've been to tea parties that were more menacing! Come on, Emperor, you can do better than this! Give us blood! Give us suspense! Give us *absolute terror!*"

Mrs. Evergreen stared up at the emperor with large, exhilarated eyes, as if she was *daring* him to order a more gruesome death for her son. Justice Evergreen groaned and gave his family members a dirty scowl.

"Guys! We all agreed to stick to the script! Stop going rogue!"

"You can't expect a mother to remain silent at a time like this!" Mrs. Evergreen proclaimed. "I want the best for my son—and that includes his execution!"

Justice Evergreen winced and slapped an open palm against his forehead.

"Had I known you were going to act like this, *Mrs. Evergreen*, I never would have asked you to be my wife!" he grumbled. "Everyone just shut up! I'll do all the talking from now on!"

The observing citizens found the family discussion peculiar. Confused looks were exchanged throughout the coliseum—even the Righteous Brotherhood were scrunching their foreheads under their masks. The emperor, on the other hand, wasn't paying any attention to the Evergreens. He had *other* concerns.

"Something is wrong...," Seven muttered to himself. "She should be here by now.... Her favorite brother is seconds away from death, and she's nowhere to be found...."

The emperor's heart was racing with anticipation. He feverishly scanned the horizon with his binoculars, worried he had missed something.

"Hang him on three!" the High Commander called to the gallows.

No, this can't be right... Seven thought. *She would rather* die *than let her family perish....*

"ONE!"

So where is she? Why hasn't she flown to their rescue? What is she waiting for?

"TWO!"

"Unless..." Seven said as he was struck by a troubling thought. *"She's already here!"*

"THREE!"

The emperor spun around and faced the gallows. The floor dropped out from below Barrie's feet, and his body fell straight through the wooden platform. The horrified crowd gasped; however, the prisoner's neck didn't snap as they expected. Instead, Barrie Evergreen's neck began to stretch and stretch like a rubber band until both of his feet touched the ground. All the citizens throughout the arena screamed—a few even fainted.

"THAT'S NOT BARRIE EVERGREEN!" Seven shouted from the balcony.

"The jig is up!" Justice Evergreen told his family. *"It's go time!"*

Suddenly, the chains wrapped around the Evergreens' bodies evaporated into thin air. The family pulled the skin off their faces and the hair off their heads—they had been wearing enchanted disguises the entire time! As the wigs and masks were removed, the imposters' true identities were revealed. Justice Evergreen was a chubby young woman with white feathers for hair, Mrs. Evergreen was an enormous doll with button eyes and burlap flesh, Brooks was a walking plant with chlorophyll skin and leaves growing from its scalp, and Penny had wings, bulging eyes, and a stinger like a giant insect.

As if his skull was made of clay, Barrie's head slipped completely out of the noose, and when he removed his disguise, he turned into a young woman with whiskers and a skunk tail.

"WE'VE BEEN DECEIVED BY *WITCHES!*"
Seven screeched.

If that wasn't enough to shock the crowded arena, the five clansmen at the gallows abruptly flung off their silver uniforms and five very colorful young people appeared. The first was a young man in a metallic golden suit with fire burning on his head and shoulders. The second was a young woman with curly dark hair who wore a robe made of gleaming emeralds. The third was a girl with a bright orange beehive and a dress made from dripping patches of honeycomb. The fourth was a girl in a sapphire bathing suit whose hair flowed down her body like a continuously flowing waterfall. And finally, the fifth was a beautiful young woman in a sparkling pantsuit, wielding a crystal wand.

"IT'S THE FAIRY COUNCIL!" Seven roared. "KILL THEM! KILL THEM ALL!"

The archers throughout the coliseum aimed their crossbows at the newcomers. Brystal Evergreen pointed her wand at Stitches, Sprout, Beebee, and Pip and broomsticks appeared in their hands. The witches hopped aboard the brooms and flew in circles around the arena. The citizens and clansmen ducked and dived out of the way as the witches looped through the air mere inches above their heads. The motion discombobulated the archers and they didn't know where or who to shoot first.

"FOOLS! DON'T LET THEM DISTRACT YOU!" Seven ordered. "FIRE AT THE FAIRY GODMOTHER! SHE'S THE PRIORITY!"

"Xanthous! Skylene! Give me some steam!" Brystal said.

A fiery jet erupted from Xanthous's outstretched palms and a geyser of water sprayed from Skylene's index fingers. The fire collided with the water, creating an enormous cloud of steam. Brystal waved her wand and a strong wind blew the steam around the center of the coliseum, blocking the fairies and the prisoners from the archers' sight.

"WHY AREN'T YOU SHOOTING?!" Seven screamed.

"Sir, the archers can't see where they're firing! And we still have men down there!" the High Commander said.

"I DON'T CARE WHO OR WHAT THEY HIT! JUST FIRE!" Seven ordered.

The archers fired their crossbows, and bloodstone

arrows whizzed through the center of the coliseum, barely missing Brystal and her friends. The clansmen among them tried to use the prisoners as human shields. Brystal waved her wand again and the cowardly clansmen joined the cloud of steam and whirled around the fairies like they were caught in a powerful tornado. The archers lowered their crossbows, afraid they might hit fellow clansmen.

The emperor howled with rage at the Brotherhood's incompetence. He dashed to the other side of his balcony and called to the dead soldiers patrolling the entrances.

"GUARDS! GET IN HERE AND ATTACK THESE HEATHENS! NOT A SINGLE WITCH OR FAIRY LEAVES THIS COLISEUM ALIVE!"

"Emerelda! Quick! Free the rest of the prisoners from their chains!" Brystal instructed.

While the Army of the Dead rushed inside, Emerelda dashed from prisoner to prisoner and turned their chains into a weak talc stone that crumbled off their hands and feet.

"Lucy! Tangerina! Block the entrances before the soldiers get in!" Brystal said.

The girls raced to the entrances on opposite sides

of the coliseum. Lucy hit the ground with a fist and a giant crack zigzagged across the earth. The crack hit the first entrance like a bolt of lightning, causing the doorway to implode before the dead soldiers could get through it. Tangerina sent her swarm of bumblebees into the second entrance and the bees doused the approaching soldiers in honey, sticking them to the floor and walls. Soon the entrance was jammed by sticky skeletons.

"The entrances are blocked, but that means the exits are, too!" Lucy announced. "How are we going to get the prisoners to safety?"

"Leave that to me!" Brystal said.

Brystal pointed her wand at the prisoners and each one's body was surrounded by a giant bubble. To the prisoners' amazement, the bubbles rose into the air, carrying them high into the evening sky. Once all the prisoners had floated out of the coliseum, Brystal pointed her wand at Emerelda, Xanthous, Tangerina, Skylene, and Lucy, and then waved it around herself. She and her friends joined the prisoners in bubbles of their own and Stitches, Sprout, Beebee, and Pip followed on their broomsticks.

After the fairies' departure, the cloud of steam in

the arena slowly faded away and the whirling clansmen dropped to the ground. The citizens cheered for the escapees but then quickly fell silent, remembering that such *sympathies* were illegal. The emperor was so enraged to see the fairies and witches floating away with his prisoners he began foaming at the mouth.

"HIGH COMMANDER, ALERT THE ARCHERS IN THE CITY!" he ordered. "IF YOU LET THE FAIRIES GET AWAY, I WILL HAVE YOUR HEAD ON A PLATTER!"

"Yes, my lord!" the High Commander said.

The High Commander blew a horn to notify the archers positioned on the rooftops throughout the capital. The archers were quick to comply, firing hundreds and hundreds of bloodstone arrows as the escapees drifted over the city. The bubbles were pelted by the arrows, which caused many of them to pop and the prisoners to fall from the sky. Brystal waved her wand and restored their bubbles, but she couldn't keep up.

"Stitches! Sprout! Beebee! Pip! Help me catch them!" Brystal said.

The witches immediately dived through the air and caught the falling prisoners just moments before they hit the ground. Unfortunately, the archers' relentless attack showed no signs of slowing down, and the witches quickly ran out of space on their broomsticks.

"YES!" Seven cheered as he watched the bubbles burst. "They'll never make it out of the capital! They're all going to drop like flies!"

"Emerelda!" Brystal called over her shoulder. "Call for backup!"

Emerelda nodded and pressed a small emerald whistle against her lips. She blew the whistle with all her might and a sharp tone echoed through the sky.

"Sir, look!" the High Commander said. "Something's approaching the capital!"

The emperor peered into the distance and every ounce of celebration drained from his spirits. An enormous black shadow appeared on the horizon, moving through the air like a veil caught in the wind. As the shadow flew closer and closer, the emperor realized it wasn't just one object but *thousands* moving together. He raised his binoculars for a closer look and discovered *a massive flock of gryphons* had entered the city!

The magical creatures soared between the buildings of Chariot Hills and attacked the archers throughout the capital. They knocked the clansmen off rooftops with strokes of their wings, they ripped crossbows out of the men's hands with their beaks, and they snatched handfuls of bloodstone arrows with their claws. The archers were completely caught off guard by the majestic beasts and many abandoned their posts. While the gryphons assaulted the clansmen, the fairies, witches, and prisoners drifted far away from Chariot Hills. Once they were out of the archers' reach, the magical creatures joined the procession of bubbles, and they all soared safely into the horizon.

"NOOOOOOOOOO!" Seven roared so loudly the entire city could hear him. "HOW IS THIS EVEN POSSIBLE?! HOW COULD WE LET THEM ESCAPE?! *AGAIN!*"

The High Commander gulped and took a cautious step back.

"My sincerest apologies, my lord," he said. "I thought our plan was foolproof!"

The emperor's binoculars began to crunch under his tight grip, but he suddenly went very still and very quiet. His fury was interrupted by something strange he had spotted in the sky.

"Wait a second," Seven said. "Where did the Fairy Godmother go? She and the fat witch aren't with the others!"

The emperor scanned the horizon over and over again, but Brystal and Lucy had disappeared.

"Your orders, my lord?" the High Commander asked.

"Gather your men and search the city at once!" Seven demanded. *"They're still here!"*

· • ★ • ·

Brystal's and Lucy's bubbles descended into the Chariot Hills town square and popped on impact. As soon as they landed, Brystal took off running and Lucy sprinted after her.

"Well, the rescue was a smash but the performance was a *flop*!" Lucy griped. "I guess that's what I get for casting amateurs. There's nothing worse in show business than a novice who thinks they can improvise."

Brystal abruptly stopped in her tracks and looked around like she was lost. *She barely recognized the city she had grown up in.* All the buildings were covered in silver banners bearing the emperor's face or the Righteous Brotherhood's white wolf symbol, all the doors and windows were boarded up or chained shut, and all the statues and tributes to past rulers had been removed or demolished. The streets were also covered in large piles of ashes, although Brystal couldn't tell what had been burned. A smoky haze still lingered in the air, making it hard to see more than a few yards in each direction.

"Brystal, what's wrong?" Lucy asked. "Why did we stop moving?"

"Everything looks so different I can't tell which building is which anymore," she said.

"Is there a town directory somewhere?"

"No—but maybe I can make one."

Brystal closed her eyes and visualized the Chariot Hills from her childhood. She waved one arm in a large circle, and thousands of tiny lights emanated from the tip of her wand, as if she was spraying the streets in a glittery mist. However, the lights didn't stick to the buildings as they were now, but re-created the city as Brystal remembered it. After she opened her eyes and got her whereabouts, the lights disappeared.

"The library's over there!" she said. "Follow me! We don't have much time!"

Brystal grabbed Lucy's hand and pulled her toward a building with a glass dome, at the far end of the town square. Just like the other buildings, the library was covered in silver banners, but unlike the others, the library's front steps were surrounded by a tall metal fence. A sign bolted to the fence read:

SUBJECTS BEWARE!

*Under Section Two of the Emperor's
Righteous Constitution,
This Building Is Officially Closed to the Public.
Unauthorized Access Is Forbidden.
Trespassers Will Be Sentenced to Death.*

The warning made Brystal's blood boil. She blasted the fence with her wand, and then Lucy hurried up the front steps and kicked the double doors open. As soon as they stepped inside the dark building, Brystal's stomach turned. *The library had been ransacked beyond recognition!* All the furniture was knocked over and the seat cushions had been ripped apart. The large silver globe that once stood regally in the center of the first floor now lay in pieces across the carpet. And most horrifying of all, every bookshelf in the three-story library was *empty*.

"Slim pickings," Lucy said.

"No, this isn't right," Brystal said. "This place used to be *full* of books!"

"What do you think happened to them?" Lucy asked.

"Seven must have hidden them somewhere," she said. "Let's have a look around and see if they left anything behind."

Brystal and Lucy wandered through the aisles of the spacious library like rats in a multilevel maze. Unfortunately, not a single page had survived the emperor's purge. Even the Justices' secret chamber, which Brystal had discovered when she worked as a maid, was completely vacant. Defeated, Brystal began pacing by a window on the third floor. Her gaze drifted toward the town square outside and her whole body went tense. It had suddenly dawned on her *what* had created all the ashes in the streets.

"Seven didn't hide the books—*he burned them!*" Brystal said in disbelief.

"I'm confused," Lucy said. "Why would Seven burn a bunch of books?"

Brystal sighed and shook her head. "Because reading inspires *thinking*, thinking inspires *ideas*, ideas inspire *change*, and nothing threatens a tyrant more than *change*."

Lucy groaned and made fists with both hands. "*God, I HATE that guy!*" she declared. "Just when I think it isn't possible to loathe someone more, he always proves me wrong!"

"Luckily, books can be replaced," Brystal said. "Well... *most* books can be replaced."

Lucy gulped. "Do you think *it* was destroyed with the others?"

"Honestly, I doubt *it* was even here to begin with. A book like that would definitely have caught my attention when I was a maid, and I don't remember seeing anything even remotely like it—not even in the Justices' private collection."

"But this is the only library we haven't searched. If it isn't *here*, then where is it?"

Brystal went quiet as she asked herself the same question. However, her train of thought was interrupted by a strange red light that began to glow around them. She and Lucy turned around and saw the Righteous Emperor standing at the end of the aisle. His bloodstone wardrobe radiated crimson light through the dark library and his unwavering scowl radiated pure hatred.

"Seven."

At first, Brystal was glad to see the emperor. Part of her wanted to believe Seven was the dashing young prince who had swept her off her feet—not the dangerous young man who had tried to kill her.

"I'm guessing your real family is alive and well," Seven sneered.

"They've been safe and sound for months," Brystal said.

The emperor's mouth curved into a sinister grin but the hatred never faded from his eyes.

"I have to give credit where credit is due," he said. "That was quite a *stunt* you pulled off at the coliseum. Sadly, your most impressive charade will be your last."

The emperor snapped his fingers and he was joined by his High Commander and the Righteous Brotherhood. The clansmen backed Brystal and Lucy into a wall at the very end of the aisle. Brystal desperately wanted to wave her wand and knock the men across the library, but she knew her magic was useless against their bloodstone weapons. With his guards in place, the emperor strolled toward the girls and looked Brystal closely in the eye.

"Tell me, Brystal, exactly how many lives do you have?" Seven asked. "On second thought, let it be a surprise. I'm willing to kill you as many times as it takes."

"Killing me won't ensure your victory," Brystal said. "It doesn't matter how many laws you enforce, how many lies you tell, or how many books you burn—your day of reckoning *will* come. Your people are much smarter and stronger than you think. With or without me, it's only a matter of time before they get sick of your tyranny and rise against you."

"And that's where you're wrong," he said. "You see, a successful resistance takes *courage*, it takes *intelligence*, it takes *resilience*—and people aren't *born* with those qualities. No, no, no. Bravery has to be *inspired*, brilliance has to be *championed*, boldness has to be *encouraged*— but if you destroy everything that *nurtures* a society, then society will never gain the tools to destroy you. And nothing will dishearten my people more than seeing *the great Fairy Godmother's head on a pike!*"

"DISHEARTEN *THIS*, YOU WALKING SUN- BURN!" Lucy shouted.

SWOOSH! Lucy shoved the nearest bookcase with all her might and *WHAM!* The bookcase fell directly on top of the emperor, pinning him to the floor. He moaned and struggled to free himself, but the bookcase was too heavy.

"Now *that's* how you improvise," Lucy said. "Sorry, Brystal, you didn't want to keep chatting with him, did you?"

"I'm just jealous I didn't think of that first," Brystal said.

"DON'T JUST STAND THERE! KILL THEM!" Seven screamed at his men.

The clansmen charged toward Brystal and Lucy with their swords and spears raised. Lucy hit the floor with a fist and sent a giant ripple through the carpet. The ripple made all the bookcases in the aisle begin to teeter until, one by one, the bookcases came crashing down on the clansmen.

"Nice one!" Brystal told Lucy.

"Thanks," she said. "I did the same thing to escape a distillery once, but that's a story for another time! Let's get out of here!"

Brystal and Lucy raced down the aisle, leaping over the bookcases and the clansmen trapped beneath

31

them. Unfortunately, Lucy's ripple was much more powerful than she intended. As she and Brystal hurried into the next aisle, the bookcases began crashing down all around them!

"Lucy, make it stop!" Brystal said.

"You know I can't stop anything I start!" Lucy said. "My magic is like eating junk food!"

Without time to think, the only thing the girls could do was run while the falling bookcases chased them through the third floor like a giant game of dominoes! As they reached the stairs, bookcases began toppling over the railings. The cases crashed into the lower levels, trigging similar domino effects across *all* the aisles in the library. By the time Brystal and Lucy reached the ground floor every bookcase in the library had been knocked over.

Lucy let out a nervous laugh as she eyed the wreckage. "I bet you're glad you aren't the maid anymore," she said.

The girls dashed to the exit, but as soon as they reached the double doors, they came to an abrupt halt—*the library was surrounded by the Army of the Dead*! Brystal and Lucy were trapped! Once the girls were spotted, the dead soldiers charged inside.

"Gosh, these guys are like cockroaches! They just

keep coming and coming!" Lucy said. "How are we going to get past them?"

Brystal glanced around the library, looking for a quick escape, and her eyes landed on the glass dome in the ceiling.

"Quick! Hold on to my waist!" she said.

"Why?" Lucy asked.

"It's my turn to *improvise*!"

Lucy wrapped her arms around Brystal's waist as tightly as she could. Brystal raised her hand toward the ceiling and a bright light blasted from the tip of her wand. The light engulfed Brystal and Lucy and, suddenly, they shot through the dome like a shooting star. The dome shattered and glass rained down on the skeleton soldiers.

On the third floor, the High Commander and the Righteous Brotherhood began to crawl out from underneath the heavy bookcases. Once they were free, the clansmen raced to the emperor and helped push the bookcase off his body.

"My lord, are you hurt?" the High Commander asked.

"I'm fine!" the emperor said as he got to his feet. "Where is the Fairy Godmother?"

"She and her accomplice escaped the library, sir."

"They *WHAT*?!"

The news sent the emperor into a furious rage. He grabbed the High Commander by the shoulders and pushed him through the nearest window.

"*The High Commander has been dismissed!*" Seven said, and then pointed to the nearest clansman. "*You!* You're the new High Commander! Disappoint me and you'll suffer the same fate! Is that understood?"

The clansman's eyes grew wide under his silver mask and he dived into a quick bow.

"I'm at your service, my lord," he said with a nervous quiver in his voice.

"Good," Seven said. "Now, the Fairy Godmother is up to something—I can feel it in my bones! We have to figure out what she's planning!"

"What was she doing in the library, sir?"

"Isn't it obvious?" Seven snapped. "She was looking for a *book*."

"But what *sort* of book, sir?"

The emperor gazed through the broken window as if he might find the answer in the desolate town square, but nothing came to him.

"I don't know," he said. "But whatever it is, we need to find it before *she* does."

CHAPTER TWO

THE COUNTDOWN

*T*ick… *Tick*… *Tick*… *Tick*…

Brystal always resented the sound of a ticking clock. Whether she was counting down the hours before she could escape the School for Future Wives and Mothers, or counting down the minutes she had left to secretly read books in the Chariot Hills Library, Brystal didn't think a clock could sound any more ominous than it already did. But she was dead wrong.

Tick... Tick... Tick... Tick...

Brystal glanced down at the silver pocket watch attached to her waist. To someone else, the watch would have shown it was a few minutes before noon. And to someone else, the watch's soft ticking would have barely been noticeable. But to Brystal, the gentle gears were *deafening.* Her watch wasn't counting down the hours of her day—it was counting down the days of her life.

Two weeks...

That's all you have left...

To locate the ancient spell book...

To destroy the Immortal...

And you still haven't found either of them yet.

Tick... Tick... Tick... Tick...

You're no closer now than you were a year ago....

You have to accept the truth....

You're out of time....

In thirteen days ...

You *will* die.

The curse on Brystal's mind rarely surfaced these days. She had become so good at ignoring the disturbing thoughts that she barely noticed them anymore. Even when they occasionally got her attention, Brystal loved putting them in their place. For her, the disturbing thoughts were no longer a powerful curse—they were an old friend she enjoyed arguing with.

You may be right..., she thought.

But who isn't on borrowed time?

Whose days aren't numbered?

Knowing when my life ends means I can make the most of the time I have left...

And I'm not going to waste a second of it.

Brystal clicked the watch shut and tucked it into the pocket of her pantsuit. She was standing at the windows of her office in the Academy of Magic, taking in the view of the rolling green hills, the sparkling blue ocean, and the shimmering golden castle around her. Brystal made a point to admire the Fairy Territory whenever she could, knowing each opportunity might be her last. However, she didn't let herself linger for long—death or no death, she had a lot of work to do.

Thankfully, Brystal didn't bear the burden of finding the ancient spell book and the Immortal alone. For the first time, instead of sparing her friends from the truth, Brystal had *confided* in them. They knew all about her deal with Death, they knew Brystal only had one year to find the Immortal and destroy her with an ancient spell book, or her life would end. And before Brystal could even *ask* for her friends' help, they went straight to work.

Over the past eleven months and two weeks, Brystal's office had turned into the center of a thorough investigation. The fairies covered every surface of the glass furniture with stacks of maps and address books of every known library, bookstore, and book collector in the world. While they worked tirelessly on locating the ancient spell book, the witches worked diligently on identifying the Immortal. All the walls in the office were filled with birth certificates, death certificates, and portraits of very, very old ladies.

After Brystal and Lucy's trip to the Chariot Hills Library, all the libraries had officially been searched, so the fairies focused their efforts on contacting bookstores and renowned book collectors. The fairies wrote under pseudonyms to keep the mission a secret, asking the sellers and collectors about any *older publications* they might have in their possession. Each morning, Horence the knight heaved a heavy sack of mail into the office and the fairies dug through the letters, hoping for a positive lead.

"I just got a letter from the Book Worm Bookshop in Tinzel Heights!" Emerelda announced. "I guess the bookstore closed a while ago and was turned into a coffee shop. *Dang, that's the fourth one this month.* They say they donated their books to their local orphanage but none of them were older than a decade or two."

"The book collector from Fort Longsworth finally wrote me back!" Tangerina said. "Mr. Gibbinson says he would be happy to show us his collection of old textbooks *and* his collection of taxidermy raccoons.

The second part is a little concerning, but the first part is promising!"

"I have an update from the Eastern Kingdom!" Xanthous said. "The Page Turner Bookstore in Iron-hand says they specialize in antique books from all over the globe. They even have a few titles dating back to the reign of King Champion I! We should go and check it out!"

Along with the mail, every morning Horence also delivered a stack of newspapers from various cities around the world. The witches scanned through the obituaries to help them eliminate potential Immortal suspects.

"Another one bites the dust!" Lucy proclaimed. "Faradean Fairtucket officially kicked the bucket last week at one hundred and twelve years old. She is survived by four children, fifteen grandchildren, and seven much younger ex-husbands—*well, way to go, Faradean*! Her last words were 'Oh, there you are, God. I thought you forgot about me.'"

"I have some sad news, too," Pip said. "Ester Ester-wig passed away at the age of one hundred and three. She was laid to rest yesterday in the Tinzel Heights Forever Cemetery. It says she died peacefully in her husband's sleep—apparently Ester was an insomniac. Dang it, I was really hoping she'd be the one."

"Looks like Windella Parkweed is no longer with us either," Sprout said. "She passed just days before her one hundred and fifth birthday. Windella is survived by her beloved felines Mayor Whiskers, Purr Baby, Snow Mittens, Doctor Hairball, Angel Toes, and Grumpy Puss II. Her cause of death is still unknown because the cats ate her corpse."

"*Awesome*," Stitches said with a wide grin. "Mind if I hang on to that one?"

Stitches cut the obituary out of the newspaper and pasted it into a scrapbook she kept of gruesome obituaries. While Stitches saved the clipping, Beebee flew around the office and drew a big red *X* on the portraits that belonged to Faradean Fairtucket, Ester Esterwig, and Windella Parkweed.

"We're r-r-running out of centenarian s-s-suspects," Beebee said.

"*Alleged* centenarians," Stitches said. "I keep telling you guys, it doesn't matter what the newspapers say, these obituaries could be fake! The only way we'll know for sure is if we dig these women up and make sure they're actually dead!"

Pip gulped and raised her hand. "Brystal, can I be reassigned to the ancient spell book? The Immortal investigation is taking a turn."

"I hate to validate her, but Stitches has a point," Emerelda said. "Who knows how many times the Immortal has had to fake her death to avoid suspicion? If we're going to track her down, we'll have to think outside of the box. It's not like the oldest woman in the world is just going to walk through the door."

Suddenly, the office doors swung open and Mrs. Vee stepped inside.

"*Hello, hello, hello!*" the bubbly housekeeper sang. "I thought you might be hungry so I whipped you up some boysenberry soufflé! You aren't going to believe this, but one of the prisoners you rescued from the Righteous Empire yesterday is an award-winning pastry chef! How lucky is that? We've been exchanging recipes all morning. Stitches, Sprout, and Beebee, per your dietary requests, I sprinkled some spider legs in your soufflés to remind you of home. But that's not the first time I've put a bug in someone's food! HA-HA!"

Skylene's eyes grew wide and she pointed an accusatory finger at the housekeeper.

"Oh my God! *Mrs. Vee is the Immortal!*" she

declared. "Why didn't we think of this sooner?! She's the oldest person we know! Even her jokes are ancient!"

Mrs. Vee rolled her eyes and set the tray of boysenberry soufflés on the tea table.

"Once again, Skylene, I'm *humbled* by your high opinion of me," the housekeeper said. "If I was the Immortal do you think I would look like *this*?"

"What do you mean, Mrs. Vee?" Tangerina asked.

"I imagine the best part of being Immortal is that you *don't age*," she explained. "Otherwise, why would anyone want to live forever? I wouldn't want to spend eternity getting older and older, and weaker and weaker. I don't even like raisins in salad, I certainly wouldn't want one in a mirror! HA-HA!"

The fairies and witches froze and looked to one another with collective dread.

"Of course!" Pip said, and anxiously tugged on her ears. "This whole time we've been looking for an old woman! But the Immortal could be *any age*! That means she could be *anybody*!"

"That's like f-f-finding a needle in a m-m-mountain of hay!" Beebee said. "How are w-w-we supposed to track her d-d-down?"

"Everybody relax!" Stitches said. "There's a very simple solution to this. We'll just have to dig up every woman who's ever lived. I'm more than happy to lead the charge."

The fairies and witches moped around the office, moaning and groaning despairingly. Strangely, the one person the revelation affected the most seemed affected the least. Brystal remained surprisingly calm, as if the development was as trivial as a weather forecast.

"We'll just have to expand the search, that's all," she said with a shrug. "Now let's get back to the ancient spell book. Tangerina, I want you and Skylene to visit the book collector in Fort Longsworth as soon as possible. Bring back anything that resembles what we're looking for. And Xanthous, I want you and Emerelda to go to the Eastern Kingdom straightaway and check out the Page Turner Bookstore. Make sure you all dress as civilians and hide your magic—we don't want word getting out that the Fairy Council is looking for an ancient book."

Emerelda crossed her arms and gave Brystal a stern look, like she was reading her mind—and to Brystal's dismay, Emerelda usually could.

"Is it just my imagination, or are you more interested in finding the ancient spell book than the Immortal?" Emerelda asked.

Brystal sighed. "At this point, I think finding the book is a better use of our time."

"But we need *both* of them to save you from Death," Emerelda said. "I hope your curse isn't trying to confuse you."

"This isn't the curse talking, I promise," she said. "I only have two weeks left to live and I want to be as productive and practical as possible. Finding the Immortal will only save *me*, but finding the ancient spell book will save *the entire world*. Whatever spell is powerful enough to destroy the Immortal is also powerful enough to destroy the Army of the Dead—it would put an end to Seven and the Righteous Brotherhood's reign of terror once and for all! I'll die much happier knowing you have the tools to finally defeat them."

"That's very noble of you, but like you said, we still have *two whole weeks*," Emerelda said. "Even if our chances of finding the Immortal are slim, we still have to try our best, otherwise we'll always regret not doing more to save you."

The fairies and the witches nodded along with Emerelda's remarks. Brystal was touched by their devotion.

"All right then," she said. "I won't give up just yet."

Lucy cleared her throat. "Can I throw my two cents into this tip jar? If you're looking for something practical and productive to do with your time, there's a *very practical* and *very productive* source of information we *still* haven't consulted yet," she said, raising her eyebrows impatiently. "If anyone knows how to find the Immortal or the ancient spell book, it's going to be Madame Weatherberry."

Brystal took a deep breath and looked to the floor. "I know, I know," she said. "It's just...asking her for help means I have to tell her the truth about *everything*. And she was so happy to hear about the legalization of magic—I can't imagine how helpless she'll feel knowing about the Army of the Dead and my deal with Death. It seems cruel to trouble her."

Lucy placed her hands on her hips. "Brystal, the woman is frozen in a block of ice in the middle of nowhere. She's not exactly *living the good life*."

Brystal turned to the enchanted globe beside her desk and gazed at the twinkling lights above the

Northern Mountains. Unbeknownst to the others, Brystal had a very specific reason for not seeking Madame Weatherberry's help, but it had nothing to do with making Madame Weatherberry feel *helpless*. Unfortunately, Brystal had put the meeting off for as long as she could.

"You're right, I should speak to her while I still have a chance," she said. "So we all have our assignments. Xanthous and Emerelda will travel to the Eastern Kingdom, Tangerina and Skylene will visit the book collector in Fort Longsworth, and Stitches, Sprout, Beebee, and Pip will start searching for women who look *really, really good for their age*. In the meantime, Lucy and I will head north."

CHAPTER THREE

THE ICY TRUTH

Brystal and Lucy dressed in their warmest clothes and left for the Northern Mountains that afternoon. They departed the Academy of Magic in a giant bubble, soared high above the Troll and Goblin Territories, and were descending into the chilly Northern Kingdom by nightfall. The bubble landed safely on a slope directly below the shimmering Northern Lights and the girls searched the snowy terrain for

Madame Weatherberry's cave. Thankfully, the weather was kind tonight and the entrance was easy to spot.

It had been over a year since Brystal visited Madame Weatherberry, but as she and Lucy wandered down the long entrance tunnel and emerged into the spacious cave, everything felt eerily familiar—as if the cold air had frozen *time* itself.

Brystal waved her wand and covered all the stalactites above them in twinkling lights that illuminated the cave like a dozen chandeliers. The girls headed to the back of the cave where the grisly Snow Queen was frozen in a wall of ice. Every inch of the witch's monstrous appearance—from her cracked and frostbitten skin to her jagged and rotten teeth—was just as terrifying as they remembered, if not more.

"Well, this is a pleasant surprise," said a soft voice behind them.

Brystal and Lucy turned around and discovered the spirit of a beautiful woman standing behind them. She wore an elegant plum dress that matched the color of her bright eyes and her dark hair was styled beneath an elaborate fascinator with feathers and ribbons. The woman's smile was so warm Brystal could have sworn the temperature rose a few degrees.

"Hello, Madame Weatherberry," Brystal said. "It's wonderful to see you again."

"Holy egg whites—*you look fantastic!*" Lucy declared. "Isolation has done you wonders! If I didn't know better, I'd ask for your magic surgeon."

Madame Weatherberry chuckled. "It's nice to see you, too, Lucy," she said. "I'm guessing Brystal has told you the truth about why I'm here."

"Actually, the others know about it, too," Brystal confessed.

"I can't imagine the disappointment I've caused," Madame Weatherberry said, and somberly shook her head. "Finding out I lied is one thing, but learning I was behind the Snow Queen all along is indefensible. I am profoundly sorry and hope you can forgive me."

"*Forgive you?* Madame Weatherberry, I'm here to option the play rights!" Lucy said.

"Pardon?" she asked.

"I mean, your life story is a theatrical smash waiting to happen," Lucy said. "Think about it! The Snow Queen grew inside of you like a parasite, feeding off a lifetime of suppressed heartbreak and rage—*that's every actor's dream role*! And how you unleashed the

Snow Queen on a world that hated magic just to prove how much the world needed magic—*man, what a genius third act twist*! And now you're stuck in an icy cavern, with a spirit detached from your former body, forced to relive your mistakes over and over again until the end of time—*I smell awards*! This show is going to run longer than *Bats*!"

Madame Weatherberry didn't know what to say. She never thought her personal tragedies could be so *profitable*.

"I'm glad you find my life so entertaining, Lucy," she said.

"I'll draw up the contracts on another day," Lucy said. "Right now, we've got much bigger fish to fry. Go ahead, Brystal."

Lucy gave Brystal an aggressive pat on the back that nudged her forward. Brystal's body immediately went tense and she gazed at the snowy ground to avoid making eye contact. Before saying a word, Brystal already regretted speaking.

"Madame Weatherberry, do you remember our last conversation?" she asked.

"How could I forget?" Madame Weatherberry asked. "You told me the wonderful news about the legalization of magic. . . . You had concerns about your friend Pip joining a school of witchcraft. . . . You mentioned you had been feeling sad and couldn't explain why. . . . And you told me about the unfortunate return of the Righteous Brotherhood."

Brystal nodded sheepishly and focused all her attention on the snow beneath her shoes.

"Right," she said. "Well, there have been a few *updates*."

"Good updates?" the fairy asked.

Brystal and Lucy exchanged a discouraging glance and Madame Weatherberry's bright smile faded.

"Treat it like a bandage, Brystal," Lucy said. "The quicker the better!"

Brystal took a deep breath, straightened her posture, and began her summary of the previous year. She started by telling Madame Weatherberry that her disturbing thoughts had been caused by a horrible *curse*, but thankfully, she had learned to manage it. Brystal told her she had been cursed by Mistress Mara, the founder of the Ravencrest School of Witchcraft, and how the witch was using the school as a front to create a *Shadow Beast* to boost her powers. Next, Brystal explained that Mistress Mara had teamed up with the

Righteous Brotherhood, and together, they had used the Shadow Beast to bring back the invincible Army of the Dead. And finally, Brystal had the unfortunate task of telling Madame Weatherberry that the Righteous Brotherhood had taken over the Southern Kingdom and turned it into an oppressive Righteous Empire.

"My word," Madame Weatherberry gasped. "Even in my worst nightmares I never dreamed of something so terrible."

"But wait, there's *more*," Lucy said.

Clearly, Madame Weatherberry couldn't imagine how things could possibly be worse. Just the thought of telling her the next part made Brystal feel physically ill. She closed her eyes and clenched her fists, as if she was squeezing the information out of her body.

"At one point the curse convinced me to surrender to the Righteous Brotherhood," she said. "They took me to their fortress and . . . and . . . and . . ."

"*And they killed her!*" Lucy exclaimed.

Madame Weatherberry shook her head as if her ears were betraying her.

"Did you say the Righteous Brotherhood *killed her*?" she asked.

Brystal and Lucy nodded.

"But how is that possible? You're standing right in front of me!"

"They covered me in chains made of bloodstone," Brystal recalled. "I tried to fight it off, but the chains made me weaker and weaker, and I eventually drifted to the other side. I traveled to a big gray field floating somewhere between the world of the living and the great unknown. There were stars and planets and galaxies all around me that I could *feel* and *hear* just as easily as I could *see* them. The field was covered with hundreds of gorgeous white trees. Each tree had the name of a different person and a silver clock that was counting down their time left on earth. It was all so strange and frightening, and yet beautiful and peaceful at the same time."

Until now, Madame Weatherberry had been glancing back and forth at the girls as if they were telling her a morbid joke, but after Brystal's detailed account of the afterlife, her expression became very serious.

"How did you come back to life?" she asked, almost afraid to hear the answer.

"Oh, buckle up, Madame Weatherberry," Lucy warned. "This part makes your third act surprise seem like an intermission raffle!"

Brystal's posture sank. "I made a deal with Death."

"*Death?*" Madame Weatherberry gasped. "Are you saying Death is a *person*?"

"Yes," Brystal said. "He looked exactly like I always imagined—and yet, I wasn't afraid of him. It's hard to explain."

"And what sort of deal did you make with him?" Madame Weatherberry pressed.

"Apparently, several centuries ago, a woman tricked Death into gifting her with immortality. Since then, this woman—this *Immortal*—has roamed the earth, making a mockery of everything life and death stand for. Death said if I agreed to find and destroy the Immortal, he would give me back my life. But the only way to destroy her is by using a spell from an ancient spell book. He also said I could use the same spell to annihilate the Army of the Dead. Once I knew that, I couldn't turn him down."

"*But,*" Lucy said.

Brystal groaned—*whose story was this?*

"*But* Death only gave me a year to complete the mission. He said if I don't find the ancient spell book and destroy the Immortal in twelve months, he's going to take my life back."

"How much time do you have left?" Madame Weatherberry asked.

Brystal winced—she knew this was going to be the hardest part to hear.

"Two weeks."

Madame Weatherberry was just a spirit, but the news was so shocking, even *she* needed to sit down. Her knees buckled and her body dropped through the air, as if she had sunk into an invisible seat.

"Why didn't you tell me sooner?" the fairy asked.

"For the record, I told her this cave should have been our first stop," Lucy said. "Brystal didn't want to burden you with more problems. She thought your plate was full enough with—well, you know—*the guilt of unintentionally murdering thousands of innocent people and damaging massive amounts of property as the Snow Queen*. Wow, now that I say that out loud, I suddenly understand where she was coming from."

Madame Weatherberry studied Brystal's face with a suspicious gaze—*there was something Brystal wasn't telling her.*

"Lucy's right—I didn't want to trouble you," Brystal said, and then quickly changed the subject. "We're hoping you can help us find the ancient spell book.

We've searched every library and nearly every bookstore in the world, and so far, we haven't found a trace of it anywhere. Madame Weatherberry, have *you* ever heard of a spell that's powerful enough to destroy an Immortal? Or what book it's in?"

Madame Weatherberry got to her feet and quietly paced around the frigid cave. Her translucent hand rubbed her translucent chin as she went deeper and deeper into thought. As she searched her memory for an answer, the girls could tell one idea in particular kept coming back to her. No matter how many times Madame Weatherberry waved the notion off, it returned again and again like a hungry pet. Finally, she had no choice but to acknowledge it.

"As a matter of fact, I *have* heard of a book that fits that description," Madame Weatherberry said. "I believe Death was referring to the Book of Sorcery."

Hearing the title sent shivers down Brystal's and Lucy's spines. They both stood straight up—eager to learn more.

"What's the Book of Sorcery?" Lucy asked.

"Isn't *sorcery* just another word to describe magic?" Brystal asked.

"Traditionally, *sorcery* is used to describe the most

ancient practices of magic," Madame Weatherberry explained. "And according to legend, the Book of Sorcery is the most powerful spell book ever created. They say in ancient times a group of sorcerers and sorceresses, both good and evil, gathered together and catalogued their greatest enchantments in one manuscript. The book has the power to control all the elements in the universe. There are spells to take life away from the living, spells to give life to the dying, and even spells to resurrect the dead. The book can bestow extraordinary gifts to the weak and strip abilities from the strong, it can take someone through space and time, and it can summon a choir of angels from heaven or an army of demons from the depths of hell. Naturally, if a book like that fell into the wrong hands it could bring about the end of existence as we know it. So the sorcerers and sorceresses hid the Book of Sorcery far away, in the only place it would be safe."

"Where?" Brystal and Lucy asked in unison.

"The Temple of Knowledge," Madame Weatherberry said.

Brystal and Lucy were fascinated, but neither had heard of such a place.

"Madame Weatherberry, I've traveled to every

corner of the kingdoms and I've never seen a Temple of Knowledge before," Brystal said.

"That's because it's not part of the *known world*," she said. "The location is magically concealed from all maps and globes to protect the objects inside it. Just like the Book of Sorcery, the temple contains a vault that harbors *other* extraordinary objects with remarkable capabilities."

"Is the temple difficult to get into?" Lucy asked.

"Extremely," Madame Weatherberry said. "Legend says the temple is also protected by a tribe of *unlikely guardians* who've dedicated their lives to keeping it safe from intruders. Even if you get past them, you must survive a series of physical, mental, and emotional tests waiting inside the temple. And finally, before entering the vault you must come face-to-face with the deadliest and most dangerous creature ever to roam the earth."

"Oh, is that all?" Lucy said with a nervous laugh. "It sounds like a jazz club I snuck into once. Maybe there's a bouncer we can bribe."

Brystal appreciated Lucy's attempt to make light of the situation, but just the *thought* of finding and surviving the Temple of Knowledge made her feel light-headed.

"We've got to get back to the academy and tell the others," Brystal said. "The sooner we start looking for the Temple of Knowledge, the better off we'll be."

Brystal headed out of the tunnel without saying good-bye to Madame Weatherberry. Lucy cleared her throat to get her attention.

"Aren't you forgetting something?" she asked.

"What?" Brystal asked.

Lucy rolled her eyes. "The Book of Sorcery and the Temple of Knowledge are a great start, but we need to find the Immortal, too, otherwise you're toast!" she reminded her. "Madame Weatherberry, do you have any clue who the Immortal is?"

The fairy went quiet again as she thought about it, but unfortunately, nothing came to mind.

"I'm sorry," Madame Weatherberry said. "But perhaps I can give guidance on *how* to find her?"

"Fantastic! We're all ears!" Lucy said.

"First, I suspect the Immortal would gain a lot of attention if they stayed in one place for long, so I would look for women who've lived in many different parts of the world," she said. "Second, I also suspect the Immortal wouldn't want to spend eternity *working*, so I bet she's found a way to remain wealthy. Keep an eye on women in the upper classes. Third, someone with that much life experience is bound to leave an impression on someone else. I would consult the elders of each village—maybe they have old *and* recent memories of the same person."

"Worldly, wealthy, and wild—got it!"

Lucy clung to every word of Madame Weatherberry's advice and started taking notes of her suggestions. Brystal stayed silent and pretended to listen, but mentally, she was focused only on finding the Temple of Knowledge. Eventually, she became so fixated on it, her attentive facade dissolved completely and her eyes darted around the cave.

"You aren't listening to a word I'm saying."

The voice came out of nowhere and startled Brystal. She looked over her shoulder and saw Madame Weatherberry was standing right behind her. But strangely, when she looked back in front of her, Madame Weatherberry was still talking to Lucy, too.

"How are you in two places at once?" Brystal asked.

"You'd be amazed at the things a spirit can do without a body weighing it down," Madame Weatherberry said. "Now, why aren't you listening to my advice about the Immortal?"

"I *am* listening," Brystal said.

Madame Weatherberry raised an eyebrow at her. "Brystal, you're the best student I've ever had—I can tell when you're interested in a subject and when you're not."

Brystal could feel her heart rate starting to rise.

"I . . . I . . . I just think finding the Book of Sorcery is a better use of our time," she said. "Finding the book will help us save *the world* from the Righteous Brotherhood, but destroying the Immortal will only save *me*. And what are the chances we'll actually find her in two weeks?"

"Ah, I see," Madame Weatherberry said. "You don't *want* to find her."

"Of course I want to find her!" Brystal lied. "What makes you think I don't?"

"Because you always accomplish what you set your mind on, despite how impossible it seems," Madame Weatherberry said. "So there's only one logical explanation for why you aren't setting your mind on the Immortal—you don't *want* to find her. And I'm not letting you leave this cave until you tell me why."

Brystal took a deep breath and let out a long sigh. This was the moment she had spent the past year trying to avoid. And now that it was finally here, Brystal knew it was useless to hide the truth.

"There's no point in searching for the Immortal," she said. "Even if we did find her, I could never go through with it—I couldn't *kill* someone."

"So you're just going to let yourself *die*?"

"I don't want to die, but I can't justify taking someone's life to save my own—especially a woman whose only crime is *living*."

"Is *that* why you waited so long to see me?" she asked.

Brystal nodded. "I knew it would break your heart."

"But what about your friends? They must be beside themselves."

"I haven't told them yet," Brystal said. "Trust me, I've spent months agonizing over this, but I don't see another option. Even if I did destroy the Immortal, I couldn't live with myself afterward. I'd much rather die twice than kill once. There's nothing you can do to help me."

Brystal expected Madame Weatherberry to passionately object and continue the argument for as long as possible, but surprisingly, the fairy didn't try to change her mind. Instead, Madame Weatherberry looked toward the back of the cave, somberly staring at the Snow Queen.

"No, you're right...," she said softly. "I wouldn't wish that kind of guilt on anyone.... It's far worse than death...."

Until now, Brystal had never realized how much pain Madame Weatherberry was in. Being trapped in the cave with the Snow Queen's frozen body was a constant reminder of all the mistakes she had made and the people she had hurt. Brystal could tell what a tremendous toll it had taken on Madame Weatherberry's soul. Before she could think of something comforting to say, Madame Weatherberry disappeared from Brystal's side. At the same time, the other Madame Weatherberry wrapped up her conversation with Lucy.

"Last but not least, I would search for women who own a lot of antiques," the fairy suggested. "The Immortal's collection could be mementos in disguise."

"That sure beats chasing old ladies and obituaries! Thanks for all the tips, Madame Weatherberry!" Lucy said. "Okay, Brystal, *now* we leave."

"Will I see you again?" Madame Weatherberry asked.

Brystal knew this might be the last time she ever

saw Madame Weatherberry, but she didn't have the heart to tell her. Saying a final good-bye to Madame Weatherberry was too painful to bear.

"I'll try to come back as soon as I can," she said.

"Please do," the fairy said. "Good luck, girls. I'm here whenever you need me."

Brystal and Lucy headed out of the cave and Madame Weatherberry waved happily as they left, but once they were out of sight, her cheerful expression drained away. Brystal's situation made Madame Weatherberry feel more powerless and trapped than ever before. Her anguished eyes drifted toward the Snow Queen once more, but this time, the sight of the dreadful witch gave the fairy a surprisingly hopeful idea.

Perhaps Brystal was wrong—perhaps there *was* something Madame Weatherberry could do to help her....

CHAPTER FOUR

THE MESSAGE

The Eastern Kingdom was the proud global leader of metal manufacturing. Under the leadership of their beloved Queen Endustria, the country ingeniously combined the natural minerals in its rich soil with the natural heat of its many active volcanoes and created the world's most productive steel, iron, and copper factories. The kingdom's capital, Ironhand, was a testament to its prosperous trade. The city was a

bustling metropolis of tall buildings, multilevel walkways, and crowded streets—and every inch of the busy
town, from the tips of the towers to the bricks of the bou-
levards, was made from the kingdom's prized metals.

Unfortunately, the endless smoke bellowing from
the factories meant the kingdom lived in a constant
haze of pollution, but the citizens thought that was a
small price to pay for a—*cough*—booming economy.

The day after Brystal sent them to the Eastern Kingdom, Emerelda and Xanthous arrived in Ironhand
on a passenger boat in the late afternoon. As the boat
sailed down the Eastern River that snaked through the
center of the capital, the duo was in awe of the tow-
ering structures around them. They had visited Ironhand many times in the past, with the Fairy Council,
but the energetic city never ceased to amaze them.
There was something about Ironhand that made them
feel like they were at the center of the world.

"Okay, remember our story," Emerelda said. "I'm
Emmy Teardrop and you're Xach Fairchild. We're students from the Western Lake Finishing School in Fort
Longsworth. We're staying with my cousin, Ruby, and
are planning to visit the Museum of Unnatural History
and see the Goblin Tenors at the Old Spinster Theater."

"Gosh, do we really need a story *that* elaborate?" Xanthous asked.

"Probably not, but it's kind of fun to be undercover," she said with a playful grin.

Emerelda checked her reflection in a small hand mirror. She was wearing a dark green hat with a wide brim, a long coat with a high collar, and a pair of thick emerald sunglasses. In fact, Emerelda's disguise was so stylish, she was actually *drawing attention* from the other passengers on the boat. Xanthous, on the other hand, had kept it simple with just a plain white shirt, a burlap vest, and black trousers. He had extinguished the flames on his head and shoulders and exposed his short blond hair for the first time in years.

As Emerelda made little adjustments to her appearance, Xanthous noticed she was still wearing the diamond bracelet she usually wore.

"*Em, you forgot to take off your jewelry,*" he whispered.

"No, I didn't," Emerelda said. "Just because Emmy is a civilian doesn't mean she can't have style."

Xanthous laughed. He reached into the pocket of his vest and removed one of his trademark golden bow ties.

"Would you help me with this?" he asked. "I think Xach could use a pop of color."

A few minutes later, the boat docked at a steel pier and Emerelda and Xanthous departed with the other passengers. They unfolded a large map of the capital and searched for the location of the Page Turner Bookstore. All the streets in Ironhand crisscrossed like a giant grid and they found the bookstore on the corner of Industry Street and Revenue Avenue. They followed the map to the intersection—narrowly avoiding getting hit by speeding carriages and trampled by pushy pedestrians along the way—and eventually arrived at the bookstore. A sign hanging over the entrance read:

THE
PAGE TURNER
BOOKSTORE
SPECIALIZING IN USED AND ANTIQUE PUBLICATIONS
FAMILY OWNED AND OPERATED SINCE 289

Emerelda and Xanthous didn't need the sign to know the bookstore had been around for centuries. The Page Turner Bookstore was the only building in

Ironhand that was built out of logs. It stood out in the metallic city like a sore, wooden thumb.

The duo hurried across the street and pushed through the store's heavy wooden doors. As they stepped inside, they were greeted by the musky smell of old paper and leather, which was a nice change from the polluted air outside. However, their first sight of the bookstore was anything but a relief. The store was so big they couldn't see where it ended. The shelves seemed to go on and on forever without a back wall in sight. Old books not only filled the shelves to max capacity, but they were also stacked across the floor and on every available surface.

As the door shut behind them, a bell tied to the handle announced the presence of customers. The elderly shopkeeper peeked his head out from a stack of books at the front counter. He was a handsome man with bright white hair that was neatly slicked back. He wore a crisp blue suit with a pink tie that matched his round spectacles.

"Why, hello there," the shopkeeper said. "May I help you?"

"Hello, sir," Emerelda said with a shallow curtsy. "My name is Emmy Teardrop and this is my friend Xach Fairchild. We're civilian students from the

Western Lake Finishing School in Fort Longsworth and we've come to the city to visit the Unnatural History Museum and see the Goblin Tenors perform."

The shopkeeper gave her a curious look.

"Good for you," he said. "Do you need directions?"

"Oh no, we're here to look at your books," Emerelda said.

The shopkeeper was pleasantly surprised.

"In that case, welcome, Miss Teardrop and Mr. Fairchild," he said. "You'll have to forgive me. People your age are rarely interested in old books—heck, people *my* age are rarely interested in old books. My name is Mr. Turner, of the *Page Turner* Turners. Can I help you find anything in particular?"

Emerelda stared at him blankly—she hadn't thought of *that* part of their cover story yet.

"We're searching for a *gift*," Xanthous decided. "You see, Emmy's cousin, Ruby, is letting us stay with her during our visit. We thought an antique book would be the perfect way to thank her."

"Then you've come to the right place," Mr. Turner said. "Feel free to look around and let me know if anything pops out. That's the magic of old books— sometimes *they're* the ones who find *you*."

"If only," Xanthous said with an awkward laugh.

Emerelda pulled him aside to whisper in his ear.

"I'll start in the back, you start in the front, and we'll meet in the middle," she said.

"Deal," Xanthous whispered.

Emerelda wandered off to find the back of the store—wherever that might be—and Xanthous started searching the shelves in the front. As Xanthous scanned through the old books he felt the strange sensation of being watched. He looked up and saw Mr. Turner peering at him through the stacks of books on the counter. The shopkeeper watched Xanthous with a friendly smile, as if there was something amusing about him.

"What's so funny?" Xanthous asked.

"I'm sorry, I don't mean to stare," Mr. Turner said. "You just remind me of someone."

Xanthous became paranoid. *Had he blown his cover without realizing it?*

"Who might that be?" he asked.

"Myself," the shopkeeper said with a light chuckle. "I used to have a bow tie just like that when I was your age—one in every color, as a matter of fact. Bow ties were, well, *how we knew each other* back then."

Xanthous was confused. "Knew *what*?" he asked.

"Oh, nothing," Mr. Turner said, and waved the notion off. "It was a different time."

Xanthous had the feeling the shopkeeper was trying to imply something—like they had more in common than just bow ties—but Mr. Turner didn't allude to anything more. Xanthous didn't know what to say so he just smiled and kept searching through the books.

A few hours later, Xanthous had combed through thousands and thousands of titles. His fingers were covered in paper cuts after searching through the mysteries, fantasies, adventures, and autobiographies. Eventually, he came to a section of romances.

The love stories were filled with illustrations of young lovers—some tragic, some comedic, and some not appropriate for his adolescent eyes. The images became annoyingly predictable after a while. Each featured one *young man* and one *young woman* who shared the same dreamy, doe-eyed expression. It made Xanthous laugh at first, but the longer he flipped through the romances, the lonelier and lonelier he felt. There were hundreds and hundreds of love stories in the store, and yet not a single one depicted the kind of love *he* could relate to.

"I'm afraid they don't write love stories for people like us."

Xanthous looked up and saw Mr. Turner standing over him.

"Excuse me?" he asked.

The shopkeeper let out a sad sigh. "Things have changed so much over the years, but the world just isn't ready for us yet," he said. "But that doesn't mean we should give up the fight."

"I don't understand," Xanthous said. "What do you mean *people like us*?"

"How old are you, son?" Mr. Turner asked.

"Fourteen."

A bittersweet smile came to the shopkeeper's face.

"You'll learn soon enough," he said. "I wasn't certain when I was your age either."

It took Xanthous a moment to realize what the shopkeeper was referring to, and as soon as he understood, his face went pale and his stomach dropped. Apparently, Xanthous *had* blown his cover, it just wasn't the cover he thought.

"Well, I unfortunately have to lock up now," Mr. Turner said. "The store will be open again tomorrow at eight o'clock if you and your friend want to come back."

"Thanks for letting me know," he said.

Xanthous raced out of the store with the urgency of escaping a tiger, but in reality, he was trying to escape the truth. Outside, the noise of the intersection was deafening. People fought for space on the walkways, carriages fought for dominance of the roads, and street performers competed for spare change—but Xanthous didn't hear any of it. He was lost in his own head, with one distressing thought repeating itself. *How did he know? How did he know?*

"Who would have thought there would be so many old books in one place?" Emerelda said as she stepped outside. "What sections did you get through?"

"Um..." Xanthous struggled to recall—his current state of mind made it hard to think of anything else. "Mystery, fantasy, adventure, autobiography, and romances."

"Lucky," Emerelda said. "I was stuck in the medical and self-help section. Do you know how misguided medical advice was in olden times? They thought leeches and sacrificing sheep were the answers to everything! It's a miracle any of our ancestors survived. I guess we'll have to come back tomorrow and finish searching."

"Should we head to the academy for the night?" Xanthous asked, desperate to get as far away from the bookstore as possible.

"It'd be easier if we stayed in the city tonight," she said. "Let's find the nearest inn and come back first thing in the morning."

Emerelda and Xanthous searched the map for the closest hotel and found a tavern called Copper Mugs and Suites down the road. To say the tavern was run-down was putting it mildly—the building was about five decades overdue for an upgrade—but Emerelda was certain no one would suspect members of the Fairy Council were staying in a place like this. They tried to book two rooms for the night, but the innkeeper insisted the tavern had a no-minors-allowed-without-an-adult policy. So Emerelda slid a handful of jewels across the counter.

"*Now* can we book two rooms?" she asked.

The innkeeper suddenly had a change of heart and was more than happy to accommodate them. He led the duo across the pub, through a storage room, and down a rickety flight of stairs to the basement where the last available suites were located.

"The bathroom is down the hall," the innkeeper said as he handed them the keys. "Stay out of trouble, and if anyone asks, you're both *short* for your age."

Xanthous's "suite" was the size of a large closet. It had four metal walls that were covered in peeling wallpaper, no window, and a lumpy bed with feathers poking out of the mattress. However, Xanthous couldn't have cared less about the drab room. Mentally, he was still at the Page Turner Bookstore, reliving his conversation with Mr. Turner.

How could a complete stranger have known so much about him? How could his biggest secret have been detected so easily? Was it more than just his bow tie? Was there something about the way he talked or walked that made it obvious? And if Mr. Turner had figured it out, would his friends start figuring it out, too? Would they still want to be his friend after they learned the truth? Would he still be welcome at the academy?

The endless questions were torturous and replayed in his mind over and over again. He couldn't stop thinking about the phrases Mr. Turner had used, like,

That's how we knew each other back then, *They don't write love stories for people like us*, and *The world just isn't ready for us yet.*

Indeed, it wasn't. Xanthous knew all too well how the world treated people like him—he saw it every day growing up in his small village. And it was even worse than the discrimination against *magic*.

It always started with a *rumor*. The rumor would inspire *jokes*, the jokes would turn into *slurs*, the slurs would turn into *harassment*, and eventually, the harassment would lead to *arrests* or *disappearances*. Xanthous's father must have grown suspicious about him because he had warned Xanthous of the consequences since he was a small child, and occasionally, he even tried to beat it out of him.

Unlike magic, *this* was something Xanthous could easily hide. So he learned how to tuck the truth away—convinced if he pushed it down deep enough, it couldn't hurt him.

Perhaps he had gotten too comfortable over the years—perhaps the acceptance of magic made him forget about the parts of him that *weren't* accepted. Unfortunately, the day had been a brutal reminder and Xanthous had never felt so vulnerable in his life.

The thought of returning to the bookstore the next morning—and the thought of seeing Mr. Turner again—made Xanthous feel sick to his stomach.

Fortunately, Xanthous was temporarily distracted from his concerns by a knock on the door. Emerelda let herself inside and took a good look at his suite.

"I came to see if your room was better than mine," she said. "It's like comparing rotten apples to rotten oranges."

Emerelda expected Xanthous to laugh, but he didn't even smile.

"Are you okay?" she asked. "You don't seem like yourself."

"I'll be fine," Xanthous said. "There's just a lot on my mind."

Emerelda shut the door and stretched out on the lumpy mattress beside him.

"Good, I could use a distraction," she said. "One of those street performers got his lousy song stuck in my head. What are *you* thinking about?"

"I don't want to talk about it," he said.

"Come on, Xanthous," she pleaded. "It's impossible to sleep in this place. We can either talk or play Guess What Died in the Walls. The choice is yours."

Xanthous groaned. "If you must know, I've been thinking about *love*," he said.

Emerelda clenched her teeth. "Ooooooh," she said. "I think I know what this is about."

"You do?" Xanthous asked in a panic.

"Yeah," she said with a confident nod. "Listen, I'm really flattered—and I think the absolute world of you—but I've always thought of you as a *brother*."

Xanthous did a double take. "*What?!*" he exclaimed.

"I suspected you had feelings for me, and I've been meaning to let you down gently, but I didn't want to make things awkward between us."

Xanthous waved his hands back and forth like he was trying to stop a speeding carriage.

"Whoa, whoa, whoa!" he said. "Em, I don't have a crush on *you!*"

"Why not?" she asked with a scowl. "What's wrong with *me?*"

"Nothing! I didn't mean it like that! You're amazing and smart and talented and—"

Emerelda burst out laughing. "Relax, I'm only teasing you!" She chuckled. "You're one of my best friends! I know I'm not your type—no *girl* is. But you should have seen the look on your face when I—"

Suddenly, Xanthous's face turned bright red and his hands started shaking. At first Emerelda didn't know what his problem was, but as his horrified eyes welled with tears, it quickly dawned on her what was wrong. She sat straight up on the bed and covered her mouth.

"Xanthous, I'm so sorry!" she said. "I didn't realize it was a secret."

"How long have you known?" he said.

"I guess I've always known," she said with a shrug.

"And you weren't ... *repulsed*?"

Emerelda smacked his arm. "Of course not! How could you ask such a thing?"

Xanthous let out a deep sigh. "Because *I* was repulsed," he confessed. "Or at least, that's how I was *told* to feel."

"Well, that's just silly," she said. "You couldn't be repulsive if you tried. And shame on anyone for making you feel that way. When did *you* figure it out?"

"Part of me has always known, too," he said. "It was just like magic. I was afraid of what people would think—I was afraid of what they might do to me—so I tried to hide it. I suppose I wasn't very good at hiding either."

"There's nothing you need to hide from me—or the other fairies for that matter," Emerelda said. "We're a family, Xanthous. We care much more about *who* you are than *what* you are. Besides, if the academy can accept *Stitches*, we can accept anyone."

Xanthous let out a soft chuckle and tears spilled down his cheeks.

"I wish everyone saw it that way," he said. "The world has advanced in so many ways, but it's still so stuck when it comes to people like me. And the world can be a really lonely place when you're not allowed to love."

Emerelda dried his tears with the sleeve of her coat and took both of his hands in hers.

"You want to know *how* I knew the truth about you?" she asked with a playful smile. "The moment I met you, you reminded me of my uncle, Mopes the Dwarf."

Xanthous couldn't tell if this was a good thing.

"*Mopes* the Dwarf?" he asked.

Emerelda nodded. "Of course, *Mopes* wasn't his real name," she said. "Everyone called him that because he was always so miserable. He used to mope around the mines, day and night, and never had a nice thing to say about anything. But then one day, all that changed."

"What happened to him?" Xanthous asked.

"Uncle Mopes met my uncle Fancy, and suddenly, we had to change his name to Smiles," Emerelda said. "Unfortunately, that sort of thing—the love that Smiles and Fancy shared—wasn't accepted in the mines. *Dwarfs are horribly old-fashioned.* So Smiles and Fancy ran away and started a mine that *would* accept dwarfs like them. I think that's one of the reasons my papa was so adamant that I went to live with Madame Weatherberry. Just like my uncle, he knew I would never be happy living in the mine forever—he knew that eventually, I would need to find someone like *me* to love."

Xanthous scratched his head. "Are you saying I should run away and start a mine?" he asked.

Emerelda laughed. "No, I'm saying the world may be backward and stubborn, but you can still find a world that loves and accepts you for exactly who you are," she said. "The Academy of Magic is living proof of that. And one day, when you're ready, you *will* find someone to love. It may take you a little longer than some people, and you may have to search a little harder, but I promise, for every Mopes there's a Fancy."

Xanthous gave Emerelda his first smile of the night. Apparently, there *were* love stories for people like him, they just hadn't been published yet.

"Thanks, Em," he said. "You're the greatest."

"I know," Emerelda said, and let out a big yawn. "On second thought, maybe we should try to get some rest. We only have about *ten thousand* more books to search through tomorrow."

Emerelda kissed him on the forehead and headed back to her suite. Xanthous curled up on the lumpy mattress and got as comfortable as he could. After the long and emotional evening, Xanthous had never been so eager to drift off to sleep and leave the real world behind.

At least in his dreams, Xanthous was free to be himself and love whoever he wanted.

Xanthous awoke in the middle of the night to the smell of smoke. This was no cause for alarm—he was used to waking up to the smell of smoke at the Academy of Magic. Sometimes during the night, if he was having a particularly eventful dream, Xanthous would produce fire while he slept, which was why his oven-like chambers were so well suited for him.

However, two strange thoughts crossed Xanthous's mind as his sleepy eyes fluttered open. *One*, he hadn't had a fiery nightmare in years—his abilities were entirely under his control now, even while he slept. And *two*, he *wasn't at the academy*!

Xanthous sat straight sat up in the lumpy bed of his hotel room. *His entire suite was on fire!* Xanthous tried to extinguish the flames with magic—but the flames wouldn't die down! On the contrary, the fire only grew higher and higher, stronger and stronger the more he tried to stop it. Whatever was happening, *the flames weren't coming from him*!

The fire wasn't the only shock Xanthous woke to. As if someone had written on the wallpaper with a hot metal poker, a message had been burned across the wall while he was sleeping:

WE KNOW WHAT YOU ARE!

"EMERELDA!" Xanthous shouted. "COME QUICK! SOMETHING IS HAPPENING!"

His panicked voice carried through the wall, and a moment later, he heard Emerelda's frantic footsteps running down the hall. She burst through the door and couldn't believe her eyes.

"Xanthous, what are you doing?!" she exclaimed.

"I'm not doing anything!" he yelled. "The fire isn't coming from me!"

The fire rose and spread so rapidly, the entire suite was consumed in a matter of seconds. Emerelda had to jump backward into the hall to avoid being singed. The metal walls turned bright orange from the heat and began to warp, causing the ceiling to implode chunk by chunk.

"Xanthous! You have to stop this before someone gets hurt!" Emerelda shouted from the hall.

Xanthous looked around the room in absolute terror—in all his years, he had never seen fire like *this* before.

"It's not me!" he cried. "I swear it isn't me!"

CHAPTER FIVE

THE ALCHEMIST

I t was the early hours of the morning in the Righteous Empire, and the young emperor was wide awake. He paced up and down the throne room of his Righteous Palace—previously known as the Champion Castle—muttering insults to imaginary figures in his head.

Even with a fire raging in the spacious fireplace, the throne room was freezing and the emperor could see his breath as he talked to himself. The emperor burned portraits of former kings and deceased relatives to keep warm. A map of the four kingdoms and five territories had been painted over the marble floor. Colorful pawns were placed throughout the map to represent different leaders and the size of their armies.

Seven hadn't slept in two days; in fact, he *rarely* slept at all anymore. His desire to kill the Fairy Godmother stayed with him day and night like a stain on his consciousness. After everything he had done, he couldn't believe she was *still alive*. The frustration was unbearable and ate at him like a disease. Seven had always been an attractive young man, but the last year had aged him significantly. His handsome face was now adorned with wrinkles and heavy bags under his bloodshot eyes. His tall and muscular build had withered into a skeletal frame. And at just seventeen years old, Seven's dark hair had begun to gray at his temples.

Why was she at the library? Seven repeated the question to himself over and over again. *What was she looking for? What sort of book could she need?*

There was a knock on the door and the High Commander entered with five dead soldiers.

"My lord, we've completed the cleanse," he said.

"*And?*" Seven pressed.

"We searched every residence in the kingdom and destroyed every book we found, just as you asked," he reported.

"Did you find anything out of the ordinary?" Seven asked.

"No, sir," the High Commander said. "It was mostly encyclopedias and scrapbooks—one woman had a collection of stolen menus—but nothing we believe would be of any interest to *her.*"

Seven growled and angrily kicked the pawns representing the Fairy Council across the floor.

"So whatever she's looking for, it isn't in *our* kingdom," he said.

The High Commander nervously cleared his throat.

"My lord, when this Empire was formed, there was talk of *expanding our borders,*" he said. "The Empire is running low on food and supplies. If we don't do something drastic, many will start to starve. Perhaps the book is the perfect excuse to start invading other territories."

"We will begin the invasions once the Fairy God-mother is dead!" Seven took a deep breath, trying to calm his rage. "She remains our greatest threat. We must eliminate *her* before we make other enemies. So bring me Brystal Evergreen's head on a platter, and *then* we can talk about conquering the world."

"That's assuming there's a world left to conquer!"

The emperor and High Commander exchanged a curious glance—the comment hadn't come from either of them. They turned to the back of the room and saw a *third* person had appeared out of thin air. A short and stout man had seated himself on the emperor's throne. His legs weren't long enough to touch the floor and his tiny feet dangled over the seat cushion. The man had a wide face like a toad and squinty eyes behind a pair of glasses with round frames that were shaped like the gears of a clock. He wore a long robe and a matching pointed cap made from a bronze material. His robe and hat were embroidered with numbers and mathematical equations Seven had never seen before. The strange man also carried a bronze cane that was engraved with more complicated formulas.

"Forgive the intrusion," the man said, and hopped down from the throne. "It's horribly rude to enter someone's home unannounced, but I promise my rudeness is warranted."

For being completely alone and defenseless, the intruder had an unusually calm and jolly disposition. He hobbled toward the emperor and offered him a handshake.

"GUARDS! SEIZE THIS TRESPASSER!" Seven ordered.

The dead soldiers charged after him. The man tapped his cane on the floor, and suddenly, the soldiers flew into the air and were held against the ceiling by an invisible force. Alarmed, the emperor and the High Commander raced for the doors, but with another tap of the man's cane, the doors slammed shut.

"Not to worry, I take no offense at your hostility," the man said with a friendly laugh. "The *fight or flight* response is a perfectly normal reaction to the unexpected presence of a stranger. It's one of many primitive and predictable traits of our human nature—although, in my opinion, the *primitive* and the *predictable* are one and the same. It'll take your overstimulated senses exactly twelve seconds to calm down and return your brain to a functioning state. I'll time you."

The man checked his watch. True to his word,

exactly twelve seconds later, the emperor's fear wore off and he was able to form words again.

"*Who are you?*" Seven roared.

"Splendid, you've moved on from *fight or flight* and have reached the *questioning* portion of our conversation," he said. "Since the mind processes information in a *who, how, what, why,* and *when* sequence, I find it's best to give information in that order. *So who am I?* My name is Dr. States. It's a pleasure to make your acquaintance."

Once again, the man offered Seven a handshake, but the emperor did not accept.

"*How did you get in here?*" Seven demanded.

"Ah, the *how*—right on schedule," Dr. States said. "This may be difficult to comprehend, being a man bound by locks and keys yourself, but I simply willed myself here, and here I am."

"So you're one of them!" Seven exclaimed. "You're magic scum!"

"And now for the *what*," Dr. States said. "Yes, your suspicion is correct. I am a member of the magical community. However, I'm not what you would consider a fairy or witch. I happen to be an *alchemist*."

"What in God's name is an *alchemist?*" Seven sneered.

"It means I am a devoted steward of *alchemy*—the age-old practice of combining all things magic with all things science."

"Science?"

"Yes—it's *the study of things,*" Dr. States said with a patronizing wink.

The emperor's nostrils flared. "I know what science is! I'm trying to understand how it could be associated with something as vile as magic!"

"On the contrary, it's a beautiful marriage," Dr. States said. "Examining the wonders of science with the advantages of magic, and the wonders of magic with the advantages of science has given alchemists a deeper understanding of how the universe operates. You see, just like fairies and witches, every alchemist is born with a magical specialty—except our specialties have a *scientific nature.* For example, I was born with a unique ability to manipulate the laws of physics."

"What are *physics?*" Seven asked.

"It's the study of motion," he explained. "For instance, *everything that goes up, must come down!*"

Dr. States tapped his cane on the floor and the dead soldiers fell from the ceiling. With a second tap, the soldiers were thrown against the walls and held in place.

"I happen to be the director of the great Alchemy Institute," Dr. States said. "We study a great number of subjects at the institute. Chemistry, biology, astrology, zoology, and geology—to name a few—although, to you it probably sounds like I'm speaking a different language. There are many things about the institute I don't expect the common man to comprehend."

Seven scowled at the alchemist. He couldn't think of a bigger insult than being called *common*.

"Why have I never seen or heard of this *Alchemy Institute*?" he asked.

A coy grin stretched across Dr. States's wide face. "We like to keep to ourselves," he said. "You see, alchemists are not only committed to studying the planet—we're also her devoted *protectors*. The Alchemy Institute has been around for thousands of years but we only interact with humanity when absolutely necessary. And as of last night, I'm afraid to report the world has entered its gravest period of peril in recorded history."

"So *that's* why you're here!" Seven yelled. "You've come to stop me and my Empire!"

Dr. States giggled like the emperor was a foolish child.

"Um...*no*," he said. "Alchemists do not concern themselves with social or political affairs. We couldn't care less about your aspirations of global domination—*good luck with that*! We find every civilization destroys themselves eventually—so why bother getting involved? As I said before, our priority is *protecting the planet*. And right now, if we do not take immediate action, every living creature on earth may perish."

Dr. States tapped the floor with his cane and a black shadow moved through the painting of the world below their feet. Soon all the kingdoms and territories were consumed in total darkness and the pawns crumbled into mounds of dust. The alchemist had the emperor's undivided attention now.

"What are we in danger *from*?" Seven asked.

"Late last night, the Eastern Kingdom suffered a horrible tragedy," Dr. States said. "More than half of Ironhand was destroyed in a massive fire. But this was no ordinary fire. In fact, we have reason to believe it was an *attack*. And we think it was just the first of many more to come."

The emperor and the High Commander looked to each other with concern.

"So what do you want with me?" Seven asked.

Dr. States removed his glasses and casually cleaned them as he explained.

"Whenever a crisis of this magnitude occurs, alchemists turn to diplomacy for a solution. We invite the leaders of each independent nation to the Alchemy Institute for a gathering known as the Conference of Kings. There, we discuss the matter at hand and determine the best way to resolve it. Being the emperor of the Righteous Empire makes you the *King of the South*, and therefore, you are eligible to attend the next gathering. I've come to formally extend the invitation."

"When is this *conference*?" Seven asked.

"Tonight," Dr. States said. "This evening, at five o'clock sharp, the institute will send transportation to the home of every world leader. Each leader is welcome to bring two guests to help represent their territory. I highly recommend you take your seat at the table."

Seven gave him a suspicious glare. "How can I trust you?" he asked. "How do I know this isn't an ambush?"

"Technically speaking, you don't," Dr. States said

with a shrug. "All I can give you is my word that you'll be protected while attending the conference. However, if I *did* have any ill intentions, it would be much easier to kill you here and now and save myself the trouble of inviting you to my home, don't you agree?"

The emperor raised an eyebrow at the alchemist— he made a good point.

"All right, then," he said. "I will *consider* attending."

"Splendid," Dr. States said with a wide grin. "We hope to see you soon."

Dr. States tapped his cane twice and vanished from the throne room. Seven rubbed his graying temples as he processed all the information the alchemist had shared. But oddly, the Eastern Kingdom fire wasn't what worried him the most. He couldn't put his finger on it, but there was something *very* unsettling about the Alchemy Institute. The more he thought about it, the more intimidated he became, and Seven grew desperate to see the institute with his own eyes.

"Were you serious about attending the gathering, my lord?" the High Commander asked.

"As a matter of fact, I was," Seven said. "It appears I may have been mistaken. The Fairy Godmother might *not* be our greatest threat after all."

CHAPTER SIX

A NECESSARY INTERVENTION

Tick... Tick... Tick... Tick...

From the moment Brystal and Lucy returned from the Northern Mountains, Brystal hadn't left the enchanted globe beside her desk. The globe showed her what the world looked like from space, and she scanned every inch of the land and sea, desperate to spot something new or out of the ordinary.

Tick... Tick... Tick... Tick...

Brystal knew the Temple of Knowledge was *somewhere* among the mountains, the valleys, the fields, and the oceans before her—she just didn't know *where*. Madame Weatherberry said it wasn't part of the *known world*, but what did that mean? Was the temple in a secluded area that hadn't been explored yet, like Madame Weatherberry's cave? Was it hidden from view by a powerful enchantment, like Greenhouse Canyon? Or was it in plain sight but disguised to look like something else, like the Justices' secret room at the Chariot Hills Library?

Tick... Tick... Tick... Tick...

And as her pocket watch constantly reminded her, the only thing Brystal knew for certain was that she was running out of time to find it. While Brystal searched the globe, she named off locations where she thought the Temple of Knowledge *might* be hiding, and Pip took notes on a pad of paper.

"The Western Shore is filled with sea coves—it could be in one of those," she said. "Also, we should do a thorough aerial search of the Northern Mountains, the Eastern Volcanoes, and the Southern Foothills, just in case there's something peculiar I've never noticed in the past. Let's also write to our allies in the Dwarf, Elf, Troll, and Goblin Territories and ask if they've discovered anything unusual. For all we know, the Temple of Knowledge could be in the back of an abandoned dwarf mine or at the bottom of an empty goblin colony. When the fairies return we'll divide the areas and start looking."

"Copy that," Pip said. "I'll start writing to our allies."

While Brystal and Pip worked on locating the Temple of Knowledge, Lucy intensified the witches' search for the Immortal with Madame Weatherberry's suggestions. She walked among the witches' work stations, barking out orders like an army general.

"All right, witches, it's time to hoist up our stockings, grease up our caldrons, and put our *double double, toil and trouble* into double-double overdrive," Lucy said. "We are to cease Operation Death and Dames immediately, I repeat, we are to cease Operation Death and Dames immediately. Obituaries and old ladies are a dead end—no pun intended."

"*Sir, yes, sir!*" the witches said, and saluted her.

"Beebee, I want you to reach out to the elders of every village in every kingdom. Ask them if they've met anyone recently who reminds them of someone they might have met when they were much younger. Sprout, I want you to get your hands on the property records of every major city. Keep an eye out for any names that pop up more than once—especially over long durations of time. And Stitches, I want you to write to all the major antique stores. Ask them about their oldest pieces and the names of the people who sold them."

"*Sir, yes, sir!*" the witches said, and scattered across the office to start their assignments.

Brystal felt a spark of guilt begin to grow in the pit of her stomach. She appreciated Lucy's and the witches' devotion more than words could describe, but she couldn't bring herself to tell them it was a waste of time. They worked so diligently, part of Brystal began to worry the witches *would* discover the Immortal. She couldn't imagine how disappointed her friends would be when they realized it was all for nothing.

"Don't worry, Brystal, we're going to find this broad," Lucy said with a confident nod.

"I know you will," she replied—secretly hoping for the opposite.

Brystal quickly glanced out the window so Lucy

didn't notice the guilt in her eyes. In the distance, at the very edge of the academy grounds, Brystal saw the hedge barrier begin to open. Emerelda was returning to the Fairy Territory, riding a unicorn into the property.

"Em and Xanthous are back from the Eastern Kingdom," Brystal announced to the others. "Perfect timing, too. They may have an idea about where the Temple of Knowledge is hidden."

Lucy glanced out the window, too. "That's funny, Xanthous isn't with her," she noted.

Brystal took a second look and realized Emerelda was alone. Even more alarming, Emerelda was riding the unicorn across the grounds at an urgent pace. Other fairies throughout the property waved as she passed by, but Emerelda didn't acknowledge any of them. She hopped off the magical steed near the academy's front steps and ran inside as quickly as she could. Brystal and Lucy looked to each other thinking the exact same thing.

"Something's wrong," they said in unison.

A few moments later, the fairies and witches could hear Emerelda rushing up the floating steps in the entrance hall. She charged through the office's double doors and slammed them shut behind her. Her eyes were wide with panic and her coat and brimmed hat had been scorched, like she had survived a terrible fire.

"Em, what happened?" Brystal asked. "Why isn't Xanthous with you?"

At the mention of his name, Emerelda slid to the floor and burst into tears. It was shocking for the fairies and witches to witness—Emerelda had always been the most calm and collected of all of them. They couldn't remember the last time Emerelda was even teary-eyed, but now, she was *sobbing hysterically.* Brystal and Lucy helped her off the floor and sat her down on the glass sofa.

"I'm so sorry—it was a rough night." Emerelda sniffled.

"Em, what's going on? Where's Xanthous?" Lucy pressed.

"I don't know!" Emerelda cried. "I tried to follow him! But he just kept running and running! And it eventually became too strong!"

"What became too strong?" Brystal asked.

"The flames!" she said. "They were everywhere!"

The fairies and witches were confused and looked

to one another for answers, but no one knew what Emerelda was talking about.

"Em, take a deep breath and start from the beginning," Lucy said.

Brystal waved her wand at the tea table and a glass of water appeared. Once Emerelda had a sip and took a few deep breaths, she was ready to explain.

"The Page Turner Bookstore was much bigger than we anticipated," Emerelda said. "We only had time to search through about a quarter of the books yesterday, so we decided to stay the night in Ironhand and start again the next morning. Xanthous and I found a cheap tavern down the street and booked two awful rooms in their basement. At some point in the middle of the night, I woke up to the sound of *screaming*! Xanthous was yelling for help! I ran to his suite and when I got there, the whole room was on fire!"

"But Xanthous hasn't lost control of his powers in years," Brystal said.

"I told him to make it stop, but he kept saying the fire wasn't his," Emerelda said. "At first I thought he was just embarrassed—you know how hard Xanthous can be on himself. But as the night went on, I started to believe him. He tried desperately to extinguish the fire, but it only grew stronger and stronger. I tried to trap the flames in his suite by turning the walls into diamond, but the fire *burned through it*!"

"It burned through *diamond*?" Sprout asked.

"So what d-d-did you d-d-do?" Beebee asked.

"Xanthous and I ran through the tavern and alerted the other guests," Emerelda said. "By the time we got everyone outside, the tavern was a burning inferno! The floors began collapsing on top of one another! The fire spread into the buildings beside the tavern and...and...and..."

Emerelda shook her head in disbelief. Clearly, she was still trying to make sense of what she had seen.

"And what, Em?" Pip asked.

"*It followed us into the street!*" Emerelda recalled. "I've never seen fire move like that before! There was nothing to burn in the street, and yet, it moved directly toward us! Xanthous and I didn't know what to do so we ran—but the fire *chased after us*! As we ran, the fire jumped from building to building on either side of us. The buildings burned down in a matter of seconds—like it was *hotter* than regular fire! Eventually we reached the Eastern River. Xanthous and I jumped in—but the current was strong and we got separated! Xanthous made it to the other side before I did—but the river didn't stop the fire! *The flames glided across the surface of the water and chased Xanthous into the Eastern countryside!*"

"The fire burned *across the water*?" Sprout gasped.

Emerelda nodded. "I begged Xanthous to stop—I begged him to turn around and come back—but he kept running! By the time I climbed out of the river the whole countryside was ablaze, half the city had been destroyed, and Xanthous was gone!"

The fairies and witches were absolutely dumbfounded by Emerelda's dramatic story and couldn't form words. The office went so quiet everyone could hear the watch ticking in Brystal's pocket. As if locating the Temple of Knowledge and finding the Immortal weren't enough to overwhelm them, the news of Xanthous made their heads spin and their hearts ache.

"Where do you think he went?" Lucy asked.

"I have no idea," Emerelda said. "I've never seen him look so terrified! The whole time he kept shouting, '*This isn't me! Em, you have to believe me!*'"

"Then what could it be? Who else could create fire like that?" Pip asked.

Brystal moved to the fireplace and stared up at the

Map of Magic above the mantel. There were thousands of lights representing the different fairies and witches throughout the world. It could take a couple hours before they determined Xanthous's location.

"Change of plans," Brystal said. "We're going to pause our search for the Temple of Knowledge and the Immortal and focus all our effort on Xanthous. The last time something like this happened, he was so ashamed, he almost drowned himself in a lake. We have to find him before he does something drastic."

All the fairies and witches nodded in agreement.

"Well, I just have one question," Stitches asked the room.

"What?" Brystal asked.

"Who the heck is *that* guy?"

Stitches pointed to the back of the room and everyone turned to look. To their surprise, a strange man had appeared out of thin air. He was short and stout and had seated himself behind Brystal's glass desk. The man had a wide face and squinty eyes that were enlarged thanks to a pair of round glasses. He wore a long robe and a pointed cap made from a bronze fabric that was stitched with different mathematical symbols and equations.

"Forgive the intrusion," the man said in a cheerful tone. "It's horribly rude to enter a place of business without making a proper appointment, but I promise my rudeness is warranted. I was going to notify you of my presence as soon as I arrived, but I didn't want to interrupt the young lady in the middle of her story."

Lucy crossed her arms and scowled at him. "Excuse me?" she asked. "Did you need help finding the little boys' room or something?"

"Not to worry, I do not take your sarcastic remarks about my height personally," the man said with a friendly laugh. "The *run or make-fun* response is a perfectly normal reaction to the unexpected presence of a stranger. However intentionally mean-spirited your wit may be, choosing to disarm me with words rather than physical force is a sign of intelligence and self-confidence—although, in my opinion, there is nothing *passive* about the *passive aggressive*."

The man got to his feet and hobbled out from behind the desk, using a bronze cane to help him walk. Brystal gripped her wand as he approached them.

"Who are you?" she asked.

"Splendid, we've already moved on to the *questioning* portion of our discussion," the man said. "Since the mind processes information in a *who, how, what, why,* and *when* sequence, I find it's best to give information in that order. Although, I must admit, you're handling my visit much better than your peers. This is the first time someone hasn't called for their guards or sicced their dogs on me."

"Get to the point, shorty!" Lucy exclaimed.

"My name is Dr. States," he said with a quick bow. "It's a pleasure to make your acquaintance."

Brystal looked the curious man up and down. "Are you a fairy or a warlock?"

"Oh, how efficient—you've skipped the *how* and are ready for the *what*," he said. "While I am indeed a member of the magical community, I'm neither a fairy nor a warlock. I am an *alchemist*."

"An al-cha-what?" Lucy asked.

"An *al-chem-ist*." Dr. States sounded it out for her. "It means I am a devoted steward of *alchemy*, the age-old practice of combining all things magic with all things science."

Brystal scrunched her forehead. "I wasn't aware such a practice existed," she said. "How does someone combine science with magic?"

"Oh, it's a marvelous partnership," Dr. States was

delighted to explain. "Examining the wonders of science with the advantages of magic, and the wonders of magic with the advantages of science has helped alchemists discover the secrets of our universe. You see, just like fairies and witches, every alchemist is born with a magical specialty—except our specialties have a *scientific nature*. Alchemists are the rarest members of the magical community, and once an alchemist is detected, they're brought to live at the great Alchemy Institute, where their abilities can be put to good use."

Brystal couldn't believe there was a branch of magic she wasn't aware of, and judging by the baffled faces around her, the others weren't familiar with *alchemy* either.

"Why haven't I heard of the Alchemy Institute before?" Brystal asked.

"That's by design," Dr. States said. "You see, the Alchemy Institute has been around for thousands of years. In ancient times, it was a very well-known and very well-respected establishment. However, the more science advanced, the more humanity felt *threatened* by it. Breakthroughs in astronomy proved religious beliefs were wrong about the origin of the world— so religious leaders declared science was a *demonic practice*. Breakthroughs in physiology proved that kings were no different from the peasants who served them—so monarchs declared science was a *treasonous act*. Eventually, the world began to hunt down scientists as ruthlessly as it hunted down the magical community. So the institute relocated to a place where humanity would never find it. Alchemists have lived there ever since, secretly conducting experiments and studies that have deepened our understanding of the planet and the worlds beyond it."

"So what are you doing here?" Brystal asked.

"Ah, I see we've reached the *why* portion already—how resourceful," Dr. States said. "In short, I'm here on very urgent business. You see, alchemists not only dedicate our lives to studying the wonders of the planet, we are also her devoted *protectors*. To keep our research safe, we only interact with humanity when absolutely necessary. And as of last night, I'm afraid the world is in very serious danger."

Lucy groaned and rolled her eyes. "Let me guess, *and for just fifty gold coins a day, you, too, can save the spotted platypus from going extinct*," she said. "Look, buddy, maybe you missed the NO SOLICITING sign on our front door, but we ain't buying whatever you're selling. Now, if you wouldn't mind showing yourself out, our friend is missing and we'd like to find him."

Dr. States's friendly smile melted into a serious frown.

"Actually, your friend *is* the danger I'm referring to," he said.

"What does Xanthous have to do with this?" Brystal asked.

"Perhaps we should all have a seat?" the alchemist suggested. "What I'm about to tell you may be difficult to hear."

Dr. States gestured to the glass sofas and the fairies and witches all had a seat. The alchemist tapped his cane on the floor and a large armchair made from bronze leather appeared. He sank into the chair and casually cleaned his glasses while he spoke.

"Now, we have a major problem on our hands," the alchemist began. "As the young lady recalled, last night one of the biggest cities in the world was destroyed by a massive fire. And as she suspected, this was no *ordinary* fire—it was created by someone with extraordinary abilities. And it's not a coincidence that a young fairy with a specialty for *fire* was at the scene of the crime."

"The fire wasn't Xanthous's fault!" Emerelda objected. "I watched him try to extinguish it! He couldn't control it because it wasn't his magic!"

"Young lady, I assure you, I have no ill will toward your friend," Dr. States said. "A good scientist reviews all the facts before making a theory, and the facts are not in his favor. The Alchemy Institute has been observing Mr. Hayfield since his abilities surfaced. He has a long history of *magical mishaps*, to say the least. Two years ago, we almost intervened when, after the death of his father, Mr. Hayfield started the largest brush fire in the Southern Kingdom's history. Fortunately, Madame Weatherberry found him and temporarily muted his abilities before anyone else was hurt. Unfortunately, last night, Mr. Hayfield proved once again that he is a danger to the planet. We believe Mr. Hayfield's abilities have outgrown his control and comprehension. As accidental as his actions may be, the threat remains. If we don't stop him, mark my words, what happened last night in the Eastern Kingdom will be one of *many* catastrophes to come."

"So what are you planning to do? *Kill him?*" Lucy asked.

The fairies and witches went tense at the idea, but the alchemist didn't deny the possibility.

"That will be decided by a vote," Dr. States said. "Whenever a crisis of this magnitude occurs, alchemists turn to diplomacy for a solution. We invite the leaders of each independent nation to the Alchemy Institute for a gathering known as the Conference of Kings. There, we discuss the matter at hand and determine the best way to resolve it. Since the Fairy Godmother is your current leader—or the King of Fairies, as the position was traditionally called—I've come to formally invite her to the next gathering."

Everyone went quiet as they waited to see how Brystal would react to the invitation. Learning there was a place like the Alchemy Institute—a place of experiments and education—would normally have thrilled her. But the more she thought about the alchemists and their secrecy, the angrier Brystal became.

"Explain something to me," she said. "If the alchemists are as advanced as you say, then where were you when the magical community was being imprisoned and executed? Surely there's something you could have done to help us!"

"Alchemists do not concern themselves with social or political affairs," Dr. States said. "We find *protecting people* is a lost cause. Regimes come and go, and laws change so frequently, there is no point in stepping in. As I said before, our priority is *protecting the planet*."

"Then where were you when the Snow Queen was attacking the North? Why didn't you step in and save the planet from her?"

"Fire *destroys*—ice *preserves*," Dr. States said matter-of-factly. "Life can survive a cold world, but it cannot survive a scorched one. If Xanthous's destruction spreads like we predict, the sky will fill with enough smoke and ash to block the sun, and then *everything* on earth will perish."

Brystal locked eyes with Dr. States for an intense moment. She found the alchemists' policies horribly selfish and inhumane, but if they were going to host a discussion that put Xanthous at risk, she couldn't miss it.

"When is the Conference of Kings?" she asked.

"Tonight," Dr. States said. "This evening, at five o'clock sharp, we will send transportation to the institute. I highly recommend you join us so your voice is heard."

"All right, I'll be there," Brystal said.

"Splendid," Dr. States said. "Now that the Fairy

King will be accounted for, there is still the question of who will be representing the witches. Brystal's position within the fairy community is obvious, but witches have always been less organized than fairies. Would one of you ladies tell me *which witch is the Witch King*?"

"You mean, one of *us* is invited to the gathering, too?" Stitches asked.

"To represent all witches everywhere?" Pip asked.

"Correct," the alchemist said.

"Why does it have to be a witch *king*?" Sprout asked. "Couldn't there be a Witch Queen or Witch Empress or Witch Sovereign or Witch Ambassador or—"

"We g-g-get it, Sprout," Beebee said. "S-s-sexism is alive and w-w-well."

"Forgive the term, it's merely a formality," Dr. States said. "If there is any confusion on who holds the title, perhaps it's best if you put it to a vote?"

The witches exchanged eager grins.

"In that case, I vote for *Lucy*!" Stitches announced.

"That's a great idea! I vote for Lucy, too!" Sprout said.

"Me th-th-three!" Beebee said.

"Me four!" Pip said.

Lucy jerked her head toward the witches. "I can't be *the Witch King!*" she exclaimed. "I don't even consider myself a full witch! I'm magically fluid!"

"Lucy, do it for *Xanthous*," Emerelda said. "He'll need all the support he can get at that conference. And we shouldn't put his life in the hands of someone like *Stitches*."

"We shouldn't put *any* life in the hands of *Stitches*," Pip said.

"*Thank you!*" Stitches said with a proud smile.

Lucy let out a reluctant sigh. "Fiiiine." She moaned. "Well, butter my butt and smack a crown on it—looks like I'm going to the gathering, too."

"Marvelous," Dr. States said, and got to his feet. "Each leader is welcome to bring two guests to help them represent their territory. And remember, transportation to the Alchemy Institute will arrive at five o'clock sharp. We look forward to hosting you both."

The alchemist tapped his cane on the floor two times and vanished from the office. After his departure, the fairies and witches sat in complete silence—it wasn't even noon and the day had already been an emotional and mental triathlon.

"I feel like my mind has been drawn and quartered," Lucy said. "First it was the Immortal, then the Temple of Knowledge, and now we have to worry about Xanthous and an Institute of Alchemy, too?"

Brystal began pacing and bit her lip as she thought it over.

"Actually, the Alchemy Institute may be *exactly* what we need," she said. "An educational facility that's hidden from humanity sounds awfully familiar, doesn't it?"

Lucy gasped. "You think the institute is the Temple of Knowledge?"

"Possibly," she said. "Even if it's not, maybe someone there knows how to find it."

Suddenly, the office doors swung open and Tangerina and Skylene stepped inside, returning from the Western Kingdom. The girls wore matching coonskin caps and they each carried a taxidermy raccoon that was dressed in a glamorous ball gown.

"You aren't going to believe what happened to us!" Tangerina said with a laugh.

The girls were eager to discuss their trip, but their friends were so preoccupied, Tangerina and Skylene's arrival wasn't met with the enthusiasm they had expected.

"Why all the long faces?" Skylene asked. "Did something happen while we were gone?"

CHAPTER SEVEN

THE ALCHEMY INSTITUTE

At 4:55 that afternoon, the fairies and witches were standing on the front steps of the academy, eagerly waiting for the transportation to the Alchemy Institute. Brystal had asked Emerelda and Tangerina to help her represent the fairies at the Conference of Kings. After hours of constant begging and bribing, Stitches and Sprout had finally convinced Lucy—against her better judgment—to take *them* as her guests. So the Academy of Magic was left in the hands of Skylene, Beebee, Pip, and Mrs. Vee.

The fairies' and witches' full attention was on the hedge barrier surrounding the Fairy Territory. At any moment, they knew their ride to the institute would appear, although they didn't know what to expect. Not only were they curious about *what* was coming, they also had no idea *how* it would get inside the property. Two additional walls of emerald and fire had been added to the border as extra protection from the Army of the Dead, so entering the grounds was not an easy task.

"Did Dr. States say *how* we'd get there?" Tangerina asked.

"He didn't mention that part," Lucy said.

"Did he say *where* the Alchemy Institute is?" Tangerina asked.

"He didn't mention that part either," Lucy said. "For a man of science, he was pretty vague about the details."

"So let me get this straight," Tangerina said. "A complete stranger shows up out of nowhere, he tells you Xanthous has become a danger to the planet, then he invites us to an undisclosed location for a conference that may or may not threaten Xanthous's life, *and none of you asked any questions?!*"

The fairies and witches shrugged with guilt.

"It had been a long morning," Lucy said.

"Well, I don't care where it is or how we get there, I'm just excited to go!" Sprout said. "I've visited preschools, grade schools, middle schools, high schools, beauty schools, trade schools, performing arts schools, academies, colleges, universities, and grad schools, but this will be my very first *institute!*"

"Won't be my first time around scientists," Stitches said proudly. "I'm what they call a *case study.*"

Emerelda checked the emerald sundial around her wrist. "It's five o'clock on the dot," she said. "Where are they?"

As five o'clock turned into 5:01, the fairies and witches began to worry there had been a miscommunication. However, the Academy of Magic was suddenly shaded by a quick eclipse, and the girls realized they had been looking in the wrong direction.

The fairies and witches gazed up and saw a floating carriage descending from the clouds at a rapid pace. The carriage was bronze, with a large balloon attached to its roof, and it was pulled through the sky by four enormous birds. As the carriage swooped lower and lower to the ground, the fairies and witches gasped—the birds weren't living animals but *machines*! Instead of feathers, the birds were covered in small pieces of scrap metal, and instead of having muscles or ligaments, they moved thanks to a series of gears turning inside their hollow bodies. Big golden keys stuck straight out of their backs like they were large windup toys.

The carriage landed on the ground, ripping up chunks of grass on impact, and the mechanical birds waddled toward the academy's front steps. The coach was also operated by a number of turning gears and cogs, and when the carriage came to a complete stop, the doors opened on their own and a chime announced its arrival.

The fairies' and witches' mouths were agape as they observed the strange vehicle.

"Um . . . what the heck is *this*?" Lucy asked.

"I guess *this* is alchemy," Brystal said.

"Is alchemy safe?" Tangerina asked.

"It got *here* in one piece," Emerelda said with a shrug.

"*I wanna ride one of the birds!*" Stitches said.

"*Me too!*" Sprout said.

The witches ran to the carriage and hopped on the backs of the two mechanical birds at the very front. Meanwhile, Brystal, Lucy, Emerelda, and Tangerina sat themselves inside the coach. Once they were seated, the doors closed behind them and another chime announced the carriage's departure. The mechanical birds raced forward and glided back into the sky. The takeoff was much more jarring than the fairies expected and they were almost thrown out of their seats. Stitches and Sprout cackled with excitement and urged the birds to go faster.

Soon the carriage was so high the Academy of Magic disappeared below them. The birds flew south over the sparkling ocean and soared into a sea of fluffy white clouds. The farther they traveled, the more inquisitive the fairies became about their destination. Even after an hour into the flight, there was no land in sight. All they could see outside their windows were clouds and ocean, and the birds never changed course.

"Where is this thing taking us? The South Pole?" Tangerina asked.

"I didn't realize there *was* anything this far south," Brystal said.

"The Alchemy Institute must be on a desert island or something," Lucy said.

Emerelda gulped. "Guess again," she said, and pointed ahead.

Everyone turned to the front window and their mouths dropped open again. Perched on top of the clouds on the horizon was what looked like a small city. The city was made of gold, silver, and bronze buildings that bobbed up and down as the clouds drifted through the sky. The buildings were connected by floating paths that continuously grew or shrank depending on how far the wind blew the structures apart.

As the carriage flew closer, the fairies and witches noticed the buildings all resembled scientific tools. There were domes and roofs that looked like test tubes and flasks, towers were shaped like gigantic telescopes and microscopes, and spires and poles were equipped with spinning weather vanes and anemometers. Dozens of exhaust pipes let out fire, smoke, and steam while several cranes and conveyor belts moved materials to and from different laboratories. And in the very center of the institute, placed on top of the tallest building, was a gigantic golden armillary sphere—clearly a proud symbol of the institute's grand ingenuity.

The fairies and witches were speechless as the carriage descended toward the Alchemy Institute's breathtaking campus. Brystal couldn't tell if she was more shocked that such a place existed, or regretful that she had never seen it until now.

"It's remarkable," Brystal said with wide eyes. "Absolutely remarkable."

"Now I get why the alchemists are so secretive," Lucy said. "If I lived in a place like this *I* wouldn't want visitors messing it up either."

The carriage dived toward a long landing strip at the very front of the campus and the vehicle came to a bumpy stop. As the fairies and witches stepped out of the coach and climbed off the birds, they saw Dr. States waiting on the landing strip. He was accompanied by twelve other alchemists, who stood in a tight row behind him.

"Welcome to the Alchemy Institute," Dr. States said. "I hope you had a pleasant flight."

There was so much to look at, the alchemist's friendly greeting was almost ignored.

"Dr. States, this place is incredible," Brystal said breathlessly.

"I've lived here since I was a child and it never gets

old," Dr. States said, and then turned to the alchemists behind him. "Allow me to introduce my colleagues. This is Dr. Strand, head of Biology. Dr. Steam, head of Chemistry. Dr. Stats, head of Mathematics. Dr. Stent, head of Physiology. Dr. Strait, head of Geography. Dr. Star, head of Astronomy. Dr. Stump, head of Botany. Dr. Storm, head of Meteorology. Dr. Stage, head of Anthropology. Dr. Stone, head of Geology. Dr. Stag, head of Zoology. And last but not least, Dr. Sting, head of Entomology."

All the alchemists were dressed in long robes and pointed caps made from gold, silver, and bronze fabrics. The only exception was Dr. Sting, head of Entomology—who wore a hornets' nest on his head with actual hornets buzzing around it. Just like Dr. States, the other alchemists' wardrobes were embroidered with symbols and equations pertaining to their respective sciences. Unlike Dr. States, the majority of his colleagues were very young and attractive men— some looked just a few years older than Brystal. Dr. Strait, head of Geography, was the only young woman among the alchemists. Her short silver hair matched her robe and she wore tiny compasses as earrings.

After one glance at his hornets, Tangerina was immediately smitten with Dr. Sting. She strolled directly to the young alchemist's side with a playful bounce in her step.

"Why, hello there, kind sir," she said. "I'm Tangerina Turkin—*Miss* Tangerina Turkin."

She batted her eyes and offered Dr. Sting her hand. The alchemist was so fascinated by the bees flying in and out of her orange hair he didn't notice the gesture.

"I've never seen a eusocial colony residing in human hair before," Dr. Sting said. "May I take one of your bees for examination?"

"Perhaps you could take me to lunch first," she said with a flirty wink.

Emerelda cleared her throat. "Tangerina, remember what we're here for," she said.

"Speaking of, where are the other representatives?" Brystal asked.

"You're the first to arrive," Dr. States said. "I'm guessing the others weren't as keen to board our mechanical carriages as you were—human precaution can be *so* inconvenient when there is a schedule to follow. I imagine we'll have some time to kill while we wait for the others to join us. Would you ladies like a tour of the institute in the meantime?"

"Absolutely!" Stitches exclaimed.

"I thought you'd never ask!" Sprout said.

The fairies and witches followed the alchemists up a winding path toward the campus. As they went, they passed through a giant gear that rotated around the path like a spinning arch. The gear was engraved with a welcoming message:

THE ALCHEMY INSTITUTE
WHERE EXCEPTIONAL INNOVATION MEETS EXTRAORDINARY IMAGINATION

For the first stop on the tour, Dr. States led the fairies and witches into a bronze building in the center of the campus. The entrance was engraved with the formula $E = mc^2$ and opened into a very tall room with four white walls and no windows.

As soon as the fairies and witches stepped inside, they had to constantly duck and dive from several colorful objects hurtling through the air. Thousands of bright red balls bounced from wall to wall, hundreds of yellow yo-yos repeatedly dropped from the high ceiling and then rolled back upward, and tons of small paper clips were compelled from corner to corner by different-size magnets.

As Dr. States walked through the room, he miraculously avoided colliding with any of the moving objects, as if he was protected by a magic shield. The alchemist tapped his cane on the floor and all the balls, yo-yos, and paper clips froze in place.

"This is the Physics Department, where we study the laws of motion," Dr. States said. "Whether through gravity, propulsion, or magnetic charges, understanding *why* and *how* something moves is one of the most fundamental principles of science."

Besides all the colorful objects, the room was also filled with a very peculiar team of workers. A dozen short people with wide rectangular heads wandered around the department, taking notes and making measurements of the frozen balls, yo-yos, and paper clips. However, just like the birds that pulled the floating carriage, the workers were made entirely of *metal*! They moved around the department thanks to gears spinning inside their hollow torsos and springs under their feet.

"Are those *people*?" Brystal asked in awe.

"We call them *Magbots*—short for Magic-Robotics," Dr. States explained. "The Magbots are a perfect example of alchemy at its finest. With some complex engineering and a dash of magic, we've created the perfect assistants to help us conduct our research. The Magbots are motivated entirely by work and don't require food or sleep to function, just a little oil and a light polish every now and then. You'll see many of them working throughout the institute."

The alchemist tapped his cane on the floor and all the balls, yo-yos, and paper clips started whizzing around the room once more.

After their tour of the Physics Department, Dr. Steam led the fairies and witches into the Chemistry Department next door. The department was covered in long glass tubes that stretched, looped, and zigzagged across a spacious laboratory. The girls became dizzy as they watched vibrant gases and chemicals moving through the tubes at different speeds. The floor was tiled and each square was labeled with an abbreviation like *He*, *Ti*, or *Ca*. The girls noticed the tiles each contained a different solid, liquid, or gas below their feet.

"What's inside the tiles?" Emerelda asked.

"Each tile holds an element of the periodic table," Dr. Steam said. "Think of elements as small bricks. And everything in the known universe—from the oxygen we breathe to the rocks at the bottom of the ocean—is made from a combination of these bricks."

"Ooooooh, what's that pretty one?" Tangerina asked.

She pointed to an element that was more like a *sparkle* than a solid, liquid, or gas.

"That's *Ma*—it stands for *magic*," Dr. Steam said.

"Magic is an element?" Brystal asked.

The alchemist nodded. "It's unlike any other element in the periodic table. Its atoms aren't made from traditional electrons, protons, and neutrons, but from a particle we call *magtron*. The magtrons can turn into as many electrons, protons, and neutrons as they wish—meaning *Ma* can transform into any element it wants. We find *Ma* in the blood of magical people and animals, but so far, we haven't been able to re-create it."

"Aw," Lucy said. "It's just like *talent*."

Next, the fairies and witches were given a tour of the Biology Department. The girls were very surprised to see the department was like a giant prison. Three stories of prison cells were wrapped around a massive microscope, and each of the cells contained a very ugly and oddly shaped creature. Some of the creatures were round and squishy, others had long tails or thousands of wiggling hairs.

"Is this a *monster jail*?" Stitches asked with a hopeful smile.

"It's a containment facility for magically magnified microorganisms," Dr. Strand said.

"Could you simplify that?" Sprout asked.

"Cells for cells," he clarified. "It's much easier to examine microorganisms when they aren't so micro— so we make them bigger with magic. Most of these cells are human, some are animal, but we also have a few troublemakers like viruses and bacteria."

A purple microorganism that looked like a giant sea urchin started growling at Lucy.

"What kind of microorganism is that?" she asked.

"That's Carole, the common cold," Dr. Strand said. "Stay away from her—she bites."

After Biology, Dr. Sting gave the girls a tour of the Entomology Department. Four of the five walls contained colonies of ants, bees, termites, and wasps. The fifth wall was a giant canvas with thousands of exotic insects pinned to it—but as the girls took a closer look, they realized the bugs weren't pinned, they had just been trained to sit very, very still. The rafters were covered in cobwebs and home to thousands of spider species. A million moths flew around a large lantern and it illuminated the department like a fluttering chandelier.

In the middle of the department, a massive magnifying glass was used as a table, and Dr. Sting invited the fairies and witches to pull up a chair.

"Most people are creeped out by insects, but they're essential to our survival," Dr. Sting said. "Without bees and butterflies, there would be nothing to pollenate plants. Without earthworms and centipedes, there would be nothing to aerate soil. And without predators like dragonflies and spiders, the earth would be overrun by pests. *Oh no—Amy and Tina are fighting again! Excuse me!*"

The alchemist quickly scooped up a queen ant and a queen termite that had escaped their colonies.

"Do *all* your bugs have names?" Tangerina asked.

"Every single one," Dr. Sting was proud to report. "And they all have different hobbies and personalities!"

The alchemist retrieved a handful of bugs from the canvas and held them beneath the giant magnifying glass for the girls to see.

"This is Lori the ladybug—she *loves* romance

novels. This is Gary the grasshopper—he is *obsessed* with gambling. This is Betty the dung beetle—she has *raging* OCD. This is Derrick the daddy longlegs— he is an *excellent* tap dancer. And this is Mandy the mantis—she is *very* conservative, so don't mention politics around—"

SMACK! Emerelda suddenly slapped a mosquito that had landed on the side of her neck. Dr. Sting's eyes went wide with horror.

"*That was Mitchell!*" he exclaimed. "*He was almost finished with medical school!*"

"Oops," Emerelda said, and wiped his remains off on her pants. "Sorry, Mitchell."

After the fairies and witches were kicked out of Entomology, Dr. Stag escorted them to the Zoology Department. The department was a gigantic aviary— not just for birds, but for every animal the girls had ever heard of. Eagles soared above artificial trees, monkeys swung on artificial vines, lions prowled through artificial fields, and elephants bathed themselves in artificial streams. There were also enormous aquariums that were big enough to hold a blue whale and a giant squid—and the natural enemies exchanged dirty looks from opposite sides of the department.

The department was also home to animals the girls *didn't* recognize. They saw a wolf walking upright like a human, a dolphin running on four legs as it chased after a stick, and a tiger with opposable thumbs that slowly—*very slowly*—climbed a tree.

"While we take great pride in studying preexisting species, magic has allowed us to create hybrid species of our own," Dr. Stag said. "Here we have a *bearwolf*, over there is *dogfin*, and this is a *slothger*."

"A *slothger*?" Stitches asked.

"Yes—he's very dangerous, but too lazy to care," Dr. Stag said.

"How do you prevent the animals from preying on one another?" Brystal asked.

"That's simple. We just keep the animals fed and they don't attack."

"Funny, we do the same thing with Lucy," Tangerina quipped.

"*Hey!*" Lucy said.

When the girls were finished looking around the Zoology Department, Dr. Stump led them up the path to a massive five-story greenhouse. The Botany Department contained every plant imaginable, from the vegetables that Brystal used to grow in her family's garden to the snapping Venus flytraps the fairies had seen in Greenhouse Canyon. The Magbots watered and pruned the plants, but strangely, they also played pianos, violins, and tubas for the plants, too.

"Why are the Magbots playing instruments?" Brystal asked.

"We've discovered plants grow quicker and stronger when they're exposed to classical music," Dr. Stump explained.

In a corner of the greenhouse, one of the Magbots stood on a small stage reciting jokes into a bullhorn.

"Knock knock," he said in a lifeless, monotone voice.

"*Who's there?*" the other Magbots responded.

"A little orchid."

"*A little orchid who?*"

"I had no idea you could yodel."

"*Ha. Ha. Ha. Ha.*"

The Magbots' lifeless laughter echoed through the greenhouse. The fairies and witches winced at the terrible pun.

"What's up with the bad jokes?" Lucy asked.

"We've also discovered some plants thrive on bad stand-up comedy," Dr. Stump explained.

"That explains Mrs. Vee's healthy vegetable garden," Emerelda said.

The fairies and witches left the Botany Department as quickly as they could and Dr. Stent escorted them to a nine-story building that was shaped like a person. The path spiraled around the Physiology Department, and they entered it from the top of the building, or rather, through its *mouth*. Once they were inside, the fairies and witches were shocked to see the interior of the department was an anatomically correct replica of the human body. They boarded a small boat that sailed down the building's throat and through its digestive system like a piece of food. As they floated through the department, Dr. Stent pointed out the different body parts around them.

"Here we have the gallbladder, above us is the liver, behind us are the kidneys, and just ahead is the pancreas," Dr. Stent said. "Each body part is actually a room dedicated to studying that particular organ, muscle, or gland. Now, everyone hang on! We're about to enter the large intestine and it's a windy ride!"

"I can't wait to see how this ride ends—if you know what I mean!" Stitches said with an eager grin.

"Please let it be a gift shop," Tangerina whispered to the others.

As they continued the tour of the Alchemy Institute, the fairies and witches found each department more wondrous than the last. The Meteorology Department was located in a tower with thermometers built into every door and a roof shaped like a massive umbrella. A different type of storm was contained in each of the tower's floors. As the Magbots monitored the weather patterns, the poor robots were tossed around by powerful tornadoes, they were drenched by tropical hurricanes, they were frozen by icy blizzards, and they were electrocuted by lightning.

Inside the Mathematics Department, dozens of Magbots sat at desks doing complicated equations by hand and swiping the beads on counting frames. The walls were made of chalkboards and every inch of them was covered by an endless equation that Dr. Stats referred to as "*pi.*" The equation started as *3.14159265* and continued for thousands and thousands of digits. A floating piece of chalk kept adding numbers to the end, and as the equation grew, the chalkboard walls magically grew with it.

The Anthropology Department was an enormous cave that was covered in handprints and artwork from ancient times. The department also displayed several fossils that had been magically reanimated. Talking skulls told Magbots everything about *when* and *where* they came from, trilobites struggled to free themselves from the stones they were trapped in, and prehistoric tools rebuilt prehistoric structures from rubble. Skeletons of cavemen battled skeletons of dinosaurs and woolly mammoths while the Magbots took notes of the interactions.

The Geography Department was laid out like a formal ballroom. It had curtains made from maps and flags, a glimmering chandelier made from large compasses, and a grand staircase made from stacks of atlases. A beautiful silver globe was positioned in the very center of the department, and as different locations were pinned with a magic pin, the spacious floor rose and sunk to create a miniature model of different location's terrain.

However, the most astonishing part of the tour was what the fairies and witches learned in the Astrology Department. The department was under a humongous dome and equipped with a six-story golden telescope. Magic holograms of distant planets, stars, and galaxies drifted through the air all around them—the holograms were so realistic, the girls used each other as shields to protect themselves from unexpected comets and meteor showers.

"There are eight planets orbiting our star, over one hundred thousand million stars in our galaxy, and an estimated one hundred and twenty billion galaxies in our universe," Dr. Star enthusiastically told the girls. "That means there could be more than seven hundred quintillion planets out there! And some just like our own!"

"Are you saying there could be *life* on other planets?" Emerelda asked.

"Not just on other planets," Dr. Star said. "Although we can't prove it, evidence suggests there are an *infinite* number of multiverses and dimensions, too!"

The idea gave Brystal goose bumps, but she wasn't altogether surprised. It reminded her of her visit to the gray field between life and the great unknown. Even a number in the *quintillions* seemed too small to describe all the planets, stars, and galaxies she had seen. There were too many for *one* universe to hold.

"Wow, other *dimensions*," she said to herself. "Now *that's* something I would love to see."

After Astronomy, Dr. Stone took them to the Geology Department. Unfortunately, the final stop on the tour was the most disappointing. The Geology Department was a narrow room with a couple of piles of rocks—and *only* a couple of piles of rocks.

"Well, *this* is underwhelming," Lucy said.

"Is something going to happen?" Tangerina asked.

"Not *all* science can be entertaining," Dr. Stone said. "In fact, some might say geology is between a rock and a hard place." The alchemist slapped his knee and howled with laughter. "Get it? Because geology is *literally* between a rock and a hard place!"

The fairies and witches collectively sighed at the bad joke.

"And I thought *rocks* were a tough crowd," Dr. Stone said, and laughed again.

"Are you sure *botany* isn't your calling?" Emerelda asked.

Thankfully, the fairies and witches were saved from the alchemist's questionable humor when a chime rang through the entire institute. The fairies and witches didn't know what the chime meant but all the alchemists went outside. Everyone looked toward the front of the institute and, in the distance, they could see more floating carriages were approaching the institute.

"Splendid, the other representatives are starting to arrive," Dr. States said. "Ladies, please excuse us while we greet our guests. Dr. Stone, would you kindly escort the fairies and witches to the conference chambers? We'll begin the Conference of Kings once everyone is here."

Dr. States and the alchemists headed for the landing strip, and Dr. Stone led the girls toward the center of campus. As they walked, Lucy pulled Brystal aside for a private word.

"*So what do you think?*" Lucy whispered. "*Is this the Temple of Knowledge?*"

"*I'm not sure,*" Brystal whispered back. "*On the one hand, there's certainly a lot of knowledge here, but on the other hand, it doesn't fit the other parts of the legend. There were no unlikely warriors protecting it and all the departments were easy to get into.*"

"Maybe the legend is false advertising to keep people away?" Lucy suggested.

"It's possible," Brystal said. "If everything goes well at the conference, I'm going to ask Dr. Strait if she's ever heard of the Temple of Knowledge before."

"You think she'll give you an honest answer?" Lucy asked.

"Probably not, but I can usually tell when someone is lying to me," Brystal said. "If she doesn't give us the information voluntarily, we'll have to sneak into the Geography Department after the conference and find it ourselves."

While the fairies and witches made their way to the conference chambers, the floating carriages started to land and the emerging passengers caught the girls' attention.

The first to arrive was King White from the Northern Kingdom. The fairies instantly recognized him from his black hair and rugged good looks. Even though King White had been on the throne for more than two years, he still chose to wear the uniform of a knight.

The next arrival was King Warworth from the Western Kingdom. An obnoxious feathered hat covered his bald head and his mustache had become so bushy it covered his mouth. Both King White and King Warworth brought two armed knights as their guests.

The kings were followed by Queen Endustria from

the Eastern Kingdom. The elderly queen wore a gown made from a metallic fabric—a tribute to her kingdom's most prized export—and her white hair was styled underneath a silver headdress that resembled the jaws of a wrench. Her face was pale and wrinkled and she walked slowly with the help of a cane. Queen Endustria had brought a knight and her granddaughter, Princess Proxima, as her guests. The princess wore a dress and hairstyle very similar to her grandmother's, and even though there were several decades between them, they shared a strong family resemblance.

The fourth arrival was the Goblin Elder, leader of the Goblin Territory. Goblins were known for their glossy green skin, pointed ears, and sharp nails—and the Goblin Elder was no exception. He traveled with two goblin warriors, one male and one female. The female goblin was about seven feet tall and very muscular. She had messy pink hair, wore armor and breastplates made from hubcaps, and she carried a tall staff.

Shortly after the goblins arrived, the fifth carriage touched down and the Troll Chief stepped outside. The leader of the Troll Territory also traveled with two guards for his protection. The trolls were harder to tell apart than the goblins were. All three of them were short and hairy, with big noses, big teeth, big feet, and tiny horns.

The sixth carriage landed at the institute and King Elvin, leader of the Elf Territory, emerged. Unlike other elves, who were traditionally small and slender, the royal family were tall and broad shouldered. The king had long dark hair, and he wore a wide crown made from tree branches and a black-and-white-checkered suit. Unfortunately, the elves were infamous for their poor tailoring skills, and the king's sleeves and pant legs were asymmetrical. King Elvin only traveled with one guest—his eldest son, Prince Elron. The prince was the spitting image of his father, but wore a much smaller crown made from sticks.

Next, the fairies were thrilled to see that Emerelda's adoptive father, Mr. Slate, had been chosen to represent the dwarfs. He arrived in the seventh carriage with two dwarfs from his mine. It looked like all three had just gotten off work because they were covered in dirt and all three wielded pickaxes.

The eighth carriage landed immediately after the dwarfs and brought a single ogre to the institute. The ogre barely fit inside the coach and had trouble squeezing out the door. He was about nine feet tall, had brown bumpy skin, and his large nose was pierced with a bone. The ogre was the only representative the fairies had never met before. He seemed just as confused as they were about why he was there.

Just like the fairies and witches, all the representatives were speechless as they took in their first sight of the Alchemy Institute. They stood motionless, their eyes darting from department to department, and they didn't even notice their peers standing beside them.

Brystal was relieved to see all the leaders together. Although they had had their differences in the past— especially with the trolls and goblins—the fairies were on good terms with the representatives. In fact, Brystal was the reason the elves, trolls, goblins, and dwarfs had territories to call their own. She was confident the Conference of Kings would go smoothly and they'd find a conclusion that wouldn't put Xanthous's life in jeopardy.

Unfortunately, Brystal quickly realized her relief was premature when a *ninth* carriage appeared in the sky. The carriage landed on the strip beside the others and the door was kicked open before the vehicle came to a complete stop. To the fairies' and witches' dismay, the Righteous Emperor stepped out, joined by his High Commander and the largest skeleton from his Army of the Dead.

"What is *he* doing here?!" Lucy shouted.

"He was invited like the rest of you," Dr. Stone told them.

"How could you invite *him*?" Emerelda asked. "He's a monster!"

"Regardless of his cruel tactics, the Righteous Emperor is *still* the leader of the South," Dr. Stone said. "The main objective of the Conference of Kings is *diplomacy*—and it wouldn't be very diplomatic to exclude someone just because we disagree with them."

Unlike the other leaders, Seven gazed at the institute the same way he looked at everything—as if it was something to *conquer*. Just the sight of his smug face made Brystal's blood boil.

"I have a feeling this conference is going to be anything *but* diplomatic," she said.

CHAPTER EIGHT

THE CONFERENCE OF KINGS

The conference was held in a large circular room at the top of the institute's tallest building. From there, the guests had a magnificent view of the surrounding campus, the grand armillary sphere spinning directly above them, and the endless ocean sparkling below. However, the beautiful view wasn't enough to ease the tension among the representatives. The marvel and majesty of the Alchemy

Institute was no match for the guests' collective resentment toward the Righteous Emperor, and from the moment he arrived, Seven had been the center of their attention. It took the representatives every ounce of self-control not to tackle the emperor on the spot. Even the elderly Queen Endustria looked like she was ready to throw a few punches.

Brystal, Lucy, and the other representatives were seated at an enormous round table while their guests stood beside them. Dr. States had the twelfth seat at the table and the other alchemists stood in a tight group behind him.

"Before we begin, I want to thank you all for joining us today," Dr. States said.

Lucy angrily slammed both hands on the table and glared at Seven.

"How could you invite that monster here?!" she shouted. "He doesn't care about *protecting* the planet! He's planning to conquer the world with an army of dead soldiers!"

The room erupted in agreement, echoing Lucy's concerns. A snide smile grew across the Righteous Emperor's face as he watched the others objecting to his attendance. He leaned back in his chair and rested his feet on the table, enjoying every moment of the disruption. Dr. States raised a hand to silence the room.

"I understand your frustration," the alchemist said. "However, the current crisis is much more important than any conflicts between us. I trust you will all work out your differences in good time, but right now, we have to work together to save the only planet we have."

The representatives sank into their seats bitterly and went quiet.

"Now, are there any other concerns we should address before we start?" Dr. States asked.

The ogre sheepishly raised his hand. "I have a question," he said. "*What am I doing here?* I've never held office or sat on a throne in my life—I don't even own furniture!"

"You were the only ogre who agreed to come," the alchemist said.

The ogre shrugged. "Fair enough," he said. "Please proceed."

Dr. States tapped his cane on the floor and the drapes shut by themselves, shrouding the conference room in darkness. The alchemist nodded to Dr. Strait and she rolled a map across the table. Once the map was exposed, a bright three-dimensional image of the world rose off the parchment. The image zoomed toward the Eastern Kingdom, and soon a miniature Ironhand appeared across the table. The leaders were amazed by the magical diorama.

"For situations like this, I believe it's best to start with the *facts*," Dr. States said. "Once all the facts are presented, we can come up with *probable conclusions* to fill in any blanks or answer any remaining questions. And once we're all on the same page, we can pitch different *resolutions* to address the matter and then vote on the best one."

The alchemist's plan seemed very reasonable and the representatives nodded.

"Now here are the facts," Dr. States began. "Last night, at precisely ten minutes past midnight, a fire started in the basement of the Copper Mugs and Suites Tavern in central Ironhand. The fire spread rapidly through the city and continued into the Eastern countryside. Over a hundred square blocks and over three hundred thousand acres were destroyed in a matter of *minutes*."

As Dr. States recited the facts, a fire moved through the diorama of Ironhand, destroying everything in its path. Queen Endustria shuddered at the reenactment.

"It was the greatest tragedy in my kingdom's history," she said. "The fire was only two streets away from the Eastern Palace. If it hadn't turned west and headed across the river, Princess Proxima and I would have been burned alive."

"The fire also moved quicker and burned hotter than any fire we've ever recorded," Dr. States continued. "On a scale of one to ten—one being a lit candle and ten being a volcanic eruption—the heat emitting from last night's fire was a *fifteen*. At this time, we are not certain of *what* or *who* caused the abnormal fire. *But* we do know that Xanthous Hayfield, a fairy with a magical specialty for fire, was staying at the Copper Mugs and Suites Tavern when the fire started. We also know the fire began in Mr. Hayfield's suite and that the fire moved with him as he traveled through the city and fled into the countryside. It is also a fact that the fire stopped burning in Ironhand as soon Mr. Hayfield was gone."

"Well, that settles it then," King Warworth said. "The boy is clearly responsible."

"No, it wasn't Xanthous's fault!" Emerelda exclaimed. "I was there! I saw it with my own eyes! The fire moved through the city because it was *chasing* him! It wasn't coming from his magic!"

"But what *else* could have caused such a disaster?" the Troll Chief asked.

Once again, Dr. States raised his hand and the room went quiet.

"Please—I know this is a sensitive matter, but let me present *all* the facts before we jump to any conclusions," the alchemist said. "While I'm not accusing Mr. Hayfield of anything just yet, it's worth mentioning that he has a history of losing control of his abilities. Two years ago, he caused a massive wildfire in the Northwest Foothills of the Southern Kingdom. And that fire *also* traveled with his movements. It ended when Mr. Hayfield's late mentor, Madame Weatherberry, temporarily muted his magic abilities. Last night, for reasons unknown to us, the Ironhand fire ended shortly before crossing the border of the Troll Territory. And the last time Mr. Hayfield was seen, he was headed in that direction."

The representatives glanced at one another with grave concern. An unsettling feeling began to grow in the pit of Brystal's stomach—convincing her peers of Xanthous's innocence would be more difficult than she had hoped.

"Where is the boy now?" King White asked.

"We don't know," Dr. States said. "No one has seen or heard from him since last night."

"If he's innocent, then why is he hiding?" the Goblin Elder asked.

"Obviously, he's worried people will blame him for the fire," Brystal said. "Look, I understand the facts are against him, but I *know* Xanthous. He would never do something like this! And he hasn't lost control of his abilities in years!"

"His *intentions* are beside the point," Dr. States said. "Whether deliberate or not, the fire *happened*. This conference is about ensuring it doesn't happen again."

"Personally, I don't see another logical explanation," King Elvin said. "Especially if the boy has a history of causing damage. It's far too big of a coincidence."

"I'm afraid I have to agree," Mr. Slate said.

"*Papa!*" Emerelda gasped.

"I'm sorry, Em," her father said. "If your friend didn't cause the fire, then what did?"

The fairies and witches looked around, desperate to come up with an explanation that contradicted the evidence, but none came to mind. Then Brystal's gaze drifted toward Seven's spiteful smile and it gave her an idea.

"We don't know—but let *me* present some facts," she told the room. "There are many people in this world who *hate* the Fairy Council. In fact, there are people in this room who are determined to destroy everything we stand for. So it isn't a stretch to think an enemy would want to hurt one of us. And if someone was planning to attack Ironhand with a *new type of fire*, Xanthous would be the perfect person to frame. If you ask me, the fire seems *suspiciously* coincidental. It could have been in the works for months! Maybe even years!"

The representatives scratched their heads as they considered Brystal's theory. Although convincing, she could tell it wasn't enough to persuade them. Dr. States cleared his throat to get the room's attention.

"The Fairy Godmother has presented *her* conclusion, now allow me to present *ours*," the alchemist said. "Given the information, my colleagues and I believe that Mr. Hayfield's abilities have evolved beyond his control. Fortunately, he was able to extinguish the fire before it crossed into the Troll Territory, but we may not be so lucky next time. We fear Mr. Hayfield may cause another fire—possibly even *stronger* than the one last night—and if he creates a fire that cannot be stopped, the world will most certainly perish."

The magical diorama zoomed out to show the entire planet. The representatives were horrified as a powerful fire burned through the continent and obliterated all the kingdoms and territories. The atmosphere filled with smoke, turning the sky black and the oceans gray. *Nothing* could survive a disaster like that.

"We have to find the boy at once!" King White exclaimed.

"He must be stopped by any means necessary!" Queen Endustria said.

"Wait!" Brystal pleaded. "I agree, we have to do everything in our power to prevent another disaster—but we still aren't *positive* Xanthous caused the fire! We need to collect more evidence before we make any decisions!"

The other representatives groaned and scoffed at her remark.

"What more do you need?" the Goblin Elder asked.

"The facts speak for themselves," King Elvin said.

"We have to act before he destroys us all!" the Troll Chief said.

Brystal wasn't ready to give up, but she didn't know what else to say.

"Respectfully, Fairy Godmother, it's important to

separate yourself from the situation," Dr. States said. "The world's greatest threat has never been famine, disaster, or disease—but the *ignorance* that fails to prevent those conditions. For too long, the truth has been at war with people who are too stubborn to accept it. Think of all the pain and suffering we could stop if everyone valued *facts* over *feelings*. Think of all the pain and suffering *you* would have been spared from."

The comment made Brystal speechless. She thought about what it had been like to grow up in a society that oppressed women and a world that hated the magical community. Brystal couldn't imagine all the sorrow and heartache she might have avoided if the people in power had prioritized *finding the truth*, instead of *spreading lies* to validate their prejudices. And now Brystal was doing the exact same thing. She was willing to ignore all the evidence to protect something *she* treasured. If she didn't at least *listen* to what the facts were saying, was she any better than the Justices of the Southern Kingdom? Or the clansmen of the Righteous Brotherhood?

"All right," she said. "For argument's sake, let's say Xanthous *accidentally* caused the fire. How do we stop him from starting another one? What sort of resolution do you recommend?"

The representatives sat in silence and avoided making eye contact with Brystal. She could tell they all had the same thing in mind but were too afraid to mention it.

"Well, if no one else is going to say it, I will," Seven said. "Obviously, the boy must be *eliminated*. It's the only way to guarantee the world's safety."

"Oh, shut up, you murderous rat!" Lucy shouted.

"You think killing fairies is the answer to everything!" Emerelda yelled.

"Am I wrong?" Seven asked the room. "You said it yourself, Dr. States—Xanthous can't control his abilities. It doesn't matter how many times they're muted or controlled, history keeps repeating itself. Therefore, as long as he's alive, the world will always be in danger."

The fairies and witches rolled their eyes at the preposterous statement. However, none of the other representatives objected. In fact, all the kings of the conference looked to one another and slowly started nodding.

"It pains me greatly to say this, but the Righteous Emperor is correct," King White said.

"Your Majesty!" Brystal exclaimed. "You aren't serious!"

"Forgive me, Fairy Godmother," King White said. "The Northern Kingdom will always be profoundly grateful to you and the Fairy Council for saving us from the Snow Queen, but I can't in good conscience stand by and allow that kind of threat to surface again. There is no question in my mind: ending *one life* to save *every other life* on earth is a sacrifice we must make."

"I couldn't agree more," Queen Endustria said. "Our people are depending on us to act. We must do whatever is necessary to protect them."

"Hear! Hear!" King Warworth said.

"Then let's put it to a vote," Dr. States said. "All in favor of eliminating Xanthous Hayfield to ensure the planet's survival, say *aye*."

"Aye," King White said.

"Aye," King Warworth said.

"Aye," King Elvin said.

"Definitely aye," Seven said with a wicked grin.

"Aye," the Goblin Elder said.

"Aye," the Troll Chief said.

"Aye," the Ogre said.

"Well, I say *nay*!" Lucy exclaimed. *"Heck nay!"*

Queen Endustria looked over her shoulder to Princess Proxima.

"Well, what will it be, dear?" she asked.

"Grandmother? You want *me* to cast the vote?" the princess asked.

"I'm on borrowed time as it is," Queen Endustria said. "You'll be sitting on the throne sooner than either of us would like to admit. I won't have to live with today's decision, you will. So the choice is yours."

The princess was taken back by the unexpected responsibility.

"Then I vote *aye*," she said. "We cannot let our people relive the horrors of last night."

Mr. Slate sighed and sadly shook his head.

"I am so sorry, Em, but I don't see another choice," the dwarf said. *"Aye."*

"My condolences, ladies," Dr. States told the fairies and witches. "The *ayes* have it.

Looking around the table, Brystal was reminded of her battle with the Snow Queen—and not just because King White was there. The representative's *consensus* was the new monster she had to defeat.

"Now we must discuss the *method* of elimination," Dr. States told the room. "The alchemists and I are prepared to find the boy and carry out the execution. I will personally lead a team to complete the task. I'd prefer to use the quickest and most humane method possible. In my opinion, it's unnecessary to make a painful situation more painful by committing a—"

Brystal's eyes darted around the conference room as she desperately tried to think of something— *anything*—that could change the outcome. Fortunately, an idea came to her—and she couldn't believe she was about to say it out loud:

"*Wait!!*" Brystal interrupted, and the room went silent. "We don't have to kill him. There's another way we can prevent Xanthous from starting another fire ever again."

The representatives and the alchemists were confused. Even the fairies and witches were eager to hear what Brystal was thinking.

"And how do you propose we do that?" Dr. States asked.

Brystal took a deep breath—it was now or never.

"By using the Book of Sorcery," she said.

"What's the Book of Sorcery?" King Warworth asked.

"It's the most powerful spell book ever created," Brystal said. "According to legend, the book contains a spell that can render someone powerless. If your theory is correct, and Xanthous *is* the source of the fire, we can use the book to strip him of all magic ability—and if my theory is correct, and Xanthous *isn't* responsible, we could use the book to defeat whatever *is* causing the fire."

The representatives had never heard of such a book before. They turned to the alchemists and waited for them to confirm its existence. However, the scientists only seemed tickled by Brystal's suggestion, and they were trying not to laugh at her.

"Fairy Godmother, I'm afraid the Book of Sorcery is *just* a legend," Dr. Stage said. "In all my years of studying history, I've come across many myths written about it, but no evidence to prove it exists."

"Actually, the Book of Sorcery *does* exist," Dr. States said.

Unlike his colleagues, Dr. States looked anything but amused. The alchemist stared at Brystal with a gravely serious scowl, as if she had just revealed something she wasn't supposed to know about.

"Sir? Are you certain?" Dr. Storm asked.

"It's as real as the nose on my face," Dr. States said.

The confirmation bewildered the other alchemists.

"Why have you never told us this before?" Dr. Steam asked.

"Because too many talented alchemists have lost their lives trying to find it," Dr. States said. "The book contains the most powerful spells the world has ever known. And yes, the Fairy Godmother is correct—the Book of Sorcery holds a spell to render someone powerless. But retrieving the book is impossible—it's a suicide mission for anyone who has ever attempted it."

"Respectfully, Dr. States, I eat the impossible for breakfast," Brystal said.

The comment made the fairies and witches whistle and snap. The representatives and the alchemists were rather surprised to hear such a bold remark come from the Fairy Godmother. Dr. States seemed intrigued by Brystal's confidence.

"My dear, are you aware of what retrieving the Book of Sorcery entails?" he pressed. "Do you know where it's located? And what horrors are waiting inside?"

Brystal nodded. "I know it's in the Temple of Knowledge and the temple is guarded by a tribe of *unlikely warriors*," she said. "I also know once you're inside the temple, there are physical, mental, and emotional challenges you must pass. And if you make it past the challenges, before you can enter the vault where the Book of Sorcery is located, you must come face-to-face with the deadliest and most dangerous creature that's ever graced the earth."

The mood of the conference became very tense. The representatives broke out in a nervous murmur, each one speculating what that creature might be.

"That doesn't seem so bad," the ogre said. "What's the most dangerous creature to grace the earth? A bear? A lion? A wolf? One of those snakes that lives in toilets?"

All the alchemists turned to Dr. Stag with curiosity. If anyone knew the answer, it would be the zoologist.

"A *dragon*," Dr. Stag said with a gulp. "Dragons are the most violent and destructive species to ever live. They've been extinct for thousands of years and, although we have the capability of bringing one back to life, no zoologist in his right mind would ever dream of it.

Dragons are capable of catastrophic damage. In fact, the last time the Conference of Kings was held, our ancestors decided to *exterminate* dragons to save the planet."

The whole room shuddered at the thought of such a ferocious creature.

"And the Fairy Godmother wants to face a dragon to save a friend?" King Elvin asked.

Brystal locked eyes with the fairies and witches—they all knew she had more than one reason for wanting the Book of Sorcery. It was their only hope of destroying the Army of the Dead, too.

"Xanthous would do the same for me," Brystal said. "But I still don't know how to find the temple. We've been to every corner of the globe but have never seen anything like it. I was hoping Dr. Strait might point me in the right direction."

The request caught Dr. Strait off guard. "I'm sorry," she said. "I've never heard of the temple until now, and I've never seen it on any of my maps."

"That's because you won't find it on any map," Dr. States said. "The temple's location is concealed by powerful sorcery. Although I've never seen it myself, *I* know how to find it."

The fairies' and witches' postures rose with their spirits.

"Please, Dr. States, you have to tell us!" Emerelda pleaded.

"We're *begging* you!" Tangerina cried.

The alchemist hesitated as he weighed the pros and cons.

"Are you *sure* you want to do this?" he asked.

"Positive," Brystal said. "If there's even a *chance* that the Book of Sorcery can help me save Xanthous's life, I *have* to find it. Give me a week to travel to the temple and retrieve the book. And if I'm not back by then, you can carry out the elimination as planned."

Dr. States squinted at Brystal and rubbed his chin as he considered.

"Fine," he said. "If you retrieve the Book of Sorcery and strip Mr. Hayfield of his magic abilities, we will spare his life. However, we cannot wait a week and risk the possibility of him starting another fire. We must proceed with the elimination as planned and hope you find the book before we find him. Is that clear?"

Brystal felt like she had been punched in the stomach. She didn't think the pressure of finding the Book of Sorcery could be greater than it already was, but what choice did she have?

"I understand," she said.

The Righteous Emperor was growing more uptight by the second. Obviously, the Book of Sorcery was the book she had been searching for in the Chariot Hills Library—but that was days before the Ironhand fires. Regardless of what she told the alchemists, he knew Brystal had more plans for the book than she was letting on. He could *smell* her desperation.

"*This is absurd!*" Seven proclaimed. "We can't trust *her* with the Book of Sorcery! If she survives the journey, who knows what she might do with it!"

"We certainly know what *you* would do with it!" Lucy snapped.

"The Righteous Emperor and the fat witch both have a point," the Troll Chief said. "I trust the Fairy Godmother, but what if the book falls into the wrong hands? No one should have that kind of power!"

"I agree with the Troll Chief," the Goblin Elder said. "If the Fairy Godmother finds the Book of Sorcery, after she uses the spell on her friend, the book should be kept somewhere safe!"

"We'd be happy to keep the book here with us," Dr. States said.

"And how can we trust *you*?" Seven sneered.

"As this institute proves, alchemists can be trusted with *many things* the rest of the world isn't ready to handle," Dr. States said. "You all have my word: the Book of Sorcery will be kept safe and faithfully looked after."

Seven fumed—still unsatisfied. "*But*," he continued, "there's nothing stopping the Fairy Godmother from using the Book of Sorcery *before* the spell on her friend!"

"Perhaps we can send someone to supervise the Fairy Godmother," Dr. States suggested.

The Righteous Emperor went quiet as he considered. The more he thought about it, the more a sinister grin spread across his face.

"Yes, that's *exactly* what we should do," Seven said. "Each of us should send a *delegate* with the Fairy Godmother to make sure she keeps her word."

The fairies and witches groaned at the proposal.

"Why not just put a bell around her neck while you're at it!" Lucy shouted.

"It's not entirely unreasonable," Dr. States said. "Fairy Godmother, do you have any objection to being accompanied by delegates?"

Naturally, Brystal had *many* objections to traveling with chaperones, but she would do *anything* to get her hands on the Book of Sorcery—and she would never get there without Dr. States's help.

"I don't mind at all," she said, and glared at Seven. "In fact, I *welcome* the company. I'm going to need all the help I can get."

"Very well," Dr. States said. "If they wish, each king may appoint a delegate to travel with the Fairy Godmother to the Temple of Knowledge."

The representatives spoke privately with their guests to determine who should join the mission. Brystal and Lucy pulled the fairies and witches into a tight huddle.

"Brystal, are you sure you're up for this?" Emerelda asked. "Shouldn't you send one of *us* to the temple so you can keep looking for the Immortal?"

"Of course not," Brystal said. "The temple is dangerous and I have less than two weeks left to live anyway. If I don't return by then, you can send someone else in my place. Even if I don't get the Book of Sorcery, hopefully I can make the temple safer for whoever replaces me. In the meantime, the rest of you need to search for Xanthous. We need to track him down and keep him somewhere the alchemists won't find him."

The fairies and witches nodded.

"Who's going to be the witches' delegate?" Tangerina asked.

"Obviously, *I'm* the best choice," Stitches said.

"No, *I'm* the best choice!" Sprout said.

"Are you two crazy?" Lucy asked them. "You're both *flammable*! I'm not sending you into a temple with a fire-breathing dragon. *I'll* go."

"Lucy, no!" Brystal said. "I can't let you do this—it's too dangerous!"

"And I can't let you face a dragon alone!" Lucy said. "Besides, it's not your decision to make. The Witch King has spoken."

Brystal sighed and shook her head, but she knew there was no use arguing with her.

"Thanks, Lucy," she said. "I'm really going to owe you one if we survive this."

Lucy smiled. "I'll add it to your tab," she said.

After several minutes of deliberating, all the representatives had made their decisions.

"I trust you've all made wise choices," Dr. States said. "Which witch has the Witch King selected?"

"I'll be representing the witches," Lucy said.

"Very well," Dr. States asked. "King of the North?"

"The Northern Kingdom will be sending Sir Rain," King White said, and nodded to the knight standing beside him. "Two years ago, he was instrumental in helping me battle the Snow Queen. If anyone can face a dragon and live to tell the tale, it's him."

"King of the East?"

"The Eastern Kingdom will be sending Sir Hammer," Princess Proxima said, and turned to the guard behind her. "He has been protecting me and my grandmother for my entire life. I would trust him with the Book of Sorcery more than anyone else in the world."

"King of the West?"

"The Western Kingdom will be sending Sir Timber," King Warworth said, and gestured to the solider at his side. "He is as sharp as he is brave and will easily outsmart or outfight whatever the temple has in store."

"King of the South?"

The Righteous Emperor nodded to the tall skeleton guarding him.

"*Him*—whoever he was," he said.

"King of the Trolls?"

"The Troll Territory will be sending Butternut," the Troll Chief said, and slapped the back of the troll next to him. "Although small and smelly, Butternut is the fiercest and most loyal protector I've ever had."

"King of the Goblins?"

"The Goblin Territory will be sending Gobzella," the Goblin Elder said, and pointed to his female companion. "She is the strongest and loudest warrior the goblins have ever known and I am confident she will return, even if the others don't."

"I'm honored to *SERVE*!" Gobzella yelled, and everyone in the room covered their ears.

"King of the Dwarfs?"

"The Dwarf Territory will send Spanky the Minor," Mr. Slate said, and patted the shoulder of the dwarf standing next to him. "Do not let his height fool you. Spanky is masterful with the pickax. The dragon won't see him coming."

"King of the Ogres?"

"If it's all the same to you, I think I'm going to sit this mission out," he said. "I barely fit in the carriage—I'll probably just get in the way."

"Fine by me," Dr. States said. "And finally, who will the King of the Elves be sending?"

"The Elf Territory will be sending Prince Elron," King Elvin announced, and then shot his son a very stern look. "Do *not* disappoint me."

Prince Elron gulped. "I won't, Father."

The others were surprised the Elf king had selected his own son—but no one looked more surprised than the prince himself.

"Very well," Dr. States said. "The delegates will leave for the Temple of Knowledge at once, and in the meantime, the alchemists and I will start searching for Mr. Hayfield."

The alchemist tapped the table with his cane like a judge with a gavel.

"The Conference of Kings is adjourned," he declared.

Brystal closed her eyes and took a deep breath.

"*Hang on, Xanthous,*" she whispered to herself. "*Help is on the way.*"

CHAPTER NINE

WATCH YOUR STEP

"X*anthous? Xanthous?"*

Xanthous was hoping it had all been a bad dream. While he slept he was haunted by images of burning buildings, the sounds of people screaming, and the smell of scorched earth. Unfortunately, when Xanthous's eyes fluttered open, the nightmare awoke with him.

At first, Xanthous didn't know where he was. He

was exhausted, his head was throbbing, and his whole body ached as if he had run a marathon. He quickly sat up and looked around to get his whereabouts. He had been sleeping on a pile of hay on the top floor of an old windmill. He got to his feet and glanced out the nearest window. The windmill was in the middle of a field and surrounded by a tall forest—although *which* forest, he couldn't tell. It was evening and the sun was starting to set in the distance.

Xanthous checked his body and saw he was still wearing his civilian disguise from the Eastern Kingdom, although it was singed and covered in ash. Strangely, he was also wearing a crystal medal with a red ribbon around his neck. After once glance at the medal, all the memories of the long night and the early morning came rushing back.

"Xanthous? Are you there?"

Xanthous jumped at the sound of the voice. He thought it had been part of his dream, but it was coming from *somewhere in the windmill below him*! Xanthous cautiously climbed down the ladder and inspected the lower floors. Each level was completely empty except for cobwebs and rusty gears.

"Xanthous, if you can hear me, give me a sign!" the voice persisted.

"He's d-d-definitely not in there," said another.

"This windmill is as empty as a politician's promise! HA-HA!" laughed a third.

"We should move on," suggested a fourth. "According to the map, it looks like there's a barn about a mile away. Maybe he's in there?"

"No, wait!" the first voice insisted. "I have a good feeling about this place."

"That could b-b-be gas," said the second.

Xanthous eventually made it to the ground floor. The first level of the windmill housed a small living area, but besides a table and a few chairs, it was just as vacant as the other floors. However, something strange caught Xanthous's eye. In a corner of the room was a full-length mirror, but instead of seeing his own reflection, he saw the reflection of a *friend*.

"*Skylene?*" he asked in shock.

"Xanthous! Thank God you're all right!" she exclaimed, and then looked over her shoulder. "See! I told you I had a good feeling! It wasn't gas!"

In the mirror, Skylene was joined by the reflections

of Mrs. Vee, Pip, and Beebee. Beyond them, Xanthous could see the glass furniture of Brystal's office. He rubbed his aching temples, worried he might be hallucinating.

"How am I seeing you guys right now?" Xanthous asked.

"We're using a *m-m-magic m-m-mirror!*" Beebee said.

"Isn't it neat?" Pip said. "It allows us to see through any other mirror in the world!"

"But how did you find me?" Xanthous asked.

"We've been following your star on the Map of Magic all day, but then earlier this afternoon it disappeared!" Skylene said. "That's when Mrs. Vee recommended we use the mirror to find you. So we started peeking into all the cottages and shops near the spot where you vanished!"

Xanthous scratched his head. "You've been looking into people's homes? Isn't that a violation of privacy?"

The fairies and witches looked to one another with guilty eyes.

"You d-d-don't want to know what w-w-we've seen," Beebee said.

"Mrs. Vee, have you *always* had a magic mirror?" Xanthous asked.

"I forgot I had one in storage," Mrs. Vee said with a shrug. "When I was younger, I was madly in love with a traveling tradesman—unfortunately, he had a reputation for being *quite* the ladies' man. So I got a magic mirror to spy on him while he was on the road."

"And what happened? Was he unfaithful?" Xanthous asked.

"I don't know—I had an affair and forgot all about him! *HA-HA!*" The housekeeper chuckled. "But that's a story for another time—I'm so glad to see you're all right!"

Xanthous climbed off the ladder and crawled closer to his friends' reflections—but peculiarly, he never let his feet touch the floor. He hopped from chair to chair, stool to stool, and then knelt on top of a desk in front of the mirror.

"Why are you climbing across the furniture?" Pip asked. "Are there mice?"

"No, I can't let my feet touch the ground—*that's when it starts!*" he explained.

"That's when *what* starts?" Skylene asked.

"The fire!" Xanthous exclaimed. "But it isn't coming from me! Look! I can prove it!"

He held up the crystal medal around his neck and Skylene instantly recognized it.

"You're wearing your old Muter Medal!" she said.

"That's how I know the fire isn't coming from me!" he said. "I've been wearing the medal since this afternoon, but the fire still appears whenever I make contact with the ground!"

The fairies and witches were absolutely baffled. They had so many questions they didn't know what to ask first.

"Wait, Xanthous, start from the beginning," Skylene said. "Em told us what *she* saw last night, but we want to hear it from you."

Xanthous took a deep breath and shook his head, still trying to process it himself.

"I was sleeping in my room at the tavern, when suddenly, I woke up and found my entire suite was on fire!" he recalled. "I tried to put it out with magic, but the flames wouldn't stop! Em and I alerted the rest of the tavern and got the guests to safety, but by the time we were outside, the fire was spreading everywhere! *It even chased us into the street!* So we ran! But the fire followed us! We crossed the Eastern River and the flames moved across the surface of the water! *I've never seen fire do that before!* I didn't know what else to do, so I kept running! I ran for miles and miles across the countryside, but the fire never slowed down. Eventually it caught up with me and completely surrounded me! I climbed a tree to escape it, and as soon as I reached the very top, I looked down and saw the fire had disappeared."

"Holy smokes!" Mrs. Vee said. "No pun intended. *HA-HA!*"

"I stayed in that tree for hours," Xanthous went on. "When I climbed down and put my feet on the ground, the flames returned almost instantly! For whatever reason, whenever I make physical contact with the ground, *the fire reappears*! At that point I was still terrified that I was the one causing it. I needed to stop my magic until I figured out what was happening. So I traveled to the Northern Kingdom—leaping from stone to stone, and from log to log—and went to the mountain where we battled the Snow Queen. I found the sinkhole where Squidelle was buried and retrieved my Muter Medal from her skeleton! But even with the Muter Medal around my neck, the fire *still* comes back whenever my feet touch the ground! Now I'm positive *the fire isn't coming from me*! How could I create it without magic?"

The fairies and witches were amazed by Xanthous's story and it took them a moment to gather their thoughts.

"So *that's* why you disappeared from the Map of Magic," Pip said. "The medal muted your magic *and* your location!"

"But Xanthous, you said you were *sleeping* when the fire started," Skylene said. "Surely your feet weren't on the ground then?"

"No, but my room was in the basement," Xanthous said. "Whatever it is, it must have found me when I was underground! And it's been following me ever since!"

"But if it isn't coming from you, what's causing it?" Pip asked.

"I have no idea," Xanthous said. "But I'm not leaving this windmill until we stop it!"

"We've got to tell Brystal and Lucy!" Skylene said. "They need to share this with the Conference of Kings before it's too late!"

Xanthous scrunched his forehead. "What's the Conference of Kings?" he asked.

"The C-C-Conference of Kings is a c-c-council

of elites!" Beebee blurted out. "They think you s-s-started the fire and are afraid you'll d-d-destroy the world! They're d-d-deciding your f-f-fate as we speak!"

"WHAT?" Xanthous yelled in terror. "What do you mean they're deciding my fate?! Am I in some kind of danger?!"

The fairies and witches shared anxious glances.

"Weeeeeeeeeeell, I suppose that depends on how the conference goes," Skylene said sheepishly. "Hopefully, Brystal and Lucy will convince the other representatives that you're innocent and *aren't* going to destroy the planet. But if they don't—"

"You'll be hunted d-d-down like a sheep in a w-w-wolf den!" Beebee declared.

Xanthous hadn't thought the situation could get any worse, but after hearing *this*, his skin went pale and his whole body went numb. He jumped to his feet and started frantically pacing across the desk, plotting his next move.

"I...I...I can't believe this is happening to me!" he thought out loud. "They're going to *kill me*! I have to go into hiding until I can prove I'm innocent!"

"Xanthous, let's not get carried away!" Skylene said. "So what if people think you single-handedly caused the biggest disaster in world history—life happens! *We know you're innocent, and that's all that matters.*"

She gave him a sweet smile, as if their trust solved everything. Xanthous ignored the comment and continued plotting.

"I'm sorry, girls, but no one can know where I'm headed—not even *you*," he said.

Xanthous picked up the chair beside the desk and raised it over his head.

"*Wait!*" Skylene pleaded. *"Xanthous, don't do this! We can help—"*

Xanthous slammed the chair into the mirror. The glass shattered and the fairies and witches disappeared from sight. Xanthous knew he had to get as far away from the windmill as possible—it wouldn't be long until his friends came to find him in person.

Without time to come up with a better option, Xanthous removed some rusty chains from the windmill's large gears and tied a stool to each of his feet. The makeshift stilts made him wobble as he walked, but they allowed him to move without touching the ground. Taking one small step at a time, Xanthous headed outside and journeyed into the forest, searching for a place where *no one*—not even the *fire*—could find him.

CHAPTER TEN

INTO THE NORTHEAST

After the Conference of Kings, the alchemists escorted the representatives to the front of the institute where the bronze carriages and mechanical birds were waiting to take them home. The guests noticed two additional carriages had been added to the landing strip—one to take Brystal and the delegates to the Temple of Knowledge, and the other to take the alchemists to Xanthous—wherever he might be.

Brystal's stomach was in knots as she watched the alchemists load their carriage with weapons and traps—the likes of which she had never seen before. There were cages with spikes and sharp wires, miniature handheld cannons, swords and spears that were launched by springs, and crossbows with preloaded arrows. If Brystal hadn't known better, she would have thought the *alchemists* were the ones about to face a dragon.

"Is all of that necessary?" she asked them. "I thought you said the elimination would be as quick and humane as possible."

"The weapons are just a precaution for our safety," Dr. States said. "One can never be too careful when traveling through the kingdoms of man. But I assure you, if we find Mr. Hayfield before you return with the Book of Sorcery, his elimination will be painless. It'll be like drifting off to sleep, and hopefully, he won't even see us coming."

"Sir, our carriage is ready for departure," Dr. Steam called.

"Splendid," Dr. States said, and then addressed the representatives. "I suppose it's time for us to say our farewells and go our separate ways."

Throughout the landing strip, the delegates said their own unique good-byes to their superiors. Sir Rain, Sir Hammer, and Sir Timber bowed and kissed the hands of their sovereigns, Mr. Slate and Spanky saluted with their pickaxes, the Troll Chief and Butternut butted horns like dueling bucks, and the Goblin Elder and Gobzella smacked each other's bellies and snorted like pigs.

However, not all the representatives gave their delegates a proper good-bye. King Elvin didn't say a word to Prince Elron. He only glared at his son with a disapproving scowl, as if he had *already* failed the mission. The Righteous Emperor didn't even acknowledge his dead soldier. Instead, Seven's eyes remained fixed on Brystal, as he watched her with a sinister smirk.

"He's always up to something, isn't he?" Brystal said to her friends.

The fairies and witches were too worried about *her* to care about the Righteous Emperor.

"It's going to be okay," Brystal assured them—although she wasn't sure she believed it herself. "I know there's a lot to be worried about, but we'll get through this. We always do."

"Will we?" Tangerina asked. "Yesterday we were

only worried about losing *you*—and that was hard enough to swallow. I can't imagine what it would be like to lose you, Lucy, *and* Xanthous in the same week! The Fairy Council would never be the same."

Until now, Brystal hadn't thought about how awful her friends must be feeling. Regardless of what happened in the Temple of Knowledge, Brystal knew her life was going to end—she had come to terms with it—but her friends were still taunted by *hope*. And if Brystal didn't retrieve the Book of Sorcery in time, *they* would have to endure everything *Brystal* wouldn't. She waved the fairies and witches to the side of the landing strip, where the alchemists and representatives couldn't hear them, for one last pep talk.

"*We can't let fear cloud our focus*," she whispered. "*If there's one thing the last year has taught me, it's how complicated life seems when fear takes the reins. And our goal is much simpler than our fears would like us to believe. First, we have to find Xanthous and keep him safe. Second, we have to get the Book of Sorcery.* But that's it. *If we accomplish those two things, everything will be fine.*"

The fairies and witches nodded but tears welled in their eyes.

"Promise us you're coming back," Emerelda said, trying her best not to cry. "Promise us this isn't *good-bye*."

Brystal and Lucy glanced at each other, but it wasn't a promise they could make.

"Oh, come on." Lucy laughed it off. "You can't get rid of us *that* easily. I've battled stage mothers who were *way* scarier than dragons."

Tangerina's bottom lip quivered and tears spilled down her face.

"You're awful, Lucy—but you're *our* awful!" she cried. "Who am I going to feud with if you die?"

Tangerina threw her arms around Lucy and sobbed into her shoulder. The fairies and witches were surprised by the emotional gesture—especially Lucy.

"There, there," Lucy comforted her. "You'll find someone just as terrible as me."

"No, I won't." Tangerina sniffled. "You're simply the worst."

"Ditto," Lucy said.

The two exchanged a sweet smile—knowing they each meant it from the heart.

"We can't promise anything, but *you* can promise *us* something," Brystal said. "Even if Lucy and I *don't* come back from the Temple of Knowledge, and even if the alchemists *do* eliminate Xanthous, promise us you won't let any amount of grief stop you from achieving our goal—promise me you'll find the Book of Sorcery and use it to destroy the Army of the Dead."

The fairies and witches looked at one another and gave Brystal a confident nod.

"We promise," Emerelda said.

"But if you *do* die, can Sprout and I have your bedrooms?" Stitches asked.

"Sure," Lucy said with an awkward shrug. "But don't do anything weird with my bottle cap collection. It's worth something. Someday."

Brystal saw the other delegates were starting to gather around the carriage.

"Well, this is it," she said. "Wish us luck."

Brystal and Lucy hugged the fairies and witches good-bye. When they arrived at the carriage the girls could sense there was already tension among their fellow delegates. Although the fairies were on good terms with the other kingdoms, there was a long and complicated history between the species. Gobzella, Spanky, Butternut, and Prince Elron stood in one group while Sir Rain, Sir Hammer, and Sir Timber stood in another. The men and the talking creatures didn't speak, but were engaged in a heated cross fire of dirty looks.

"Hi, everyone," Brystal said with a friendly wave. "Before we leave, I want to thank you all for coming along. I'm really grateful for your help."

Sir Rain, Sir Hammer, and Sir Timber scoffed at her.

"Is something funny?" Lucy asked.

"Please don't act like we're doing you a *favor*, Fairy Godmother," Sir Rain said. "We wouldn't be going on this mission unless we were ordered to."

"And if something dangerous *does* happen, just let us handle it," Sir Hammer said. "We'd like to come back in one piece and don't need a group of *damsels* and *beasts* getting in our way."

Lucy crossed her arms. "Who are you calling a *damsel*?" she asked.

"*Damsels* may be a stretch but *beasts* is putting it nicely." Sir Timber chuckled. "Check out that goblin. She's built like a bear and has the face of a swine!"

SWOOSH! Before Brystal or Lucy could react to

the knights' rudeness, Gobzella suddenly dropped to the ground. *FUMP!* With one swipe of her staff, the goblin knocked all three knights off their feet. Gobzella jumped back up and hovered over the men, raising both of her fists.

"You see *THESE?*" she asked them. "This is *WRATH* and this is *VENGENCE!* Run your mouth again and I'd be happy to make an *INTRODUCTION!*"

The knights remained on the ground until Gobzella backed away. Lucy turned to Brystal with a big grin.

"*I like her,*" Lucy whispered.

Brystal groaned. "*This is going to be a long trip,*" she whispered back.

Across the way, Dr. Steam, Dr. Storm, and Dr. Stag boarded the carriage with all the weapons. Dr. States hobbled toward the delegates, and with one tap of his cane, their coach's doors opened on their own.

"I'm afraid the coach isn't big enough to seat all of you," the alchemist said. "Some of you will have to ride on the Magbirds."

"Please, allow us," Sir Rain said.

The knights were happy to separate themselves from the talking creatures and climbed on top of the mechanical birds. The delegates squeezed inside the coach but they were still missing the dead soldier from the Righteous Empire. Brystal gazed across the landing strip and saw Seven was whispering something into the skeleton's ear. When he was finished, the Righteous Emperor pushed the dead solider toward the carriage. The skeleton climbed inside and had a seat with the others. The smell of the soldier's rotting corpse instantly made the delegates gag.

"We *definitely* need to roll down a window or something," Lucy said.

Brystal waved her wand and masked the skeleton's smell with a flowery scent. Once everyone was aboard, the carriage door closed behind them. Brystal used her foot to block it from shutting and looked to Dr. States.

"Are you going to tell us how to get to the Temple of Knowledge?" she asked.

"The Magbirds have been instructed to fly northeast," the alchemist said.

Brystal waited for more instructions but that was all Dr. States said.

"That's it?" she asked. "We just fly northeast and we'll find the temple?"

"No," Dr. States said. "Fly northeast and *it* will find you."

The simple instructions made Brystal a little uneasy, but she lifted her foot and allowed the carriage door to shut behind her. Dr. States hobbled back across the landing strip and joined Dr. Steam, Dr. Storm, and Dr. Stag in the other carriage. Two chimes announced the vehicles' departure and both sets of mechanical birds lunged forward. The carriages soared into the sky, one taking the delegates into the Northeast, and the other taking the alchemists into the Northwest.

The representatives and the remaining alchemists waved to the vehicles as they disappeared into opposite horizons. Once they were out of sight, the remaining alchemists headed back to the institute and the guests headed to their carriages home. As the fairies and witches climbed inside, they noticed the Righteous Emperor and King Elvin were lingering behind. The men were in the middle of a private conversation, and judging by how close they were standing to each other, it was *clearly* a conversation they didn't want anyone else to hear.

"Brystal was right," Emerelda said. "Seven is absolutely up to something."

"Oh *gooooosh*," Tangerina moaned. "Can't he take a break from being evil?"

Seven and King Elvin's discussion ended in a handshake. The men covertly went their separate ways, as if the conversation had never happened.

"Looks like King Elvin is in on it, too," Stitches said.

"But what could the elf king want with the Righteous Emperor?" Sprout asked.

Emerelda studied the men with a suspicious gaze, asking herself the same question.

"I don't know," she said. "But we should keep an eye on *both* of them until Brystal gets back."

· · ★ · ·

TICK-TICK… TICK-TICK… TICK-TICK…

Brystal didn't know if her anxiety was playing tricks on her, or if it was just the close quarters of the carriage, but she could have sworn her pocket watch was ticking much louder than usual.

TICK-TICK… TICK-TICK… TICK-TICK…

She tried her best to ignore the daunting sound, but something about it felt more persistent, as if the watch *wanted* to be heard. The noise was practically an invitation for her disturbing thoughts to resurface. With every tick, she could feel the curse growing stronger inside her mind.

TICK-TICK… TICK-TICK… TICK-TICK…

Well, well, well…

Isn't this an unexpected turn of events?

You finally found the location of the Book of Sorcery…

But you may lose a friend before you find it.…

Life is always a game of give and take…

But do *you* have what it takes?

TICK-TICK… TICK-TICK… TICK-TICK…

Can you survive the Temple of Knowledge?

Unlikely.…

Can you save Xanthous ?

Doubtful....

Can you stop the Righteous Emperor before Death collects you?

Impossible.

TICK-TICK... TICK-TICK... TICK-TICK...

Yes, I will, Brystal told her thoughts.

And after Xanthous has been saved...

After we discover the true source of the fire...

After we finally put an end to Seven and his Army of the Dead...

You'll have nothing to taunt me with...

And I'll spend my last moments in peace.

TICK-TICK… TICK-TICK… TICK-TICK…

I hope you're right….

You don't have time to be wrong….

Eleven more days…

That's all you have left….

Good luck…

You'll need it.

TICK-TICK… TICK-TICK… TICK-TICK…

Finally, the disturbing thoughts faded away and left Brystal alone. As she sighed with relief at the silence in her mind, Lucy sighed with restlessness due to the silence in the carriage. The delegates had been traveling for hours and hadn't said a single word to one another.

"Soooooooo," Lucy said to break the silence. "Anybody interested in a game?"

"I love *GAMES*!" Gobzella declared.

The goblin's loud voice made the other delegates cringe.

"Do you always talk like that?" Prince Elron asked.

"Like *WHAT*?" Gobzella asked.

"Like you're screaming down a long tunnel," the elf said.

Gobzella shrugged. "I'm a goblin—we're *ALWAYS* screaming down long tunnels," she said. "Now what game do we want to *PLAY*? I should warn you I'm *VERY COMPETITIVE* and I don't tolerate *CHEAT-ING*! The last person who cheated me lost his *TOENAILS!*"

"In that case let's *not* play a game," Lucy said. "Why don't we just chat and get to know one another? I'll go first. My name is Lucy Goose and I'm fifteen years old. You all know me as a member of the Fairy Council, but before that, I was the tambourine player in the world-famous Goose Troupe."

"Never heard of them," Butternut grumbled.

"And with *those* ears I imagine you've heard just about everything," Prince Elron sneered.

"Look who's talking, you pointy-ear tree nymph!" Butternut said.

Prince Elron gasped. "How dare you!" he exclaimed. "I'd say that was below the belt—but that's probably as far as you can reach!"

Lucy quickly changed the subject before a physical fight broke out.

"So, *Gobzella*," she said with a nervous laugh. "You certainly taught those knights a lesson back at the institute. Besides being my hero, what do you like to do for fun?"

"I like to *FIGHT!* And *WIN!*" the goblin said. "And not necessarily in that *ORDER!*"

Lucy nodded politely. "Solid hobbies," she said. "You also must enjoy exercising to have such a muscular body. Is everyone in your family as big and strong as you?"

"I don't have *FAMILY*," Gobzella said. "I ate all my siblings in the *WOMB!*"

Lucy gulped. "What about your parents?"

"No *PARENTS!*" Gobzella said. "I was still hungry when I came *OUT!*"

The passengers scooted as far away from the goblin as they could.

"Butternut, tell us more about yourself," Lucy asked. "Do you have any special pastimes?"

"Actually, I like to write poetry," the troll said.

"Oh, really?" Lucy asked. "Anything you'd like to share with us?"

Butternut eagerly sat up in his seat and removed a folded piece of parchment from his moleskin vest. The troll cleared his throat—which sounded like a choking hyena—and read a few poems aloud.

"Trolls like bridges,
Trolls love caves,
Trolls like ditches,
And trolls love slaves.

"Puppies are cute,
Kittens are precious,
Bunnies are mute,
And they all taste delicious.

"Your teeth are rotten,
And sharp as a knife,
Your beard's like cotton,
But you're still my wife."

The delegates sat in awkward silence, greatly disturbed by the troll's poetry. Gobzella, on the other hand, wiped tears from her eyes.

"Those were *BEAUTIFUL*, Butternut!" the goblin said. *"BRAVO!"*

"Deep stuff," Lucy said. "I'll be thinking about those for a while."

"Especially in my nightmares," Prince Elron said.

Butternut took the elf's comment as a compliment. "Thank you," he said bashfully, and tucked his poems back into his vest.

"What about you, Your Highness?" Lucy asked the elf. "What are your interests?"

"Privacy," Prince Elron said with a cold glare.

"Copy that," Lucy said. "Last but not least, we have Spanky. Is there a fun fact you'd like to share? How'd you get a name like *Spanky*, anyway?"

"I was a horrible child," the dwarf said.

"And what do you like to do when you're not digging in the mines?" Lucy asked.

Spanky eyed his fellow passengers with a suspicious gaze, wondering if they were worthy of his trust.

"I'm not sure if I should mention it," he said. "Most people can't handle it."

The comment made everyone sit on the edge of their seats.

"Okay, now you *have* to tell us," Lucy said.

Spanky looked cautiously to his left and right, then leaned close toward the others, as if the clouds outside were listening.

"I search for *mole people*," the dwarf said.

"For *what*?" Butternut asked.

"*Mole people!*" Spanky repeated. "They're a secret society that live deep under the ground. They feed on tree roots and recruit lost children into their colonies. The mole people only come to the surface to sabotage us and spread chaos. They're behind all the worst events in history—attacks, assassinations, rigged elections, you name it! The mole people want to take over the world and will stop at nothing until all the sun dwellers—*that's what they call us*—have destroyed themselves!"

The delegates stared blankly at Spanky, assuming the dwarf was only kidding. Unfortunately, he wasn't—Spanky believed every word of the outlandish conspiracy theory.

"Spanky, I live underground and I've never heard of *MOLE PEOPLE*!" Gobzella said.

"Trust me, they've definitely heard *you*," Prince Elron quipped.

"You can't find what you aren't looking for," the dwarf said.

"And you've seen a *mole person* before?" Butternut asked.

"Not personally, but I've heard enough stories to be certain," Spanky said. "Even as we speak, the mole people are somewhere below us plotting their next move! In fact, I wouldn't be surprised if *they* were the ones starting the fires your friend is being framed for!"

Lucy leaned close to Brystal and whispered in her ear.

"*We're doomed,*" she said. "*These people aren't from the top shelf, if you get my drift.*"

"*They're just a little eccentric—that's all,*" Brystal said.

"*No wonder the representatives chose them as delegates—they couldn't wait to get rid of them!*" Lucy said.

Brystal didn't respond, but the colorful delegates were starting to give her doubts about the mission, too.

· • ★ • ·

TICK-TICK… TICK-TICK… TICK-TICK…

The carriage continued flying through the sky with no destination in sight. With every passing hour the sun sank a little more into the horizon ahead, but it never disappeared. They had traveled so far northeast Brystal wondered if they would eventually reach the Southwest.

The longer the carriage flew, the more Brystal became paranoid, wondering if there *was* no Temple of Knowledge. Perhaps Dr. States had sent them on a wild goose chase? Perhaps he made it all up so he had more time to find and eliminate Xanthous? Just when Brystal started thinking they should turn around, Sir Timber tapped on the window from outside.

"Fairy Godmother!" the knight called. "There's something you should see!"

Brystal, Lucy, and the other delegates faced the front window. In the distance, floating on the ocean's surface, was an enormous white dome. It was the height and width of a mountain range, but was so perfectly round, Brystal knew it couldn't be a natural formation.

"What is *that*?" Lucy asked.

"It looks like some sort of shield," Brystal said.

"Whatever it is, the Magbirds are taking us straight toward it," Butternut noted.

"Are we going to *CRASH*?" Gobzella asked.

Brystal took a better look at the mysterious structure and discovered it was made entirely of *clouds*.

"I don't think so—it doesn't look solid," she said, and the notion made her smile. "Wait a second—that's not a shield, that's a *cover*! The dome must be *hiding* the Temple of Knowledge!"

The carriage proceeded toward the dome and flew through its thick, cloudy surface. Strangely, even though the dome wasn't solid, Brystal and Lucy felt like they were passing through something—or rather, something was passing through *them*. A cold chill traveled down their bodies, causing them to shiver and buckle at the knees.

"Did you guys feel that?" Lucy asked the others.

"Feel what?" Spanky asked.

"I don't know—I just felt *weak* all of a sudden," Lucy said.

"Me too," Brystal said.

"Must be altitude sickness," Butternut said.

Once the mechanical birds and the carriage were

past the cloudy dome, they entered an environment that was completely hidden from the rest of the world. The air was smoky and carried the scent of sulfur. The ocean waves were much choppier and a strong wind rattled the carriage. The dome protected a chain of *islands* and each of the islands hosted an active volcano that spewed a long trail of smoke into the sky.

"What is this place?" Lucy asked.

All the delegates went dead silent as they stared at the mysterious islands, asking themselves the same question. The carriage started to descend through the sky and the Magbirds prepared for landing.

TICK-TICK… TICK-TICK… TICK-TICK…

"Thank goodness we're here," Butternut said. "That awful ticking noise has been driving me nuts."

Brystal did a double take. "*You* can hear it, too?" she asked.

"Of course I can," Butternut said.

"I apologize, it's coming from my watch," she said.

Brystal reached into her pocket and showed the troll her silver pocket watch.

Tick… Tick… Tick… Tick…

Butternut shook his head. "No, that's not it," he

said. "What I'm hearing is louder and ticking much faster."

All the delegates went quiet and noticed the sound themselves. Brystal realized the persistent ticking *wasn't* coming from her pocket watch after all—it was from something *else* inside the carriage.

TICK-TICK… TICK-TICK… TICK-TICK…

"That's bizarre," Brystal said. "I don't see anything that could be causing it."

Butternut raised one of his ears and followed the sound, like a dog following a scent. He moved throughout the coach—crawling over the other passengers' laps—and stopped near the chest of the dead soldier.

"It's coming from inside *him*!" the troll declared.

The dead soldier hadn't moved since the delegates left the institute—in fact, many of them had forgotten he was even there. Upon Butternut's accusation, the skeleton suddenly jumped up and retrieved his sword. He swung the weapon at the delegates and they ducked and dived out of his way. *BONK!* Gobzella knocked the sword out of the soldier's bony hands. She wrapped one arm around his neck and held his hands behind his back with the other.

"Sounds like the dead guy has a skeleton in his *CLOSET*!" Gobzella said.

While the solider was restrained, Spanky used his pickax to pry the armor off the skeleton's torso. Inside the soldier's hollow rib cage was a strange contraption with several bags of gunpowder and a ticking clock.

TICK-TICK… TICK-TICK… TICK-TICK…

"*It's a BOMB!*" Lucy shouted.

Everyone screamed and immediately backed away.

"*Why is the skeleton carrying a BOMB?*" Gobzella asked.

"*It's the mole people!*" Spanky exclaimed. "*They're trying to sabotage the mission!*"

Brystal grunted—she knew exactly why the soldier was armed.

"No, it's *Seven!*" she said. "That's why he recommended I travel with delegates! He's trying to blow me up before we reach the Temple of Knowledge!"

"*Well, don't just stand there! Someone stop it!*" Prince Elron yelled.

Brystal retrieved her wand and waved it at the bomb. Nothing happened. She waved it a second time with more intensity. Still, *nothing happened*. Even after a third and fourth attempt, the bomb remained exactly the same.

"Brystal, what's happening?" Lucy asked.

"My magic isn't working!" she said.

Brystal desperately waved her wand a fifth and sixth time, but nothing changed.

TICK-TICK... TICK-TICK... TICK.

Butternut sighed with relief. "Oh good, it stopped," he said. "Well done."

"It wasn't me!" Brystal said. "I was trying to turn it into a bouquet of flowers!"

RING-RING-RING-RING! The ticking was replaced by the sound of an alarm. The dead solider gazed up at the other passengers and gave them an eerie wave good-bye.

"*He's about to blow!*" Lucy yelled.

"*What do we do?*" Prince Elron asked.

"*ABANDON SHIP!*" Gobzella shouted.

The goblin forcefully kicked open the door. The coach instantly filled with the smoky wind from outside. Gobzella grabbed Spanky and Butternut by the collars and threw them outside and then pushed Prince Elron after them. Brystal banged on the front window to warn the knights.

"*Get off the carriage!*" she yelled.

"What?" Sir Rain called back.

"*There's a bomb on board!*" Brystal cried. "*You have to jump!*"

"We can't hear what you're saying," Sir Hammer said. "The wind is too loud!"

RIIING-RIIING-RIIING-RIIING-RIIING! The bomb's alarm intensified.

"*WE GOTTA GO!*" Gobzella shouted.

Before Brystal knew what was happening, the goblin wrapped her arms around her and Lucy and then jumped outside. Brystal, Lucy, and Gobzella fell hundreds of feet through the air toward the choppy ocean below. *BANG!* The bomb went off and the carriage exploded above them. The force from the blast hit them like a brick wall, causing them to fall even faster.

SPLASH! Brystal plummeted into the ocean.... The impact knocked the wind out of her lungs.... The waves crashed over her, pushing her deeper and deeper below the surface.... Her body thrashed and spun through the powerful current.... Her wand slipped out from her tight grip and disappeared into the ocean's depths....

Debris from the explosion plunked into the water and sank all around her.... Brystal tried to swim to the surface but was too weak.... Her arms and legs moved slower and slower, and gradually became still.... She searched for Lucy and Gobzella but couldn't find them.... All she could see was the dark ocean stretching for miles around her....

CHAPTER ELEVEN

THE ELVISH PRINCE

Xanthous had been walking all night—and unfortunately, he hadn't gotten very far. Thanks to the stools tied to his feet, he had managed to travel only a few miles away from the windmill. When the sun began to rise the next morning, Xanthous was still in the same forest as the night before, and he knew it was only a matter of time before the fairies and witches caught up with him. If he wanted to find a permanent place to hide, he first needed to come up with a better method of transportation. So Xanthous had a seat on a boulder to rest his tired legs and brainstorm his next move.

As Xanthous contemplated the odds of finding a bicycle or a horse-drawn carriage in the forest, he was distracted by the sound of thumping. The thumping grew louder and stronger as something traveled through the woods. Xanthous looked around but didn't know where to hide without making the fire reappear—all the nearby bushes and boulders were too close to the ground. With no other option, Xanthous pulled himself into the nearest tree and kicked the stools off his feet. He climbed to the very top branch and hid behind the leaves.

A few moments later, Xanthous was surprised to discover the source of the strange commotion. A silver chariot was being pulled through the woods by six jackalopes the size of large dogs. The horned rabbits were steered by a young man who wore black-and-white-checkered armor. The young man had floppy dark hair, large gray eyes, and a slight point to his nose. A slingshot and a bag of stones were attached to his belt. Xanthous assumed the young man was about fifteen, and although he didn't seem threatening, Xanthous remained as quiet as possible.

To Xanthous's dismay, as the chariot passed beneath his tree, the young man pulled on the reins and his jackalopes came to an abrupt halt. The young man sniffed the air and then scanned the forest around him with an intense scowl. He hopped off the chariot and inspected the ground, running his fingers over the strange tracks Xanthous had left in the dirt. Curious, Xanthous leaned a few inches to his right to take a closer look at the young man, and the branch beneath him gave a slight *creak*.

Suddenly, the young man whipped around and retrieved his slingshot in one quick move. He fired three stones—one right after the other—directly at Xanthous. Xanthous ducked to avoid the stones and lost his balance.

"*WHOAAAAA!*" he yelled as he fell out of the tree. But thankfully, his fall was broken by a thick blueberry bush. The young man instantly leaned over him, aiming his slingshot at Xanthous's throat.

"Don't shoot!" he pleaded, and raised his arms. "I'm unarmed!"

The young man studied Xanthous for a moment.

After a brief inspection, he slumped and lowered the slingshot.

"Dang it," he said under his breath. "I was hoping you were a bear."

"Pardon?" Xanthous asked.

"I've been hunting all morning and thought I had finally gotten lucky," the young man said.

"Sorry to disappoint you," Xanthous said.

The young man tilted his head like a curious puppy. "Why were you hiding in a tree?"

Xanthous knew he was a horrible liar—especially under pressure—but he did his best.

"I wasn't *hiding*," he said with an anxious laugh. "I just like to quietly climb trees to clear my head."

The young man raised an eyebrow at him. "So you physically exert yourself in dangerous woods to . . . *relax*?"

Xanthous looked around the forest for inspiration to help his lie.

"Well, I wasn't *just* relaxing . . . I was also *practicing*," he said. "I happen to be a tree-climbing champion. See this? I won it in my last competition."

Xanthous showed the young man his Muter Medal.

The young man didn't seem convinced—but nodded like Xanthous was a child showing him a toy.

"A *tree-climbing* champion, huh?" he asked. "I didn't realize it was a competitive sport."

"Oh, it's *very* competitive," Xanthous said.

"And you like to wear your awards even when you're practicing?"

"It's good motivation," Xanthous said.

"And what are the stools for? Are they also part of your *tree-climbing process*?"

The young man pointed to the stools Xanthous had left under the tree.

"Well...," Xanthous said as he struggled to think of an answer. "Technically it's cheating, but sometimes I need a boost. But this isn't an official competition—so no harm there."

"And why do you have *two* of them? In case one of them breaks?"

The young man gave Xanthous a playful grin—clearly, he was enjoying poking at all the holes in Xanthous's story. Until now, Xanthous hadn't noticed how *handsome* the young man was. It almost made him forget about the outlandish lie he was trying to sell.

"What's with all the questions?" Xanthous asked. "Are you writing a book about strangers in the woods?"

The young man laughed. "If I did, you would certainly be the weirdest," he said.

Xanthous scoffed at the comment. "*I'm* weird? *You're* the one hunting for bears with jackalopes!"

"Oh, I never claimed to be normal," the young man said. "I thrive on weird—it keeps things interesting. And weird usually *attracts* weird, if you know what I mean."

Xanthous didn't know what the young man meant, but something about the way he said it made him blush.

"Who are you?" he asked.

"My name's Elrik Elderwood. And you?"

"I'm Xan—I mean, *Xach*! Xach Fairchild."

"Nice to meet you, Xach. Can I help you out of that bush?"

The young man offered Xanthous a hand but he quickly pulled away from the gesture.

"I promise I won't hurt you," the young man said.

"Sorry—it's not you," he said. "I can't touch the ground."

"Come again?"

"Um...I twisted my ankle," Xanthous said, and winced from the fake pain. "I shouldn't put any weight on it."

"So you were climbing a tree with a twisted ankle?"

"No...I was climbing the tree *when* I twisted my ankle."

"Why didn't you climb down?"

"Because...I needed help."

"Then why didn't you ask *me* for help?"

Xanthous's face flushed and his nostrils flared—he had lied himself into a corner.

"Because...because...," he said, but he couldn't think of anything to say. "*Because I'm hiding from someone, okay!* Happy?"

Elrik gave him a slow clap. "Well, *that* was a journey but I knew we'd get to the truth eventually," he said. "So who are you hiding from?"

Xanthous was both annoyed and a little flattered by Elrik's unwavering interest in him. He went quiet for a moment and wondered how to answer his question. Clearly *lying* wasn't working—but he couldn't tell him the truth either. Xanthous decided to tell him the truth about the *past* instead of the *present*.

"If you must know, I was running away from my father," Xanthous said.

"Not a nice man?" Elrik asked.

"To say the least."

Elrik let out a long sigh and sat on the boulder next to the bush. He removed apple slices from his pocket and fed his jackalopes.

"Boy, I know what *that's* like," he said.

"You do?" Xanthous asked.

"Oh yeah—big-time," Elrik said. "My father is an awful man. He's always pitting me and my siblings against one another. He makes everything a competition and assigns us different tasks to impress him. *Swim across that river! Climb that mountain! Hunt a bear!* He always acts like we'll win his approval if we succeed, but no matter what we do, *nothing* makes him happy. Sometimes I think all his happiness died with our mother."

Xanthous nodded sadly, empathizing more than Elrik realized.

"My mom's gone, too," he said. "She died giving birth to me, and my dad has always blamed *me* for it."

"Really?"

"That's only the half of it," Xanthous went on. "He

used to beat me whenever he caught me doing some-thing he thought *normal boys shouldn't*. I desperately tried to please him, but he always found a new reason to resent me. I spent a long time thinking there was something wrong with me, but the truth was, *he* was the broken one—not me."

The boys locked eyes and gave each other a bitter-sweet smile. However, the longer they stared at each other, the less bitter and the more *sweet* it became. Xanthous couldn't explain why, especially given the circumstances, but there was something in Elrik that he trusted—and *really liked*.

"It sounds like we have a *lot* in common," Elrik said.

Xanthous blushed again. "Weird attracts weird, right?"

The boys held their smile until the silence was on the brink of becoming awkward. Elrik finished feed-ing his jackalopes and hopped back to his feet.

"I'd be more than happy to give you a lift into the next town," he offered.

Xanthous was excited by the idea of going *anywhere* with Elrik, but he quickly reminded himself of *why* he was in the woods in the first place.

"Actually, I think it's better if I stay out of sight—at

least until I figure out a plan," he said. "You know, to avoid my father."

"You can't expect me to leave a cute boy stranded and wounded in a dangerous forest."

Xanthous couldn't believe his ears. "What did you just call me?"

"Wounded," the young man repeated.

"No—before that," Xanthous said.

"Stranded?"

"Did you say I was *cute*?"

Elrik looked around like someone else was there. "I don't think so," he said. "If I did, that would be rather *forward* of me."

Xanthous was stunned and his heart began thumping louder than all the jackalopes put together. Elrik gave him a smirk and tucked his floppy hair behind his ears. Xanthous's bashful daze was interrupted when he noticed Elrik's ears were *pointed*.

"Wait a second—you're an *elf*?" he asked.

"Is that a problem?" Elrik asked.

"Of course not—I'm just surprised," he said. "You're so much *taller* than any elf I've seen."

Elrik winced as if it was an embarrassing subject.

"Yeah, I'm sort of a *prince*," he said. "Aristocratic

elves are bigger than other elves. It's just the way our species evolved over time. My family says it's because we're *superior*, but honestly, I think my ancestors just hogged all the milk and vegetables."

Xanthous was suddenly struck by an idea. Of all the kingdoms and territories in the world, the Fairy Council had visited the Elf Territory the least in their travels, but Xanthous could never forget laying eyes on the territory for the first time. All the elves lived in tiny homes that hung from the branches of a massive tree in the Northeast. It was one of the greatest wonders of the world—*and it was the perfect place for him to hide.*

"Could you take me to the Elf Territory?" Xanthous asked.

"Why do you want to go there?" Elrik asked.

"Because my father would never find me with elves! And I've always wanted to see it!"

Elrik bit his lip as he thought it over. "I suppose I could—but on *one condition*," he said.

"What's that?"

Elrik smirked. "You have to tell my father I *saved* you from a bear."

"Just one?" Xanthous asked. "I remember there being a whole *pack* of them!"

"That's the spirit," the elf said. "Well, we better get a move on then."

Elrik headed for the chariot and motioned for Xanthous to follow him. Xanthous lingered behind, anxiously eyeing the ground.

"What's wrong?" Elrik asked.

"I ... I wasn't lying about my ankle," Xanthous said. "I hate to ask but would you mind carrying me to your chariot?"

"And I thought *I* was a prince," the elf said.

Elrik scooped Xanthous out of the bush like a baby and gently placed him down in the chariot. The elf whipped the reins and the jackalopes raced forward, headed for the Elf Territory—and the higher ground Xanthous desperately needed.

Chapter Twelve

The Unlikely Guardians

After tumbling through the ocean for what felt like forever, Brystal finally felt sand brush past the tips of her toes. The next thing she knew, a powerful tide threw her onto the shore of an island. She tried to stand but the waves kept crashing on top of her, knocking her back to the ground. Brystal was so exhausted she could barely lift her head, let alone get to her feet.

"*Lucy?!*" she called. "*Luuuuucy?!*"

Brystal looked around the island. The beach was covered in pale sand and piles of black jagged boulders were scattered across the land. The air was so smoky she could barely see the sun through all the haze. Nothing about this strange place seemed welcoming—in fact, Brystal felt like she was on another planet entirely.

"*Brystal! I'm over here!*"

Hearing Lucy's voice gave Brystal the boost of energy she needed to stand. She felt a sharp pain in her right wrist as she pushed herself upward and figured she must have broken it in the fall. She trekked across the sand to the other side of the beach and found Lucy lying against a boulder. Her eyes were wide and she was clutching her left leg.

"Thank God you're alive!" Brystal said "Are you hurt?"

"I think I broke my leg." Lucy moaned. "Can you fix it?"

Brystal reached for her wand, but it wasn't there.

"My wand!" she gasped. "I lost it in the ocean!"

Lucy moaned even louder. "Can this day get any worse?!"

Brystal ran her fingers through her hair and glanced around the island in a panic. Without her wand, how would she survive the Temple of Knowledge? And now that the Magbirds and carriage had been destroyed, how would they ever get *off* the island?

As she gazed around the ocean she spotted Gobzella floating among the waves. The goblin used one hand to swim toward land while the other was wrapped around Prince Elron. The elf was unconscious and his face was blue. Butternut's and Spanky's arms were wrapped around Gobzella's neck, using her like a life raft.

"Gobzella!" Brystal shouted as she waved. "We're over here!"

"I got the little guys, but I couldn't find the *KNIGHTS*!" Gobzella called to them. "I don't think they survived the *CRASH*!"

Eventually Gobzella made it to shore. Once the goblin had dragged the others from the water, she collapsed to her knees and caught her breath. Prince Elron was laid out across the sand, but he didn't move a muscle, and his face was getting more blue by the second. Spanky began giving the elf mouth-to-mouth while Butternut jumped up and down on his belly. After a few moments, the troll placed his ear against Prince Elron's torso.

"*I don't hear a heartbeat!*" Butternut said.

Gobzella crawled to the elf's side and pushed the troll and the dwarf off his body. She pounded on the prince's chest with both of her fists.

"*Stay away from the LIGHT, Your Highness!*" she said. "*No elves are dying TODAY! I repeat, no elves are dying TODAY!*"

If the elf's heart had stopped beating, Gobzella had definitely restarted it. Prince Elron sat straight up as if he had been electrocuted, and coughed up a gallon of salt water.

"Well, *this* can't be heaven," Prince Elron said as he looked around the island.

Lucy suddenly shrieked and made all the delegates jump.

"What's wrong? Is it your leg?" Brystal asked.

"No, I saw something move!" Lucy exclaimed.

She pointed into the black boulders behind her. The others went quiet as they watched the rocks. Just when they were convinced Lucy's eyes were deceiving her, something large and dark scampered between the boulders.

"*There!* Did you see it?" Lucy asked.

"I saw it, too!" Spanky said.

"So did I!" Butternut said. "It looked like some kind of *reptile*."

The scampering happened again, but this time, in *many* places.

Brystal gulped. "We aren't *alone*."

The delegates' heads jerked back and forth as they spotted more and more figures dashing from hiding spot to hiding spot. They caught glimpses of body parts as the mysterious creatures moved around them—a tail here, a claw there, even a *tongue*. The delegates could also hear hissing and rattling as the figures moved closer and closer. Then to everyone's horror, dozens of enormous reptiles the size of tigers crawled out from the boulders. They had long scaly black bodies, forked tongues that slithered in and out of their wide mouths, and sharp claws that scraped across the rocks as they crept.

"Dear God—what are *those*?" Prince Elron asked.

"They must be the *unlikely guardians* protecting the Temple of Knowledge!" Lucy said.

"Nobody panic just yet," Spanky said. "These things could be herbivores for all we know."

"I'd say Gobzella is more likely to win a beauty pageant," Prince Elron said.

"Hey! I just saved your *LIFE*!" the goblin said.

Prince Elron rolled his eyes. "Oh, sure! Thank you for pulling me out of the ocean so I could be *eaten on the beach*!" he said. "My gratitude is *boundless*!"

The reptiles snapped their jaws at the delegates and growled with deep, raspy rattles. The delegates backed away. Lucy wrapped her arm around Brystal's shoulders and stood on her good leg.

"Say, Fairy Godmother? Now would be the *perfect* time to turn them all into seagulls!" Spanky suggested.

"I can't!" Brystal said. "My wand is at the bottom of the ocean!"

"I got this," Lucy said confidently. "Everyone stand back—I'm going to make a moat of sinkholes around us!"

She hit the sand with a clenched fist, but nothing happened. Lucy tried again and again, but no sinkholes appeared.

"I don't understand—why isn't our magic working?" Lucy asked. "You couldn't stop the bomb in the carriage and now I can't summon one of my trademark sinkholes!"

Brystal gazed around the island in terror. "We both felt strange when we entered the dome," she said. "Something about this place must be *blocking magic*."

The reptiles were multiplying by the second. Dozens became hundreds, and hundreds became *thousands*. The creatures watched the delegates with big *hungry* eyes, never looking away. Brystal knew it was only a matter of seconds before the reptiles attacked.

"Any *other* ideas?" Prince Elron asked.

"Maybe we can outrun them?" Brystal said.

"Only one way to find out!" Butternut said.

The troll took off running down the beach. With nothing else to do, Gobzella scooped Lucy up and all the delegates raced after Butternut. The reptiles charged after their prey, and unfortunately, they were *very* fast runners. As the delegates ran down the beach, even more reptiles slithered out from the boulders and joined the chase. The delegates ran until they couldn't run any more. They were gasping for air and getting weaker with every step.

"I'm so sorry," Spanky wheezed. "I can't go any farther!"

"Me neither," Butternut said.

"Tell my father I'm sorry." Prince Elron panted.

One by one, the delegates started to pass out and drop in the sand. The reptiles surrounded them, snapping their sharp teeth as they circled in closer and closer. Gobzella set Lucy down and started punching and kicking the creatures.

"Come on, you scaly *NIGHTMARES!*" she shouted. "Who wants a piece of *ME*?! I repeat, who wants a piece of *ME*?! There's plenty of Gobzella to go *AROUND!*"

Five reptiles pounced on top of the goblin, wrapping their bodies around hers like giant snakes. Gobzella tried to fight them off, but they gripped her throat with their tails. Their grip got tighter and tighter, and eventually, the goblin's eyes shut and she fell beside the others. Brystal and Lucy picked up branches of driftwood and swung them at the creatures, but they were so tired they could barely hold them up. The creatures seemed to enjoy watching the girls struggle—the more they tired themselves out, the easier it would be to kill them.

Just when Brystal and Lucy were about to be tackled, the island was suddenly eclipsed in a giant shadow. The reptiles froze and whipped their heads toward the sky. The shadow swept over the land again as something very large swooped through the air. The creatures began to squeal and scattered across the island. They took cover in the boulders and fought one another for the best hiding spots.

"Was it something I said?" Lucy asked.

"It certainly wasn't *me*," Brystal said.

Suddenly, the girls felt a strong wind coming from above. They glanced up and saw the most horrifying sight they had ever seen in their lives. Flying in the sky directly above their heads was *another* scaly creature—but this one was as big as a house.

"*It's a . . . a . . . a . . .*"

Lucy fainted before she could finish the sentence.

"*It's a dragon!*" Brystal gasped.

The massive beast landed on the beach and the whole island shook upon impact. The dragon's body was covered in red scales and several horns poked out from its skull. Its yellow eyes were so vibrant they practically glowed and puffs of smoke blew in and out of its enormous snout. To Brystal's complete bewilderment, the dragon was also wearing *reins* like a horse. And seated on a saddle at the base of the dragon's neck was a *man*. The man was dressed in armor adorned with sharp spikes.

A group of very brave reptiles tried to attack the

dragon.... The giant beast let out a thunderous roar and a fiery geyser erupted from its mouth, burning the reptiles to a crisp. Seeing the dragon, hearing its deafening roar, and feeling the warmth of its breath was all Brystal's senses could take for one day....

Brystal's eyes rolled into the back of her head and her body hit the sand.

CHAPTER THIRTEEN

THE DRAGON KEYS

Brystal was awoken by a pleasant tingling sensation on her right wrist. When her eyes slowly opened, she had no idea *where* she was or *how* she had gotten there. The first thing she noticed was a roof made of large leaves above her. The second was that she was lying in a green hammock. And the third was that her right wrist was tingling because it was on *fire*!

The alarming sight made Brystal rapidly sit up and the hammock swayed beneath her. She tried to put out the flames by rubbing her wrist on the leg of her pantsuit, but they wouldn't extinguish. As she frantically patted her wrist, Brystal realized she was hurting herself more than the fire was. On the contrary, the flames were making her injured wrist *feel better*. And strangely, instead of bright yellow or orange, the fire was a soft rosy color, like the skin of a peach.

Brystal took a look around and discovered she was in a *hut*. It was one large room and every inch of it was made entirely from palm trees—from the leaves making up the thatched roof to the floor tiled with coconut shells. Lucy, Gobzella, Prince Elron, Butternut, and Spanky were sleeping in other hammocks beside hers and different parts of their bodies had been set ablaze with the same mysterious flames.

"Hiya!"

The voice made Brystal jump and she almost fell out of the hammock. She looked up and saw a young man standing over her. He was tall and muscular and looked like he was about sixteen years old. His head was shaved and he had thick dark eyebrows and bright brown eyes. The young man also had a friendly smile and wore spiked armor the color of charcoal. Brystal thought his wardrobe looked familiar, but couldn't remember where she had seen it.

"Sorry, I didn't mean to scare you—I was just watching you sleep," he said.

"Excuse me?" Brystal asked, her eyes widening.

The man cringed at his choice of words.

"I mean, because I'm *supposed* to watch you sleep—not because I *wanted* to," he said with a nervous laugh. "Don't get me wrong, you're pretty—*very* pretty, actually. I'm sure a lot of boys *would* want to watch you sleep. Oh gosh, not that I think *that's* okay! No, *that* actually sounds really creepy! What I'm trying to say is that *I'm* not creepy—I was just doing my job."

If Brystal wasn't so concerned she would have found his awkwardness charming.

"Who are you?" she asked.

"Apologies, I should have started with that," he said. "My name's Ryder. What's yours?"

Brystal found it refreshing not to be recognized, but she was still cautious of the young man.

"I'm Brystal," she said. "Why is it your job to watch me sleep?"

"To make sure the fire is working," Ryder said, and

pointed to the flames on her wrist. "You guys were pretty banged up after I saved you. *Oh, I'm sorry!* I didn't mean to use the word *saved*—that implies I think you aren't capable of taking care of yourself. I'm sure you're capable of *whatever* you set your mind to—I'm not one of *those* men. I have a *lot* of respect for females—*Females? Seriously, Ryder?* Sorry, I'm not sure why I said *females*—I meant to say *women*. And the word I meant to use earlier was *help*—you guys were pretty banged up after I *helped* you, so I brought you here."

"What is this place?" Brystal asked.

"You're in the Healing Hut," he said. "Thankfully you and your friends' injuries weren't too severe. I've seen the boulder bandits do way worse to castaways."

Brystal looked at him like he was speaking a different language.

"*Boulder bandits?*" she asked.

Ryder was surprised she didn't remember.

"Yeah—that's what we call the reptiles that were attacking you on the beach," he said. "The outer islands are infested with them. It's a good thing I spotted your group when I did, otherwise you would have been eaten."

Suddenly, the memories of the beach flashed before Brystal's eyes. She remembered the carriage exploding above her, she remembered running from the massive reptiles, and she remembered *where* she had seen Ryder's unique armor. Brystal hopped out of the hammock in fright and slowly backed away from him.

"You were riding the dragon!" she exclaimed.

"Yeah—that was me," he said.

"Why were you riding the dragon?" she asked.

Ryder stared at her like it was a trick question. "Um . . . because she's easy to get around on?"

"Is that supposed to be a joke?"

"Um . . . no?"

"Then why are you acting like that's *normal*? Riding a dragon is *not* normal!"

Ryder shrugged. "For me it is," he said. "Oooooh, I completely forgot! You *just* got here and are probably so confused! Not that it's your fault—how could you *not* be confused? No, it's definitely my fault. I've lived here my entire life so sometimes I forget to fill people in. I'm guessing you and your friends survived a shipwreck, right?"

"Um . . . correct," Brystal lied. "We survived a *shipwreck*."

"I figured—that's usually the case when people wash ashore," Ryder said. "Well, these islands are an animal sanctuary for endangered creatures. Welcome to the *Dragon Keys!*"

The young man posed with his arms out, but quickly lowered them when he realized how strange he looked. Ryder was right about one thing—Brystal was *very* confused. Dr. States had never mentioned anything about an *animal sanctuary* being near the Temple of Knowledge.

"What *kind* of animal sanctuary is this?" she asked.

"Well...it's for *dragons*," Ryder said. "Hence the name."

Brystal was shocked. "You mean, there's more than *one* dragon here?"

Instead of giving her a verbal answer, Ryder took Brystal by the good hand and led her to the window. He opened the leafy curtains and Brystal's mouth dropped. The Healing Hut was one of many buildings built around the top of an active volcano. From the hut, Brystal had a spectacular view of all the islands in the Keys and a massive pool of magma boiling inside the volcano below them. Lava poured down the side of the volcano and moved through the island like a bright red river.

Even more shocking than the volcano, as Brystal's eyes followed the river across the island, she saw *dragons* everywhere she looked. The creatures were all different shapes and sizes, with different colors and features. Some looked just like the dragon she'd seen on the beach, with enormous wings and long tails. Others were short and stout and walked on four legs and had no wings at all. Most of the creatures were covered in scales, but others were furry or covered in feathers. The dragons soared around one another in the sky, they grazed and wrestled in fields, and Brystal spotted a few bathing and swimming in the river of lava.

"I . . . I . . . I can't believe this," Brystal said. "I thought dragons were *extinct*."

"They were almost hunted into extinction," Ryder said. "My ancestors rounded up the survivors and brought them to the islands to keep them safe. My family has been taking care of them ever since. We call ourselves the *Caretakers*."

"How many types of dragon are there?" she asked.

"We have over fifty species in the Keys," Ryder was excited to share. "You see that short fat one with scales like tree bark? That's a *treechomper*—they live off petrified wood and build nests out of logs. Do you see the flock of small ones with the yellow wings? Those are *smoke angels*—they eat clouds and their bodies are so light, they spend their whole lives in the sky. See the dragons swimming in the river, the ones that look like glowing snakes? Those are called *lavalingers*—they survive by absorbing heat from the magma. And see those hairy ones with the webbed feet? Those are *fishhoarders*—they eat seaweed and live in burrows on the shore."

"Are they dangerous?" Brystal asked.

"Dragons are just like people—they can be nice *or* aggressive," Ryder said. "It all depends on how they're raised. A lot of people don't know this, but dragons are a *subservient species*—that means they need *masters* to function properly. After their eggs hatch, the dragon imprints on the very first person it sees. If a dragon is brought up by a decent person, then it'll grow up to be gentle. But if someone cruel or corrupt gets their hands on a dragon, it can become quite hostile."

In addition to the dragons Ryder had pointed out, Brystal saw several people among the creatures. They wore spiked armor as they walked around the island, carefully observing the creatures and inspecting their habitats.

"Are all these people in your family?" Brystal asked.

"Most of them—but some are castaways like you and your friends," Ryder said. "It's our policy to help castaways get back home, but a lot of them decide to stay. All it takes is one introduction with a dragon and *boom*—they're hooked for life."

Brystal giggled as she watched some of the Caretakers teaching dragons to *sit* and *roll over* in exchange for treats.

"I never thought dragons could be so friendly," she said.

"Some dragons are more than friendly—some are downright *helpful*," Ryder said. "Do you see the dragon sitting in the nest above the volcano? The one with the shiny white scales and blue eyes? That's a *great albino dragon*—they breathe fire that *restores* instead of *destroys*. It's great for fixing damaged property or healing wounds."

Brystal glanced down at the flames burning on her wrist. Knowing they came from a dragon made them even more wondrous than before. As she studied them, they suddenly disappeared.

"What just happened? Why did the fire stop?" she asked.

"That means your wrist is done healing," he said.

Ryder glanced around the Healing Hut and saw the flames on Lucy, Gobzella, Prince Elron, Butternut, and Spanky were still burning strong. The delegates were also still out cold, snoring peacefully in their hammocks.

"Looks like your friends have a while before they're recovered," he said. "Would you like a tour of the islands while we wait for them to heal?"

Ryder's enthusiasm was contagious and Brystal couldn't resist. Besides, she figured a tour was the perfect way to scout the islands for the Temple of Knowledge.

"Absolutely," she said.

Ryder smiled and led Brystal outside the Healing Hut to the edge of the volcano. He whistled with his fingers, and a few moments later, the dragon Brystal had encountered on the beach swooped down from the sky and landed in front of them. Even though Ryder had assured Brystal the dragons were friendly, the giant beast still made her uneasy.

"This is Kitty," Ryder said. "She's a *fire-breathing horned scarlet*. They used to have the highest population until dragons were hunted. But don't worry—Kitty is harmless. I raised her myself."

"Your dragon's name is Kitty?" she asked.

Ryder shrugged. "I always wanted a cat—but they never last very long on the island, you know, for obvious reasons," he said, and then turned to the dragon. *"Kitty, can you show us your pretty smile?"*

Ryder spoke to the dragon in a high-pitched voice like she was a baby. The creature opened its massive mouth and exposed hundreds of sharp teeth. If the dragon's smile was supposed to make Brystal more comfortable, it wasn't working.

"Good girl, Kitty!" Ryder said. *"Who's a pretty dragon? Who's a pretty dragon?"*

The dragon panted and wagged her tail like a happy dog, and then rolled onto her back so Ryder could scratch her tummy.

"You wanna give the nice lady a tour? You wanna give the nice lady a tour?" he asked.

The dragon was *thrilled* by the idea and eagerly licked his face with her forked tongue.

"Hold on—you're going to give me a tour on *Kitty*?" Brystal asked.

"Of course. How else would we get around?"

"Is there a *walking* option?"

"We'll cover more ground if we ride Kitty," Ryder

said. "You'll be perfectly safe—she's the best flyer in the Keys."

The dragon raised her head and posed regally. Brystal took a step back.

"I promise it'll be a tour you'll never forget," Ryder said. "Besides, it's so rare that I get to meet people my own age—well, you're the *first* actually. Usually the only people who end up here are rowdy pirates and drunken sailors."

Brystal hesitated. "I don't know about this," she said.

"Come on—*pretty please*?"

Ryder pouted like a toddler and Kitty mimicked the expression behind his back. They both looked so pathetic it made Brystal laugh.

"Okay, fine," she said. "But go easy on me, Kitty—it's my first time."

The dragon lowered her neck to the ground and Ryder and Brystal climbed aboard her saddle. Kitty stretched out her massive wings, and with just a couple flaps, the dragon soared into the sky. The takeoff was much faster than Brystal was expecting and she wrapped her hands tightly around Ryder's waist to keep from slipping off.

"I suppose this is a good place to start the tour," Ryder said, gesturing to the buildings at the top of the volcano. "This is Caretaker Village, it's where we eat and sleep when we aren't looking after the dragons. The big hut in the middle is where the Caretaker Supreme lives."

"What's a Caretaker Supreme?" Brystal asked.

"She's sort of like our queen," Ryder explained. "It's her job to govern the islands and keep them safe. All the Caretakers report to her and all the dragons treat her like an alpha. Trust me, you don't want to get on her bad side."

"Good to know," Brystal said, and made a mental note of it.

As Kitty flew around the Dragon Keys, Ryder showed Brystal all the different islands and pointed out every dragon species they encountered. Brystal was in a constant state of amazement—she couldn't believe an entire ecosystem of *dragons* had existed in secret for thousands of years. She was so intrigued by everything she saw, Brystal almost forgot what she was doing there. In fact, Brystal was having so much fun, it made her feel guilty.

"Most of the dragons are kept separate depending

on their diets," Ryder said. "The majority of them eat fish or boulder bandits, but there are a few dragons that prey upon other dragons. We try to keep the *hunters* and the *hunted* on separate islands but they like to wander."

Kitty swooped down an island, following a river of lava from the air. The lava spilled into a lake of magma like a waterfall. Brystal could see a few Caretakers working at the edge of the lake. They walked across the lake, carefully hopping from stone to stone, as they checked on round objects floating in the magma.

"You see this lake?" Ryder pointed it out. "We call this the *birthing suite*. All the dragons lay their eggs in the magma. The hotter the magma, the faster the embryos develop. Usually it takes a few weeks for dragons to hatch, but I've seen it happen in a matter of hours!"

"It's unbelievable," Brystal said. "My friends are never going to believe this!"

"What kingdom are you from?" Ryder asked.

"The Southern Kingdom, originally," she said.

"No way!" he said excitedly. "My father was from the Southern Kingdom. He was a sailor in King Champion XIV's royal navy—although I never met him. He and his fleet washed ashore after their ship was damaged in a hurricane. They were only in the Dragon Keys long enough to repair the ship. He sailed home before my mother even knew she was pregnant."

"Have you ever thought about leaving the islands yourself?" Brystal asked.

Ryder grinned at the idea. "Maybe someday," he said. "I've always dreamed about traveling the world, but for now, I think I belong here. The dragons need me—and I like being where I'm needed. Does that make sense?"

"Perfect sense," Brystal said with a sweet smile. "I like being where I'm needed, too."

Ryder steered Kitty toward the outer islands of the Keys. Brystal noticed something very long and very big swimming in the ocean below them.

"What's that?" she asked.

"That's a *water dragon*," Ryder said.

"There are dragons that live in the *water*?" Brystal asked in awe.

Ryder nodded. "Wanna meet one?"

Before Brystal could answer, Ryder steered Kitty toward the beach of the nearest island. They landed on the shore and climbed down from the saddle. Ryder faced the ocean and whistled with his fingers. A few seconds later, a massive sea serpent with sapphire scales and turquoise fins poked its head out from the water.

"Brystal, meet Goldfish—he's one of mine," Ryder said.

Brystal's eyes went wide and she backed away from the creature.

"It's a pleasure to meet you, Goldfish," she said with a nervous quiver.

"*Goldfish, would you like to show Brystal your cave of treasures?*" Ryder asked, speaking in the same high-pitched voice he used to speak to Kitty.

"Cave of treasures?" Brystal asked.

"Goldfish likes to collect shiny objects he finds on the ocean floor," Ryder said. "It's mostly a bunch of sea glass and empty bottles, but one time, he found a whole set of crown jewels! Isn't that incredible? Who knows how long those things had been down there!"

The water dragon gave Brystal a curious look and then turned to Ryder, as if asking, *Can I trust her?*

"Don't worry, she isn't going to steal anything," he said.

Goldfish glared at Brystal—*Fine, but keep your hands where I can see them.*

The water dragon rolled out from the water and

stretched his long body across the sand. The creature was shaped like a giant snake and didn't have any arms or legs. Ryder mounted Goldfish's back and then helped Brystal sit beside him. Once they were situated, the water dragon slithered back into the water and then swam across the ocean's surface. When they were about a mile away from shore Goldfish turned to Ryder and gave him a nod—*It's time.*

"Hold your breath," Ryder told Brystal. "I mean, like *really* hold it."

Brystal took his advice and filled her lungs with as much air as possible. The water dragon dived into the water, snaking deeper and deeper into the ocean. Brystal had to grip Goldfish's fins with all her strength to keep from slipping off his back. The salty water stung her eyes and the pressure in her ears got worse and worse the farther down they dived. Just when she didn't think she could hold her breath any longer, Brystal felt air rush past her skin. She opened her eyes and discovered the water dragon had surfaced in a large underwater cave.

There were so many glittering objects, at first Brystal thought they had somehow traveled into space. As her vision improved, she realized the cave was filled with thousands and thousands of valuables. Goldfish had neatly organized his treasures into piles of old coins, jewelry, silverware, empty bottles, bottles with messages, and sea glass arranged by color. There was also a massive stack of miscellaneous junk: telescopes, oars, clocks, sails, and other pieces from sunken ships.

"Oh my goodness," Brystal gasped. "Look at all this stuff!"

"It's impressive, right?" Ryder said.

The water dragon bobbed his head proudly—*It sure is*.

"I didn't realize dragons had hobbies," Brystal said.

"They're amazing creatures," he said. "It's a shame they're so misunderstood. I suppose the world always hates and fears what it doesn't understand. But if people just *tried* to understand them, I'm sure they'd love dragons as much as I do."

"There's a lot that the rest of the world gets wrong," Brystal said. "Although I've been pleasantly surprised by the progress people have made over the years. There have been changes I never thought I'd see in my lifetime. So maybe the world will be ready to accept dragons sooner than we think?"

"I hope so," he said. "I couldn't imagine my life without them."

"They're lucky to have you," she said.

"I'm luckier to have them."

Ryder looked like a proud father as he spoke about them. Brystal was touched to see how much he cared. His passion for dragons reminded her of how she felt about the Fairy Territory. The more time she spent with the Caretaker, the more she was starting to like him—*really* like him. It had been more than a year since Brystal had felt this way about anyone. Unfortunately, Brystal knew she was on borrowed time and tried to squash the feeling before it grew any stronger. She looked around the cave for a distraction—and luckily, she found *more* than what she needed.

"Oh my God!" Brystal gasped.

"What is it?" Ryder asked.

"I don't believe it," she exclaimed. "It's . . . it's . . . *my wand!*"

Her crystal wand was sitting on top of a wine barrel in the stack of miscellaneous sea junk. It glimmered as Brystal approached it, as if it was happy to see her.

"Wait a second—that's yours?" Ryder asked.

"Yes, I'm positive," Brystal said. "I lost it in the crash—I mean, *shipwreck*."

"That's incredible!" Ryder said. *"Goldfish! You're a miracle worker!"*

Brystal reached for her wand, but before she could pick it up, the water dragon suddenly dashed between them. Goldfish growled at Brystal with a dirty scowl— *That's mine!*

"Sorry, water dragons are *very* greedy creatures," Ryder said. *"Goldfish, just because you found it doesn't mean it belongs to you! Remember what I told you? 'Finders keepers' just makes you a thief with a motto. Now give the nice lady back her wand!"*

The water dragon let out a disgruntled sigh and turned the other way. Brystal retrieved her wand, smiling from ear to ear.

"I never thought I'd see it again," she said.

"What are the chances Goldfish would find it?" Ryder said. "It's just like magic."

"Right," Brystal said with a nervous laugh. *"Magic."*

After Brystal was reunited with her wand, she and Ryder returned to the beach and continued their tour of the islands. Their damp clothes were dried while Kitty soared through the sky. As they flew, Brystal's eyes were drawn to an island with the biggest volcano in all the Keys. Although the island was large and lush with plant life, it looked completely empty.

"Why aren't there any dragons over there?" she asked.

"They're afraid of that island," Ryder said.

"Why?"

"Because that's the island with *the old temple*."

When they flew closer, Brystal suddenly understood why the dragons were intimidated. A massive fortress was built into the side of the island's spewing volcano. It was so ancient the structure had practically become *one* with the island. It was made from dark stones that perfectly matched the scorched earth surrounding the volcano. There were a thousand steps leading to the entrance and each one was consumed by weeds and vines.

From the moment she laid eyes on it, Brystal knew she was looking at the Temple of Knowledge—and the sight sent chills down her spine.

"Do you mind if we take a closer look?" Brystal asked.

"Not at all," Ryder said.

He gripped the reins and steered Kitty toward an island across from the Temple of Knowledge. They landed in an empty dragon nest with a perfect view of the island. Being so close to the temple made Kitty visibly uneasy. The dragon wrapped herself in her wings and trembled as she gazed across the water.

"You weren't kidding," Brystal said. "Why are the dragons so afraid of it?"

"There's something inside the temple—something that terrifies them," Ryder said.

"But what could be more frightening than a dragon?" Brystal asked.

Ryder shrugged. "Beats me," he said. "I've never been inside the temple personally, but I know enough to stay away from it."

Brystal acted naive. "Oh, really?" she asked. "Anything you can share?"

A mischievous grin grew across Ryder's face. He looked around the nest to make sure they were alone.

"Can I tell you a big secret?" he asked.

"Please," she said.

"They call it the *Temple of Knowledge*," he said. "It was built thousands of years ago by a group of sorcerers, and supposedly, the temple has a vault that holds the most powerful items ever created. That's why my ancestors and their dragons came to the islands— the sorcerers gave them a home hoping the presence of dragons would discourage people from going inside. Then they shielded the islands in a magical dome to hide it all from view."

Brystal was mesmerized as she gazed across the water. It suddenly made sense: the Caretakers and the dragons—not the boulder bandits—were the *unlikely guardians* that the legend described.

"How do you get inside?" she asked.

"The doors only open with a special key," Ryder said. "But trust me, you don't want to go inside. Everyone who's gone in has never come out."

"And if someone *did* want to go inside, how would they find the key?" she said.

Ryder scrunched his forehead. "Why are you so interested in the temple?"

Brystal locked eyes with him and let out a long sigh. Ryder had been so kind to her she didn't have the heart to lie to him anymore. Besides, dishonesty would only take up more time—time she didn't have.

"Ryder, I have to make a confession," she said. "My

friends and I aren't sailors. And we weren't in a shipwreck. We came to the islands to find the Temple of Knowledge."

"What?" he exclaimed. "But...but...but why?"

"Because the world is in terrible danger," she said. "Cities are being destroyed by a powerful fire—a fire unlike anything the world has ever seen before—and innocent people are being framed for it. Back home I'm known as the Fairy Godmother, and just like the Caretaker Supreme, it's my job to keep people safe. There's a powerful spell book inside the temple that could help me stop the fires. I know it's dangerous—and I know I sound crazy for even attempting it—but if you could help us get inside, we could save a lot of lives."

Ryder was shocked and it took him a few moments to comprehend everything Brystal had said.

"So...you're a *fairy*?" he asked.

"Yes—well, I *was*," she said. "My magic hasn't worked since we arrived."

"That's part of the sorcerers' spell," Ryder said. "People can't use magic while they're inside the dome. The sorcerers didn't want anyone to have an advantage in the temple."

Frustrated, Brystal closed her eyes and took a deep

breath. She had been *counting* on that advantage. The mission was getting more complicated by the minute.

"I still have to try," she said. "A lot of innocent people are going to die if we don't succeed. Can you help me?"

Brystal could tell Ryder was overwhelmed by the request.

"No one can enter the Temple of Knowledge on their own," he said. "You have to get permission from the Caretaker Supreme. She holds the key to the temple. But she's never allowed anyone to use the key before."

"Is there any way I could speak with her?" Brystal asked.

"She normally doesn't meet with strangers, but I *might* be able to arrange a meeting."

"Really? Will she listen to you?"

Ryder gulped. "I think so," he said. "She's my *mother*."

· • ★ • ·

That evening, Brystal stayed in the Healing Hut while Ryder went to speak with the Caretaker Supreme. Brystal paced between the hammocks as she waited for him to return. By now the healing flames had started to shrink on the delegates' bodies and, one by one, they started to wake up.

Lucy yawned and lazily stretched out in her hammock, but became alarmed when she opened her eyes.

"What happened to us?" she asked. "I haven't been this sore since the morning after the Tinzel Heights music festival."

"Lucy, you're on *FIRE*!" Gobzella shouted.

"Thanks—but that wasn't a joke," she said.

"No, you're *literally* on fire!" Butternut exclaimed.

Lucy shrieked when she saw the peach-colored flames burning her broken leg.

"It's not just her! We're *all* on fire!" Prince Elron yelled.

All the delegates screamed and hopped down from their hammocks in panic. They frantically ran around the Healing Hut trying to extinguish the flames. Brystal whistled as loudly as she could to get their attention.

"Everyone calm down!" she said. "The fire isn't hurting you—it's *helping* you! It'll stop once all your injuries are healed!"

At first the delegates didn't believe her, but once they realized the fire wasn't causing them pain, they relaxed. In fact, they discovered the flames felt rather *nice*. Gobzella lay back in her hammock and placed her hands behind her head.

"She's *RIGHT!*" the goblin said. "This feels *GREAT!* It's like a *TICKLE* and a *MASSAGE* at the same time!"

"My knees haven't felt this good since I was a dwarf-ling," Spanky said.

"Brystal, are you doing this to us? Is your magic working again?" Lucy asked.

"No and no," Brystal said. "But I can explain everything."

"The last thing I remember was being surrounded by those mutant lizards!" Butternut said. "How did we escape them?"

"Was it *ME?* Did I *WIN?*" Gobzella asked.

"We're safe now—and *that's* what's important," Brystal said. "Nobody freak out when I tell you this, but we were actually saved by a dragon."

Lucy gasped. "You mean, that wasn't a dream!"

The other delegates looked at Brystal like she was crazy. Instead of wasting time trying to convince them, Brystal walked over to the window and opened the leafy blinds. The delegates were flabbergasted as they caught sight of the volcano, the islands, and all the dragons roaming and flying throughout the Keys.

"No, no, no, no," Lucy said, and shook her head. "This can't be real. Someone must have slipped us purple-spotted clover when we weren't looking. In about five minutes, all of this is going to fade away and a group of preteen tuba players will be laughing at us. The same thing happened to me at band camp."

"What you're seeing is real, I promise," Brystal said. "The islands hold more than the Temple of Knowledge—they're also a *sanctuary for dragons.* When the sorcerers created the temple, they invited the dragons to the islands to help them protect it. *They're* the *unlikely guardians* the legend warns about."

"How do you know all of this?" Prince Elron asked.

Brystal filled the delegates in on everything that had happened while they were asleep. She told them about Ryder's tour of the islands, how a water dragon had found her wand at the bottom of the ocean, and now, she was waiting to speak with the Caretaker Supreme.

"Apparently the key is the only way to get inside," Brystal said. "If she doesn't give it to us, we don't stand a chance."

"And you think we can convince her?" Lucy said.

"We *have* to," Brystal said.

The front door swung open and Ryder stepped inside. Brystal was so anxious she didn't even think about introducing him to the others.

"Well?" she asked. "What did your mother say?"

Ryder sighed, and Brystal knew it wasn't good news.

"She said there's absolutely no way she would ever give you the key—*but* she agreed to meet with you," he said. "That was the best I could do."

"All right then," Brystal said. "Let's meet. Maybe I can change her mind."

Ryder led Brystal and the delegates out of the Healing Hut. They walked down a long rope bridge that snaked through Caretaker Village toward the building at the very top of the volcano. The entrance was guarded by two intimidating Caretaker guards armed with spears made from dragon teeth. Brystal and the delegates followed Ryder through the doors, entering a throne room that hovered over the volcano like a large balcony. The throne room had a glass floor and the delegates could see directly into the pool of magma below them.

"Come closer," said a woman's voice.

The Caretaker Supreme was seated at the far end of the room on a giant throne created from dragon ribs. She wore a horned headdress, spiked shoulder pads, and a tight white gown made from molted dragon skin. With just one glance at the Caretaker Supreme, Brystal knew why all the dragons treated her like an alpha. Her stoic gaze radiated confidence and wisdom. She was already one of the most intimidating people Brystal had ever met.

Ryder bowed as he approached his mother, and the delegates copied him.

"Mother, these are the people I was telling you about," he said.

The Caretaker Supreme was only interested in Brystal.

"So you're the great Fairy Godmother," the Caretaker Supreme said. "Word of your remarkable power has traveled far and wide. It's a pleasure to make your acquaintance."

"Thank you, ma'am," Brystal said. "I wish I could say I've heard about you, too, but you've done a good job at keeping the Dragon Keys a secret."

"My son tells me you've come for the Temple of Knowledge," she said.

"That's correct," Brystal said. "We're hoping to retrieve the Book of Sorcery from the vault."

"And why would someone with *your power* need such a thing?" she asked.

"It isn't about gaining power, it's about rendering someone else *powerless*," Brystal explained. "Two nights ago, the Eastern Kingdom was attacked by a very dangerous fire. It's unlike anything the world has ever seen—it burns much quicker and much hotter than normal fire. More than half of Ironhand was destroyed in a matter of minutes. Our friend Xanthous is a fairy with a specialty for fire. He was at the scene of the attack and is now being blamed for it. We know he's innocent—we know something *else* must be causing the fires, but we just can't prove it."

The Caretaker Supreme slowly nodded. "So the *Devil's Breath* has returned," she said.

"Pardon?"

"The fire you speak of is called *Devil's Breath*," the Caretaker Supreme said. "Thousands of years ago, Devil's Breath destroyed much of the ancient world."

"You mean, it *isn't* Xanthous's fault after all?" Brystal asked.

"Unless your friend is thousands of years old, I sincerely doubt it," she said.

"So what happened the first time? How was the Devil's Breath stopped?" Brystal asked.

"It wasn't stopped," the Caretaker Supreme said. "The fire disappeared as quickly as it appeared. To this day no one knows where it came from or where it went. Unfortunately, that didn't stop people from assigning blame. A group of men known as alchemists held a conference with world leaders to address the situation. They determined dragons were causing the destruction, and so they decided to exterminate the entire species to save the planet. If it weren't for the heroic efforts of my ancestors, dragons would be extinct."

Brystal couldn't believe her ears. *History was repeating itself.*

"And now the same thing is happening to our friend!" Brystal exclaimed. "We just came from the Alchemy Institute! The Conference of Kings determined Xanthous was causing the fires! They insisted the only way to prevent future fires was to eliminate him—but he's just as innocent and misunderstood as the dragons were!"

"It appears *killing* is the alchemists' answer for everything," the Caretaker Supreme said. "My condolences for the loss of your friend."

"But we can still save him!" Brystal said. "If we get the Book of Sorcery, and use it to strip Xanthous of his magic, the alchemists said they would spare his life!"

"I'm sorry, my dear, but that is *not* going to happen," the Caretaker Supreme said. "Opening the temple comes with a great risk—a risk that is not worth saving *one* life."

"But we could use the Book of Sorcery to stop the Devil's Breath once and for all," Brystal said. "And if I'm being completely honest, the fairies and witches have been searching for it long before the fires began. There's *another* reason we need it."

The Caretaker Supreme was surprised to hear this—and she wasn't the only one. Brystal's alternative motives were news to the delegates, too. She could feel their confused gazes on the back of her head without having to look.

"Do tell," the Caretaker Supreme said.

"The world is being threatened by much more than the Devil's Breath," Brystal went on. "Last year, the Southern Kingdom was taken over by a ruthless tyrant known as the Righteous Emperor. He partnered with a powerful witch to raise an unstoppable Army of the Dead. The emperor has plans to invade and conquer all the kingdoms and territories in the world. If we don't stop him, people will be stripped of their rights, talking creatures will lose their homes, and the entire magical community will be hunted down."

"You mean, the Army of the Dead can be *defeated*?" Spanky asked.

"Why didn't you mention this before?" Prince Elron asked.

"The alchemists would have never told me where the Temple of Knowledge was if they knew the *real* reason I wanted the Book of Sorcery," Brystal said. "The fires may destroy all life on earth, but the Army of the Dead will destroy everything worth living for. But with the Book of Sorcery, we can stop *all of it*. We just need the key."

Brystal didn't know what else to say to make her case. The Caretaker Supreme tapped her long fingernails on the armrest of her throne while she considered.

"No," the Caretaker Supreme said.

"*No?*" the delegates gasped together.

"Mother, you can't be serious?" Ryder objected.

"The odds aren't in their favor," the Caretaker Supreme said. "Yes, the fires *might* destroy the planet. And yes, the Righteous Emperor *might* destroy everything worth living for. But if the Book of Sorcery falls into the wrong hands, the world *will* perish. That is certain."

"But Mother, we can't just stand back and—"

The Caretaker Supreme raised a hand to silence her son.

"I've made my decision," she said. "Besides, I couldn't help you if I wanted to. As soon as I inherited the key, I made sure it would never see the light of day again. Our ancestors led enough people to their doom."

"Ma'am, please tell us where it is!" Brystal pleaded. "You're our last hope!"

"Tomorrow morning, I will arrange for a ship to transport you and your friends back to the continent—but that is *all* I'm willing to offer," the Caretaker Supreme said. "Ryder, please escort our visitors to the Healing Hut. They are welcome to stay there until their departure."

With nothing left to do or say, Brystal and the delegates followed Ryder out of the throne room. Their heads hung low while they walked down the rope bridge through Caretaker Village. As far as they knew, the mission wasn't over—*the world was.*

"Is there some sort of *appeal* we could file?" Lucy asked.

"Unfortunately not," Ryder said. "My mother's will is the law around here. And she never takes back a decision once her mind has been made up."

"This can't be the *END!*" Gobzella moaned. "We've got to talk some *SENSE* into her!"

Ryder held open the door of the Healing Hut while the delegates filed in. However, once they were inside, they realized Ryder had escorted them to a completely different part of Caretaker Village. Instead of the green hammocks and peach-colored flames, the new hut was filled with swords, spears, crossbows, and spiked armor.

"Ryder, what is this place?" Brystal asked.

"Everyone suit up," he said. "You can't go into the Temple of Knowledge dressed like that."

"But your mother said she wouldn't help us," Lucy said.

"Oh, and she was serious, too," he said. "My mother is a very practical speaker. She chooses her words very carefully and never says something she doesn't mean. When she said the key would *never see the light of day again*, that wasn't a metaphor."

"And *why* is your mother's frankness a good thing?" Lucy asked.

"Because she unintentionally told us *where* she hid the key," Ryder said. "There are only so many places where the sun doesn't shine—especially around here."

Brystal's eyes grew large when she realized what Ryder was implying.

"The *ocean*," she gasped. "Your mother threw the key into the ocean!"

Ryder smiled. "And if I'm right, I might know someone who's already found it."

CHAPTER FOURTEEN

DINNER WITH ELVES

The jackalopes pulled Elrik and Xanthous through the hills of the Northwestern Woods as they raced toward the Elf Territory. The boys took turns steering the horned rabbits and Xanthous was pleasantly surprised by how swiftly the animals moved through the trees. He wouldn't have thought it was possible to laugh and smile at a time like this, but Xanthous found every tight turn more amusing than the one before. And despite the dangerous forest surrounding them, just being beside Elrik made Xanthous feel safe. He felt butterflies in the pit of his stomach after every bump and jolt that pushed them closer together.

Soon the great tree of the Elf Territory appeared in the distance. It stood regally in the center of the Northwestern Woods like a giant among men. The tree was over a thousand feet tall and hundreds of feet wide. An entire village of small homes were hanging from the enormous branches like a community of birdhouses. The homes and shops were all different colors and styles with clever asymmetrical floor plans to maximize the limited space. Xanthous could see the small elf citizens walking along bridges and pathways between the leaves.

At the base of the tree, the jackalopes passed through wooden gates patrolled by elvish soldiers. Elrik steered the chariot up a path that moved toward the tree's enormous roots and then spiraled up its massive trunk. The higher the rabbits climbed the more relieved Xanthous became—he was so far above the ground the fire would *never* find him.

The chariot traveled to the very top of the territory

and stopped at a miniature castle the tree wore like a crown. The castle was made from checkered panels of black-and-white wood; it had four identical towers, and the entire building was covered in impressive leafy carvings. As soon as the chariot was parked, servants emerged from the castle to collect it from Elrik.

Xanthous stepped down from the chariot and spun around as he took in all the sights of the Elf Territory.

"Wow," he said. "This place never gets old."

"I thought you said you'd never been here before," Elrik said.

"I mean—it *must* never get old, right?" Xanthous corrected himself.

"It sure doesn't," Elrik said. "How's the ankle? Feeling better?"

Xanthous had completely forgotten about his fake injury.

"Good as new," he said. "I always bounce back pretty quick."

"That's good," Elrik said with a laugh. "I was worried I would have to carry you all the way to the guest chambers. Come on, I'll show you to your room."

Just like the outside, everything inside the castle was black and white. The floors were covered in black-and-white tiles and the tall white walls were painted with black symbols that matched the carvings on the exterior. The castle was bustling with elvish maids, butlers, and other servants who wore matching black-and-white uniforms.

Xanthous followed Elrik up a curvy staircase and down a hall on the second floor to the guest chambers. The bedroom had a four-poster bed, a lounge chair, and a wardrobe, but the furnishings were so small it looked like the room was made for children.

"Sorry about the furniture," Elrik said. "We're used to *smaller* company."

"Don't worry, I can make it work," Xanthous said. "I'm just so grateful to—"

Xanthous stopped midsentence when he noticed a mirror in the corner of the room. He became paranoid the fairies might spy on him and quickly yanked a sheet off the bed and draped it over the glass.

"Not a fan of mirrors?" Elrik asked.

"I just caught a glimpse of myself and didn't realize how dirty I was," Xanthous said.

Elrik went to a miniature wardrobe and pulled out a white suit with black lapels.

"Here, you can change into this if you'd like," he

said. "It's an extra-extra-elf-large, so it should fit you. There's also a bathroom next door if you want to freshen up."

"Thank you," Xanthous said, and took the suit from him. "It's so kind of you to bring me here. I don't think I'll ever be able to repay you."

Elrik shrugged it off. "Don't mention it," he said. "Boys like us have to stick together."

The prince and the fairy shared a sweet smile, but the moment was interrupted when something suddenly flew past the window. Xanthous and Elrik rushed to the window and saw a big bronze carriage swooping down from the sky. The carriage was kept afloat by a large balloon and it was pulled through the air by four mechanical birds.

"What is *that*?" Xanthous asked.

Elrik gulped. "Father's home," he said.

"Is *that* how he gets around?" Xanthous asked.

"No, he was invited to a special meeting yesterday," Elrik said. "All the world leaders attended something called a Conference of Kings at a place called the Alchemy Institute. The institute provided the transportation."

Xanthous suddenly felt butterflies in his stomach

again, but this time they were nerves. He knew Elrik must be talking about the meeting Skylene had warned him about—but he had never heard such names before.

"What's a Conference of Kings?" Xanthous asked.

"I guess it's where kings go when there's an emergency," Elrik said.

"And what's the Alchemy Institute?" he asked.

"Beats me," the elf said. "Although I was hoping father would be gone longer."

Xanthous and Elrik watched the bronze carriage as it landed in front of the castle. Servants hurried toward the carriage to welcome their sovereign home. As King Elvin emerged from the coach, the tree branches in his crown were so wide the servants had to help him maneuver through the door. Xanthous grew tense as King Elvin entered the castle. He had met the king a few times with the Fairy Council in the past. If Xanthous didn't want to be recognized, he'd have to keep his distance.

"That's strange," Elrik said. "My brother isn't with him. I wonder why Father left Elron at the institute? Oh well, you'll enjoy dinner much more without him. Elron's a jerk."

Xanthous's eyes went wide. "You mean, *I'm* invited to dinner? With your *father*?"

"Of course you are—you're a guest of the prince." Elrik laughed. "The dining hall is on the first floor. We eat every night at seven seventeen on the dot. Now, I should change beforehand. I've got a long day's worth of hunting to wash off."

Elrik excused himself from the guest quarters. As soon as the prince was out of sight, Xanthous began to pace the room in a frenzy. Apparently keeping a low profile wouldn't be a possibility. If Xanthous didn't want the king to notice him, he'd have to make himself *unrecognizable*. So he hurried next door and took a bath in the miniature elf tub. After he'd bathed, Xanthous slicked back his blond hair, hoping a different hairstyle would help disguise him. He was so used to having flames on his head he couldn't remember the last time he'd used a comb.

Next, Xanthous went back to his room and dressed in the white suit Elrik had provided. He carefully tucked his Muter Medal under his shirt and checked his reflection in the mirror as quickly as he could, just in case the fairies were watching from the other side. However, Xanthous stared at his reflection longer than he intended. The new suit and hairstyle made him look so *grown-up* he barely recognized himself. At some point in the recent past, Xanthous had officially crossed the line between boyhood and manhood—but he must have missed the memo of *when* it had happened.

"Not bad," he said to his reflection. "Not bad at all."

At 7:16, Xanthous climbed down the curvy staircase and found the dining hall on the first floor. When he arrived, an elf girl who looked about six years old was already seated at the long dining table. She wore a white dress with black patches, a tiara made from white flowers, and her hair was styled in three buns on the top of her head. The girl was holding a fluffy red squirrel and feeding it milk with a baster.

"Oh—Princess Elvina," Xanthous said, and quickly bowed.

The princess raised an eyebrow at him. "Have we met?" she asked.

Xanthous had definitely met Princess Elvina with the Fairy Council before, but she clearly didn't remember him—his disguise must be working.

"No, but I've *heard* a lot about you," he said. "I'm Xach Fairchild. I'm a friend of your brother Elrik."

"I didn't realize Elrik *had* any friends," the princess said.

"At least one," Xanthous said with a shrug. "I see *you* have a friend, too. Does your squirrel have a name?"

"Acorn," Princess Elvina said. "I'm trying to train him."

"I didn't know squirrels *could* be trained," Xanthous said.

Princess Elvina let out a discouraged sigh and placed the squirrel in a cage under the table.

"I'm starting to think it's impossible," she said. "Father told me to catch and train a wild animal—it's one of his *assignments*, but I'm not sure how it's supposed to make me a better leader. The last time I checked, elves don't bury their food and pee on everything when you're not looking."

"Thankfully not," Xanthous said.

A very handsome young elf entered the dining hall wearing a black suit with a white lapel—the exact opposite design of Xanthous's suit. The elf also wore a crown made of sticks and his dark hair was pulled into a short ponytail behind his pointed ears. It took Xanthous a couple of moments before he realized he was looking at *Elrik*. He had no idea the elf prince could look so *princely*.

"Gosh," Xanthous said. "You clean up well."

Elrik looked Xanthous up and down, clearly thinking the same thing about him.

"You do, too," Elrik said. "*Very* well."

Xanthous blushed and didn't know what to say—but thankfully, he didn't have a chance to say anything. The doors burst open and King Elvin stomped inside. Elvina jumped to her feet and the elves bowed to their father. Xanthous copied them but he was a little delayed.

"Good evening, Father," the elves said.

King Elvin took a seat at the head of the table without acknowledging his children. Once the king was seated, the elves took their seats, too. Xanthous didn't know where to go so he took the chair beside Elrik.

"*I'm starving! Let's eat!*" the king shouted.

Almost instantaneously, a parade of elf servants entered the dining room with plates full of food. The elves' diet was completely vegetarian and the servants placed piles of almonds, fruit, and vegetables on the table. There was enough food to feed an army, let alone four people. Princess Elvina eyed the empty seat beside her.

"Where's Elron?" she asked.

"He's on an assignment," King Elvin said. "Speaking of, is that animal trained yet?"

"So far he can sit and stay but I'm still potty training him," she said.

"Good," the king said. "And Elrik? Did you hunt a bear like I instructed?"

Elrik glanced to Xanthous with nervous eyes.

"Actually, Your Majesty, Elrik hunted *several* bears," Xanthous said.

The king looked up for the first time and was surprised to see a *visitor*.

"What is this *human* doing at my dinner table?" he asked.

Xanthous was grateful the king didn't recognize him, but also terrified to have his full attention.

"I'm Xach Fairchild, sir," he said. "Your son saved my life in the forest. You see, I got lost in the woods and was attacked by a pack of bears. Had Elrik not showed up at the exact moment he did, I would have been eaten."

Elrik nodded along to the story. The king wasn't convinced, though, and his eyes darted back and forth between the boys. Even Princess Elvina seemed suspicious.

"I didn't realize bears traveled in *packs*," King Elvin said.

"Well . . . there were quite a few of them," Elrik said.

"How many?" Princess Elvina asked.

"*Five*," Xanthous said.

"*Six*," Elrik said.

The boys went tense—they should have clarified the details of their lie beforehand.

"Six including a *cub*, sir," Xanthous said.

"And I imagine you brought back the bodies as souvenirs?" King Elvin asked.

"The chariot was only big enough for the two of us, Father," Elrik said.

"You're telling me you slaughtered *six bears* and brought back *nothing* to show for it?!"

"I couldn't just leave Xach in the woods alone," Elrik said. "What if more bears showed up?"

King Elvin groaned under his breath and shook his head.

"Next time I give you an assignment, I want *proof* you completed it," he said.

"Yes, Father," Elrik said.

The dining hall filled with an awkward silence. Xanthous was curious about the king's trip to the Alchemy Institute but didn't know the appropriate way to inquire about it. So he raised his hand as if he were a student in a classroom.

"Do you have a question?" King Elvin asked.

"How was your trip, Your Majesty?" Xanthous asked.

"Long," he grumbled.

Xanthous was hoping the king would elaborate but he didn't share any other details.

"Elrik told me you attended a Conference of Kings at a place called the Alchemy Institute? Is that right?" he asked.

"Correct," King Elvin said.

"I'm curious, what *is* the Alchemy Institute?" Xanthous asked.

"It's a large campus that floats in the sky," the king said. "It's where alchemists live and conduct experiments."

The more Xanthous learned, the more confused he became.

"*Alchemists*, sir?" he asked. "I'm not familiar with the term."

"That's because they live in secret," King Elvin said. "Apparently, alchemists are a type of fairy or witch that studies *science*. They have a department for every scientific subject you can think of—physics, chemistry, biology—you name it. I've never seen the point of *science*, personally. Why waste time on matters you can't control?"

"Perhaps to learn *how* to control them?" Elrik suggested.

King Elvin shot his son a dirty look as if the prince was insulting his intelligence. Xanthous was desperate to learn more and raised his hand again before the tension escalated. The king rolled his eyes at Xanthous's persistence.

"Yes?" he grunted.

"Forgive my curiosity, Your Majesty, but what did you discuss at the Conference of Kings?" he asked. "Elrik mentioned there was an emergency?"

"It seems a fairy has lost control of his powers and is spreading fires," King Elvin said. "The alchemists were worried the boy might destroy the planet if he isn't stopped. So the conference decided it was best to eliminate him before he causes any more damage. The alchemists are tracking him down as we speak."

Xanthous's mouth dropped open and all the color drained from his face.

"But . . . but . . . but what if he's *innocent*?" he asked.

"Doubtful," King Elvin said. "The evidence spoke for itself."

"But . . . but . . . but what if the evidence is *wrong*? What if it's a misunderstanding?"

Princess Elvina squinted at him. "You seem very *invested* in this story," she said.

"Sorry, it just seems unfair to *execute* someone without a trial, don't you think?" Xanthous said. "I hope someone at least *defended* the poor boy."

"Unfortunately so," King Elvin said. "The whole conference could have been an hour shorter, but the Fairy Godmother *insisted* her friend was being framed. But you know how *she* is—her heart is too big for her own good. The Fairy Godmother begged the alchemists for a chance to prove he was innocent."

"And how is she going to do that?" Xanthous asked.

"She and a team of delegates are on their way to some sort of *temple* to retrieve a special *spell book*—although I can't recall the specific names," King Elvin said. "If they make it back in time, the spell book is supposed to contain a spell that will render the boy powerless, and therefore prove his innocence. But it's very unlikely the Fairy Godmother will return before the alchemists find and kill the boy. Apparently, once people enter the temple, they never come out."

Xanthous was consumed with so much anxiety he couldn't form words to ask any more questions. At that exact moment, a team of sophisticated scientists were *hunting him down*. He suddenly felt very unsafe—the Elf Territory might be protecting him from the mysterious fires, but where could he possibly go to hide from the alchemists? How far would he have to travel? How long would he have to stay there for?

And if that wasn't enough to worry about, one of his best friends was risking her life on a mission to save him. Would Brystal even return from the temple? Was the spell book the same book she needed to defeat the Army of the Dead and destroy the Immortal? Or would Brystal spend her last moments alive trying to prove his innocence instead of focusing on her own needs?

Elrik must have sensed his distress because he gently squeezed his hand under the table.

"Father?" Princess Elvina asked. "Did you say the Fairy Godmother took a team of *delegates* to the temple?"

"Yes," King Elvin said. "One was chosen from each kingdom and territory."

"Please tell me *that* isn't the assignment you gave Elron," Elrik exclaimed.

"As a matter of fact, it was," King Elvin said. "We all know your brother has acted like a coward in the past. This was the perfect opportunity for him to prove himself."

Neither the prince nor the princess could believe the words coming out of the king's mouth.

"Father, how could you?" Elrik asked. "What if Elron gets hurt? What if he gets *killed*?"

King Elvin slammed a fist on the table, causing all the plates to rattle.

"Then he doesn't deserve to inherit my throne," he declared. "It is my duty—*my sacred duty*—to leave this territory in proper hands when I die. And so far, *none* of my children have proven themselves worthy of it.

All three of you continue to be *complete and utter disappointments*! So unless you'd like me to send *you* on a task I'm certain you won't return from, I suggest you *keep your mouths shut*!"

Elrik went pale and quietly stared down at his plate. The king's outburst was enough to break Xanthous out of his anxious trance. For a moment, he forgot all about his own troubles and felt nothing but sympathy for the elf prince. Xanthous knew exactly what it was like to be humiliated by someone who was supposed to love you—he had experienced it every day living with his own father.

Xanthous squeezed Elrik's hand under the table. The corner of Elrik's mouth curved into a small grin and he squeezed him back. The boys secretly held hands for the rest of the evening, and even when the dinner came to an end, neither wanted to let go.

That night after their tumultuous dinner with the king, Elrik took Xanthous to a grand balcony on the fourth floor of the castle. From there the boys could see the entire Elf Territory below them. All the tiny elf homes were lit up and the glowing windows made the giant tree look like a small universe. The boys were emotionally drained from the distressing meal, but the longer they took in the spectacular view, the more it recharged their spirits.

"I didn't think this place could be more beautiful," Xanthous said.

"This is my favorite time of night, too," Elrik said. "When all the shops are closed, when all the work is finished, and everyone goes home, I love how *peaceful* and *simple* everything becomes."

"I know what you mean," Xanthous said. "It's like the world is taking a deep breath."

"Exactly," Elrik said. "I wish *all* moments were like this one. I wish you could wrap a moment up and take it out whenever you need it. But I suppose that's why they tell us to cherish each one—because the good moments never last."

The prince let out a sad sigh and Xanthous could feel the pain behind it.

"I'm sorry your father is so cruel to you," he said. "You deserve better."

"I'm sorry about your father, too," Elrik said. "But

it's just like you said back in the forest—*they're* the broken ones, right?"

Xanthous was touched the prince remembered the sentiment.

"Moments like this may not last forever, but I'll certainly *cherish* it forever," he said.

"Me too," the elf said. "I really like you, Xach."

"I really like you, too, Elrik," Xanthous said.

"Of all the people in the world, what are the chances a couple of boys like us would find each other in the middle of the woods?" Elrik asked. "Makes me wonder if some things are just meant to be."

Xanthous couldn't agree more. Meeting someone like Elrik seemed like a miracle. If Xanthous could wish for anything it would be to spend more time with the prince. Unfortunately, he knew their time was over. If Xanthous wanted to survive the alchemists, he needed to leave the Elf Territory as soon as possible.

"Elrik, there's something I need to tell you," Xanthous said. "I haven't been completely honest with you. My name isn't Xach—it's Xanthous—and the real reason you found me in the woods is because—"

"You're the fairy the alchemists are looking for," Elrik said.

Xanthous was shocked.

"How did you know?" he asked.

"When Father was talking about the Conference of Kings your pulse was racing," the elf said.

"And you weren't *concerned*?" Xanthous asked.

"If you were going to start a fire, I figured you would have done it already," Elrik said.

"Then you probably understand *why* I have to leave," Xanthous said.

"I do," Elrik said.

"I wish I could stay," Xanthous said. "Honestly, I wish I could spend every minute of every day with you—you've been a dream in the middle of a nightmare. It just isn't safe for me here."

Elrik nodded. "I feel the same way about you," he said. "So you probably understand why I have no choice but to come with you."

Xanthous thought his ears were playing tricks on his mind.

"*What?* Elrik, you can't come with me!"

"Why not?" the prince asked.

"Because it's too dangerous!" Xanthous said. "You

heard your father—the alchemists are coming to kill me! I have to go somewhere they'll never find me! I have to hide until the Fairy Godmother retrieves the spell book from the temple!"

"No offense, but I've seen your hiding technique, and without my help you'll be dead by morning," Elrik said. "You're going to need someone to keep a lookout, someone who can gather food and water, and someone who can guide you through the woods—and no one knows the Northwestern Woods better than me. I've discovered caves and caverns that no one else in the world has ever heard of, let alone been to. And most important, you're going to need someone to contact the Fairy Godmother when she returns."

Xanthous was speechless. He knew Elrik was right—hiding from the alchemists would be impossible without someone's help—but he couldn't let the prince put himself in jeopardy.

"Elrik, I can't let you do that for me," he said.

The prince grabbed Xanthous by the shoulders and looked deeply into his eyes.

"I can't tell you how many times I've looked down at those gates and dreamed of running away. I've made plenty of excuses to stay, but *you're* the first excuse I have to leave. I know it feels like the whole world is against you, but it's not—you've got *me*. And I'm not ready to lose you just yet."

"But what if the Fairy Godmother doesn't return?" Xanthous said. "What if I have to stay in hiding forever?"

"I can think of worse fates than being stuck with a cute fairy," Elrik said with a wink. "So what do you say? You want to run away together?"

Suddenly, Xanthous's greatest nightmare had turned into a dream come true. Even a life on the run seemed like a paradise with Elrik by his side.

"All right," Xanthous said. "Let's do it—let's run away together."

Elrik gave him the biggest smile Xanthous had ever seen.

"Wonderful," the prince said. "We'll leave at once. I'm going to pack some supplies and get my chariot ready. You stay here—I'll be back as soon as I'm finished!"

Elrik kissed Xanthous and quickly ran inside the castle. Xanthous's eyes grew twice in size and he held a shaky hand over his lips. *Did that just happen?* Xanthous pinched himself to make sure he wasn't dreaming. *No, it definitely happened!* Muter Medal or not, Xanthous was blushing so hard he was surprised his cheeks didn't catch on fire. He looked out at the Elf Territory in awe, beaming brighter than all the stars in the night sky.

Perhaps Emerelda was right about love. Perhaps there *was* a Fancy for every Mopes.

CHAPTER FIFTEEN

THE TEMPLE OF KNOWLEDGE

Inside the arsenal at Caretaker Village, Brystal, Lucy, and the delegates changed into dragon-skin jumpsuits, boots, and spiked pads for their shoulders, knees, and elbows. Ryder insisted they arm themselves with weapons, too, and Brystal and Lucy had a difficult time choosing one. The girls were so used to protecting themselves with magic they couldn't imagine swinging a sword or spear in combat. Still, they listened to Ryder's advice and selected swords made from sharpened dragon teeth. Brystal tucked her wand into her boot for safekeeping, eager for the chance to use it again.

"This is quite a makeover," Brystal said as she eyed their new outfits.

"We look like the world's toughest kickball team," Lucy said. "I'm not mad at it."

"Everyone ready?" Ryder asked.

The delegates nodded and gave him a thumbs-up.

"Good," he said. "Now, we're going to sneak out of the village and climb down the volcano on foot. We have to be as quiet as possible. If my mother's guards catch us, she'll have us all thrown in Caretaker jail."

"Copy *THAT*!" Gobzella said. "I'll be as quiet as a *FOX*!"

Prince Elron cringed. "Gobzella, you're not allowed to *speak* until we get there!" he said.

Gobzella mimed zipping her mouth shut and locking it with a key. Ryder opened the door a crack and peeked outside.

"*The coast is clear*," he whispered. "*Come on.*"

The delegates followed Ryder onto the rope bridge outside. It was late and besides the glowing and gurgling magma in the volcano below, everything was dark and quiet in Caretaker Village. They climbed under the rope bridge and crawled along beneath it, except for Butternut and Spanky—there was enough room for the dwarf and troll to walk upright. As they covertly moved through the village, Ryder would occasionally raise a hand and pause the procession whenever he heard a Caretaker moving above them.

Once they reached the edge of Caretaker Village, Ryder scanned the land surrounding the volcano and then checked the sky. When he was certain there were no Caretakers or dragons nearby, he slid down the volcano's steep hillside, zipping from ridge to ridge, until he reached the base of the volcano. Brystal, Lucy, and the other delegates followed his pattern and made it to the base very smoothly, except Gobzella—the goblin tumbled down the volcano like a one-woman avalanche.

Once the delegates picked Gobzella up and dusted her off, they dashed across the island. They tiptoed through a herd of sleeping treechompers, they hopped across a river of snoozing lavalingers, and they snuck past a colony of fishhoarders snoring in their dams. Ryder led the delegates to a vacant section of the beach and whistled toward the ocean. A few moments later,

Goldfish stuck his giant head out of the water. The water dragon glared at Ryder with sleepy eyes—*Do you know what time it is?*

"Hey, Goldfish, sorry to wake you," Ryder apologized.

"*Its name is Goldfish?*" Spanky whispered to the others.

"*He names all his dragons after pets he wished he had*," Brystal whispered back.

"Listen, I promise I wouldn't be bothering you in the middle of the night unless it was extremely important," Ryder said. "Can you take us to your cave of treasures?"

The water dragon gave him a suspicious look—*Why?*

"Because I think you have something we need," Ryder explained. "Several years ago, my mother tossed a special key into the ocean. We have no clue what it looks like but I have a hunch you might have found it by now."

Goldfish turned to Brystal and he noticed the wand tucked into her boot. The water dragon groaned and shook his head—*Haven't you taken enough from me?*

"Please, Goldfish?" Brystal said. "I'd be happy to make a trade this time."

Goldfish raised an eyebrow—*You have my attention*.

"My friend Emerelda can turn anything she touches into jewels," Brystal said. "If you let us take the key, I could give you all the diamonds, rubies, and emeralds you've ever dreamed of. What do you think?"

The water dragon didn't seem impressed—*I have enough jewels, thank you very much*. Brystal and Ryder looked at each other, each hoping the other had another idea, but neither knew *how* to convince him. Lucy cleared her throat and pushed past Brystal and Ryder.

"Stand back—I can handle this," she declared.

"How?" Brystal asked.

"I've negotiated in the sleaziest pawnshops in the world—these *collector types* are all cut from the same cloth," she said, looking up at the dragon. "Hello, Mr. Goldfish—may I call you Mr. Goldfish?"

The water dragon nodded—*If you must*.

"Well, Mr. Goldfish, I can tell you're a dragon with good taste," Lucy said. "You know a good deal isn't necessarily about the *price*—it's about the *value*. Diamonds and jewels are way too *common* to be interesting. What you really want is something *priceless*—something that *can't be replaced*."

300

Goldfish squinted at her—*Go on*. Lucy removed her bottle-cap necklace and showed it to him.

"See this?" she asked. "This bottle cap is from a bottle of Fabubblous Fizz that the Duchess of Downsouthington sent me *personally*. She attended a Goose Troupe concert at the Appleton Music Hall and was so blown away by my tambourine solo, she sent me a gift. I shared the beverage with the world-famous Goblin Tenors, made this necklace from the bottle cap, and have worn it ever since. It means the absolute world to me—and something that means the world to *one person*, is much *rarer* than something that's important to *everyone*. Right?"

The water dragon scratched his head with his tail as he thought about it. Even Brystal was confused about where Lucy was going with this.

"So what do you say?" Lucy asked. "I'll give you my most prized possession in exchange for some discarded junk you found at the bottom of the ocean. You can't beat a deal like that."

The water dragon was visibly intrigued. He looked back and forth between Ryder and Lucy with her bottle cap as he contemplated. Eventually, Goldfish made his decision and nodded eagerly.

"Thanks, Lucy," Brystal whispered. *"I'm sorry you had to trade something so valuable."*

"Relax, there is no Duchess of Downsouthington," she whispered back. *"I'm just conning a con man."*

Goldfish took the necklace with his teeth and then rolled onto the beach and stretched out across the sand. The delegates climbed on his back, and once they were situated, Goldfish slithered back into the water and snaked across the ocean. When they were about a mile away from the beach, the delegates held their breath and the water dragon dived deep underwater. Two minutes later, Goldfish and the delegates surfaced in his underwater cave. The delegates gasped for air and looked around in amazement at the piles of coins, sea glass, silverware, bottles, and ship parts.

"Whoa," Lucy said with wide eyes. "Talk about an *offshore account.*"

While the delegates searched the cave, the water dragon lay on his back and played with his new necklace like a cat with a ball of yarn. An hour later, the delegates had found over a hundred keys in Goldfish's stack of miscellaneous sea junk. They laid all the keys out in a row to inspect them. Some were made of gold, others of steel, and a few even had jewels.

"Well? Which one is the key to the temple?" Butternut asked.

Brystal studied the pile of keys. Despite all the glittering ones, her eyes kept coming back to a small and rusted key. She picked it up and raised it for the others to see it.

"It's this one," she said.

Prince Elron grunted. "You can't be serious," he said. "There's no way *that's* the key to the most valuable vault in the world!"

"If *you* hid all your valuables in one place, what would you want the key to look like?" Brystal asked him. "This key is the most inconspicuous and misleading—and that's exactly what the sorcerers would have wanted."

Ryder took the key from her and examined it himself.

"She's right," he said. "Look, this key is made from *volcanic stone*. Just like the temple itself."

Gobzella clapped her hands in celebration. "All right, we got ourselves a *KEY*!" she said. "Now all we need is a *DOOR*!"

"How are we going to get to the Temple of Knowledge from here?" Spanky asked.

Ryder winced. "I didn't think about that part," he

said. "I suppose we'll have to convince Goldfish to give us a ride."

The delegates turned to Lucy, hoping she had another valuable she could negotiate with.

"Hey, Mr. Goldfish?" Lucy called to the dragon. "Did I mention I have a lucky *toe ring* from the *Duke of Uppereastshire*?"

· · ★ · ·

The water dragon transported the delegates across the Dragon Keys to the island of the Temple of Knowledge. Brystal could feel Goldfish getting more and more tense as the ancient structure came into view. Although she couldn't blame the dragon. Even *her* stomach was tightening as they approached the island. And judging by the wide eyes and pale faces of her peers, the feeling of intimidation was mutual.

Tick... Tick... Tick... Tick...

Don't worry....

You won't be in there very long....

Temple or no temple...

Challenges or no challenges...

Eight days is all you have left....

But you'll be dead much sooner than that.

Brystal tried to ignore the disturbing thoughts, but she had plenty of vulnerability for them to feed on. *Tick... Tick... Tick... Tick...*

How can you possibly survive...

The physical challenge...

The mental challenge...

The emotional challenge...

Without magic?

The closer Goldfish swam to the Temple of Knowledge, the louder Brystal's pocket watch and disturbing thoughts became.
Tick... Tick... Tick... Tick...

And let's not forget . . .

If you want the Book of Sorcery . . .

You'll have to face the deadliest and most dangerous creature ever to roam the earth. . . .

What could it be if not a dragon?

What kind of terrifying beast is waiting inside?

I doubt you'll make it far enough to find out.

When they were a few yards away from land, Goldfish came to an abrupt halt. The dragon rapidly arched his back and catapulted all seven passengers toward the beach. Once they hit the sand, the timid dragon dived under the water and didn't return. The delegates got to their feet, brushed themselves off, and gazed up at the temple and the spewing volcano that engulfed it.

"So *this* is the Temple of Knowledge, huh?" Spanky asked.

"Should be called the Temple of *CARNAGE!*" Gobzella said.

"Where's the entrance?" Butternut asked.

"It's at the top of the steps," Ryder said.

The delegates moaned when they noticed the steps stretched all the way to the very top of the temple—except for Gobzella. The goblin excitedly rubbed her hands together and started stretching.

"All right, time for some *CARDIO!*" she said. "Let's get our blood *PUMPING!*"

Gobzella's enthusiasm made Prince Elron groan and he held his face in his hands.

"I hate her," the elf said under his breath. "I hate her so much."

The goblin led the charge and the delegates followed her up the endless stairs. The stone steps were chipped and cracked from years of exposure to the elements and they were covered in weeds and vines, making it difficult to hike. As they climbed, the sun started to rise and it helped the delegates see where they were going. Unfortunately, the sunlight also illuminated how *high* they were—if anyone slipped it would be a long tumble back to the ground. By the time they reached the top of the stairs, everyone in the group was panting and sweating profusely.

"Please tell me *that* was the physical challenge," Lucy wheezed.

"I sincerely doubt it," Brystal said.

The stairs led to a tall archway carved into the side of the volcano. Underneath the arch was a massive stone door that towered high above their heads. The door was completely solid and didn't have any handles or knobs, only a small keyhole. Brystal stuck the key inside the hole and sighed with relief when it was a perfect fit. She turned the key and suddenly, the whole temple began to rumble as the heavy stone door opened. A burst of dusty air blew out from inside the temple, causing all the delegates to cough.

"If anyone wants to turn around, now is your last chance," Brystal said. "Once we step inside, there's no going back."

The delegates were visibly frightened, but they mustered the courage they needed and shared a confident nod.

"There's too much at stake to give up now," Lucy said.

"I couldn't agree more," Butternut said. "We can't let the world be destroyed by fiery tyrants or tyrannical fires."

"Besides, we've come too far," Prince Elron said. "I'm not climbing down those stairs."

"Let's get the *BOOK OF SORCERY* so we can stop the *DEVIL'S BREATH* and kick some *RIGHTEOUS BUTT*!" Gobzella declared.

"And then *the mole people*!" Spanky said, and raised his fist.

The delegates rolled their eyes at the dwarf.

"Sure, Spanky," Lucy said. "And *then* the mole people."

The delegates' determination was contagious. Brystal felt her first spark of hope since they had left the Alchemy Institute.

"All right, here we go," she said. "No matter what happens in there, we have to keep moving. Too many people are counting on us to fail."

Brystal, Lucy, Ryder, Gobzella, Prince Elron, Spanky, and Butternut all took a deep breath and walked into the temple. As soon as they were inside, the heavy door closed behind them and sealed itself shut. At first, the delegates saw nothing but complete darkness. When their eyes adjusted, they found themselves in a dark tunnel. They saw light in the distance and felt heat coming from the other end. They clutched their weapons and cautiously walked toward it, keeping their eyes and ears on high alert.

When they reached the end of the tunnel, the delegates discovered they were *inside* the island's volcano. A long stone bridge stretched across an enormous lake of magma that violently bubbled and splashed below them. The bridge connected the tunnel to a round platform at the volcano's core. Seven giant statues were seated on thrones around the platform—four sorcerers and three sorceresses. The statues had wrinkled faces, the men had long bushy beards, the women had long stringy hair, and all seven were dressed in hooded cloaks. The statues' eye sockets were empty—as if they were watching *nothing* and *everything* at once.

The delegates carefully crossed the bridge and went to the platform one at a time. The very center of the platform's floor was covered in a large pentagram made from black metal. Brystal and the delegates gathered on top of the pentagram and noticed its star was circled by carvings in an ancient language.

"What do you think it says?" Ryder asked.

"It's probably a warning," Brystal said.

Suddenly, the platform began to vibrate and the sound of scraping stone echoed through the volcano. The pentagram started sinking through the platform, taking all seven delegates with it.

"It must be taking us to the first challenge," Brystal said. "Everybody get ready! And be prepared for anything!"

The delegates stood back to back as the pentagram sank deeper and deeper. It moved faster and faster, descending through the hollow platform as if it were a deep well. Stone walls rose around them, and the farther the pentagram went, the hotter the air became. A bad feeling grew in the pit of Brystal's stomach when she heard sloshing beneath them.

"I don't like this!" Brystal exclaimed. "We need to get off this thing!"

The delegates jumped off the pentagram and hung from the stone bricks on the walls. A few seconds later, Brystal's intuition proved itself right. The pentagram sank into a pool of magma at the bottom of the well. As they looked down in terror, the delegates noticed the magma was slowly starting to rise.

"*It's coming toward us!*" Spanky shouted.

"*We have to climb!*" Brystal yelled.

While the delegates frantically scaled the walls, an empty doorway appeared several feet above them.

"That must be the way out!" Ryder said.

"This is *definitely* the physical challenge!" Brystal said. "Everyone head for the doorway!"

Unfortunately for the delegates, the task was *just* getting started. All the stone bricks in the well started moving *in and out of the walls*! The movement happened at different speeds and in no particular order or pattern, making it impossible to predict. The delegates lost their grips and slipped farther and farther down the well as the magma rose higher and higher toward them.

To make matters worse, the delegates heard a loud banging coming from above. They all looked up and gasped as *giant stone boulders began rolling into the well*! The boulders ricocheted toward them, smashing the bricks into pieces and leaving huge dents in the walls. The delegates had to leap and dive from brick to brick to avoid being crushed.

"Seriously?" Lucy shouted. "The bricks and the magma weren't challenging enough?! The sorcerers had to add BOULDERS to this?!"

"Butternut! Look out!" Ryder yelled.

The troll glanced up and saw a boulder headed straight for him. Butternut leaped out of its way just in time and jumped to the other side of the well. Tragically, when he reached the opposite wall, the brick he was aiming for suddenly retracted. There was nothing for the troll to grab hold of and he slid down the well. His long fingernails scratched the stone wall as he desperately tried to grab hold of something.

"*AHHHHHHH!*" Butternut shrieked.

"*Butternut!*" the delegates yelled.

The troll plunged directly into the magma and never resurfaced. The delegates screamed as they looked down in horror. Sadly, they didn't have time to mourn the fallen troll. The longer they were inside the well, more and more boulders came rolling in from above.

"This is pointless!" Prince Elron said. "We'll never make it out of here!"

"Everyone stay *CALM*!" Gobzella said. "I've got an *IDEA*!"

The goblin swung from brick to brick like a monkey swinging through trees, narrowly avoiding the boulders raining down around her. She moved through the well and scooped up each delegate, throwing them over her shoulder. Brystal, Lucy, Ryder, Spanky, and Prince Elron held on to Gobzella as she painstakingly climbed higher and higher.

"No more death TODAY! No more death TODAY!" Gobzella repeated to herself as she went.

Finally, the goblin reached the doorway at the top of the well. The delegates climbed to safety and pulled Gobzella in behind them. As the goblin lay down to catch her breath, Prince Elron leaned over to her and repeatedly kissed her face.

"Gobzella, you're our hero!" the elf declared. "I promise I will never make fun of your volume for as long as I live!"

The celebratory moment was cut short when the delegates remembered their team was one delegate short. Tears filled their eyes as they stared down at the rising magma that had consumed the troll.

"I can't believe Butternut's gone," Lucy said. "It happened so fast."

"Lord, why'd you have to take *BUTTERNUT*?" Gobzella sniffled. "The world needed his beautiful *POETRY*!"

"Farewell, friend," Spanky said. "Just like you, your life was far too short."

The delegates had known the temple would be dangerous, they had known they were risking their lives by joining the mission, but until now, the reality hadn't sunk in. Butternut's death was likely only the first of many.

"We have to keep moving," Brystal said, reminding herself as much as the others. "The world is counting on us."

CHAPTER SIXTEEN

BAIT

While Xanthous waited on the balcony for Elrik, he kept himself busy by day-dreaming of their future life on the run. He imagined them traveling the world as they dashed from hiding place to hiding place, sharing exotic meals in exotic locations, and happily holding hands as they ran from the alchemists. The thoughts were so cheerful, Xanthous had to remind himself of the *danger* he was in.

However, after waiting more than an hour for the elf prince to return, Xanthous's giddiness turned into impatience. And as the second and third hour rolled by, his impatience evolved into full-blown *worry*.

Xanthous couldn't imagine what was taking Elrik so long. He leaned over the railing and looked around the castle grounds but didn't see the prince or his chariot anywhere. As he searched, Xanthous was relieved when he heard the sound of footsteps coming from behind him.

"Elrik?" he asked, and whipped around with a big smile. "Where have you been?"

Unfortunately, Xanthous discovered the wrong royal.

"Princess Elvina?" he asked. "What are you doing out here?"

"My brother asked me to come and get you," the princess said. "I found him loading a chariot in the stables. He said he was going to give you a *night tour* of the kingdom."

"Um ... that's right," Xanthous said with a nervous

laugh. "The Elf Territory is so beautiful at night I wanted to see everything up close."

Princess Elvina crossed her arms.

"Uh-huh," she mumbled. "Well, follow me. I'll show you to the stables."

Xanthous was grateful nothing bad had happened to Elrik and was embarrassed for letting his paranoia get the best of him. Once again, his head was filled with daydreams of the future and Xanthous practically floated as he followed Princess Elvina through the castle. They climbed the curvy staircase to the first floor and then the princess led him down a steep flight of stairs to the lower levels of the castle. She escorted him down a narrow hall, where they entered a room that was pitch-black.

"We're almost there," Princess Elvina said.

"The stables are all the way down here?" Xanthous asked.

"They're my family's *secret stables*," she explained. "In case the castle is ever attacked, it gives us a quick way to escape. It's just on the other side of this door— watch your head."

Although Xanthous couldn't see the princess, he

heard her open a door. He ducked through the tight doorway and had to crawl on his hands and knees to fit in the short hall behind it. Xanthous was only inside the hall for a couple of seconds before he bumped into a set of steel bars.

"Princess Elvina?" he asked. "I think there's something blocking the—"

WHAM! The princess slammed the door behind him. Xanthous heard the sound of rattling chains and a lock being clicked shut. He tried to move to his right and left, but he could barely turn around. The princess had tricked him into some kind of metal box.

"What's going on?" he asked. "Where am I?"

FFFFHT! Princess Elvina's face was illuminated for a brief moment as she lit a match. She tossed the match into a pile of dry logs beneath Xanthous. As the flames rose around him, Xanthous realized he wasn't in a hall—*he was trapped inside a cage in the middle of a fireplace!* The warmth of the fire turned the metal bars red-hot and it singed the edges of Xanthous's white suit.

"Elvina, what are you doing to me?" he cried.

A malevolent grin grew across the elf princess's face

while she watched the fire rise higher and higher. Even as the cage was completely engulfed in the flames, Xanthous remained unharmed.

"See, Father? I told you it was him!" Princess Elvina said. "I recognized him the minute he walked into the dining room!"

Xanthous saw a pair of hands appear in a corner of the dark room. King Elvin clapped for his daughter as he slowly stepped out from the shadows. The king walked closer to the fireplace and was joined by four soldiers from the Army of the Dead.

"Well done, Elvina," the king said. "I have never been prouder of you. You have proven yourself far more cunning and capable than your brothers. You'll make an excellent queen when I am gone."

Princess Elvina beamed victoriously. "Thank you, Father," she said.

Xanthous shook the bars of his cage but they didn't budge.

"Where's Elrik?!" he exclaimed. "What have you done to him?!"

"I'm afraid you'll never see my son again," King Elvin said. "You see, lying to the king comes with severe consequences—especially for a prince. By the time Elrik has served his sentence, you'll be long gone."

"If you're turning me in, then where are the alchemists?" Xanthous asked. "Why are those soldiers here?"

"The Righteous Emperor made me an offer I couldn't refuse," King Elvin said. "In exchange for you, he promised to spare the Elf Territory from invasion."

"But *why*?" Xanthous gasped. "What does Seven want with *me*?"

"I don't care what his reasons are—I have a territory to protect," King Elvin said. "The Righteous Emperor's army is impossible to defeat. Regardless of what the Fairy Godmother believes, it's only a matter of time before he annihilates everything standing in his way. Turning you over to him is the only way I can guarantee the elves' safety."

"He's lying to you!" Xanthous shouted. "You can't trust the emperor! He's going to betray you just like he betrays everyone else! You have to let me out!"

"I'm sorry, son, but I have no choice," King Elvin said, and then he gave the dead soldiers a nod. "Take him away."

Dr. States and the alchemists had been searching for two whole days and still hadn't found a trace of Xanthous Hayfield anywhere. However, as dawn broke on the morning of the third day, the alchemists thought their luck was about to change. While their bronze carriage flew through the northwestern sky of the Righteous Empire, they spotted a trail of smoke billowing in the distance.

The alchemists steered the Magbirds in the direction of the smoke and landed beside a small brush fire in the foothills. Strangely, instead of finding Xanthous Hayfield at the scene, they discovered the Righteous Emperor himself, holding a lit torch. He was there with his High Commander and a fleet of his dead soldiers.

"Gentlemen, it's good to see you again," Seven said.

"What is the meaning of this?" Dr. States asked.

"Forgive the theatrics, I have good news and didn't know how else to get your attention," Seven said.

"Did you find Mr. Hayfield's location?" Dr. States asked.

"Even better," Seven teased. "Xanthous Hayfield

has been captured, bound, and disarmed by a Muter Medal. He's in my custody as we speak."

The alchemists looked at one another and sighed with relief.

"That *is* wonderful news!" Dr. States said. "Great work, Your Majesty! Tell us where he is and we'll head there immediately."

The emperor scrunched his nose and shook his head as he considered.

"Actually, I'm not sure that's a good idea," Seven said.

"What are you talking about?" Dr. States asked. "We have to eliminate him as soon as possible!"

"But like you said, Xanthous Hayfield is *very* powerful," Seven said. "I don't think it's *wise* or *responsible* to perform his execution in my Empire. What if something went wrong? If one of my citizens was injured in the process, well, I'd *never* forgive myself."

It had been so long since the emperor felt empathy for anyone but himself, he had to remind himself which face muscles to use.

"Your Majesty, we are *more* than capable of handling this," Dr. Steam said.

"If it makes you more comfortable, we can transport the boy back to the institute and perform the elimination there," Dr. Stag said.

"*And risk him escaping midflight?* No, no, no—that wouldn't be very smart either," Seven said, and he sighed dramatically. "If only there was a way to bring the institute *closer* to the Righteous Empire. That way, I could hand Mr. Hayfield over *safely* without putting my people or my kingdom in jeopardy."

The alchemists shared a patronizing laugh at the emperor's expense.

"The Alchemy Institute can go wherever *we* tell it to," Dr. Storm boasted. "It sits on a foundation of clouds—clouds that can travel anywhere in the world."

Seven put a hand over his chest and dropped his jaw, pretending to be amazed.

"It can?" he exclaimed. "My, my, my—you scientists are full of surprises! Well, that solves everything, doesn't it?"

Dr. States gave the emperor a peculiar glare, as if he had caught a foul stench.

"Unfortunately, moving the institute comes with its own set of risks," he said. "We wouldn't want to spoil the institute's secrecy by exposing it to your people."

The emperor waved off the concern like it was a harmless fly.

"Oh, there's no need to worry about that," he insisted. "My Empire is under a very strict curfew. All the citizens are required to be indoors by sundown. If you bring the Alchemy Institute to the Righteous Palace after dark—let's say *midnight* tonight—no one will ever know you were there."

The alchemists scrunched their brows and scratched their foreheads as they considered the emperor's proposal. It seemed like Seven was making the situation more complicated than necessary, but they would do anything to get their hands on the boy.

"Very well, Your Majesty," Dr. States said. "We will bring the Alchemy Institute to the Righteous Palace tonight at midnight."

"Terrific," Seven said. "I will sleep *much easier* once this nightmare is behind us."

After the decision was reached, the alchemists returned to their bronze carriage. The Magbirds carried the scientists into the sky and the emperor waved as they disappeared over the southern horizon. When the alchemists were out of sight, the emperor's friendly smile turned into a cunning smirk.

"What do you think, High Commander?" Seven said. "Was I convincing?"

"Without question, my lord," the High Commander said. "You acted like an *absolute idiot*. The alchemists aren't expecting a thing."

"Good," Seven sneered. "I'm counting on it."

CHAPTER SEVENTEEN

THE RIDDLE OF FOUR DOORS

After their narrow escape, the delegates finally understood why no one had survived the Temple of Knowledge before, and they were starting to doubt *their* fate would be any different. Their arms and shoulders were aching horribly from climbing the stone bricks, their palms and knuckles were covered in scrapes and blisters, and their fingernails were filled with blood. Gobzella had pulled every muscle in her body while helping the others to safety. The goblin was so sore she could barely walk and used Spanky as a living crutch. It was a miracle the delegates were still *standing* let alone *moving* at all, but the party kept going, taking one determined step at a time, ready to face whatever obstacle was next.

The doorway at the top of the physical challenge led to a long and dark corridor. As the delegates walked inside, torches mounted to the walls were magically lit as they passed them. The longer they walked, the deeper the corridor slanted, and the air began to cool. The delegates assumed they had traveled beyond the island's volcano and were somewhere below the ocean.

Eventually, they reached the end of the corridor and discovered a wide chamber. The chamber was completely empty except for four identical doors on the far wall. The doors were cracked open and a faint pale light shone out from whatever was behind them. A single plaque was bolted to the wall above the doors and carved with a message written in the same ancient language they saw before.

"This doesn't seem fair," Lucy said. "How are we supposed to know what the plaque says?"

"You should file a complaint," Prince Elron scoffed.

Suddenly, as if the plaque was listening to Lucy, all the letters started rearranging themselves into a language the delegates *could* understand. They gathered in a tight clump below it to read the inscribed message:

Each door leads to A DIFFERENT PATH.
Each path leads to THE SAME DESTINATION.
The path behind door one is the quickest.
The path behind door two is the shortest.
The path behind door three is the slowest.
The path behind door four is the longest.
Choose wisely.
Once a door shuts, it will not reopen.

The delegates stared at the plaque with the same crestfallen expression. They read the message over and over again, but none of them understood what it meant.

"Are those supposed to be directions?" Spanky asked.

"No, it's a riddle," Brystal said. "This must be the mental challenge."

"Why do riddles always have to be so *PASSIVE AGGRESSIVE!*" Gobzella said.

"It seems pretty simple to me," Ryder said. "If each door leads to the same destination, then it's letting us pick our route to the next challenge."

"That's too easy—there's got to be a catch," Brystal said. "Riddles choose their words very carefully, and they're designed to be misleading. It doesn't say each door leads to *the next challenge*, it says each door leads to the *same destination*. So what's a *destination* that we'll all reach even if we *don't* choose the right door?'"

All the delegates went silent as they contemplated the question. Suddenly, their train of thought was interrupted when Prince Elron bolted for the first door.

"Your *HIGHNESS*? What are you *DOING*?" Gobzella said.

"I'm picking the quickest path!" the elf called.

"But we haven't solved the riddle yet!" Spanky said.

Prince Elron froze in the doorway of the first door. He looked over his shoulder with a scheming smile.

"I'm not here to help you stop the Righteous Empire or the Devil's Breath," he confessed. "My father sent me to this temple to retrieve the Book of Sorcery for *the elves*—and if I survive, he promised to name me as the heir to his throne! And once we have the book in our possession, the Elf Territory will become the mightiest nation the world has ever known!"

"You shady little tree parasite!" Lucy shouted.

"You've been lying to us this whole *TIME*?!" Gobzella asked.

The delegates charged toward the elf, but Brystal held out her hand to stop them.

"Elron, wait!" she pleaded. "I understand your desire to prove yourself to your father—believe me! I spent my whole childhood desperate for my father's approval, too! But that door is *not* the way forward! The riddle is trying to trick you! And no matter what you do here, it doesn't guarantee your father's respect! Some people can't be pleased no matter how hard we try!"

Prince Elron looked to the floor for a moment while he considered Brystal's words, but a conniving grin quickly returned to his face.

"Nice try," he said. "I'm sorry, Fairy Godmother, but this is where *your* journey ends and *mine* finally begins!"

Prince Elron stepped through the first door and

slammed it shut behind him. As soon as the door was closed, it dissolved into the wall and disappeared from sight. The delegates could hear the elf's footsteps behind the wall as he raced farther into the temple.

"Elron, come back! It isn't safe!" Brystal yelled.

"I'll tell the world you all died noble deaths!" Prince Elron called to them. "Your memories will be cherished for—*AHHHHHHHHHHH*!"

Suddenly, the chamber began to rattle with the power of a massive earthquake. A thunderous noise boomed from behind the wall as an avalanche of giant stones crushed the elf. Prince Elron's screams grew louder and louder, until finally, there was dead silence. The delegates gazed at one another with large, horrified eyes.

"Wrong door," Lucy said.

"Tragically, Prince Elron just solved the riddle for us," Brystal said. "The destination isn't the next challenge—it's *death*. That's the one destination everyone reaches regardless of the choices they make."

"Elron chose the door with the *quickest path*, so he had a *quick demise*," Ryder thought aloud. "So now we have to figure out if the shortest, the slowest, or the longest path leads to the next challenge."

"What's the difference between a *QUICK* death and a *SHORT* death?" Gobzella asked.

"Height," Spanky said, and nodded with conviction. "I bet there are razors behind door two that will slice us all in half! And Gobzella into thirds!"

"Then it's between door number three and four," Ryder said. "But what's the difference between a *slow* death and a *long* death? Aren't they the same thing?"

Brystal went quiet and paced in front of the doors as she thought about it.

"When I think of the word *slow*, I think of *time*," she said. "But when I think of the word *long*, I think of *length*. Last year, when I was in the realm between life and death, all the clocks on the trees were spinning at different speeds—"

Ryder did a double take. "Sorry—did you just say *realm between life and death*?"

"We'll explain later—just focus," Lucy told him. "Keep going, Brystal."

"Mistress Mara said the clocks moved at different speeds because people experience time differently," Brystal went on. "Time is *relative*, but length is not—length is a measurement and measurements by definition are *exact*. And technically, we all start to die from the moment we're born—therefore, life and death could be perceived as *the same thing*. So if we want to survive this challenge, we would want the option that gives us a *long death!*"

The delegates stared at her like she was speaking a different language.

"I'm saying we should pick the fourth door," Brystal clarified.

"Great, we've got ourselves a *DOOR!*" Gobzella cheered.

The delegates were confident in Brystal's decision and they headed for the fourth door. However, Spanky stayed put, scratching his beard as he thought about Brystal's analysis.

"Hold on," the dwarf said. "I understand what the Fairy Godmother is saying, *but* her theory depends entirely on the translation. What if *slow and long* or *quick and short* aren't synonyms in the ancient language? What if the translation is purposely trying to mislead us?"

The delegates collectively moaned and started pulling out their hair. They were so confused it gave them headaches.

"This mental challenge is going to drive me *INSANE!*" Gobzella said.

"I'm starting to think Prince Elron picked the right door!" Lucy said.

Ryder calmly raised his hands to get everyone's attention.

"I think we're making this more complicated than we need to," he said. "Even if the translation was flawless, there's no guarantee the riddle is honest. But there are *three* doors left and *five* of us. The most logical thing to do is split up—that way, at least *one* of us will make it to the next challenge."

The delegates gazed at one another, hoping someone would suggest a better option, but splitting up made the most sense.

"I suppose dragon boy is right," Lucy said. "Gosh, if only we had magic to point us in the right direction."

Brystal's posture suddenly straightened—Lucy had unintentionally given her an idea.

"Actually, I have something that might point us in the *wrong* direction," she said.

"Come again?" Lucy asked.

"Everyone just be quiet for a minute—I've got a plan," Brystal said. "It's absolutely crazy—but maybe we need to be a little *mental* to beat the mental challenge."

She removed the silver watch from her pocket and held it close to her ear. *Tick... Tick... Tick... Tick...* The daunting sound instantly sent a wave of anxiety through Brystal's core. *Tick... Tick... Tick... Tick...* She stayed as still and silent as possible, hoping her plan would do the trick. *Tick... Tick... Tick... Tick...*

Decisions, decisions, decisions ...

You'll go mad long before you make the right choice....

The sorcerers knew exactly what they were doing....

They didn't want anyone to actually *survive* the temple....

None of these doors leads to the next challenge....

Death is waiting behind each of them.

For the first time since the curse began, Brystal was thankful when the disturbing thoughts resurfaced. She stood in front of the second door and concentrated on what they had to say.

Ah...

The *shortest* death...

The wisest choice in my opinion...

Guaranteed to be the least painful....

Why suffer more than necessary?

Choose the second door.

Brystal made a mental note of that and moved on to the third door.

Ah...

The *slowest* death...

By far the most excruciating...

But more time to watch your life "flash" before your eyes...

And you'll always be remembered as a martyr....

Choose the third door.

Brystal took another mental note and then stood in front of the fourth and final door.

Ah...

The *longest* death...

Not something I would recommend....

If I were you, I'd get death over with....

Why wait?

Pick another door.

A big smile grew across Brystal's face and she happily tucked the watch back into her pocket.

"I was right—we should take the fourth door," she told the others.

"How do you know?" Lucy asked.

"The curse wants me to take the second or third door—and it would *never* lead me in the right direction," Brystal said.

"Holy reverse psychology!" Lucy exclaimed.

Ryder did another double take. "Sorry—did you just say *curse*?" he asked.

"The last two years have been *wild*," Lucy told him. "We'll give you the bullet points another time. Let's keep this party moving."

The delegates followed Brystal as she confidently stepped through the fourth door. Once they were all on the other side, the door shut behind them and dissolved into the wall. The delegates' hearts were racing as they waited for something dangerous to happen. After a few moments of terror, a row of mounted torches began to ignite on a wall beside them, illuminating a second corridor that led even deeper into the temple. *Brystal had made the right decision.*

"Great work, Fairy Godmother!" Spanky congratulated her.

"Two challenges down, one to go!" Ryder said.

"And don't forget we have to face the deadliest and most dangerous creature to ever *LIVE*!" Gobzella said.

Brystal let out a nervous sigh. "Trust me, *I didn't*."

CHAPTER EIGHTEEN

THE IMMORTAL AGENDA

It was the early hours of the morning and all was quiet in the Eastern Palace. Princess Proxima was wide awake and impatiently pacing the hallway outside Queen Endustria's chambers. The princess's footsteps were soft but her heart couldn't have been heavier. Shortly after she and her grandmother returned from the Conference of Kings, the queen fell gravely ill and hadn't left her bed since. Although the doctors couldn't figure out what was causing the illness, Queen Endustria was so weak she could barely raise her head off her pillow.

Given Queen Endustria's age, her ailing condition wasn't a surprise. Princess Proxima had been preparing for this moment for years, but still, the thought of losing her grandmother was just as unbearable today as it had always been. She couldn't imagine life without the queen's wise and compassionate guidance. Part of Proxima had always hoped her grandmother would live forever, so she would be spared the grief of losing her.

The door to the queen's chambers opened and the royal physician quietly stepped into the hall with a somber face.

"How is she?" Princess Proxima asked.

"She's comfortable, but I've done all I can," the doctor said. "It won't be long."

Princess Proxima burst into tears and turned the other way so the doctor wouldn't see her crying. However, the princess quickly forced herself to suppress the sadness. Soon she would be the new queen and the entire kingdom would be looking to *her* for guidance.

"Is she awake?" the princess asked.

The doctor nodded. "If there's anything you'd like to say to her, now is the time."

Proxima entered her grandmother's chambers and gently shut the door behind her. All the furniture in the spacious bedroom was made from the Eastern Kingdom's prized metals, from the queen's copper vanity to the steel frame of her large bed. The room was also decorated in portraits of past rulers dating back hundreds and hundreds of years, including Queen Immortalia, the very first woman to sit on the Eastern Kingdom's throne. The kingdom had been ruled by women ever since, and just like Queen Endustria and Princess Proxima, their ancestors all shared an uncanny family resemblance.

"Proxima, is that you?"

Queen Endustria's voice was so weak it was barely a whisper.

"Yes, Grandmother—I'm here."

Proxima rushed to the queen's side and held her grandmother's cold hand. Endustria's long white hair covered her pillow like a silver halo shining around her frail head. Although there wasn't much life behind the queen's tired eyes, she beamed at her granddaughter with enough affection to illuminate a cave.

"I'm afraid this is the end," Endustria wheezed.

"You've lived a long and wonderful life," Proxima said. "You are the most extraordinary grandmother in the world and your reign will go down in history as the Eastern Kingdom's most prosperous era. You've earned your rest."

"I am so proud of you, Proxima," she said. "It's been a privilege watching you grow into the woman you are now. Of all the things I've accomplished in my long life, *you* are my greatest success."

The princess held the queen's hand against her face as tears streamed down her cheeks.

"I love you so much, Grandmother," she cried. "Everything I am and everything I have is because of you. You've raised me well and I promise to take good care of the kingdom when you're gone."

Queen Endustria let out a long, anguished sigh.

"Yes…about *the kingdom*," she said. "Before we part, there is something I must confess…A deep family secret that I have kept from you….It pains me greatly to burden you with it now, but I'll rest much easier after I tell you….You deserve to know the truth…."

Proxima tilted her head with curiosity.

"The truth about *what*, Grandmother?" she asked.

Queen Endustria pointed to a steel liquor bar in the corner of her room.

"You'll want a drink for this," she said. "A *strong* one."

The princess's grief was immediately replaced with concern. She and her grandmother had always had a very open relationship—she couldn't imagine the queen keeping any secrets from her, let alone one she needed to confess on her deathbed. Proxima went to the bar and poured herself a generous amount of whiskey. She took a sip and then sat in the chair beside her grandmother's bed.

"All right, I'm ready," Proxima said. "What's the secret?"

"It's about your thirteenth-great-grandmother, Queen Immortalia," she said. "What do you know about her?"

Proxima shrugged. "Just what the history books tell us," she said. "I know she inherited the throne when she was about my age and became the first woman to rule the Eastern Kingdom."

Queen Endustria slowly shook her head.

"Immortalia wasn't *thirty* when she became queen—she was well over *three hundred*."

The princess looked at her grandmother with pity and checked her temperature—obviously the illness had started to affect her brain.

"Grandmother, you aren't feeling well and your mind is confused," she said.

Queen Endustria suddenly grabbed Proxima's wrist and pulled her in close. The old woman glared at her granddaughter with the most serious expression the princess had ever seen.

"Have I ever lied to you before?" the queen asked.

"Never," the princess said.

"Then why on earth would I start *now*?"

Proxima didn't know what to say. Her grandmother might have been dying, but there wasn't an ounce of dishonesty or uncertainty in her weak gaze. The princess's concern skyrocketed and she took a big gulp of her whiskey.

"Go on, then," she said. "How did Immortalia live to be three hundred?"

"Before I tell you, I have to ask you a question," Queen Endustria said. "Do you remember the stories I used to tell you when you were a little girl? In particular, the story about the Daughter of Death?"

"Vaguely," Proxima said.

"Tell me what you remember," the queen said. "Please—it's important."

Proxima did her best to recall the story, but it had been decades since she last heard it.

"In the beginning of time Death gave every person on earth a hundred years to live," the princess said. "He thought a century was plenty of time, but human beings always *mourned* after their loved ones perished, and they always wished for *more life*. To help him understand their pain, Death sent his only daughter to the world of the living. The separation made Death experience grief for the first time. Unfortunately, his daughter liked the world of the living so much, she learned to avoid her father and live forever. So Death invented *disease* and *injury* to cut people's lives short, hoping it would help him find his daughter. But the two never reunited, and Death has been searching for his daughter ever since."

"Good memory," Queen Endustria said. "Now, what about the Demon King? Do you remember that story, too?"

Proxima had to concentrate harder to remember that one.

"I believe so," she said. "According to legend, there

is a civilization of demons that lives in the center of the earth. The demons look like humans, but their bodies are made entirely of flames and they live in a world of chaos and fire. In ancient times, the Demon King led his people to the surface in an attempt to take over the planet. But luckily, the king was defeated by a group of very powerful sorcerers. The sorcerers imprisoned the demons in the center of the earth, but just in case the demons escaped and resurfaced, the sorcerers created a spell to control them. However, there's a prophecy that one day a *new* Demon King will be born among mankind. And when the new king accepts his role and takes his throne, the demons will no longer be vulnerable to the sorcerers' spell."

"Very impressive," Queen Endustria said. "You were paying attention."

"Grandmother, what do these stories have to do with Queen Immortalia?" Proxima asked.

Her grandmother paused for a moment, mustering the little energy she had left.

"Immortalia is from the times of demons and sorcerers," Queen Endustria said. "She was born into slavery and spent her early life being bought, sold, and traded from master to master. Understandably,

Immortalia developed a hatred for mankind and dreamed of seeking revenge—not just on her captors, but on *the whole world*. Eventually, she was sold to a powerful group of sorcerers—the same sorcerers that defeated the King of Demons. While Immortalia was under their control, the sorcerers combined all their most powerful spells into a single manuscript they called the Book of Sorcery—including the spell that controlled the demons. They hid the book in a vault with their most prized possessions and then forced their slaves to build a magnificent temple around the vault to protect it. Immortalia knew if she got her hands on the Book of Sorcery, there would be nothing to stop her from destroying the world. But the temple was incredibly dangerous—the sorcerers designed a series of challenges to complete before reaching the vault—and if Immortalia was going to survive, she needed help."

The princess moved to the edge of her seat.

"From who?" she asked.

"*Death*," the queen said. "Immortalia escaped the sorcerers by jumping into the heart of a fiery volcano. When she crossed into the realm between life and death, Immortalia begged Death to let her live so she could seek revenge on the world. When Death refused, Immortalia made him an offer he *couldn't* refuse. She told Death about the Book of Sorcery and claimed it contained an *elimination spell* that was capable of destroying *anything.* In exchange for eternal life, she promised Death she would retrieve the Book of Sorcery and use the elimination spell on his daughter, so they would be reunited at last."

"And Death agreed to this?" Proxima asked.

"Like a desperate fool," Queen Endustria said. "And so Death gave Immortalia the gift of *immortality*—a term he coined after *her* namesake. Immortalia spent her first two centuries inside the temple, repeating each of the challenges thousands and thousands of times until she reached the vault. By the time she got her hands on the Book of Sorcery, the sorcerers were long gone and the world had drastically changed, but Immortalia's thirst for carnage was stronger than ever. She decided to abandon her promise to Death and focus solely on gaining control of the demons."

"Did she manage it?" Proxima asked.

"There was only one problem," Queen Endustria said. "In order to control the demons, Immortalia had to *free them first.* The sorcerers had sealed the entrance to the demons' world with a mighty gate. And finding the gate wasn't a challenge Immortalia could complete on her own—she would need the resources of a *queen*. So Immortalia spent the next century seducing and marrying men of nobility, slowly working her way up the social ladder that would eventually make her queen. Once she was on the throne, she spent the next two hundred years forcing prisoners to dig long tunnels under the earth in search of the demons' gate."

"But how could she have lived so long without being discovered? Surely someone must have noticed a queen who wasn't *aging*?" Proxima asked.

"Naturally, but Immortalia knew *exactly* how to shield her immortality," Queen Endustria said. "Over the years, she had many daughters and granddaughters. As her descendants grew older, Immortalia had to wear disguises to give the illusion that *she* was getting older, too. Whenever she reached an age that was suspiciously old, Immortalia would kill one of her descendants and take their identity."

Proxima turned to the portraits on the wall and shuddered. Until now, she had never questioned her ancestors' remarkable family resemblance—but it suddenly made sense why all the queens looked so similar.

"You mean, Immortalia has been queen more than once?" she said.

"Oh yes...," her grandmother said. "Many, many, many times."

The discovery made the princess feel ill and she clutched her stomach.

"How was Immortalia stopped?" she asked.

A twinkle appeared in Queen Endustria's eyes and her wrinkled lips stretched into a sly grin. The old woman sat up in her bed with the ease of a young woman.

"She *wasn't* stopped," she said.

"Wait... *Immortalia is still alive?*" Proxima asked.

"Alive and well," Queen Endustria said. "And after centuries of searching, she *finally* found the demons' gate and set them free. Unfortunately, it wouldn't be wise for Immortalia to reveal herself until all her enemies are defeated. If she wants to conquer the world, she'll have to perform *identity theft* one more time."

Suddenly, the pain in Proxima's stomach surpassed any cramps she had experienced before. Her whiskey glass slipped from her grip and shattered across the floor. The princess dropped to her knees, wrapped her arms around her torso, and moaned in agony.

"It's . . . it's . . . it's you!" the princess gasped. "You're Immortalia!"

Immortalia's grin grew into a full smile as she watched Proxima struggle.

"I'm so glad to get that off my chest," she said. "Of all the descendants I've killed over the years, you were by far my favorite. I didn't want there to be any lies between us before you died."

"You . . . you . . . you poisoned me!" Proxima coughed.

"Please tell Death I said hello—he won't be seeing me anytime soon," Immortalia said.

Proxima's eyes fluttered shut and she collapsed on top of the broken glass. Once the princess stopped breathing, Immortalia cracked her neck and leisurely stretched out in bed.

"What a relief," she said. "This disguise was getting insufferable."

Immortalia removed the wrinkled mask, gray wig, and pair of liver-spotted gloves that had made her look like the elderly Queen Endustria. She then hopped out of bed and placed the disguise on Proxima. She also switched clothes with the princess, and then heaved her dead body into the bed. In a matter of minutes, the women had flawlessly traded identities.

A knock came from the inside of a wall that was painted with a colorful mural.

"Ma'am, have you finished?" asked a gruff voice.

"Yes, come in," Immortalia said.

A secret door slid open and a man covered in dirt stepped inside the room. His sunken eyes grew wide at the sight of the dead princess and he lowered his head in respect.

"Don't look surprised," Immortalia said. "You've known this was coming since she was born. Have all the prisoners been buried?"

"Yes, ma'am," the man said. "You and I are the only people left alive who know about the gate."

"Excellent," Immortalia said. "Then the time has finally come."

The Immortal walked to an iron desk in the corner of the chambers. She twisted and pulled the drawer's knobs in a particular order and a secret shelf popped out from the side of the desk. The shelf contained a single book with a decrepit leather cover and worn parchment pages. The cover was designed with several majestic symbols, including the earth, the sun, and the moon to represent the times of day. A rock, a breeze, a raindrop, and a flame to represent the elements of earth, wind, water, and fire. There was also a blossom, a green leaf, an autumn leaf, and a snowflake to represent spring, summer, fall, and winter. Immortalia stroked the book as if it was a beloved pet she had been reunited with.

"Ma'am, what about me?" the man asked. "Am I free to go?"

Immortalia eyed the man with a mischievous smile.

"Of course you are," she said. "After a lifetime of service, you've earned a vacation. But do me one last favor before you go?"

"What sort of favor, ma'am?" he asked.

"Let's toast to our success," she said.

Immortalia poured two glasses of the poisoned whiskey.

"To summoning demons," the man said, and raised his glass.

"To summoning demons," she said. "God knows I've waited long enough."

CHAPTER NINETEEN

THE BLESSING OF A CURSE

Deep within the Temple of Knowledge, Brystal and the delegates cautiously walked down the corridor that led to the next challenge. At the end of the corridor, the group found a square chamber that was the size of a ballroom. At the very end of the room, a flight of stone steps led to a pair of double doors that were bound shut by thick chains and a steel lock. A giant glass heart hovered in the air above their heads. The heart was hollow and contained a golden key that was so bright it illuminated the entire room. Five trails of white smoke orbited the glass heart like the ghosts of shooting stars.

"Judging by the big heart, this must be the *emotional challenge*," Lucy said.

"I'm guessing those double doors are the way out of here," Ryder speculated.

"I wonder how we're supposed to get the key," Spanky said.

"This looks like a job for a *DWARF*!" Gobzella exclaimed. "Go get it, *SPANKY*!"

Before the dwarf knew what was happening, the goblin grabbed him by the waist and launched him into the air. Spanky tried to grab the glass heart but his hands went right through it as if the heart and the key were made of air. Gobzella caught the dwarf on his way down.

"It's no use—the heart and the key aren't *solid*," Spanky said. "How can we unlock a door without a real key?"

"I bet they're more symbolic than physical," Brystal said. "Remember, this is the emotional challenge— it won't be like the other challenges. It's going to test our sentiments and our character, it could torment us with fear and existential questions, or try to attack our confidence and squash our belief systems."

"Reminds me of a director I worked with," Lucy said with a laugh.

"So how does the challenge start?" Ryder asked.

The delegates stood directly below the heart for a few minutes and waited for something to happen, but nothing changed. They looked around the chamber for a sign or a plaque with instructions, but they didn't find anything that explained the challenge.

"Check out the floor," Spanky said. "You think *those* mean something?"

The dwarf pointed to the floor and the delegates discovered five black tiles engraved with footprints. The tiles were evenly spaced in a big circle around the room, like the numbers of a clock.

"That's interesting. There are five sets of footprints and five of us," Ryder noted.

"The temple must know there are five of us left," Brystal said. "I bet the challenge will begin as soon as we each stand on a tile."

"Well, here goes nothing," Lucy said.

Each of the delegates stood on a tile, placing their feet over the engraved footprints. Once they were all in position, the tiles sank a few inches into the floor like the buttons of a machine. *CLANK!* Suddenly, four metal cages dropped from the ceiling. The cages trapped Lucy, Ryder, Spanky, and Gobzella where they stood—but strangely, a cage didn't fall over Brystal. The delegates looked toward the ceiling, expecting another cage to drop at any moment, but a fifth never appeared.

As they gazed upward, the five trails of white smoke were released from orbiting the glass heart. The trails zoomed through the chamber, bouncing off the walls and ceiling, and eventually landed inside the delegates' cages. The white smoke grew into different shapes and silhouettes, it gained color and texture, and soon apparitions of people and creatures appeared.

Ryder was astonished when a handsome man in a blue sailor uniform manifested before him.

"Father?" he asked in disbelief. "Is that you?"

"Hello, son," the sailor said.

Ryder went as pale as a ghost. He had never seen his father before, but the man wasn't hard to recognize.

The two shared so many similar features—the same eyes, nose, and jawline—it was like Ryder was looking at an older version of himself.

"Wait . . . you know who I am?" he asked.

"I've known about you since you were born," his father said. "Your mother wrote to me and told me she gave birth to a son."

"Then why haven't you tried to contact me? Why haven't you come to visit?"

The sailor laughed. "Oh please—you think I want a disappointment like *you* in my life?"

"*Disappointment?*" Ryder asked.

"What kind of man devotes his life to a dying breed of *monsters?*" the sailor asked, and scowled with disgust. "You and your mother lead *pathetic* and *pointless* existences—I'm ashamed to call you a *son.*"

Ryder was shocked by his father's cruel words and didn't know what to say.

Inside Lucy's cage, the second smoke trail materialized into a man and a woman. The man had a tall top hat and a gold earring in his left ear. The woman had several beaded necklaces and a scarf over her head. The couple also wore theatrical makeup as if they had just stepped off a stage.

"Mom? Dad?" Lucy asked. "What are you doing here?"

"Hello, Lucy," Mr. Goose said. "It's been a long time."

"Not long enough, if you ask me," Mrs. Goose sneered.

"What's *that* supposed to mean?" Lucy asked.

"Haven't you heard?" Mr. Goose asked. "The Goose Troupe is the most popular band in the world! We've been performing to sold-out crowds every night in the biggest venues around the globe!"

"That's wonderful!" Lucy said. "Maybe I could join you for a reunion show?"

"Oh sweetie," Mrs. Goose said with a patronizing laugh. "Why do you think we're so successful now? People are coming in droves to see us perform because *you're not in the band anymore.* We should have kicked you out years ago!"

Lucy shook her head in disbelief.

"You . . . you . . . *you aren't serious,*" she said.

"Let's face it, you were a *horrible tambourine player*," Mr. Goose said. "Your mother and I couldn't wait to get rid of you. We're lucky we found the perfect excuse."

Lucy's eyes welled with tears and her bottom lip quivered.

"No...no... *that's not true!*" she said. "You sent me to live with the fairies because you loved me.... You wanted me to be with people who understood me.... You wanted Madame Weatherberry to help me develop my magic!"

Mr. and Mrs. Goose looked at each other and howled with laughter.

"Sure, Lucy," Mrs. Goose said. "Keep telling yourself that."

In Gobzella's cage, the third smoke trail transformed into four rambunctious goblin boys. They had insidious grins and devious twinkles in their eyes as they bounced around Gobzella and climbed up the walls of her cage.

"I don't believe it—it's the boys from *SCHOOL!*" Gobzella exclaimed. "I haven't seen them since I was a *GOBLING!*"

"A *gobling?*" The first boy laughed. "Did you hear that, fellas?"

"Gobzella thinks she was a *gobling!*" said the second boy.

"Impossible," said the third boy. "That implies she was small."

"Gobzella has *never* been small!" The fourth boy laughed. "Well, small for a *hippo*, maybe!"

The boys chuckled like a pack of banshees and their laughter echoed throughout the chamber. Gobzella's face flushed, turning a dark shade of green, and her thin nostrils flared.

"How *DARE you*!" she told them. "You can't speak to me like *THAT* anymore! I'm *GROWN* now!"

"Oh, no arguments there," said the first boy.

"You're certainly *grown*!" said the second boy.

"Yeah, a full-grown *whale*!" said the third boy.

"Come on, fellas—don't be mean," said the fourth boy. *"That's an insult to whales!"*

Gobzella covered her ears to tune out the boys' mean comments.

"This can't be *REAL*!" she said. "I left them in the *PAST*! They can't hurt me *ANYMORE*!"

Inside Spanky's cage, the fourth trail of white smoke sank into the floor. A few moments later, nine short and hairy creatures crawled out from beneath the ground and surrounded the dwarf. Each of them had a long snout, sharp fingernails, and big front teeth. The creatures glared at the dwarf with their beady little eyes and they spoke in squeaky yet sinister voices.

"*Mole people!*" Spanky shouted.

"Hello, Spanky," said the first mole. "We meet at last."

"*I knew you were real!*" the dwarf declared. "You may have fooled the world, but you won't fool me!"

"You've been trying to expose us for *decades*," said the second mole.

"How's that working out for you? Any luck so far?" asked the third mole.

"I've been gathering evidence!" Spanky grumbled. "You've covered your tracks so far, but one day I'll have enough proof—one day everyone will know the truth!"

"Oh Spanky, who are you kidding?" asked the fourth mole.

"You'll never expose us because *we don't exist!*" said the fifth mole.

"Why do you keep lying to yourself?" asked the sixth mole.

"Isn't it time you faced the truth?" asked the seventh mole.

"You invented *us* because you couldn't take responsibility for *your* mistakes!" said the eighth mole.

"We aren't your enemy—we're your *excuse!*" said the ninth.

Spanky turned bright red and beads of sweat appeared on his forehead.

"*Lies!*" the dwarf hollered. "You've been sabotaging the world for centuries! And you've been framing me since I was a child!"

"*Framing you?*" The first mole snickered. "You mean, like your first day at the *School of Small Miners at Large?* When you dropped the bag of diamonds down the well?"

"That was *you!*" Spanky said. "You wanted to get me in trouble!"

"What about the time you hit that poor, innocent bear cub with the mine cart?" the second mole asked.

"*You* pushed him in front of the cart!" the dwarf exclaimed.

"Or that time you failed the management test and *Mr. Slate* became the leader of the mines?" the seventh mole asked.

"You *switched* our answers!" Spanky shouted.

"That's the only reason I didn't get the job! It was *you—it's always been you!*"

Suddenly, the tiles under the caged delegates' feet all turned into quicksand. Ryder, Lucy, Gobzella, and Spanky slowly started sinking into the floor—however, they were so fixated on the apparitions in their cages, none of them even noticed the sand. The more the apparitions taunted them, the faster the delegates sank.

Brystal's eyes darted back and forth, desperate to understand what was happening—and why none of it was happening to her.

"I don't get it," Brystal thought aloud. "Why isn't the challenge affecting me?"

"That's no mystery."

Brystal jumped when she heard a very familiar voice behind her. She looked over her shoulder and realized the fifth apparition had appeared—for *her.* Lounging on the steps in the back of the chamber, Brystal saw *herself*—but this version of Brystal was the exact opposite of her. She had dark makeup around her sunken eyes, she wore a pantsuit that was pitch-black, and her long hair was filled with dead flowers.

"I know you," Brystal said. "You're the voice in my head—*you're the curse!*"

"Finally, we get to meet face-to-face," the curse said. "Thank goodness, too—I was getting so bored in your subconscious all by myself."

Brystal studied the apparition, and it slowly dawned on her what was happening.

"The emotional challenge is forcing people to face their *inner demons*," she said.

The curse gave her a condescending round of applause.

"Very good," she said. "You're clever when you want to be."

"Then why aren't *we* in a cage together?" Brystal asked. "Why am I not sinking in quicksand like the others?"

"I thought that part would be obvious," the curse said. "Because *you've* already faced your inner demons."

Brystal was confused. "I have?" she asked.

"Last year, in the fortress, you learned how to silence me," the curse explained. "And if that wasn't bad enough, in the mental challenge, you learned how to use me for *good*. I'll never be able to sabotage you again after *that* little stunt. Unfortunately, your friends are still vulnerable to the negative thoughts in their heads. Until now, they've never had to confront the dark whispers that keep *them* up at night. So the challenge has trapped them each in a cage of insecurity, it's provoking them with their greatest fears, and they're sinking into the depths of their own despair. It's rather poetic, don't you think?"

Brystal checked on the delegates and saw they were already up to their waists in the quicksand. In a few short moments, they'd disappear completely.

"What happens if they sink all the way?" she asked.

"They'll die," the curse said. **"But luckily, you'll get to move on without them."**

"But if they learn how to silence their own disturbing thoughts—like I did—they can beat the challenge, too?" Brystal asked.

"Yes, but as you'll recall, it was much easier said than done," the curse said. **"It took you *months* to defeat me. And from the looks of it, your friends only have a matter of minutes before they're gone forever. If I were you, I would spend this time saying my good-byes."**

Brystal shuddered as she remembered the night she and her friends battled the Righteous Brotherhood.

"That was the toughest night of my life," she said.

"Oh, I remember," the curse said. **"You crossed an impressive bridge—a bridge your friends aren't strong enough to cross."**

"Yes, but *I* didn't have anyone to help me," Brystal said. "I had to learn to silence you all on my own. It was difficult and it was painful—I had to summon strength I didn't know I had—but now I know *exactly* how to help someone else go through it. And perhaps that's *the blessing of a curse*? I went to hell and back, but I learned where all the roads are!"

The new realization made Brystal smile from ear to ear, and judging by the curse's reaction, she figured she was onto something significant, too. The curse let out a long, disappointed sigh and slowly shook her head.

"There you go again, turning a negative into a positive," she said. **"Misery loved company until you came along. Good-bye, Brystal."**

The curse faded back into a cloud of white smoke and evaporated from the chamber.

Fueled by the new discovery, Brystal ran to the top of the steps and stood where all the delegates could see her. She removed her dragon-bone sword and banged it against the chained double doors as hard as she could. The noise temporarily distracted the delegates from the apparitions and they all turned toward her.

"Everyone, listen to me!" she pleaded. "I know exactly how you're feeling! I used to be paralyzed by fear, I used to be plagued with doubts, and I used to let my insecurities overrule my voice of reason. I thought my thoughts were telling me the truth, I thought I deserved to feel the pain and despair they caused me, and I thought I was broken in a way that couldn't be fixed—*but none of that was real*! The challenge is using your fears and insecurities to stop you from moving forward! Whatever the apparitions are saying to make you feel rejected, untalented, ugly, or ashamed is a *lie—but only you can prove them wrong*!"

As if a veil had been lifted from their eyes, the delegates finally looked down and realized they were sinking into quicksand. They grunted and screamed as they tried to pull themselves out of the challenge's trap—physically and emotionally.

"Ignore her!" the sailor told Ryder. "Listening to women is what's made you so soft! If you had been raised by a *father*, you wouldn't be such an embarrassment! You'd be a *real man* and a son I could be proud of!"

Ryder went quiet. His father's choice of words had made him realize something for the very first time.

"But I *did* have a father," he said. "My *mother* was my father—she had to be both parents because you abandoned me! She taught me to be smart, compassionate, strong, brave, loyal, and proud without any help from you! And if that's not what a *real man* is, then I have no interest in becoming one!"

"No!" the sailor barked. "You'll never feel complete without a father! *You need me!*"

"You're wrong," Ryder said. "I won't make the same mistakes as the elf prince! I've *never* needed you or your approval—and I certainly don't need you now!"

All of a sudden, Ryder stopped sinking into the quicksand. His metal cage turned into dust and the sailor vanished in a smoky haze. Brystal sprinted to Ryder's side and helped him out of the sand.

"You did it, Ryder!" she cheered. "You beat the challenge!"

"Thanks for the guidance," he said. "I couldn't have done it without you."

Across the room, Lucy was up to her chest in the quicksand. The apparitions of her parents loomed over her sinking body, blocking her friends from view.

"You won't get out of this as easily as *him*," Mr. Goose told her.

"Deep down, you know we're telling you the truth," Mrs. Goose said. "Deep down, you know you were a lousy musician and we're better off without you!"

Lucy rolled her eyes and let out a loud groan.

"*Sooooooo what?*" she snapped. "There are worse things in life than being kicked out of a family band! And who cares if I ever perform again? I don't need applause or affection from *strangers* to be fulfilled—I have *friends*! And they make me feel more *loved* than a sold-out crowd ever could! Living with the fairies was *the best* thing that ever happened to me! And I wouldn't trade it for all the praise and fame in the world!"

Just like Ryder, after confronting the apparitions, Lucy stopped sinking into the quicksand. Her cage disintegrated into a pile of dust and her parents faded from sight. Brystal and Ryder each grabbed Lucy by an arm and lifted her out of the sand.

"Way to go, Lucy!" Brystal said. "I'm so proud of you!"

"Thanks for coaching me through it," she said.

"For the record, I think you're a *great* musician," Brystal said.

"No, the apparitions were right—the Goose Troupe is better off without me," Lucy confessed. "But in my defense, what band *isn't* better off without a tambourine player?"

In the next cage, the goblin boys became more rambunctious and restless than before. They leaped from wall to wall, whacking Gobzella upside the head and taunting her with mean jokes. Gobzella tried with all her might to pull herself out of the quicksand, but she sank deeper and deeper after every cruel punch line.

"Gobzella is so big, she got a fur coat and all the mammals went extinct!" said the first boy.

"Gobzella is so ugly, she made her own reflection puke!" said the second boy.

"Gobzella is so heavy, I pictured her in my head and my neck broke!" said the third.

"Gobzella is so scary, her face emptied a haunted house!" said the fourth.

Gobzella growled angrily and slammed her hands against the sand.

"All right, that is *ENOUGH*!" she shouted. "Your

mean comments may have hurt me when I was young, but they also made me *STRONG*! And I became the best warrior the Goblin Territory has ever *SEEN*! And now look at *ME*! I'm exploring ancient temples and saving the *WORLD*! And what are *YOU* doing? What became of *YOUR* lives? You're probably sitting in your gross goblin homes, trapped in your bad goblin marriages, with a bunch of goblin kids running around breaking your *STUFF*! So who's laughing *NOW*?"

One by one, the four goblin boys disappeared, and Gobzella's cage crumbled into dust. She stopped sinking into the quicksand and was able to pull herself out of the floor. Brystal, Lucy, and Ryder cheered for the goblin—however, there was no time to celebrate her triumph. The delegates turned to Spanky's cage and saw the dwarf was up to his neck in the quicksand. The mole people circled him like predators as he struggled to keep his head above the sand.

"Poor, poor, little Spanky," said the first mole.

"If only he could admit his mistakes, he would survive the challenge," said the second mole.

"Come on, just say you were wrong," said the third mole.

"*You* dropped the diamonds down the well because *you* were clumsy," said the fourth mole.

"*You* hit the bear cub with the mine cart because *you* were careless," said the fifth mole.

"And *you* failed the management test because *you* weren't smart enough," said the sixth mole.

"You have no one to blame but yourself," said the seventh mole.

"Just confess and all of this will stop," said the eighth mole.

"*Never!*" the dwarf yelled passionately. "*None of that was my fault—it was all you!*"

While the other delegates had completed the challenge by *embracing their truths*, Brystal realized Spanky's challenge was about *embracing his dishonesty*. She knelt beside his cage, desperate to talk some sense into him before it was too late.

"Spanky, if the mole people are telling the truth, you've got to admit it!" she said.

"They can't be trusted!" he said. "Don't let them deceive you!"

"*The dwarf's in denial! The dwarf's in denial! The dwarf's in denial!*" the mole people chanted.

"Spanky, there's no shame in admitting you've made mistakes in the past," she said. "We've all done things we aren't proud of—and sometimes those things are so painful, it's easier to come up with *lies* instead of taking responsibility. When we blame our mistakes on other people—when we come up with *conspiracies* to justify our actions—we never grow from our mistakes! This is your chance to take all of that shame and turn it into something good!"

"I'm sorry, Fairy Godmother," Spanky said. "I *won't* let them win."

The dwarf took a deep breath and let the quicksand pull him out of sight. Brystal, Lucy, Ryder, and Gobzella screamed as their friend disappeared. Above them, the floating glass heart burst into hundreds of pieces and the golden key flew across the room to unlock the double doors. The delegates heard the chains and lock unraveling from the doors, but none turned to look at it. Even though they had beaten the challenge, the delegates waited with bated breath, praying that Spanky would come back, but the dwarf never returned.

"I can't believe he choose *death* over facing the truth," Lucy said.

"He was a casualty of his own *CONSPIRACIES!*" Gobzella said.

Brystal wiped the tears running down her face, wishing there was more she could have done to help the dwarf.

"The most dangerous lies are the lies we tell ourselves," she said.

CHAPTER TWENTY

RAISING DEMONS

The fairies and witches were running out of places to look for Xanthous. In the last three days, they had thoroughly searched the cold mountains of the North, they had combed through the thick forests of the West, and they had explored the foothills of the East—but still, they hadn't found a trace of their friend anywhere. If they weren't so concerned about Xanthous, his friends would have been impressed by how well he had covered his tracks.

The only place the fairies and witches hadn't searched was the Righteous Empire—and *none* of them wanted to set foot in there. However, their desire to find Xanthous outweighed their reservations, and they all agreed to go.

To attract the least amount of attention, the fairies and witches waited until it was dark to travel into the Empire. Emerelda cast a spell over their golden carriage and unicorns and disguised them as a regular coach and horses. They decided to begin their search in the south of the Empire and work their way north. As the coach and horses arrived at the southernmost point of the Southern Shore, the sight of an abandoned structure sent shivers down their spines.

"The fortress," Sprout said with a nervous lump in her throat. "There's something I was hoping to never see again."

"Do we *have* to go in there?" Skylene asked.

"Don't worry, it's probably empty," Emerelda assured them. "The Righteous Brotherhood and the Army of the Dead are all in Chariot Hills with the emperor. They have no reason to be here anymore. See, their flag isn't even raised."

"Why would Xanthous hide in *there* of all places?" Tangerina said. "Hasn't he been through enough trauma already?"

"No one in their right mind would expect Xanthous to be hiding in the fortress. That's why it would be the *perfect* place for him," Emerelda said. "It's worth taking a look."

"Mrs. Vee? Did you bring any cooking utensils with you?" Skylene asked. "That really saved our skins last time we were here."

"I packed my finest silverware and my best set of pots and pans," Mrs. Vee said. "I'm ready for battle or an impromptu dinner party—and to be honest, I'm not sure which one I'm more afraid of! *HA-HA!*"

The coach and horses parked beside the entrance to the fortress and the passengers stepped outside. The fortress was just as unsettling as the fairies and witches remembered. It seemed more like the remains of a massive creature than the ruins of an ancient structure. The weathered walls looked like the skin of a decaying carcass and its five crumpling towers stretched toward the night sky like the fingers of a giant skeletal hand.

"This p-p-place gives me the c-c-creeps!" Beebee shuddered.

Pip sniffed the air. "It reeks of *fear* and *death*," she said.

"Gosh, I've missed it," Stitches said with a crooked smirk.

The fairies and witches split into groups of two and searched the fortress. Skylene and Mrs. Vee searched the lower levels, Beebee and Pip searched the upper floors, and Stitches and Sprout searched the towers. Meanwhile, Emerelda and Tangerina walked through the vast courtyard in the very center. Everything they looked at reminded them of the horrible night when they were almost killed by the Righteous Brotherhood and the Army of the Dead. Unfortunately, they didn't find a single clue of Xanthous anywhere.

"Gosh, he's really playing hard to get," Tangerina said as she searched the courtyard. "Why is he trying so hard to stay away from *us*? We're his friends! We could help him!"

"He's trying to protect us from himself," Emerelda said. "But if *we're* having such a hard time finding him, let's hope the alchemists are, too. I just pray he can keep it up until Brystal and Lucy get back with the Book of Sorcery."

"*If* they get back with the Book of Sorcery,"

Tangerina said. "We should probably start thinking of a plan B in case they don't return."

Emerelda let out a defeated sigh and sat on a pile of rubble.

"You're right," Emerelda said. "But Brystal still has a week left to live—let's not give up on her just yet."

The girls were distracted when they noticed Stitches on the roof of the tallest tower. The witch was whistling and waving both of her arms to get the fairies' attention.

"Hey, guys—there's something you should see!" she called to them.

"This better not be another one of your pranks, Stitches!" Tangerina warned her. "If we go up there and find *another* skeleton in a suggestive position, I'm going to push you out a window!"

"No, it's nothing like that," Stitches said. "Just wait a second—you won't miss it!"

Emerelda and Tangerina exchanged a curious look, but a couple of moments later, they understood exactly what Stitches was talking about. The Southern Shore was covered in a dark shadow as a group of fluffy clouds blew in from the ocean and blocked the full moon. The girls could see the roofs and spires of the Alchemy

Institute peeking out of the clouds as the entire campus drifted over their heads and floated into the North.

"It's the Alchemy Institute!" Emerelda exclaimed.

"But why is it moving? Where are the alchemists going?" Tangerina asked.

Emerelda asked herself the same question and was suddenly filled with dread—there was only *one* reasonable explanation she could come up with.

"Oh no. *Xanthous!*" she gasped. "The alchemists must have found him! *We have to follow them!*"

· • ★ • ·

Just as Dr. States and the Righteous Emperor had discussed, that night at midnight, the alchemists arrived in Chariot Hills to safely eliminate Xanthous Hayfield. The Alchemy Institute descended into Chariot Hills and hovered above the town square. Dr. States and the other alchemists were gathered on a balcony below the grand armillary sphere in the very center of the campus. From there, the alchemists could see the entire city and the countryside surrounding it. After waiting several minutes, the Righteous Emperor, his High Commander, and the rest of the Righteous

Brotherhood appeared on the roof of the Righteous Palace to greet the visitors—but oddly, not a single soldier from the Army of the Dead was with them.

"Good morning, gentlemen," Seven called up to them. "Welcome to Chariot Hills! I hope you had a pleasant journey."

"I'm afraid we don't have time for pleasantries, Your Highness," Dr. States said. "We need to perform the elimination at once. If you could kindly hand over Mr. Hayfield, we'll get it over with."

A snide smile grew across the emperor's face.

"Actually, Dr. States, I've had second thoughts about our *agreement*," Seven said.

"What do you mean, *second thoughts*?" he asked.

"I've given the situation a lot of thought and have decided to keep the boy myself," Seven said. "I'm not sure I can *trust* you with him."

Dr. States grunted impatiently. "For God's sake, this is no time to start a debate about *trust*," he said. "The world is in danger! We have to destroy the boy before he destroys us all!"

"I agree, the world *is* in danger—but not from *the boy*," Seven said. "After visiting your institute I'm deeply concerned about you and your colleagues' intentions. You claim you have no interest in gaining power, but I say the technology you possess tells a different story. I say you're just waiting for the right opportunity to strike, and enslave us all."

Dr. States was appalled by the emperor's accusations.

"Your Highness, we are men of *science*!" the alchemist declared. "We have absolutely no interest in attacking you or your Empire!"

"That doesn't mean you won't change your mind," Seven said. "You could easily use your *sciences* against me and my people if you wanted to. What's stopping you from turning Mr. Hayfield into another one of your experiments? What's stopping you from harnessing the boy's powers and turning him into a *weapon*? No man should have *that* kind of power—and for the world's sake, I believe it's my responsibility to stop you."

BAM! BAM! The alchemists heard the sound of explosions going off all around them. *BAM! BAM!* The Army of the Dead appeared on the rooftops of the town square and fired cannons at the institute. *BAM! BAM!* Instead of cannonballs, the cannons blasted enormous harpoons connected to long chains. *BAM! BAM!* The harpoons punctured the walls of the different facilities. *BAM! BAM!* The dead soldiers cranked the chains with giant reels, pulling the Alchemy Institute deeper and deeper into the town square.

The alchemists were outraged as they watched the Army of the Dead assault their campus. Dr. States and the Righteous Emperor locked eyes, exchanging a heated glance.

"So you've led us into a trap," Dr. States said. "I should have known better. Men like *me* have been fighting men like *you* since the beginning of time. For far too long, alchemists have sat in the shadows while tyrants spread ignorance and hatred. It's time we took a stand and put an end to it! So if it's a war you want, *a war you shall get*!"

The alchemist tapped his cane on the floor four times. Suddenly, the institute was filled with the sound of marching—but instead of the thumping of boots, the Righteous Emperor heard the clanking of metal. All the doors throughout the campus burst open and hundreds of Magbots emerged. The Magbots formed a protective line around the Alchemy Institute, ready to defend the campus at all costs.

The Righteous Emperor gave the High Commander an eager nod.

"*Begin the attack*," he ordered.

The fairies and witches raced through the country-side of the Righteous Empire aboard their disguised carriage. They followed the Alchemy Institute from the ground as closely as they could, but the floating campus eventually got ahead of them and disappeared from sight. Soon, the city of Chariot Hills appeared on the horizon and Emerelda spotted the institute hovering above it.

"There it is!" Emerelda told the others. "They've stopped in Chariot Hills!"

She snapped her fingers and the horses charged ahead, racing even faster than before. However, when they were just a few miles outside the city, the horses neighed with fear and came to an unexpected halt.

"What's gotten into them?" Skylene asked.

The fairies and witches poked their heads out the window to see what had spooked the horses. A few acres away, they saw a woman standing in the middle of the countryside all by herself. The woman wore a metallic gown, a headdress that was shaped like the jaws of a wrench, and she was clutching an old book tightly to her chest.

"That's Princess Proxima from the Eastern Kingdom," Tangerina said. "What is she doing out here by herself?"

The fairies and witches stepped outside the coach to get a better look. The princess opened the book and read a passage aloud.

"*Demis-dule demis-dole, demis-see demis-sole!*" Proxima chanted.

"What did she say?" Sprout asked.

"If I didn't know any better, I'd say she was casting an old spell," Mrs. Vee said.

Pip caught a whiff of something in the air.

"Is it just me, or does anyone else smell *smoke*?" she asked.

Before the others had a chance to smell it, the ground started rumbling beneath their feet. The fairies and witches saw bright flashes of light throughout the countryside. When their eyes adjusted, they realized *fire* was rising out of the ground! In a matter of seconds, the entire countryside was covered in *flames*! And although the closest fire was a few acres away from them, the fairies and witches could feel its warmth as if it were just a few feet away.

"Why is fire coming out of the ground?!" Tangerina yelled.

Emerelda instantly recognized the fire—she would *never* forget it as long as she lived.

"This is the fire that attacked the Eastern Kingdom!" she said.

"But Xanthous isn't anywhere near here!" Skylene said. "This proves he's *innocent* after all!"

"Proxima's the one causing the fire!" Emerelda said. "*She's* been behind the fire all along!"

"Hey, dames, do you notice anything *funny* about those flames?" Stitches asked.

At first the fairies and witches didn't know what Stitches was talking about, but as they studied the flames, they quickly realized what the witch meant. The fire wasn't just hotter than regular fire—the fire was actually hundreds of *people* whose bodies were made entirely out of flames.

The fairies and witches couldn't believe what they were seeing and looked to one another in bewilderment.

"The fire's *alive*!" Sprout exclaimed.

"I've never seen anything like this in my life!" Mrs. Vee said.

"What kind of magic is this?" Tangerina asked.

"So that's why the fire was chasing us in Ironhand—*it had legs!*" Emerelda said.

Princess Proxima was ecstatic as she watched more and more fire people crawl out of the ground to join her. Soon she was surrounded by thousands and thousands of fiery bodies, but strangely, neither the princess nor her book were harmed by the heat the fire people emitted.

Proxima started marching toward Chariot Hills and the fire people followed her. As they moved across the land, they left a trail of destruction behind them. The ground was scorched under their feet, the sky filled with dark smoke, and small brush fires spread in every direction. If something didn't stop the fire soon, the whole Righteous Empire—perhaps the world— would burn to a crisp.

"Dr. States was right," Emerelda said. "The fire is going to destroy the world!"

"How can we stop it?" Tangerina asked.

Emerelda went silent as she thought about it. She recalled something Dr. States had said previously that caught her attention—and it gave her a *very* troubling idea. It was absurd, it was irresponsible, and it made her sick to her stomach just thinking about it—but Emerelda didn't see another solution.

"Fire destroys—*ice* preserves," Emerelda said. "And we're going to need a *lot* of ice."

Tangerina's whole body went stiff.

"Em, please tell me you aren't saying what I *think* you're saying," she said.

"Actually, I *am*," Emerelda confessed.

"No—absolutely not!" Tangerina objected. "There's got to be another option!"

"We don't have time to think of one! If we don't do something drastic, the entire kingdom is going to go up in smoke!" Emerelda said, and quickly turned to the witches. "Stitches? Sprout? Beebee? Pip? Did you bring your broomsticks?"

"W-w-we never leave the house w-w-without them," Beebee said.

"Good," Emerelda said. "I need you guys to fly us to the Northern Mountains. *Now*."

CHAPTER TWENTY-ONE

THE SORCERERS' VAULT

In the chamber of the emotional challenge, Brystal and the delegates stood before the double doors at the top of the steps. They were equally encouraged and exhausted after completing the physical, mental, and emotional challenges, but *nothing* could physically, mentally, or emotionally prepare them for what was about to happen next. The deadliest and most dangerous creature that ever existed was lurking somewhere beyond the doors, and even though they didn't know what to expect, they all had an eerie feeling that the creature was expecting them.

"Remember, this is the end," Brystal reminded the others. "If we survive whatever is waiting behind these doors, *we win*."

Lucy, Ryder, and Gobzella took a deep breath and tightened their grips on their weapons.

"Should we take bets on what the creature is?" Lucy asked.

"I'm guessing it's an extinct dragon species," Ryder said. "If so, we have to stay as still and silent as possible. Dragons don't attack unless they feel threatened— but the minute they think you're an enemy, there's practically nothing you can do to stop them."

"Maybe it's an animal from *MYTHOLOGY*!" Gobzella said. "I'm picturing a creature with the head of a *LION*! The body of a *BEAR*! The fangs of a *SNAKE*! The legs of a *HORSE*! I should be able to handle a creature like that—reminds me of a goblin I used to *DATE*!"

"I'm standing by my *stage mother* theory," Lucy said. "If that's the case, everyone call me *Madame Director* and get ready for a rigged audition."

"At this point nothing could be worse than the suspense," Brystal said. "Let's go in."

Brystal slowly turned the handles, pushed open the doors, and the delegates followed her into the next chamber. They discovered a very large and very dark room on the other side, but once they were all through the doors, they realized it wasn't a room—they had entered an *infinite space* that stretched for miles in each direction.

The ground was flooded in a shallow pool of crystal-clear water that came up to their ankles. The water perfectly reflected thousands of stars from the twinkling night sky above them. The reflection gave the illusion that the stars went on forever all around them, but the illusion was interrupted by the ripples their footsteps created.

The double doors shut behind the delegates and then sank into the water and disappeared. The delegates wandered around the endless space but didn't find anything except a tall, rectangular mirror. Brystal peered into the mirror but only saw her and her friends' reflections staring back.

"Why would the most dangerous creature in history need a mirror?" Ryder asked.

"Or all this *WATER*?" Gobzella asked.

Lucy shrugged. "Maybe it's a narcissistic shark?"

The delegates spread out and continued searching the space, but Brystal felt compelled to stay in front of the mirror. A strange feeling told her the mirror meant more than they realized—she just couldn't put her finger on *what*. After more than an hour of splashing through the area, the delegates still hadn't found anything or anyone else.

"What if the creature isn't here?" Ryder said. "It could have died or escaped the temple."

"You mean, this whole journey has been a waste of *TIME*?" Gobzella said.

"Holy procrastination!" Lucy exclaimed. "Gobzella, maybe that's it! Maybe the deadliest and most dangerous creature on the planet is *time*!"

Ryder and Gobzella scrunched their foreheads.

"Time?" Ryder asked.

"How'd you come up with *THAT*?" Gobzella asked.

"Brystal and my old teacher Madame Weatherberry told us *time* is the most complex thing in the universe," Lucy explained. "It's both the culprit and the solution to all problems, you always have too little or too much but never the amount you want, and in the end, *time kills us all!*"

The delegates considered Lucy's theory and convinced themselves she was right, but Brystal wasn't as sure. She stayed in front of the mirror, never looking away from her and the others' reflections.

"What does a *mirror* have to do with time, though?" she thought out loud. "If *time* was the deadliest creature, surely the temple would put us face-to-face with a *clock* instead of our own—"

Brystal went quiet—she was suddenly struck by a theory of her own. The idea was so shocking, Brystal placed a hand over her mouth.

"*Oh my gosh,*" she whispered to herself. "*I think I just figured it out!*"

The delegates gathered around Brystal and searched the mirror, looking for something hidden in the reflection.

"Where is it, Brystal?" Ryder asked.

"I don't see anything but us," Lucy said

"That's because it *is* us," Brystal said.

"What do you mean it's *US*?" Gobzella asked.

"The most dangerous and deadliest creature on the planet isn't an animal—it's *people,*" Brystal explained.

"Think about it! Can you name another species that's caused more harm to itself or the planet? People pollute the skies, they fill the oceans with waste, and they hunt other animals into extinction! People start *wars* against one another, they *hate* for sport, and they're the only creature on earth that *lies*."

The delegates took a long look at themselves in the mirror and their stomachs turned—*Brystal was right.*

"But how can we *defeat* the creature, if the creature is *people*?" Lucy asked. "Even for sorcerer standards, that seems like a tall order."

"The legend didn't say we have to *defeat* the creature—it said we had to *face* it," Brystal recalled. "Perhaps that's why the mirror is here? Before going into the vault, we have to take responsibility and acknowledge all the damage people have caused. And just like we learned from Spanky, sometimes *facing the truth* is the greatest challenge of all."

Suddenly, the mirror sank into the water and disappeared just like the double doors had before. The delegates felt a powerful rumble beneath their feet and the water began rippling wildly. Thousands and thousands of enormous golden pillars shot straight out of the water and stretched high into the night sky. The water drained away and the delegates found themselves standing on top of a silver star that was engraved into a white marble floor. The star pointed in four directions like a compass, and the delegates realized the golden pillars had formed four endless corridors around them.

As the delegates took in the amazing sight, millions of objects began materializing throughout the four corridors. Everything from gold to dirt appeared before their eyes and filled the vast spaces.

"We made it!" Brystal said breathlessly. *"We're in the sorcerers' vault!"*

The delegates cheered and Gobzella lifted them all off the ground in a celebratory hug.

As the goblin set her friends down, a swirl of twinkling lights appeared beside them. The lights spun faster and faster, and before they could tell what was happening, a tall man was standing before them. The man had a wrinkled face, a long silver beard, and he wore a thick brown cloak with a hood over his head. The delegates were intimidated by his stern and knowing gaze, and they all took a step back. Brystal recognized the man—he had the same face as one of the seven statues in the beginning of the temple.

"Are you a sorcerer?" Brystal asked him.

"I was," he replied.

Lucy gulped. "So you're a *ghost*?"

"I am neither living nor dead—I am a *memory*," the sorcerer said. "Now that you have passed the challenges, you are welcome to take *one* item from the temple. I am here to assist you with your decision and help you navigate our vault. Would you like me to show you what the temple has to offer?"

"Yes, *PLEASE*!" Gobzella exclaimed.

The sorcerer turned to the first corridor with a grand gesture. It had mountains of gold coins, jewelry, furniture, clothing, food, wine, carriages, and ships.

"If it's *material possessions* you desire, this is the Gallery of Goods," he said. "Anything a person could ever need or want is within this gallery. All of these items belonged to the sorcerers when we were alive, and everything is still in pristine condition."

The sorcerer walked around the delegates and gestured to the second corridor. It held a never-ending library with shelves so high they disappeared into the sky.

"If it's *knowledge* you crave, this is the Library of Life," he said. "Our library has a copy of every book that has ever been published, written, or just *imagined* in an author's mind. Even though the founders passed away many centuries ago, you'll find our collection is very current."

The sorcerer stood before the opening of the third corridor. It was lined with cupboards containing billions of scrolls, and the air was filled with floating quills taking notes on floating pieces of parchment.

"If it's *answers* you seek, this is the Foyer of Facts," he said. "Everything that ever happened, is happening, or *will* happen has been documented in these archives. The answers to the greatest mysteries on earth can be found within the sorcerers' scrolls."

The sorcerer gestured to the fourth and final corridor. The fourth corridor contained five open doorways—and each of the doorways led to a room that was filled with thousands and thousands of *bubbles*.

"If it's *insight* you wish for, these are the Halls of Humanity," he said. "By gazing into the bubbles within these doorways, you can see every present emotion on earth. In the Hall of Dreams, each bubble contains insight into someone's greatest desires. In the Hall of Nightmares, each bubble contains insight into someone's worst fears. In the Hall of Ideas, each bubble contains insight into someone's thoughts and opinions. In the Hall of Love, each bubble contains insight into someone's deepest affection. And in the Hall of Hatred, each bubble contains insight into someone's most shameful prejudice."

Brystal was drawn into the Halls of Humanity like a moth to a flame. She peered into each of the doorways and marveled at how beautiful and unique the bubbles were. The dreams sparkled and floated whimsically through the air; the nightmares were cloudy and flew erratically across the hall; the ideas had flashes of lightning and energetically bounced off each other; the love bubbles looked as if they were blushing and drifted in leisurely circles around one another; and the hate bubbles were pitch-black and frozen in place.

Brystal was very intrigued by the Halls of Humanity—she couldn't imagine all the good someone could spread with insight into people's wildest dreams—but at the same time, there was something about the halls that Brystal found greatly disturbing.

"Why are the Hall of Nightmares and the Hall of Hatred fuller than the others?" she asked the sorcerer.

"That's an unfortunate reality about humanity,"

he said. "Their dreams, ideas, and love have never exceeded their hatred or fear. And until that changes, I'm afraid they'll always be the deadliest and most dangerous species on the planet."

Hearing that made Brystal feel like she had been punched—not anywhere in the body, but in her soul. She knew humanity was capable of changing—she had *seen* the world make profound changes with her own eyes. But sadly, Brystal knew she'd never live to see the day when the Halls of Dreams, Ideas, and Love were the fullest. She only had a week left to live, and right now, she couldn't waste a moment of it.

"Sir, we know exactly what we want to take," Brystal said.

"Oh?" the sorcerer said with a peculiar look. "Are you sure you don't want more time to browse the corridors?"

"Unfortunately, time is a luxury we don't have," Brystal said. "We've come to the Temple of Knowledge for the Book of Sorcery."

The sorcerer raised his eyebrow curiously and stroked his long beard.

"How interesting," he said. "Of all the possessions

in this vault, the Book of Sorcery is the only object that has *already* been taken."

"It's been *TAKEN*?" Gobzella exclaimed.

"You mean, this whole thing has been a complete waste?" Lucy asked.

"But *who* beat all the challenges before us?" Ryder asked.

"Only one other person has survived this far," the sorcerer said. "Several centuries ago, a woman traveled to the temple and completed the challenges by herself. It took her over three hundred years to finish, but she eventually reached the vault."

Brystal and Lucy gasped in unison, thinking the same thing:

"*The Immortal!*" they said.

"So she *did* get the Book of Sorcery after all!" Brystal said.

"But if the Immortal got the book, why didn't she use it to destroy the Daughter of Death? Why not keep her end of the bargain?" Lucy asked.

Ryder did a double take. "Sorry—did you just say *Daughter of Death* and *the Immortal*?"

Lucy waved the subject off like it wasn't important.

"One day we'll take you to lunch and explain everything," she told him.

"The Immortal must have wanted it *before* she made her deal with Death," Brystal determined. "Otherwise, how would she have known to bring it up in the first place? Perhaps immortality wasn't what she wanted after all—perhaps she just needed immortality to help her *get* the Book of Sorcery!"

"So you're telling me there's something in the Book of Sorcery that's *flashier* than immortality?" Lucy asked.

Brystal winced at the thought and turned back to the sorcerer.

"Sir, do you remember who the woman was? Or where she might have taken the book?"

"I'm sorry, but I do not recall the woman's name," the sorcerer said.

"Sir, I used to work in a library," Brystal said. "If the Library of Life is as grand as you say it is, surely there must be some sort of *card catalog* to keep track of the books."

The sorcerer gave her another peculiar look—but this time, he was impressed.

"Follow me," he said.

The delegates followed the sorcerer into the Library of Life. After walking through more than a mile of endless bookshelves, they stopped at a massive cabinet. The cabinet had thousands of small drawers and, like the shelves surrounding it, it was so tall it disappeared into the night sky. The sorcerer levitated out of sight, floating toward the cabinet's highest drawers, and a few minutes later, he returned with a card.

"Here you are," he said.

Brystal took the card from the sorcerer and read the name written on it.

"*Immortalia*," she said.

"Sounds like a lounge singer," Lucy said.

"Wait a second, I've heard that name before," Brystal said. "Quick! I need a history book!"

The sorcerer led the delegates another mile into the Library of Life to a section that held hundreds of thousands of history books. Brystal rummaged through the collection until she found one dedicated to the Eastern Kingdom. She found Queen Endustria's name at the bottom of a royal family tree and then traced it backward, going up the line of succession. Her finger landed on the portrait of a young queen with very familiar features. Brystal flipped the book over and showed the portrait to the others.

"I knew I recognized that name," she said. "*Queen Immortalia* was the first woman to ever sit on the throne of the Eastern Kingdom! And there's been a woman on the throne ever since!"

"Whoa," Lucy said. "She looks just like Queen Endustria and Princess Proxima!"

"Immortalia looks like *all* the queens!"

Brystal flipped through the history book and showed her friends the portraits of all the queens from the last three centuries.

"Something tells me that's more than strong genetics," Lucy said.

"The Immortal has been right under our nose the entire time!" Brystal said. "We have to get to the Eastern Kingdom as soon as possible! *Queen Endustria has the Book of Sorcery!*"

CHAPTER TWENTY TWO

THE KING OF DEMONS AND THE QUEEN OF SNOW

Xanthous had no idea why he had been brought to the Righteous Empire, but he knew his chances of escaping were near impossible. He was curled up on the floor of his tiny cage with his hands and feet tied behind his back and a cloth wrapped around his mouth. Xanthous was the only prisoner in the dungeon of the Righteous Palace and his cage was surrounded by a dozen soldiers of the Army of the Dead. At any moment, he expected the Righteous Emperor to come stomping down the dungeon steps and use him as a prop in some macabre scheme—and that was only if the alchemists didn't find and execute him *first*. Either way, Xanthous would need nothing short of a *miracle* to survive the night.

Just as Xanthous started to accept his grim fate, a loud *crash* came from the top of the steps. Two of the dead soldiers hurried up the stairs to inspect the source of the noise and disappeared from view. A moment later, there was another *crash* as the first soldier toppled down the steps without his skull attached to his neck. A young man in black-and-white-checkered armor emerged down the stairs, riding the second soldier like a surfboard. He raised a slingshot as he slid down the steps, launching rocks at the skeletal guards, and one by one, he knocked their skulls clean off their bony necks.

"*Mmmhhhk!*" Xanthous mumbled under the cloth.

While the headless skeletons searched the dungeon for their decapitated skulls, Elrik snatched a ring of keys off a soldier's belt and raced toward Xanthous's cage.

"Xanthous! Thank God you're still alive!" Elrik said. "I was worried I'd be too late!"

The elf unlocked the cage door and untied the cloth wrapped around the fairy's mouth.

"Elrik! How did you get here? Your father said he locked you up!" Xanthous said.

"Oh—*he did*, but I escaped," Elrik said. "Elves are horrible tailors, but luckily, they're even worse architects. Would you believe our prison is made out of *sticks*?"

Xanthous was so overwhelmed with joy, tears welled in his eyes.

"I'm so happy to see you!" he said. "Thanks for coming to rescue me!"

"Don't mention it," Elrik said. "I couldn't let the Righteous Emperor hurt such a cute—"

"Elrik, behind you!"

The dead soldiers had screwed their skulls back on their necks and were now charging toward the elf. Elrik dived out of the way, barely missing getting struck by the blades of their swords. The soldiers' blades slammed into the bars of Xanthous's cage and knocked it over. Xanthous rolled onto the floor and desperately tried to get up, but his restraints made it impossible to stand.

"Elrik, you've got to help me!" he cried. "I've got to get off the ground or the fires will start!"

"One second—I'm a little busy!" Elrik said.

The elf was fighting off the soldiers, twelve to one. He rapidly fired his slingshot, shooting off their arms and legs, but he couldn't keep up with their assault. A skeleton kicked Elrik's legs out from underneath him, the elf landed hard on his back, and his slingshot was ripped out of his hands.

"*Leave him alone!*" Xanthous yelled.

The fairy rolled across the floor and knocked the soldiers off their feet, but they quickly bounced back. The skeletons surrounded Xanthous and Elrik, looming toward the boys with their swords raised high above their heads. The boys winced as they anticipated being sliced, but suddenly, the dark dungeon was filled with bright lights. Xanthous and Elrik shielded their eyes, but when their vision adjusted, they saw *fire* bursting up from the ground all around them! The fire distracted the skeletons and they turned toward the flames in amazement.

The temperature in the dungeon instantly rose to sweltering heights. Xanthous sat up on his knees and used his body to shield Elrik from the heat.

"Get out of the dungeon before the fire kills you!" he said.

The elf's mouth dropped open as he watched the fire.

"You mean before *they* kill me," he said, and pointed to the flames.

Xanthous turned toward the fire and squinted at the flames. After watching for a few moments, he understood why Elrik was so stunned. The dungeon wasn't filled with *one* powerful fire, but *twelve* small fires—and each set of flames was shaped like a *person*.

"Oh my God," Xanthous gasped. "They're *people*!"

The dead soldiers zeroed in on their new target, swinging their swords and thrusting their shields at the fire people—but the skeletons' weapons went right through them. Each fire person grabbed a soldier, wrapping their flaming arms and legs tightly around the skeletons' hollow torsos. The skeletons ran amok as they tried to extinguish the flames, slamming into the walls and each other, but the fire people never loosened their grip. They held on to the soldiers until each of their bodies crumpled into a pile of charred bones. The skeletons' ashy remains still twitched with life, but they were damaged far beyond the point of repair.

Once the fire people had defeated the soldiers, they gathered around Xanthous and Elrik. The elf quickly untied Xanthous's restraints and they tried to escape the dungeon, but the fires backed them into a corner. However, the fire people didn't try to harm the boys like the skeletons—on the contrary, they kept their distance to make sure Elrik wasn't burned.

The fire people stood eerily still with their flaming heads pointed in Xanthous's direction. The longer he waited for them to do something, the angrier Xanthous became.

"You've ruined my life!" he yelled. *"Why are you doing this to me?!"*

One of the fire people walked to the nearest wall and waved their hand over it, burning a message into the stone bricks:

WE KNOW WHAT YOU ARE.

Frustrated, Xanthous got to his feet and walked closer to the wall. He inspected the message as if the answer was hidden somewhere within the burned letters.

"I don't understand," he told them. "Who are you? And *what* do you think I am?"

The fire person waved their hand over the wall again and a new message appeared:

WE'RE YOUR FAMILY.
WE'VE BEEN SEARCHING FOR YOU.
WE NEED YOUR HELP.

"*What?*" Xanthous asked. "How are *we* family?"

YOU'RE A DEMON AMONG MEN.
AND THE HEIR TO THE DEMON
THRONE.
IT'S YOUR DESTINY TO RULE US.

Xanthous was so baffled he felt light-headed.

"I'm sorry, but you must have me mistaken for

someone else," he said. "I don't even know what a *demon* is."

"Ooooh," Elrik said. "They're *demons*!"

"Elrik? You know who these people are?" he asked.

"Yes—well, sort of—I didn't know the stories were *real*!"

"What stories?"

"Haven't you ever heard the Legend of the Demon King?" Elrik asked.

Xanthous stared at Elrik like he was speaking a different language.

"It's a fable my mother told me when I was younger," he said. "According to an ancient myth, the center of the earth is inhabited by a fiery race of people known as *demons*. They protect our planet's core and keep the world spinning—they've always been a peaceful people, but a few thousand years ago, the Demon King became corrupt and waged war with humanity. He led his demons to the surface and caused fires that almost destroyed the planet. Thankfully, a group of sorcerers killed the Demon King and imprisoned the other demons. Without a ruler, the demons have lived in utter chaos ever since—but the Legend of the Demon King states that one day a *new king* will be born among mankind. It's his destiny to sit on the Demon Throne and restore the demons to the peaceful race they once were."

"And they think *I'm* the Demon King?" he asked.

"Can you blame them?" Elrik asked. "You're a fairy who controls *fire*! Who would be a better candidate?"

The fire person waved their hand over the wall and wrote another message:

SEARCH YOUR HEART, XANTHOUS. YOU'VE BEEN SEARCHING FOR US AS MUCH AS WE'VE BEEN SEARCHING FOR YOU. WE'RE YOUR MISSING PIECE.

Xanthous was speechless. For as long as he could remember, Xanthous had always been trying to fill a void in his heart. Over the years he tried to fill it with approval, friendships, adventures—and most recently—*love*. However, no matter where he lived or who he met, the emptiness always returned. But what if Xanthous wasn't *supposed* to be fulfilled by magic, fairies, or even Elrik? Perhaps the demons *were* his missing piece all along.

Unfortunately, Xanthous didn't have time to find out. As if the demons were being dragged underground by an invisible lasso, they abruptly started dropping through the floor. They held on to the ground with all their might, desperate to stay above the surface, but they weren't strong enough to fight whatever force was pulling them down.

"What's happening to you?" Xanthous asked.

Only one demon remained and they used their last bit of strength to burn another message on the wall beside them:

SHE'S COMPELLING US! YOU HAVE TO FREE US FROM HER!

Xanthous threw himself onto the ground and grabbed the demon's hand before they disappeared belowground.

"Free you from *who*?" Xanthous asked. "Who's compelling you?"

THE ONE WHO RELEASED US FROM THE CORE! SHE'S CONTROLLING US WITH THE BOOK! SHE'S GOING TO ATTACK THE CITY! SHE'LL DESTROY EVERYTHING IF YOU DON'T STOP HER!

Xanthous's mind was racing with dozens of questions, but he knew he only had time to ask one before the demon was pulled away.

"How do I stop her?" he asked.

FIND THE BOOK!
RECITE THE OATH!
AND THE THRONE IS YOURS!

The demon's flaming hand slipped from Xanthous's grip and they were dragged underground.

"We've got to find that book," Xanthous said.

"Are you ready for that? Do you even *want* to be the Demon King?" Elrik asked.

The question had never entered Xanthous's mind.

"What choice do I have?" he asked. "You saw what the demons did to the soldiers—if we don't stop whoever is controlling them, the whole world will burn!"

BAM! BAM! The boys heard a powerful commotion coming from outside. *BAM! BAM!* They ran to the dungeon's barred window and gazed into the Chariot Hills town square. *BAM! BAM!* Xanthous and Elrik were shocked to see an entire city of gold, silver, and bronze buildings perched on clouds over the capital. *BAM! BAM!* And even more shocking, the

Army of the Dead was attacking it with cannons and harpoons.

"That must be the Alchemy Institute!" Xanthous exclaimed.

"What is it doing in Chariot Hills?" Elrik asked.

"So *that's* why the emperor wanted me here," he said. "He was using me as bait for the alchemists! He led them into a trap!"

"But why is the Righteous Emperor attacking the alchemists?" Elrik asked.

"Seven wants to eliminate *everyone* who poses a threat to him," Xanthous said. "This could be the exact distraction we need! While the alchemists and the Army of the Dead are busy fighting, let's sneak out of the Righteous Palace and find the woman controlling the demons! We've got to catch her before she reaches the city! *Come on!*"

· • ★ • ·

As the fairies and witches moved down the icy tunnel in the Northern Mountains, they stayed in a tight huddle for warmth and protection. The girls expected the terrifying Snow Queen to lunge out from the darkness at every twist and turn, so they tiptoed through the tunnel as quietly and cautiously as possible. Pip led the shivering and trembling procession nose-first, sniffing the air after every step.

"Do you smell her yet?" Tangerina asked.

"Will you stop asking me that," Pip griped.

"I'm sorry, but these mountains are huge!" Tangerina said. "I want to make sure we're headed in the right direction."

"I told you, this is the only tunnel where I caught a whiff of something besides rocks and icicles," Pip said. "Either the Snow Queen is rotting at the end of this tunnel or we're about to find a decomposing moose."

"Sounds like a win-win to me," Stitches said.

The fairies and witches finally reached the end of the tunnel and entered an enormous frozen cavern. Emerelda waved her hands and covered all the stalagmites and stalactites with glowing jewels to illuminate the area.

"I can't imagine Madame Weatherberry living here," Mrs. Vee said. "Then again, it's amazing how far people will move for more square footage and high ceilings! *HA-HA!*"

"Living isn't how I would describe it."

The fairies and witches turned toward the unexpected voice. They were completely mesmerized when they noticed that a beautiful woman with dark hair had appeared in the back of the cavern. She wore a plum gown, a stylish fascinator, and a smile that was brighter than all of Emerelda's jewels combined.

"Madame Weatherberry!" Tangerina and Skylene cheered.

The girls ran to embrace their old teacher with open arms, but sadly, they moved right through the fairy.

"Sorry, I almost forgot," Skylene said. "Brystal told us you're *dimensionally challenged* now."

"Unfortunately so," Madame Weatherberry said. "It's so wonderful to see you girls! I can't believe what beautiful young women you've become! Who are your friends?"

"This is Stitches, Sprout, Beebee, and Pip," Emerelda said. "They came to live with us after the Ravencrest School of Witchcraft closed down."

"You want to know *why* they call me Stitches?" the witch asked.

"Ignore her—*we do*," Tangerina said.

"It's a pleasure to meet you, ladies," Madame Weatherberry said. "Brystal has kept me updated on all your trials and tribulations. I am so proud of everything you've accomplished. I was hoping Brystal would bring you to visit me one day so I could congratulate you personally."

Madame Weatherberry looked around at her guests, but didn't see everyone she'd expected.

"Wait a second, why aren't Brystal and Lucy with you?" she asked.

The fairies and witches glanced at one another with distress written all over their faces. Madame Weatherberry instantly knew something was wrong.

"So this isn't a *social* visit," the fairy said. "Tell me what's happened."

Emerelda quickly summarized the events from the past week. She told Madame Weatherberry about the fire that had destroyed more than half of Ironhand, how all the world leaders were invited to a Conference of Kings at the Alchemy Institute to discuss the matter, how the alchemists were planning to eliminate Xanthous, and how Brystal was currently leading a team of delegates through the Temple of Knowledge to find the Book of Sorcery.

"We all knew Xanthous was innocent, but until

a couple of hours ago, we didn't have any proof," Emerelda said. "Just now in the Righteous Empire, we saw Princess Proxima summoning the fire with a spell! The alchemists may be wrong about Xanthous, but they're right about the fire! It's spreading through the Southern countryside as we speak and destroying *everything* in its path! If we don't stop it soon, the whole world is going to go up in flames!"

"Then why travel all the way here?" Madame Weatherberry asked.

Emerelda cringed. "Because there's only *one person* we know of who's powerful enough to stop a fire like that," she said.

Madame Weatherberry went very tense when she realized *who* Emerelda was talking about. The fairy looked over her shoulder to the frozen Snow Queen. Her guests shrieked when they discovered the monstrous witch in the wall of ice behind her.

"So you've come to set her free," Madame Weatherberry said.

"I know that sounds bananas—but I don't know what to else to do," Emerelda said. "There's no way of telling *if* or *when* Brystal will get back with the Book of Sorcery, so we have to do something drastic before—"

Emerelda stopped talking mid-sentence when she noticed something bizarre about the Snow Queen's frozen prison. The wall was *dripping* and one of the witch's frostbitten hands was already poking through the ice.

"Madame Weatherberry, are you *defrosting her*?" Emerelda asked.

The fairy turned back to the girls and let out a heavy sigh.

"I am," she said.

"But . . . but . . . but *why*?" Tangerina asked.

"I have my own reasons to free her," Madame Weatherberry said. "Although it sounds like yours are far more pressing than mine."

The fairies and witches couldn't believe their ears.

"You mean, you aren't going to talk us out of it?" Skylene asked.

On the contrary, Madame Weatherberry wanted to dissuade them with every fiber of her being. However, the fairy had her *own* plan in motion—and she knew she would accomplish it much sooner with her former students' help.

"I'm afraid I agree with you," Madame Weatherberry said. "If the world is in danger, then we must do whatever is necessary to save it. But if you're going to free the Snow Queen, you must be prepared to stop her by any means necessary, too. Are you prepared to do that?"

Emerelda gulped. "We are," she said with a confident nod.

"Good," Madame Weatherberry said, and stepped out of their way. *"Release her."*

CHAPTER TWENTY~THREE

A WAR OF FIRE, ICE, AND ALCHEMY

Curfew or no curfew, the citizens of Chariot Hills were *getting out*. Shortly after midnight, everyone in the capital was awoken by the thunderous blasts of cannons being fired in the town square. The citizens peeked out their windows to see what was causing the commotion and were astonished to see the Alchemy Institute floating above their heads.

However, their shock quickly turned into terror when they saw the Army of the Dead attacking the campus with harpoons. In a matter of minutes, the sleepy capital had turned into a dangerous battleground. The citizens began to panic, knowing if they didn't leave Chariot Hills straightaway, they might not survive until morning.

While the streets became chaotic with fleeing citizens, the Army of the Dead continued their ambush on the Alchemy Institute. The dead soldiers reeled in the chains of their harpoons until all thirteen facilities slammed down in the town square. Upon impact, the clouds beneath the campus completely vaporized. The alchemists were still stationed on the balcony below the grand armillary sphere and they watched in horror as the skeleton army marched into the town square and crept toward the institute.

"They've surrounded us!" Dr. Steam cried.

"How are *we* going to stop *them*?" Dr. Storm asked.

"We're scientists—not soldiers!" Dr. Stage said.

Dr. States didn't seem nearly as distraught as his colleagues. The alchemist observed their approaching enemy like he was looking down at an opponent's chess pieces. He tapped his cane on the ground three times and all the Magbots along the perimeter of the campus linked arms, forming a protective barrier around the institute.

"The Magbots won't hold them off for long!" Dr. Strand said.

"The soldiers outnumber them ten to one!" Dr. Stats said.

"The Magbots aren't supposed to *stop* the soldiers," Dr. States said. "They're merely a distraction while we get *our* own troops ready."

"But, sir, we don't *have* an army!" Dr. Star said.

"Of course we do!" Dr. States grumbled. "Stop being scientists for one minute and use your imaginations! We have the greatest army the world has ever seen, right at our fingertips! Everyone report to your departments at once and wait for my commands! The Army of the Dead may outnumber us, but we can outsmart them! Now go!"

The alchemists dispersed and hurried to their departments. Across the town square, on the roof of the Righteous Palace, the Righteous Emperor was perched on a cushy throne being served wine and desserts while he watched the battle begin. The clansmen of the Righteous Brotherhood cheered for the

Army of the Dead like they were observing a sporting match.

"High Commander, send for the champagne," Seven ordered. "This battle is going to be finished before we know it."

From what he could see, the Righteous Emperor had good reason to feel victorious. His Army of the Dead pelted the Magbots with their swords and shields, denting and bending their metal limbs. Eventually the dead soldiers hacked their way through the magic robots and broke through their perimeter. Once all the skeletons were past the Magbots, the dead soldiers raced toward the institute with nothing to stop them—or so they thought.

Dr. States glared at the approaching army.

"You heathens have already broken the laws of *nature*," he said under his breath. "But let's see how well you do against the laws of *physics*."

The alchemist tapped his cane on the floor three times, and the doors of the Physics Department burst open. Thousands of bright red balls, hundreds of yellow yo-yos, and dozens of magnets came rolling out of the facility and clashed with the oncoming soldiers. The red balls bounced off the skeletons' bony bodies, knocking off fingers and toes. The yellow yo-yos wrapped their strings around the soldiers' feet and tripped them as they ran. The magnets magnetized the skeletons' armor, causing the soldiers to slam into one another and stick together.

The Righteous Emperor scoffed at the institute's first wave of defense.

"The scientists are putting up a bigger fight than I predicted," Seven said. "But they're going to need more than *children's toys* to defeat us."

"*Dr. Strand! Release the microorganisms!*" Dr. States commanded, his voice echoing through the institute.

The biologist kicked open the doors to the Biology Department and a stampede of giant cells, viruses, and bacteria charged toward the army. White blood cells gobbled up the dead soldiers and held them prisoner inside their nuclei. Neurons thrashed their long bodies like whips and wrapped themselves around the skeletons. Viruses rolled through the army, infecting each of the soldiers they touched, and the skeletons' joints became too achy to move. A small bacterium was cornered by a dozen dead soldiers, but the bacterium began multiplying and quickly outnumbered them.

The Righteous Emperor spit out his wine as he witnessed the microorganisms devour his army.

"It's just beginner's luck," Seven said with a cocky laugh. "This battle is going to be more entertaining than we thought!"

"*Dr. Storm! Release the weather!*" Dr. States instructed.

The Meteorology Department's umbrella roof rose like the lid of a teakettle and several miniature storms erupted from inside. Tornadoes spun across the institute, sucking the soldiers into their vortexes. A miniature hurricane blew through the army, tossing the skeletons across the city with powerful winds. Dark clouds hovered over the soldiers, drenching them with rain and striking them with lightning. Blizzards chased the skeletons across the campus and froze their feet to the ground.

The Righteous Emperor and the clansmen were growing more nervous by the second.

"That has to be it, right?!" Seven asked the clansmen. "They can't *possibly* have anything more up their sleeves!"

"*Dr. Stage! Release the artifacts!*" Dr. States ordered. "*And Dr. Sting! Release the swarms!*"

The remains of a massive T. rex, a woolly mammoth, and a dozen cavemen came running out from the Anthropology Department. The dinosaur flattened the dead soldiers with its enormous tail, the mammoth smashed into them with its huge tusks, and the cavemen beat them to the ground with their clubs. Next, the windows of the Entomology Department were flung open and plagues of locusts, swarms of wasps, and colonies of ants rained down on the dead soldiers. The locusts piled on top of the skeletons until they couldn't move, the wasps covered their bodies in nests, and the ants picked their bones apart.

The Righteous Emperor growled angrily and ripped out handfuls of his hair.

"Shall I cancel the champagne, my lord?" the High Commander asked.

"We need more soldiers! Send in every man we have!" Seven yelled.

"Sir, we don't have any more soldiers," the High Commander said.

"Then fetch some crossbows and cannons!" Seven ordered. "The clansmen will attack from the roofs!"

"My lord, you armed the Army of the Dead with our

entire arsenal," the High Commander said. "There are no more crossbows or cannons."

The Righteous Emperor's eyes bulged and the veins on his neck throbbed. He grabbed the High Commander by the collar of his uniform and held him over the edge of the roof.

"Are you saying we have NOTHING left to defend ourselves with?" Seven roared.

"We may have a couple butter knives in the kitchen," the High Commander peeped.

"My lord?" said a clansman. "Forgive the interruption, but we might have a *bigger* problem than the alchemists."

"*Are you out of your mind?*" Seven screamed. "*What could possibly be bigger?!*"

The clansmen quickly parted to two sides of the roof so the Righteous Emperor could see for himself. While the clansmen had been fixated on the battle in the town square, the Eastern countryside had turned into a blazing inferno. The sky was covered in thick black smoke, wildfires were spreading rapidly, and from what the Righteous Emperor could see, it appeared the flames were headed *straight toward them.*

"What the devil is *that*?!" he seethed.

Brystal, Lucy, Ryder, and Gobzella soared over the Northeast Ocean aboard Kitty's back. Ryder steered the dragon southwest toward the kingdoms and territories and she flew as fast as her wings could carry them. The continent eventually appeared on the horizon and the dragon flew above the border between the Northern and Eastern Kingdoms as she descended toward the city of Ironhand.

"We should touch down in about twenty minutes!" Ryder told the others.

They were so high in the sky the delegates could see for hundreds of miles in each direction. As Brystal scanned the cold Northern Mountains to her right, she suddenly *screeched*—not because of something she saw, but rather, because of something she *didn't* see.

"What's wrong?" Lucy asked. "Did you see a gremlin on the wing?"

"No!" she said. *"Look!"*

Brystal pointed toward the Northern Mountains in a panic.

"I don't see anything," Lucy said.

"Exactly!" Brystal said. "The northern lights are gone!"

The girls were horrified, but their friends didn't understand.

"What's so special about the *NORTHERN LIGHTS*?" Gobzella asked.

"The northern lights mark the presence of the Snow Queen!" Lucy explained. "As long as they're in the sky, that means the Snow Queen is trapped in the Northern Mountains!"

"And if the northern lights are *NOT* in the sky?" Gobzella asked.

"It means she's *escaped*!" Brystal said.

Ryder did a double take. "Sorry—but who's the *Snow Queen*?"

Lucy rolled her eyes. "Boy, you really need to get out more!" she said.

Everyone aboard the dragon suddenly went quiet. Their attention was drawn to something rising straight ahead on the southern horizon. A gargantuan cloud of thick black smoke was billowing up from the countryside, drifting across the full moon like a floating mountain.

"I've never seen so much smoke in my life!" Ryder said. "And I live on a volcano with dragons!"

"That's not a normal fire!" Brystal said. "The Devil's Breath has returned!"

"Oh no—*Xanthous*!" Lucy said. "He's going to get blamed for this, too!"

"Change of plans," Brystal told the others. "The Book of Sorcery can wait another day! We've got to stop the fire before it spreads around the world! *Follow that smoke!*"

· • ★ • ·

Immortalia triumphantly led the demons through the countryside and toward Chariot Hills. By two o'clock in the morning, they finally reached the outskirts of the capital, and Immortalia paused the fiery procession at the top of a high hill. From there, Immortalia could see the entire city below her. She was thrilled to discover the Army of the Dead was engaged in a heated battle with the Alchemy Institute.

"Well, well, well—isn't *this* lucky," Immortalia told the demons. "We can get rid of the Righteous Empire and the Alchemy Institute with one shot."

A wicked laugh erupted from the Immortal's

mouth. *This* was the moment she had been waiting *centuries* for—she was *finally* going to get her revenge by attacking one of the greatest cities in the world—and nothing was standing in her way except a few acres of farmland.

"*Demons! Burn that city to the ground!*" she ordered.

The demons were magically compelled to follow her commands and they headed toward the city. However, shortly after they began their approach, all the demons stopped in their tracks—something very strange was hovering in the sky above them. A giant block of ice appeared through the smoky haze as it was flown into the countryside. The ice was hanging from four flying broomsticks. Each of the brooms was steered by a witch and carried a fairy passenger.

"What on earth is *that*?" Immortalia asked.

"Put her down over there!" Emerelda instructed her friends.

The witches gently set the block of ice down in the field between the demons and Chariot Hills. Once the ice was on the ground, the witches and fairies hopped off the broomsticks and stood in a row behind it. From the hill, Immortalia could see the silhouette of something *monstrous* inside the ice. After one glimpse of the creature's tall snowflake crown, she knew *exactly* who it was.

"Aren't they *clever*," Immortalia muttered. "They've resurrected the Snow Queen to stop me—but they're going to need more than a little *ice* to extinguish *my* fires. *Demons! Vaporize that frigid witch!*"

The demons sprinted toward the block of ice and the fairies and witches backed away. The demons formed a tight circle around the ice and pressed their flaming bodies against it. Steam surged into the night sky as the ice melted at a rapid pace.

"Here we go!" Emerelda told her friends. "Remember to keep her focused on the fire! And don't let her get near the city!"

Suddenly, the entire countryside was covered in a blinding white flash. The demons surrounding the ice were blasted across the field. When the light faded, the block of ice was gone, and the Snow Queen was *awake*. The witch let out a horrendous moan as she stretched her stiff body for the first time in two years. She gritted her rotten teeth, sniffed the smoky air, and growled angrily like an animal recently released from a cage.

"Don't just stand there!" Immortalia shouted. *"Demons! Destroy her!"*

Although the Snow Queen was blind, she could feel the warmth emitting from the demons' bodies. The witch extended her right hand and a brand-new icicle scepter grew from her palm. The Snow Queen struck the ground with her scepter and sent a powerful frost in every direction. The cold breeze knocked the fairies, witches, and demons off their feet. The frost spread across the countryside and instantly extinguished all the wildfires in the Empire. Only the demons themselves were left ablaze.

The fairies and witches helped one another off the ground and stared at the Snow Queen in terror.

"She seems more *powerful* than she was before," Tangerina said.

"She's *angrier*," Emerelda said.

Once the demons were back on their feet, they charged the witch again. The Snow Queen pointed her scepter at the ground, creating thick walls of ice in their path. The demons slammed into the icy barriers, but their bodies were so warm the ice didn't stay standing for long. The fairies and witches were relieved as they watched the Snow Queen duel the demons.

"It's working," Skylene said.

"She's stopped the fires *and* she's keeping them away from the city!" Mrs. Vee said.

"Let's hope it stays that way," Emerelda said.

The fairies and witches felt a strong wind as something large swooped down from the sky. They looked up and were shocked to see a massive dragon flying above their heads—but even more alarming was seeing the four people who were *riding* the dragon.

"*Brystal!*" the fairies gasped.

"*Lucy!*" the witches cried.

"*You're alive!*" the girls cheered together.

Kitty landed in the field behind the fairies and witches. Brystal, Lucy, Ryder, and Gobzella quickly climbed off the dragon's back. The fairies and witches were so excited to see Brystal and Lucy they tackled the girls to the ground. However, the happy reunion was cut short when the newcomers caught sight of the Snow Queen.

"Can someone tell me what *she's* doing here?" Brystal asked.

"You first!" Tangerina said. "Where did that *dragon* come from?"

"It's a long story—we'll chat later," Lucy said.

"Did you get the Book of Sorcery?" Emerelda asked.

"No—someone already took it!" Brystal said.

"Who?" Skylene asked.

Lucy gazed into the distance and dramatically pointed to the hill.

"As a matter of fact—*she did*!" she announced.

"Wait, *Princess Proxima* has the Book of Sorcery?" Mrs. Vee asked.

"That's not Princess Proxima," Brystal told them. "That's Queen Immortalia—*she's the Immortal*! She took the Book of Sorcery from the Temple of Knowledge centuries ago!"

"So *that's* the book she was reading from!" Pip said. "The Book of Sorcery must contain a spell that controls the fire people!"

"Wait, *fire people*?" Lucy asked.

Pip pointed toward the demons battling the Snow Queen. Lucy and Brystal felt as if the wind had been knocked out of their lungs.

"The fire's moving like *people*!" Lucy said.

"Pretty awesome, huh?" Stitches asked.

"This p-p-proves Xanthous is in-in-innocent!" Beebee said.

"We saw Proxima summon the fire in the countryside!" Emerelda said. "We were afraid the fire was going to destroy the whole Empire. So we went into the Northern Mountains and brought back the Snow Queen."

"And Madame Weatherberry let you?" Brystal asked.

"Are you kidding? She encouraged it!" Tangerina said.

"And so far, so good!" Skylene noted.

Brystal was overwhelmed by all the information her friends were giving her. Her eyes darted around the countryside—from the Snow Queen to the fire people to the Book of Sorcery clutched tightly in Immortalia's arms—while she plotted their next move.

"First things first—we have to get the Book of Sorcery away from Immortalia," Brystal said. "There's a spell inside the book that can stop the Snow Queen and the fires!"

"Then we might want to hurry," Lucy said. *"Looks like someone is about to beat us to it!"*

The fairies and witches looked to the hill where Immortalia was standing. To their surprise, a chariot pulled by four enormous jackalopes was sneaking up behind her. The horned rabbits were steered by a young man in black-and-white-checkered armor while another young man stood behind him. Before Immortalia heard them coming, the chariot sped right past her and the second young man snatched the Book of Sorcery out of her hands.

The fairies and witches were overjoyed when they recognized the passenger.

"Xanthous!" they cheered.

"He's all right!" Tangerina said.

"And he's got the book!" Skylene said.

"Wait, why does *he* want the book?" Emerelda asked.

"Who cares?! Don't look a gift mallard in the beak!" Lucy said.

The Immortal was enraged as she watched the elf and the fairy get away.

"*Noooooooooo!*" she howled. *"Demons! After them! Bring me back my book!"*

Upon her command, the demons abandoned their

duel with the Snow Queen and chased after the chariot. The demons' silhouettes changed from the shape of *people* into the shape of *tigers*. The fiery felines raced after the boys. Elrik steered the jackalopes in erratic loops to avoid being struck by the demons' flaming paws.

"They need our help!" Brystal told her friends. "*Stitches, Sprout, Beebee, and Pip!* Get on your brooms and try to get the book from Xanthous! Ryder and I will follow behind you! *Emerelda, Tangerina, Skylene, and Mrs. Vee!* Make sure the Snow Queen doesn't leave the countryside! *Lucy and Gobzella!* Keep an eye on the Immortal!"

Without a moment to lose, everyone separated to follow Brystal's instructions. The fairies lined up behind the Snow Queen, Lucy and Gobzella sped across the field toward Immortalia, and the witches hopped onto their brooms and flew to Xanthous's aid. When the witches arrived, the demons were closing in on the chariot and getting ready to pounce.

"Hey, Xanthous!" Stitches called down. "Up here!"

Xanthous was surprised to see the witches following him from the air.

"What are you guys doing here?" he asked.

"We're trying to help you!" Sprout said.

"Toss us the Book of Sorcery before the fires get you!" Pip said.

"Wait—*this* is the Book of Sorcery?" he asked.

"Just p-p-pass us the dang b-b-book!" Beebee said.

Seconds before the demons were about to tackle the chariot, Xanthous threw the Book of Sorcery as high as he could. Pip swooped through the air and caught the book with her skunk tail.

"Don't let them get away!" Immortalia screamed from the hill. *"Demons! Fly!"*

The demons changed silhouettes again, and the fiery felines morphed into a flock of *flaming hawks!* The blazing birds soared after Pip, chasing her through the sky. As the birds zeroed in on her, Pip quickly tossed the Book of Sorcery to Beebee. The hawks abruptly changed course, but Beebee threw the book to Sprout before they got too close. Sprout covertly passed the book to Stitches as she zipped by, and the demons lost track of it.

The witches exchanged the Book of Sorcery—*from Beebee to Sprout, from Sprout to Pip, from Pip back to Beebee, from Beebee to Stitches*—and the demons became confused. Eventually, the demons caught wind of what was happening and followed the book as it returned to Stitches. The hawks surrounded Stitches in midair and blocked her from passing it to the other witches.

"Stitches! To your left!"

Kitty did a barrel turn through the air, and the dragon blew the demons across the sky with the powerful wind her massive wings created. Stitches saw Brystal and Ryder riding on Kitty's back and she tossed them the Book of Sorcery. The dragon soared higher and higher, but the demons relentlessly followed. Brystal tried to zap the hawks with her wand, but there were too many to fight on her own.

"Brystal! Down here!" Xanthous called from the ground. "I know how to stop the demons!"

"Demons?" Brystal asked.

"It's a long story!" he said. "Toss me the book!"

Brystal dropped the Book of Sorcery and it plummeted toward the earth. Xanthous dived to the ground and caught it in his arms. The demons immediately did a sharp turn and skyrocketed after the book. As the hawks flew straight toward him, Xanthous quickly flipped through the pages, but the entire book was written in a language he didn't understand.

"Which page has the oath?" Xanthous cried.

"Are there *any* words you recognize?" Elrik asked him.

"No!" Xanthous said. "What do I do?"

As the boys frantically searched through the book, they noticed each passage included a sketch. There were images of skeletons and newborn babies, a full moon and a bright sun, flowers and weeds, and every animal and insect in existence.

"Ignore the words and focus on the illustrations," Elrik said. "They should give you a hint about what each passage means!"

Xanthous found an illustration of a throne surrounded by fire. He showed it to Elrik and the boys looked at each other with the same wide-eyed expression—*that had to be it*! Above them, the demons were descending faster and faster. Xanthous took a deep breath and read the passage from the Book of Sorcery, praying it was the oath of the Demon King.

"Demonous karta, demonous marta! Demonous infintay en demonous traynata!"

Xanthous and Elrik threw their arms around each other, expecting to be hit with thousands of flaming hawks at once. However, instead of landing on top of the boys, the demons landed in a circle *around* them—and as each demon hit the ground, they took on the shape of a *person* again. Xanthous slipped out of Elrik's arms and floated into the air. His eyes started to glow, a golden crown appeared, hovering over his head like an angel's halo, and a long cape of fire grew down his back like the wings of a phoenix.

"*It's working!*" Elrik cheered. "*You did it, Xanthous!*"

The demons were finally freed from the Immortal's spell and they knelt before their new leader. Kitty landed beside the demons, and Brystal and Ryder stared at Xanthous in astonishment.

"What's happening to him?" Brystal asked. "Why is the fire bowing to him?"

"Because he's the new Demon King!" Elrik said.

Ryder did a double take. "Sorry—did he say *Demon King*?"

"This time I'm just as confused as you are," Brystal said.

Xanthous landed gently on the ground and looked at his crown and cape in awe.

"How do I look?" he asked.

"Like you were *born* for it," Elrik said with a smile.

Before Brystal had a chance to ask any more questions, Immortalia appeared out of nowhere and sprinted right past her. The Immortal yanked the Book of Sorcery out of Xanthous's hands and then ran off in the opposite direction.

"I won't let you ruin this for me!" Immortalia yelled over her shoulder. "I've waited too long to let you take it from—"

"Not so fast, you *EVIL OLD LADY*!"

Gobzella and Lucy jumped in front of Immortalia and she slammed into the goblin's muscular body like it was a brick wall. As Immortalia fell backward, Lucy hit the ground with her fist and a sinkhole appeared behind her. The Immortal rolled into the hole and hit the bottom with a hard *thump*. Immortalia moaned and groaned as she tried to climb out, but the sides of the hole were too steep—*she was trapped.*

"*You'll pay for this!*" Immortalia screamed.

"Yeah, yeah, yeah—send us a bill," Lucy said.

Gobzella reached into the hole and pulled the Book of Sorcery out of Immortalia's hands with ease.

"Heads-up, *FAIRY GODMOTHER!*" the goblin said, and tossed it to her.

Brystal couldn't believe she was holding the Book

of Sorcery. Everything the fairies needed to defeat the Army of the Dead was finally in her hands. She flipped through its ancient parchment pages, and, as with Xanthous, the illustrations helped her guess what each passage was intended for. She assumed the sketch of a wilted flower was for a spell to disarm; the sketch of a skull was for a spell to destroy; and the sketch of a newborn baby was for a spell to resurrect.

Unfortunately, Brystal was just as devastated as she was relieved. Now that the Book of Sorcery was in her possession, her friends would expect her to kill the Immortal, and Brystal would be forced to disappoint them.

"What are you waiting for?" Lucy asked. "The Immortal is right in front of you! Knock her old dusty lights out while you have the chance!"

Brystal turned toward Lucy with tears in her eyes and slowly shook her head.

"I *can't*," she confessed.

Lucy was flabbergasted. "*What?*" she asked. "But you *have* to or you'll die!"

"I would rather die than spend the rest of my life feeling like a murderer," Brystal said.

"You can't be serious!" Lucy said. "This woman

just tried to fry the whole world! She doesn't deserve to live! *You do!*"

"But I don't want to live with the guilt of taking another life," Brystal said. "Please understand."

The girls were sidetracked by the sounds of screaming. They looked across the field and were reminded the battle was only *half* over.

Emerelda, Tangerina, Skylene, and Mrs. Vee were desperately trying to block the Snow Queen from entering Chariot Hills, but the witch was too powerful. Emerelda had surrounded her in tall emerald pillars, but the Snow Queen demolished them with icy blasts from her scepter. Tangerina tried to stick the witch to the grass, but the Snow Queen froze the fairy's bumblebees before they got close enough to douse her with honey. Skylene hit the witch with geysers of water, but the water froze upon contact and shattered across the ground. Mrs. Vee pelted the witch's head with a whole set of saucers, which greatly *annoyed* the Snow Queen, but did nothing to delay her.

The Snow Queen waved her scepter and froze the fairies in giant blocks of ice. A raspy cackle erupted from deep within the witch's throat as she entered Chariot Hills and disappeared from Brystal's sight.

"*Demons! Thaw out my friends!*" Xanthous ordered. "*And please hurry!*"

While the demons raced to save the fairies, both Brystal and Lucy knew their discussion about the Immortal would have to wait.

"We have to stop the Snow Queen!" Brystal cried.

"That doesn't mean *this* conversation is over!" Lucy said.

"Gobzella, stay here and make sure Immortalia doesn't move," Brystal said. "Ryder, I need you and Kitty to take me to the city—*fast!*"

CHAPTER TWENTY-FOUR

THE FIERY FAREWELL

The Righteous Emperor's luck was starting to change. Outside the city, the wildfires had miraculously been extinguished by an unexpected frost, and inside the city, the Army of the Dead was finally gaining ground in their battle against the alchemists. No matter how many times the dead soldiers were knocked down by red balls, or trapped by enormous white blood cells, or electrocuted by lightning—the skeletons *always* got back to their feet.

Eventually, all the robots, magnets, microorganisms, storms, artifacts, and insects had been released, and the alchemists were running out of ways to defend themselves. The skeletons blocked the entrances to all thirteen departments, trapping the alchemists inside their facilities.

"It's over, Dr. States," Seven called from the roof of the Righteous Palace. "Surrender now and I promise to give you and your colleagues a *swift* execution."

"You may destroy *us*, but you'll never destroy what we stand for!" Dr. States called back. "No matter how much hatred you spread, no matter how many lies you tell, no matter how many history books you rewrite, *science is truth*—and you cannot defeat the truth!"

"We'll see about that," Seven sneered. *"Guards! Finish them!"*

Just as the Army of the Dead was about to storm inside the Alchemy Institute, a brisk chill blew through the air. The temperature dropped so significantly, the dead soldiers' jaws began chattering. The Righteous Emperor and the Righteous Brotherhood shivered as

they searched the town square for whatever was causing the cold.

"Why is the air *freezing*?" Seven asked his men.

"I don't know, my lord," the High Commander
said. "It must be *them*."

He pointed to the alchemists, but the scientists were
just as confused as the clansmen.

"Dr. Storm, is this your doing?" Dr. States asked.

"Don't look at me," the meteorologist said. "My
blizzards are all out of ice."

A few moments later the clansmen and the scientists
had their answer—and for the first time all night, they
were united by fear. The Snow Queen crept down an
alleyway and emerged into the town square, freezing
the cobblestones under her feet as she walked.

"*The Snow Queen!*" the High Commander gasped.
"*She's returned!*"

"*Guards! Obliterate that witch!*" Seven ordered.

The Army of the Dead left the Alchemy Institute
and surrounded the Snow Queen. The witch could
hear the skeletons approaching, she could smell their
decaying bones, but she couldn't *feel* their cold bodies as easily as she could sense the demons. The dead

soldiers loaded their crossbows and fired a round of bloodstone arrows at the Snow Queen. The witch shielded herself with a wall of ice, but the arrows zipped right through her magic and penetrated her frostbitten skin. The Snow Queen screamed in agony at the arrows sticking into her shoulder and legs.

"Well done!" Seven cheered. *"Now aim for her heart!"*

The Snow Queen pointed her scepter toward the sound of the Righteous Emperor's voice. An icy blast erupted from the tip of her scepter and froze Seven and all the clansmen standing on the roof. The men moaned as they tried to break through the ice covering their bodies, but it was so thick they couldn't move a muscle.

The Army of the Dead reloaded their crossbows and fired arrows again, this time piercing the witch's back and stomach. The Snow Queen wailed as black blood oozed from her wounds and ran down her body. The witch waved her scepter in a giant circle, freezing the skeletons nearby, but there were still hundreds more to go.

Kitty swooped down from the sky, carrying Ryder and Brystal aboard her back. Brystal gasped when she saw the dead soldiers pelting the witch with arrows. If the skeletons killed the Snow Queen, then Madame Weatherberry would be slaughtered in the process.

"Get me as close to the Snow Queen as you can!" Brystal told Ryder.

He gripped the dragon's reins and steered Kitty toward the center of the town square. The dragon landed next to the Snow Queen, rattling the Alchemy Institute upon impact. The alchemists were flabbergasted to see the creature.

"Sir, the Fairy Godmother has returned with a *dragon*!" Dr. Stone shouted.

Dr. States was more interested in the *book* Brystal was holding.

"My God," he said. "She did it—she got the *Book of Sorcery*!"

"What should we do, sir?" Dr. Strait asked.

"There's nothing we *can* do," Dr. States said. "It's up to *her* now."

The Army of the Dead continued firing bloodstone arrows at the Snow Queen. Brystal flipped open the Book of Sorcery and turned to the page with the sketch of the skull. She pointed her wand at the skeletons and recited the passage as loudly as she could.

"Eliminous pardomous, mortamay pardomous!"

An eerie silence fell over the town square. At first Brystal worried she had read the wrong passage but then, as if the life were being sucked out the skeletons, a thick black smoke expelled from each soldier's body. The smoke rose into the sky, spinning like a cyclone of chaotic beasts, and then disappeared into the light of the full moon. One by one, the soldiers dropped their weapons and collapsed into a pile of bones—and this time, the Army of the Dead didn't get back to their feet.

"MMMMMMHHHHHMMMMM!" Seven growled.

The Righteous Emperor's precious army had been destroyed right in front of his eyes and there was *nothing* he could do to stop it. Seven was so enraged his body temperature skyrocketed and the ice containing him began to melt. Although his mouth was covered, his furious screams echoed through the town square.

"It's over, Seven," Brystal said. *"You lost."*

Lucy, Xanthous, and Elrik ran into the town square and the fairies and witches followed them. The group was shocked by all the destruction throughout the town square—especially the battered institute. However, their uneasiness quickly turned into euphoria once they noticed the *piles of bones* around them.

"*They're gone!*" Emerelda said with tears in her eyes. "*The Army of the Dead is finally gone!*"

The fairies and witches cheered and embraced one another. Brystal wanted to join her friends' celebration, but the Snow Queen was still at large. She opened the Book of Sorcery to the page with the wilted flower and began reading the passage beside it, eager to put an end to the Snow Queen's reign of terror once and for all.

"*Inferness infanata, inferness dull—*"

"*BRYSTAL! LOOK OUT!*" Lucy shouted.

Before Brystal could turn around, she was hit by a powerful blow. The Snow Queen had propelled her, Ryder, and Kitty across the town square with an icy blast. The dragon crashed through the glass wall of the Botany Department and landed among the plants. Brystal and Ryder hit the side of the Astrology Department and were held in place by a sheet of ice. The Book of Sorcery was frozen to the wall above Brystal's head, just a few feet out of reach. Brystal struggled against the ice trapping her, but Ryder didn't move—the blow had knocked him unconscious.

"Ryder? Are you hurt?" she asked, but he didn't respond.

The Snow Queen pulled the arrows from her body and then loomed toward Brystal with her scepter raised. Just as the witch was about to strike Brystal with another powerful blow, the Snow Queen was hit in her wounded shoulder with a ball of fire.

"*Leave her alone!*" Xanthous yelled.

The Snow Queen jerked her head toward the sound of Xanthous's voice. The witch pointed her scepter in his direction and a massive blast erupted from the tip. Xanthous raised his hands and protected himself and his friends with a shield of fire. However, the Snow Queen's icy blast stayed steady, and Xanthous struggled to keep his shield up.

"She's too powerful—I can't hold it forever!" Xanthous cried.

"Don't just stand there! Ask your new friends for help!" Lucy said.

"Oh, good idea! *Demons! I could use a hand!*"

His command summoned the demons to the town square and the fiery people grew up from the ground all around him. The demons pressed their flaming bodies into Xanthous's shield, which strengthened the barrier—but unfortunately, even with the demons' help, they couldn't hold off the Snow Queen's magic.

Brystal fought against the ice pinning her to the Astrology Department, and the sheet started to crack. Eventually, the ice chipped away and Brystal wriggled out from underneath it. She pointed her wand at the Book of Sorcery—intending to free it from the ice—but the sound of *stomping* caught her off guard. Kitty emerged from the Botany Department, covered from head to toe in scrapes and leaves. The dragon roared furiously as she crept toward the Snow Queen and smoke rose from her nostrils. The witch was so fixated on destroying Xanthous, she didn't notice the giant creature sneaking up behind her. Kitty took a deep breath and a fiery geyser erupted from her mouth.

"*Noooooooooo!*" Brystal screamed.

She pointed her wand at the Snow Queen and created a protective bubble around the witch. Kitty didn't understand why her fire wasn't reaching the witch and tried again. The dragon took a deeper breath and an even stronger geyser shot out of her mouth.

"Ryder! Wake up!" Brystal said. "You have to tell Kitty to back off!"

Ryder moaned as he stirred back to consciousness, but his eyes remained closed.

The dragon's breath was so forceful, it was hard for

Brystal to stay on her feet, let alone keep her wand in position. The more time passed, the weaker Brystal's bubble became—but the Snow Queen was only getting stronger. Her icy blast backed the demons, the fairies, and the witches up against the Righteous Palace—*they were trapped*!

"Brystal, lower your wand."

The calm voice caught Brystal by surprise. She looked over her shoulder and saw that Madame Weatherberry had appeared beside her.

"I can't!" she said. "If I lower my wand the dragon will kill the Snow Queen!"

"I know," the fairy said. "I *want* the Snow Queen to die."

"But . . . but . . . *but you'll die with her*!"

Madame Weatherberry nodded somberly. "It's time for the Snow Queen's story to end," she said. "And mine with it."

Brystal thought her ears were deceiving her—she couldn't have heard the fairy correctly.

"Madame Weatherberry, you can't die!" she said. "I only have seven days left to live! The fairies will need you when I'm gone!"

"They won't need me, because you aren't going anywhere," the fairy said.

"Yes, I am! I made a deal with Death!"

"Yes, but I *also* made a deal with Death," Madame Weatherberry said. "When you told me you weren't going to kill the Immortal, I couldn't just sit back and let you die. I reached out to Death and made him an offer. I convinced him that as long as the Snow Queen remained in the ice, she and I would *also* be Immortal. Having more than one Immortal in the world didn't sit well with him, and he agreed to spare *you* in exchange for *us*. So I began defrosting the Snow Queen ever so slightly, until she started to slowly suffocate in the ice. Just before she and I crossed over, your friends arrived and asked for my help. Now here we are—and it's up to you to finish the job."

Brystal was so overwhelmed she started losing her grip on her wand.

"No!" she said. "I could never hurt you!"

"Brystal, there's no time to argue," Madame Weatherberry said. "Your friends are in trouble. The Snow Queen is much more powerful than she was before— she has two years of anger built up inside of her—and this time, I can't help you fight her. This may be your only chance to destroy her for good."

Brystal shook her head as tears spilled down her face.

"Please don't make me do this!" she cried. "I don't want to kill you!"

"You aren't killing me—you're setting me free," the fairy said. "Every day I spent in that cave was a nightmare and a constant reminder of the monster I created. I'm tired of living with the *guilt* and I'm tired of living with the *shame*. But you could save me from that misery—you could save me from an eternity of pain."

The fairies and witches screamed as Xanthous's shield buckled under the Snow Queen's steady blast. In just a few moments, they would all be obliterated. *Brystal knew what she had to do.*

"I'll never forgive myself for this!" she cried.

"There's nothing to be forgiven for," Madame Weatherberry said. "Ending the Snow Queen is the only way to save you *and* your friends. Just lower your wand and all of this will go away. Lower your wand and I'll finally be at peace."

Brystal was sobbing so hard her entire body was shaking.

"I love you, Madame Weatherberry!"

"I love you, too."

It took every ounce of strength in Brystal's body to keep her wand up, but every ounce of willpower to lower it. Her wand gradually fell to her side, the bubble disappeared around the Snow Queen, and the witch was consumed by the dragon's breath. While the Snow Queen burned alive her bloodcurdling screams echoed for miles. However, as the witch was incinerated, Madame Weatherberry had never looked so serene. The fairy beamed with gratitude and exhaled peacefully as all the guilt, shame, and pain lifted from her spirit.

Madame Weatherberry spent her final moments watching Brystal and the fairies with a loving gaze and a proud smile.

"You are my greatest dreams come true," she said.

Like a beautiful rainbow after a long storm, Madame Weatherberry slowly faded from sight, and when the dragon finished her fiery attack, not a single trace of the fairy or the Snow Queen remained. Brystal dropped to her knees and wept uncontrollably. The fairies and witches gathered around Brystal, but they couldn't stop their own grief from surfacing as they comforted her.

· • ★ • ·

Following the Snow Queen's demise, Xanthous and Skylene worked together using streams of warm water to melt all the ice covering Chariot Hills. By sunrise the whole city had been defrosted, including the Righteous Emperor and the Righteous Brotherhood. Emerelda, Tangerina, Sprout, and Mrs. Vee enjoyed putting the clansmen in shackles made from emerald, honey, vines, and tablecloths. Once the clansmen were restrained, Dr. States and the Magbots marched the men across the crumbling town square and locked them away in the prison they used to run.

While the clansmen were taken into custody, the alchemists cleaned up their battered institute and examined the wounded. Dr. Stent checked on Ryder's concussion and made him count his fingers and walk in a straight line. Dr. Stag bandaged the cuts covering Kitty's body and stealthily managed to take a sample of the dragon's blood when she wasn't looking.

The witches swept all the Army of the Dead's remains into one giant pile—and Stitches even pocketed a few skulls for her private collection.

Everyone was doing their part to clean up after the battle, but Brystal hadn't moved since the Snow Queen was slain. She stayed seated on the ground, silently staring at the spot where the witch had been incinerated. Brystal prayed with all her heart that part of Madame Weatherberry had survived the Snow Queen's death—she hoped, at any moment, she would see the fairy rising from the ashes—but she never returned.

"Well, this week has been a kick to the tail feathers," Lucy said. "I don't know about you, but I'm taking a much-needed vacation after all of this."

Lucy sat on the ground beside Brystal but she didn't look up.

"You did the right thing, you know," she said.

"Did I?" Brystal asked.

"Of course," Lucy said. "You saved our lives. If you hadn't lowered your wand, the Snow Queen would have killed us—and God only knows what she would have done after that."

"Then why do *I* feel like a murderer?" Brystal asked.

Lucy put her arm over Brystal's shoulders.

"Because you're a good person—and good people can find guilt in a salad if they look hard enough." Lucy laughed. "I know it's difficult to process now, but Madame Weatherberry *sacrificed herself* to save you—that's the truth. This was her choice, not yours. And if I have to remind you of that every hour of every day for the rest of my life, I will."

"Thanks, Lucy," she said.

"You're welcome," she said. "And for what it's worth, of all the people I know who've been forced to let a fire-breathing dragon incinerate the magically detached body of their former mentor—you're handling it the best."

A small smile came to Brystal's face.

"I suppose you're right," she said. "Madame Weatherberry gave me a gift—it'd be an insult to her memory if I wasted it on guilt."

"Atta girl," Lucy said, and patted her on the back. "Thanks to Madame Weatherberry, our adventures are *just* getting started. And we'll always have her to thank."

Without warning, the town square began to rumble with the intensity of an earthquake. The ground cracked and separated as the opening of a tunnel appeared in the middle of the city. The fairies and witches gathered around the mysterious tunnel and peered inside. It seemed to stretch for miles underground with no end in sight.

The demons walked through the capital and lined up at the tunnel's entrance. As a demon passed by Xanthous, they waved their hand over the wall of the Righteous Palace and burned a message into the bricks:

TIME TO GO HOME.

"I guess that's my cue," Xanthous told the others.

"I can't believe we're friends with the heir to *the Demon Throne*," Tangerina said.

"Who would have thought?" Skylene said.

"My father always said a boy like me would end up burning with demons, but he never said I would get to *rule* them," Xanthous said.

"Are you sure you have to live with them?" Emerelda asked him. "I mean, couldn't you rule the Demons *remotely*?"

Xanthous smiled as he watched the demons head down the tunnel.

"I'm actually looking forward to it," he said. "Look at them, Em. I've found *another* world that loves and accepts me just as I am. How lucky is that? The only difference is this one needs me. And I think part of me has always needed them, too."

"We're going to miss you so much," Brystal said.

"Have fun being a king, buddy," Lucy said.

"Don't forget to write!" Mrs. Vee said. "I want to know what demons wear, what they eat, and if there are any eligible demon bachelors my age! *HA-HA!*"

"Don't worry, I'll tell you all about it when I come back to visit," he said. "I promise."

Xanthous gave each of his friends a tight hug good-bye. When he had said good-bye to the fairies and witches, he noticed Elrik sulking near the tunnel.

"I guess this is farewell," the elf said.

The boys exchanged a bittersweet smile, not knowing what to say.

"It doesn't *have* to be," Xanthous said. "You could always come with me."

Elrik laughed like he was joking.

"I'm serious," Xanthous said. "We could rule the demons together. Who knows? I might need some help down there."

"You want me to come with you? *To the center of the earth?*" the elf asked.

"I mean, unless you *wanted* to go back to the Elf Territory."

"Of course I don't! But won't I *burn* down there?"

Xanthous offered Elrik his hand with a sweet smile.

"I control the fires now," he said. "I can protect you."

Elrik smiled from ear to ear as he considered the offer, but it didn't take long to decide. The elf eagerly took the fairy's hand and they followed the demons to their new home in the center of the earth. The fairies and witches waved as Xanthous and Elrik walked deeper and deeper underground. Once they were out of sight, the tunnel sank into the dirt and disappeared.

After the boys were gone, the fairies and witches looked around the ravished town square and the damaged Alchemy Institute and collectively sighed.

"What a *dump*," Lucy said. "It looks like a group of child stars threw a party."

"It's going to take *months* to get this place cleaned up," Brystal said.

Ryder and Kitty turned to each other with matching grins, thinking the same thing.

"Actually, *we* might be able to help with that," he said.

CHAPTER TWENTY-FIVE

A NEGLECTED SCIENCE

Although the Caretaker Supreme was furious with her son for entering the Temple of Knowledge against her will—and livid that he'd taken a dragon outside the Dragon Keys without her permission—she was very proud to learn her son's disobedient efforts had helped save the world. Ryder and Brystal told her about the damage the Army of the Dead had inflicted on Chariot Hills and the Alchemy

Institute and they convinced the Caretaker Supreme to loan them a great albino dragon. Six days later, after the dragon had consumed the city and campus in its restorative flames, the capital was as good as new, and the institute returned to its usual location over the Southern Sea.

As a thank-you for saving them from the Army of the Dead, Dr. States invited Brystal to the Alchemy Institute for tea. The alchemist was particularly excited to show off the newest resident of their Biology Department. Brystal peered into the cell next to Carole, the common cold, and found the disgraced Righteous Emperor pouting on the floor.

"We're calling him the *hate virus*," Dr. States told her. "We thought the Biology Department was the most appropriate place to keep him. That way, we can make sure he doesn't spread, just like all the other contagious microorganisms."

"It's perfect," Brystal said. "Where did you decide to keep Immortalia?"

"She's in the Anthropology Department with the other relics," Dr. States said. "Dr. Stage is very excited to have a living history book in his possession."

"It's a win-win for everyone," Brystal said.

Seven rolled his eyes at her enthusiasm and let out an aggravated moan.

"What have you done to my Empire?" he griped.

"I'm afraid it's not *your* Empire anymore," Brystal said with a cheeky smile. "The throne is being passed down to your heir."

"*Heir?*" Seven scoffed. "I don't have an heir!"

"Of course you do," Brystal said. "Remember your cousin Penny Charming?"

Seven's face turned bright red.

"Mousy little *Penny* is going to be Empress of my Righteous Empire?" he sneered.

"Oh, good heavens no," Brystal said with a laugh. "Penny is going to be *Queen of the Charming Kingdom*. She's decided to change the empire back into a kingdom, and given what her poor citizens have been through, she's also changing its name to something more *cheerful*."

"But that means your gangly brother is going to be—"

"The King Consort—I know! Isn't that exciting? Poor Barrie has been a nervous wreck since he found out. As a matter of fact, Penny's coronation is this afternoon. I better be on my way before I'm late."

"I'll walk you out," Dr. States said.

The alchemist escorted Brystal out of the Biology Department, leaving Seven alone with his grievances. As Dr. States and Brystal walked down the floating path through the institute, Brystal reached into a satchel over her shoulder and removed the Book of Sorcery.

"Before I go, I wanted to leave this with you," she said.

Dr. States was surprised by the offer.

"Are you sure you want *us* to keep it?" he asked.

"I think it's better off with you," Brystal said. "There are spells within those pages no one should *ever* have access to. We can't afford for the Book of Sorcery to fall into the wrong hands—and there are a lot fewer hands up *here* than on land."

Dr. States seemed touched by the gesture of confidence.

"We'll guard it with our lives," he said. "Before you leave, I would like to extend an apology to you and your friends."

"What for?" she asked.

"We were wrong to blame Mr. Hayfield for the fires—just like our ancestors were wrong to blame dragons in the past," he said. "We've also been wrong to turn a blind eye to tyranny and to ignore dictators like the Righteous Emperor. Had we interfered sooner, we may have prevented the attack on our institute. It's been an unfortunate but necessary wake-up call for us. Fortunately, through it all, it's forced me and my colleagues to recognize a science we've been neglecting—a science that, with proper care and attention, will guarantee we make better decisions in the future."

"What's that?" Brystal asked.

"The science of *mistakes*," Dr. States said. "One mistake can teach you just as much as any experiment. And perhaps the biggest mistake alchemists have made over the centuries is forgetting to include *compassion* into our analysis. Humanity may have its flaws, but distancing ourselves from the world hasn't been as beneficial as we thought. In many ways, we've forgotten what it means to *be* human. But we'd like to change that."

"I'm glad to hear it," Brystal said. "Although I'm not sure I can fault you for your views on humanity. At least, for now."

"Oh?" the alchemist asked.

"When we were in the Temple of Knowledge, we saw something in the sorcerers' vault that was disturbing," she said. "It was called the Halls of Humanity. There were five corridors, and each one held a living representation of all the current dreams, nightmares, ideas, love, and hatred that humanity is experiencing. And sadly, the Hall of Nightmares and the Hall of Hatred were the fullest."

"Unfortunately, I'm not surprised," he said.

"Well, it was a shock to me," Brystal said. "It has haunted me ever since we left. That's why I've decided to devote the rest of my life to changing it."

The alchemist chuckled. "You plan on *changing humanity*? All on your own?"

"Not alone," she said. "Before we left the temple, the sorcerer we met was adamant that we take something from the vault. And since the Book of Sorcery was no longer there, I decided to take the one thing I knew could help change humanity for the better."

Dr. States's eyes grew wide with curiosity.

"What did you take?" he asked.

"The Hall of Dreams," Brystal said. "I've seen how easily the world can change with just a little touch of kindness. Humanity isn't a cruel species—and it isn't destined to self-destruct. They just haven't had enough good examples to aspire to. They need someone who will champion their ideas, they need someone to encourage their ambitions, and they need someone to nurture their vulnerabilities. And hopefully, with the Hall of Dreams, we'll be able to spread so much joy and light, people like the Righteous Emperor will never rise again."

"That's quite a goal to set for yourself," Dr. States said.

"Even if I can't do it, perhaps I'll inspire the person who can," she said.

"I admire your devotion—but I'm too skeptical," the alchemist said. "I suppose that's why you're the Fairy Godmother and I'm not."

"Everyone can't save everything, Dr. States," Brystal said. "You worry about the planet, and I'll worry about its people."

"Now *that's* a goal I can get behind," he said.

The Fairy Godmother and the alchemist shook hands and said their good-byes. Brystal followed the floating path as it snaked through the Alchemy Institute and headed toward the landing strip at the front of the campus. There, Ryder and Kitty were waiting to take Brystal home.

Tick... Tick... Tick... Tick.

Brystal suddenly stopped in her tracks at an unexpected *silence*. All she heard was the ocean breeze as it whistled through the towers and spires of the institute—*but her pocket watch had stopped ticking.* It was quite a shock. She opened the watch and was amazed to see the gears had finally stopped turning, and yet: Brystal was still standing. *Madame Weatherberry's sacrifice had worked.*

An enormous smile grew across Brystal's face, and her eyes filled with happy tears.

"What are you smiling about?" Ryder asked.

"I just realized I have the rest of my life to look forward to," she said.

Ryder helped Brystal aboard Kitty and the dragon soared into the sky. Soon the Alchemy Institute disappeared from view and all they could see for miles and miles around was the sparkling ocean and the sea of fluffy white clouds. Brystal beamed brightly while she admired the beauty surrounding her.

"You doing okay back there?" Ryder asked.

"I'm great!" she replied.

However, Brystal was much better than *great*. As she flew through the picturesque sky, enjoying the wind blowing through her hair and the sunlight warming her skin, Brystal was consumed with an *exhilarating* feeling of happiness, excitement, and eagerness all at once. It was a familiar sensation, but she had never been more grateful to feel it.

Brystal was *alive*.

ACKNOWLEDGMENTS

I'd like to thank everyone on my team, especially Rob Weisbach, Derek Kroeger, Alla Plotkin, Rachel Karten, and Heather Manzutto.

I'd also like to thank the incredible people at Little, Brown Books for Young Readers, including Alvina Ling, Megan Tingley, Siena Koncsol, Stefanie Hoffman, Shawn Foster, Jackie Engel, Emilie Polster, Janelle DeLuise, Hannah Koerner, Ruqayyah Daud, Jen Graham, Sasha Illingworth, Ching Chan, Lindsay Walter-Greaney, Andrea Colvin, Jake Regier, Virginia Lawther, Chandra Wohleber, Regina Castillo, and Rosanne Lauer.

Finally, I'd like to thank Brandon Dorman for his amazing artwork and Jerry Maybrook for his terrific guidance while recording the audiobook.

Turn the page for an excerpt from

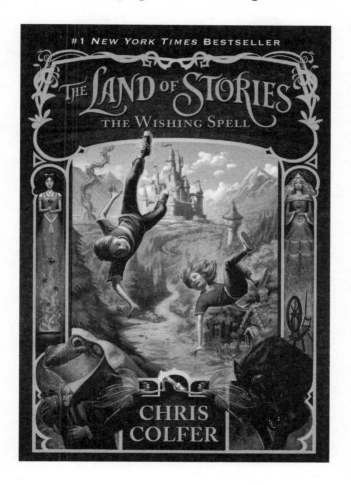

AVAILABLE NOW

THE QUEENS' VISIT

The dungeon was a miserable place. Light was scarce and flickered from the torches bolted to the stone walls. Foul-smelling water dripped inside from the moat circling the palace above. Large rats chased each other across the floor searching for food. This was no place for a queen.

It was just past midnight, and all was quiet except for the occasional rustle of a chain. Through the heavy silence a single set of footsteps echoed throughout the halls as someone climbed down the spiral steps into the dungeon.

A young woman emerged down the steps dressed head-to-toe in a long emerald cloak. She cautiously made her way past the row of cells, sparking the interest of the prisoners inside. With every step she took, her pace became slower and slower, and her heart beat faster and faster.

The prisoners were arranged according to crime. The deeper she walked into the dungeon, the crueler and more dangerous the criminals became. Her sights were set on the cell at the very end of the hall, where a prisoner of special interest was being watched by a large private guard.

The woman had come to ask a question. It was a simple question, but it consumed her thoughts every day, kept her lying awake most nights, and was the only thing she dreamed about with the little sleep she managed.

Only one person could give her the answer she needed, and that person was on the other side of the prison bars ahead.

"I wish to see her," the cloaked woman said to the guard.

"No one is allowed to see her," the guard said, almost amused by the request. "I'm on strict orders from the royal family."

The woman lowered her hood and revealed her face. Her skin was as pale as snow, her hair was as dark as coal, and her eyes were as green as a forest. Her beauty was known throughout the land, and her story was known even beyond that.

"Your Majesty, please forgive me!" the stunned guard

apologized. He quickly bent into an overly pronounced bow. "I wasn't expecting anyone from the palace."

"No apology necessary," she said. "But please do not speak of my presence here tonight."

"Of course," the guard said, nodding.

The woman faced the bars, waiting for them to be raised, but the guard hesitated.

"Are you sure you want to go in there, Your Highness?" the guard said. "There's no telling what she's capable of."

"I must see her," the woman said. "At any cost."

The guard began turning a large, circular lever, and the bars of the cell rose. The woman took a deep breath and continued past them.

She journeyed through a longer, darker hallway where a series of bars and barriers were raised and then lowered after she walked past them. Finally, she reached the end of the hall, the last set of bars was raised, and she stepped into the cell.

The prisoner was a woman. She sat on a stool in the center of the cell and stared up at a small window.

The prisoner waited a few moments before acknowledging the visitor behind her. It was the first visitor she had ever had, and she knew who it was without looking; there was only one person it could be.

"Hello, Snow White," the prisoner said softly.

"Hello, Stepmother," Snow White replied with a nervous quiver. "I hope you are well."

Although Snow White had rehearsed exactly what she

wanted to say, she was now finding it nearly impossible to speak.

"I heard that you are the queen now," her stepmother said.

"It's true," said Snow White. "I've inherited the throne as my father intended."

"So, to what do I owe this honor? Have you come to watch me wither away?" her stepmother said. There was such authority and power to her voice; it was known to make the strongest of men melt like ice.

"On the contrary," Snow White said. "I've come to understand."

"To understand *what*?" her stepmother asked harshly.

"Why..." Snow White hesitated. "Why you did what you did."

And with this finally said, Snow White felt a weight lift off of her shoulders. She had finally asked the question that had been so strongly on her mind. Half of the challenge was over.

"There are many things about this world that you don't understand," the stepmother said, and turned to look at her stepdaughter.

It was the first time in a long time that Snow White had seen her stepmother's face. It was the face of a woman who had once possessed beauty without flaw, and the face of a woman who had once been queen. Now, the woman sitting before her was just a prisoner whose looks had faded into a permanent, sorrowful scowl.

"That may be," Snow White said. "But can you blame me for trying to find some sort of reason behind your actions?"

The recent years of Snow White's life had become the most scandalous of the kingdom's royal history. Everyone knew the story of the fair princess who'd taken refuge with the Seven Dwarfs while hiding from her jealous stepmother. Everyone knew of the infamous poisoned apple and the dashing prince who had saved Snow White from a false death.

The story was simple, but the aftermath was not. Even with a new marriage and a monarchy to occupy her time, Snow White found herself constantly wondering if the theories of her stepmother's vanity were true. Something inside the new queen refused to believe that someone could be so malicious.

"Do you know what they're calling you out there?" Snow White asked. "Outside these prison walls the world refers to you as the *Evil Queen*."

"If that is what the world has labeled me, then that is the name I shall learn to live with," the Evil Queen said. "Once the world has made a decision, there is little anyone can do to change its mind."

Snow White was astonished by how little her stepmother cared, but Snow White needed her to care. She needed to know there was some humanity left in her.

"They wanted to execute you after they discovered your crimes against me! The whole kingdom wanted you dead!"

Snow White's voice faded to a faint whisper as she fought off the emotions building up inside her. "But I wouldn't allow it. I couldn't..."

"Am I supposed to thank you for sparing me?" the Evil Queen asked. "If you expect someone to fall at your feet and express gratitude, you've come to the wrong cell."

"I didn't do it for you. I did it for myself," Snow White said. "Like it or not, you are the only mother I have ever known. I refuse to believe that you are the soulless monster the rest of the world claims you to be. Whether it's true or not, I believe there is a heart deep down inside of you."

Tears rolled down Snow White's pale face. She had promised herself she would stay strong, but she had lost control of her emotions once she was in her stepmother's presence.

"Then I'm afraid you're wrong," the Evil Queen said. "The only soul I've ever had died a long time ago, and the only heart you'll find in my possession is a heart of stone."

The Evil Queen did indeed have a heart of stone, but not inside her. A rock in the shape and size of a human heart was on a small table in the corner of the cell. It was the only item the Evil Queen had been permitted to keep when she was arrested.

Snow White recognized the stone from her childhood. It had always been very precious to her stepmother, and the Evil Queen had never let it out of her sight. Snow White had never been allowed to touch it or hold it, but nothing was stopping her now.

She walked across the cell, picked it up, and curiously stared down at it. It brought back so many memories. All the neglect and sadness her stepmother had caused her as a child rushed through her.

"All my life I only wanted one thing," Snow White said. "Your love. When I was a girl, I used to spend hours hiding in the palace just hoping you would notice I was missing, but you never did. You spent your days in your chambers with your mirrors and your skin creams and this stone. You spent more time with strangers with anti-aging methods than you did with your own daughter. But why?"

The Evil Queen did not answer.

"You tried to kill me four times, three of which you attempted yourself," Snow White said, shaking her head in disbelief. "When you dressed as an old woman and came to me at the dwarfs' cottage, I knew it was you. I knew you were dangerous, but I kept letting you in. I kept hoping that you would change. I let you harm me."

Snow White had never confessed this to anyone, and she couldn't help but bury her face in the palms of her hands and cry after saying it.

"You think *you* know heartbreak?" the Evil Queen said so sharply that it startled her stepdaughter. "You know *nothing* of pain. You never received affection from me, but from the moment you were born you were loved by the whole kingdom. *Others*, however, are not so fortunate. *Others*, Snow White, sometimes have the only loves they've ever known taken from them."

Snow White didn't know what to say. What love was she referring to?

"Are you speaking of my father?" Snow White asked.

The Evil Queen closed her eyes and shook her head. "Naïveté is such a privileged trait," she said. "Believe it or not, Snow White, I had my own life before I came into yours."

Snow White grew quiet and slightly ashamed. Of course she knew her stepmother had had a life prior to marrying her father, but she had never considered what it had consisted of. Her stepmother had always been such a private person, Snow White never had reason to.

"Where is my mirror?" the Evil Queen demanded.

"It's to be destroyed," Snow White told her.

Suddenly, the Evil Queen's stone became much heavier in Snow White's hand. Snow White didn't know if this was really happening, or if she was just imagining it. Her arm became tired from holding the stone heart, and she had to put it aside.

"There's so much you're not telling me," Snow White said. "There are so many things you've kept from me all these years."

The Evil Queen lowered her head and stared at the ground. She remained silent.

"I may be the only person in the world with any compassion for you. Please tell me it isn't going to waste," Snow White pleaded. "If there were events in your past that influenced your recent decisions, please explain them to me."

Still, there was no response.

"I'm not leaving here until you tell me!" Snow White yelled, raising her voice for the first time in her life.

"Fine," the Evil Queen said.

Snow White took a seat on another stool in the cell. The Evil Queen waited a moment before beginning, and Snow White's anticipation grew.

"Your story will forever be romanticized," she told Snow White. "No one will ever think twice about mine. I will continue to be degraded into nothing but a grotesque villain until the end of time. But what the world fails to realize is that a *villain* is just a *victim* whose story hasn't been told. Everything I have done, my life's work and my crimes against you, has all been for *him*."

Snow White felt her own heart grow heavy. Her head was spinning, and curiosity had taken over her entire body.

"Who?" she asked so quickly that she forgot to hold back the desperation in her voice.

The Evil Queen closed her eyes and let her memories surface. Images of places and people from her past flew out from the back of her mind like fireflies in a cave. There was so much she had seen in her younger years, so many things she wished she remembered, and so many things she wished to forget.

"I will tell you about my past, or at least the past of someone I once was," the Evil Queen said. "But consider yourself warned. My story is not one that ends with a happily-ever-after."

Andrew Scott

Chris Colfer

is a No.1 *New York Times* bestselling author and Golden Globe–winning actor. He was honored as a member of the TIME 100, *Time* magazine's annual list of the one hun-dred most infl uential people in the world, and his books include *Struck By Lightning: The Carson Phillips Jour-nal*; *Stranger Than Fanfi ction*; the Land of Stories series: *The Wishing Spell*, *The Enchantress Returns*, *A Grimm Warning*, *Beyond the Kingdoms*, *An Author's Odyssey*, and *Worlds Collide*; and the companion books *A Tale of Magic . . .* , *A Tale of Witchcraft . . .* , and *A Tale of Sorcery . . .*

MAGIC IS NOT A
CHOICE.

THE NO. 1 *NEW YORK TIMES*
BESTSELLING SERIES

LITTLE, BROWN BOOKS
FOR YOUNG READERS

ATaleofMagic.com

Don't miss out on reading
Chris Colfer's adventure series …

THE LAND OF STORIES

Perfect for fans old and new!